PRESENCE:
THE MARKED

PRESENCE:
THE MARKED

L.J. Branch

To my parents, LeRoy and Rochelle, thank you for supporting me in finding my passion.

To my mentors, Gil Cook and Maggie Anderson, thank you for guiding me through the long journey to follow my dreams.

To my friends Denzel and Rodney, thank you for being my own personal band of thieves joining me on our journey to chase our dreams.

To you who have decided to purchase this book, thank you for your support.

Lastly, to my fans online, both old and hopefully new, thank you for putting up with my insanity over the years and helping me improve tremendously on my craft. You've all earned this badge.

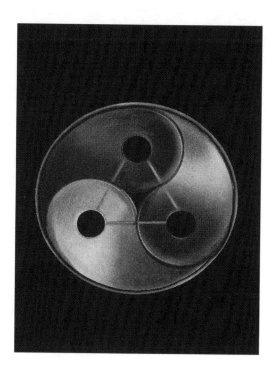

ACKNOWLEDGMENTS

• • • • • • • ● • • • • • • • •

Special thanks to Eddy Shinjuku for going above and beyond expectations when illustrating the cover for the book and further images to help support it. Another thank you to Jeannie Glickson for proofreading the story. Further gratitude to my aunts Yolanda and Nadine, for helping me develop the story and for acting as my practice audience for the plot. Final thanks to Lexie, Quentin Gerbault, and Will in particular, for helping me improve over the years. This adventure wouldn't exist without you all.

CONTENTS

Acknowledgments ix

Chapter 1: Swipe Right...1

Chapter 2: The Mark...16

Chapter 3: Band Thirteen 33

Chapter 4: Grand Theft Auto 43

Chapter 5: The Magnus Financial Job..61

Chapter 6: Xavier Romero Magnus 78

Chapter 7: Pay Day..87

Chapter 8: Power Moves 101

Chapter 9: Elders 122

Chapter 10: The Gladius Gallery Job...140

Chapter 11: Lines Crossed 152

Chapter 12: Changes 171

Chapter 13: Solstice..187

Chapter 14: The Broken Doll..203

Chapter 15: Alice 224

Chapter 16: Divine Intervention...238

Chapter 17: Healing 253

Chapter 18: Spring of Rebirth 269

Chapter 19: The Prosperity Industries Job 287

Epilogue: Presence.. 315

CHAPTER 1

SWIPE RIGHT

Santa Monica, California

"According to Diamond's manager and father, she will no longer continue her music career. In other news, we have more information about the seventh major break-in at a fortune 500 company in the last three months. With the cyber-terrorist group known as Wonderland little more than a terrible memory, authorities still are unaware of who is behind the recent crime wave…"

The sound of the news broadcast echoed throughout an old rundown apartment in the slums of Santa Monica. In her bed, one Abigail Stone stirred awake. A lot could be said about the woman but the most prominent, in her opinion anyway, was that she was definitely not a morning person. Abbie groaned when she looked at her clock and saw 6:30 a.m. flash on its screen and cursed when she saw the time. Abbie closed her eyes in frustration, a desperate attempt to calm herself, before she decided to do her best to at least get a few more minutes of sleep. However, that plan didn't last long as someone had decided it would be a good time to call her.

"Oh my God," Abbie complained as she blindly reached on her nightstand and knocked over a beer bottle in an attempt to grab her phone. Deep down, she was in disbelief. It was the year 2054

1

and apparently, people had not learned when to call at respectable hours. It took a minute, but eventually she managed to blindly grab her phone. When she opened her eyes, she couldn't help the scowl that appeared on her face when she saw the name "Eric" appear on the screen. "This had better be good," Abbie all but growled out, her annoyance clear. Eric of all people knew not to wake her up early, especially when he was the cause of the splitting headache she had woken up to. "What do you want?"

"Well good morning to you too, sunshine," Eric said sarcastically.

"Eric..." Abbie began as patiently as she could, which wasn't very patient at all at the moment. "...why did you wake me up this early, on my day off?"

"What? You're the one who told me to wake you up, remember?" Eric pointed out and Abbie couldn't help but look at the phone in confusion.

"Excuse me?"

"You told me to show up early so we could head down to Roy's and check out some new gear. Come on girl, don't tell me you forgot?" Eric questioned, and soon the memories came rushing back.

"Shit."

He was right.

"Would you believe me if I said I didn't?"

"Abbie..." Eric began and she could just picture him shaking his head. "...you know what? Doesn't matter, you're up now so hurry up! I did you a huge favor, so you owe me."

"I owe you?" Abbie couldn't help but ask. She had agreed to give him some pointers on choosing which tech to buy out of the kindness of her heart, not because she owed him. "Since when do I owe you? What favor did you do for me?"

"Ah, ah, ah, all will be explained later, just come down here," Eric ordered playfully and Abbie frowned when a chill went down her spine. Favors from him always filled her with dread because she never asked for them. Eric just did things on her behalf without telling her and then claimed he helped her out, leaving her to deal with the consequences.

"Give me, ten," Abbie eventually told him as she forced herself to sit up in her bed. It wouldn't take her long to get ready after fixing the black mess that was her bed hair.

*　　*　　*

Santa Monica, The Mad-Hatter

When they exited their 'cab-4-cash', Abbie paid their fare with an app before she and Eric made their way to a small corner store. The sound of air shuttles could be heard above them which made Abbie glance up at them every now and again. Sure, they were fun to be in but, in Abbie's opinion, that alone couldn't justify the fare needed to ride in one. Call her old-fashioned but she'd take a regular car any day, they looked much sleeker than the shuttles and got her from point "A" to point "B" like anything else.

"What's up, pops!?" Eric greeted loudly as they entered the shop. Roy looked up from his paper and grinned. The Mad-Hatter was an odd little store they frequented, a hidden gem in the city. It was easy to overlook due to the sheer size of the neighboring towers, how it stayed in business Abbie didn't know. It was filled with the latest and greatest that the tech industry had to offer along with various stylish hats. It was an odd combination, but perhaps that just added to its quirkiness. The shop was a haven for hipsters, tech nerds, or both which was surprising as Roy was an older man whose gray hair was in stark contrast with his weathered dark skin. Abbie had learned fast that, despite his age, the man definitely knew his stuff. Hell, he even taught her some tricks she didn't know which made Abbie think of him as an impromptu mentor.

"How's it hangin', lil' brotha?" Roy asked with a kind smile as he placed a white straw hat on his head. Abbie watched with a smile as Roy grabbed Eric's hand and brought him in for a quick hug before he turned to face her. "And what's this? You even got the one and only, Abigail Stone, out and about while the sun's still out?" Roy teased as he greeted Abbie the same way he had Eric.

3

"It's Cali, Roy, the sun's always out," Abbie reminded him.

"Girl, you know what I meant," Roy said with an eye roll. "So, what can I do for you?"

"Eric's tryin' to get into the tech scene," Abbie told Roy as she gestured toward Eric. "I taught him what I knew, I think he's ready for the back room," Abbie said knowingly. Roy looked at her in surprise for a moment before a smirk graced his lips.

"The back room?" Eric asked curiously.

"Come on, lil' brotha, let me show you the real merchandise," Roy said as he gestured for them to follow him. Roy led them behind the counter and pulled out a keycard to open the back room.

"Holy…" Eric began, his eyes wide as they stepped into the room and Abbie couldn't blame him. The first time she ever stepped into the backroom she thought she had stepped onto an alien ship or something. That said something because she was definitely no stranger when it came to good tech.

"You say he's ready?" Roy asked Abbie.

"He's not as good as me, of course," Abbie began, which made Eric roll his eyes. "But he ain't half bad. We could have been classmates back when I was at school down south," Abbie explained. "We can get him started so he can start makin' some change," Abbie said as Eric grinned. Eric was gifted, he was self-taught until Abbie helped him out. He soaked up knowledge in a way that almost made her envious. Whether it was program design, music production, or whatever, Eric could work his way around electronics like it was second nature. Recently, Eric decided he wanted to make music his full-time job so Abbie figured she'd help him with a few things.

"Well alright, I ain't got no problem helping you out, just understand that even with a discount, this won't be cheap," Roy pointed out.

"Don't worry about that, I got lucky on a scratch-off lottery ticket the other day so cash ain't no problem now," Eric reassured Roy. "It ain't much but it's enough for me to get a down payment on a place outside of the slums and allow me to invest in my future a bit, you know?"

"Do I know?" Roy asked with a laugh. "Boy you're young, you just got here. I know all about the grind. Come on lil' brotha, let Abbie and me hook you up. What you tryin' to do?"

"Anything will work really, but my passion is music, making beats and all that. I wanna blow up and maybe make music for artists like Diamond or something," Eric explained.

"Aim for the skies lil' brotha but stay grounded. Hopefully, you'll get to do that, but Diamond is going to have to recover first," Roy pointed out only to frown when they looked at him in confusion. "What? You kids ain't heard? The stress finally got to that girl and she's taking a break from the limelight. No telling when or if she's going to start singing again, it was on the news."

"For real? That blows," Eric said as he shook his head. Roy nodded in agreement but before the man could continue, he heard a bell ring from the front of the store.

"Abbie, you can help the lil' brotha out, right? I'm gonna see what the customers need."

"Gotcha, don't worry, I'll make sure he picks out the right stuff," Abbie reassured him before she and Eric began to look around the backroom. "By the way, what was that favor you apparently did for me? I need to know how much damage control I need to run before it's too late."

"What? Damage control? Do you have that little faith in yo' boy?" in response, Abbie just stared at him with the blankest expression she could muster as they both recalled times where his favors ended poorly. "Uh...anyway, just hand me your phone, I didn't do anything drastic, trust me."

"Those words have never ended with a result that would lead me to ever trust you again...but I do anyway...for some reason," Abbie muttered as she tossed him her phone.

"Alright, just go to the app store, download this app..." Eric muttered as he went through her phone as a frown appeared on Abbie's face.

"That better be free."

"It is, don't worry girl, I got you. It's totally free...for the first few weeks," Eric muttered the last part so quietly that Abbie almost didn't hear him. Narrowing her eyes, Abbie watched as he began to sweat under her scrutiny. "…now just log in…"

"Wait, log in to what?" Abbie asked as he tossed her back her phone.

"Your ticket to happiness," Eric said with a grin and Abbie felt the blood drain from her face as she looked at the screen.

A dating app.

He made her an account for a goddamn dating app.

"You can't be serious," Abbie finally said. As Abbie looked through the profile, her expression slowly shifted into one of horror. "What is this?"

"It's the newest dating app on the market, it uses revolutionary algorithms to make your first date your last," Eric answered proudly as Abbie looked at him, her horrified expression never changing. "You helped me so I figured I'd help you! You're the one who told me you haven't dated anyone in two years so I'd figured this could be your first step getting back into the dating scene," Eric answered as Abbie looked back at her phone as if it were the first time that she had ever seen it. He even managed to make a profile pic of her by editing himself out of a selfie they had taken the previous night. "I even went out of my way to put in your interests and make a quick bio about you," Eric said and as Abbie looked at the profile closer, she couldn't help but shake her head at how accurate it was. In fact, not only was it accurate but he had made it in a way that if she hadn't known better, she'd have sworn that she actually made it.

"You know me so well," the words were not a compliment.

"Yeah, I know," but he took them as one anyway. "All you have to do is wait for someone to take an interest in you, the app will automatically check if you're at least a ninety-percent match and alert you. If you like what you see out of them, swipe your screen right and bam there you go. Welcome to how dating works nowadays."

"You know, there was once a time you could just-you know-go out and meet someone right?" Abbie asked him, her sarcasm heavy.

"Yeah, but that's too slow for people now, this gets straight to the point. I even went out of my way to filter your preferences," Eric revealed proudly as if Abbie should have been grateful for his actions. "Give it a day or two, the ladies will be lining up."

"Newsflash, do you know how many of these accounts could be fake?" Abbie questioned skeptically. "All these apps have had that same issue for decades now. I have no interest in being catfished."

"Abbie, please, if anyone can weed out a fake account it's you," Eric stated and Abbie cursed as they both knew he was right. "Look, just humor me for a day or two alright? What happened to you and Alice was tragic, but it's been two years and that monster who took her from you is locked up," Eric said firmly. "I ain't got no kind of place to say this, but you know Alice would want you to stop wasting away, right?" Eric asked an Abbie found herself speechless at his argument, knowing it to be true. "Two days, that's all I'm asking, just make the attempt you know? Do that and I'll never bring it up again. You don't even have to search for anyone, let them come to you. You're a catch, girl, I'm sure there is someone that can see that."

"We're supposed to be finding you the right gear, right?" Abbie responded as she desperately tried to change the subject. Though by the look on his face she might as well had gone on and agreed to his stupid deal. "Wipe that look off of your face!" Abbie snapped only this just caused Eric's grin to widen even further. Two days, she could humor him for two days and put this behind her.

*   *   *

Santa Monica, Abigail's Apartment

"Home sweet home," Abbie said to no one as she stepped back into her apartment that evening. They had spent hours getting the appropriate equipment for Eric before they started the tedious task of moving it all into his new apartment, which looked leagues better than hers. Abbie was happy for Eric if anyone needed a break it was him. Abbie moved to her kitchen to raid her fridge, desperately needing a drink after the long day. When she closed it a picture of herself and Eric celebrating with drinks in their hands appeared on the door. It was taken the previous night and had the caption: "Happy twenty-second!" which made her smile a bit. Eric annoyed her at times but she'd be damned if she didn't love that idiot. Abbie's smile faded soon as the digital slideshow continued and the picture was replaced with one of her and Alice. In the picture, Abbie and the former love of her life smiled at the camera. A heart filter surrounded their faces. Abbie could vividly remember the day they took that picture, how the sun reflected off Alice's golden hair as she pestered Abbie relentlessly to take the picture. Abbie closed her eyes tightly when she was overcome with a sense of loss. For a moment, she let herself go back to that day, soaking in everything she could remember from Alice's radiant smile to her crystal blue eyes. Most of all Abbie remembered the grin she herself wore, she hadn't smiled like that since losing Alice. Perhaps Eric was right, as much as Abbie hated to admit it. Abbie missed Alice sorely but perhaps it was time to move on. No amount of grieving would bring her back at the end of the day, and Alice would want Abbie to get out of this rut she trapped herself in. It was at that moment Abbie's phone vibrated.

"Don't tell me he forgot something," Abbie muttered as she checked her phone and saw that it wasn't a text but rather an alert from that damned app Eric had given her. Apparently, someone named Katarina Umbra had shown an interest in her. Despite herself, Abbie couldn't help but check out her profile. From Katarina's pictures, Abbie could tell she was an adventurous person, there were images from all over the country. Katarina had brown hair and bright green eyes, but one thing that Abbie noted fairly quickly was that she looked young. Not that Abbie was old, but Katarina just had an air of youth that seemed to radiate from her. Checking her bio, Abbie's suspicions were proven right as she saw that Katarina was eighteen. The age gap put Abbie off a bit but before she could reject the younger woman Abbie spotted that picture of her and Alice. Abbie was younger than Alice when they dated, around four years too if she remembered correctly. Later, Abbie wouldn't know what persuaded her to swipe right only that she had felt particularly reckless in that moment. "Well Abigail, let's see what you've gotten yourself into this time."

*　　*　　*

Santa Monica, Al's Diner, One week later

Abbie hummed to herself as she finished washing the dishes. Abbie's boss, Al, looked at her as if she had grown a second head and she couldn't blame him. Abbie was not the happiest worker by far, but Al-bless his soul-had yet to fire her. Still, she couldn't help it, the day had seemed a lot less gray than it used to be. During the past week since she made that reckless decision, Katarina, or Kat as she preferred to be called, and she had started messaging each other daily. At first, Abbie swore the app had made a mistake. Kat was a very "outdoors" person, an adventure lover that was a borderline adrenaline junkie if you asked Abbie. Abbie, on the other hand, was a total shut-in. Yet, in one conversation they stumbled across a common ground with a mutual love for cars. Though Kat's love was geared more toward the engines and such, Abbie's was more toward the software in recent vehicles. Despite that, Katarina's passion was endearing, to say the least. Often, they'd lose track of time in their conversations only noticing really when one of them had to get to work. Abbie didn't know what she did but apparently it involved a lot of traveling, in fact, Abbie was pretty sure Katarina lived at the airport by this point. Somehow, they managed to set aside a time for an actual date which was today as soon as Abbie clocked out.

"You alright in the head, kid?" Al asked after Abbie dried off her hands and hung up her apron. "You've got a little pep in your step."

"Do I?" Abbie asked, genuinely curious.

"Definitely," Eric said startling Abbie as she hadn't even noticed he had entered the kitchen to get ready for the night shift. Eric had given Al his two-week notice and Al had been determined to get as much work out of him as possible. Abbie would have felt bad for him if her friend wasn't blatantly ditching her there to work alone. "Something you want to say?" Eric asked knowingly and in response, Abbie shook her head. Abbie refused to let him know that she actually used that app of his, the little pride she had left just wouldn't allow it.

"Not at all," Abbie said firmly before a bell rung, letting them know that someone had entered the diner. "Now if you don't mind, I have to go," Abbie said as she left them in the kitchen. Now, even though she had heard someone enter the diner, Abbie still found herself surprised to see Kat standing by the door. Though Abbie had seen plenty of pictures of her, she was definitely cuter in person-and thankfully not a catfish. Kat was a good margin smaller than Abbie which she expected. Abbie was a tall woman that stood at six feet exactly which was something she always hated, it made her feel like a clumsy giant most of the time.

"Abbie?" Kat asked with a grin as she placed her hands in the pockets of a thin black hoodie she'd worn in many of her profile pictures. Almost hidden behind the hoodie was a black collar with a gold and green yin and yang pendant.

"Yeah, and you're Kat, right?" Abbie asked with a small smile. "Great timing, come on let's get out of here," Abbie said before she attempted to make her escape. Before Abbie could get too far, Kat suddenly stopped and waved at someone behind Abbie. Abbie was confused until she glanced back and found a smirking Eric with a confused Al behind him. Abbie grabbed Kat's hand and led her out before she could hear Eric's mouth.

"Friend?" Kat asked curiously making Abby snort.

"More like the bane of my existence."

"So best friends, then."

"Yup," Abbie admitted despondently. It was then Kat led Abbie toward a motorcycle and handed her a helmet. Kat had told Abbie she had a bike but it didn't click that Abbie might have to ride it anytime soon.

"Hm? What's the matter? Don't wanna ride?" Kat asked in concern when she saw the cautious look Abbie had on her face. "I mean we can always catch a bus or something, no air shuttles though they aren't worth the price."

"No, no, it's fine. I'm just wonderin' where your helmet is," Abbie answered lamely though Kat didn't seem to mind as she laughed.

"I never wear one."

"Isn't that illegal?" Abbie asked but Kat just winked at her.

"Only if you get caught," Kat answered and Abbie was certain now that Kat was definitely an adrenaline junkie.

"Wait, then where did you get this one?" Abbie asked curiously and to her surprise, Kat blushed a bit, a sheepish expression on her face.

"Grabbed one on my way over here, my roommate reminded me that not everyone might be up to riding on my bike, let alone helmetless," Kat answered and Abbie was both touched and surprised by the gesture.

"Wait, you bought me a helmet?" Abbie asked incredulously and she noted the surprisingly shy expression on Kat's face. "Expectin' me to ride with you a lot?" Abbie couldn't help but tease, surprised that Kat even had a shy side.

"After I show you the time of your life, yeah," Kat answered with a small smile that only grew when Abbie placed the helmet on her head.

"Now I'm interested, let's go," Abbie said while Kat's eyes lit up with joy before she climbed onto her bike. Abbie honestly didn't know what was wrong with her, she prided herself on not being a risk taker, but Kat had made her take more risks in the past week than she had in the last year. Something about Kat just made Abbie's inhibitions crumble and for the life of her, she couldn't understand why she didn't care as much as she probably should have.

*   *   *

Santa Monica, The Back Alley

"Nice spot," Kat said with a grin as they sat at a booth in the corner of the club and ate pizza. Abbie used the term "club" lightly. The Back Alley was really just a restaurant with a dance floor. A chill spot if you had nothing to do in the afternoon or evening. At least, that's how it should have been and how it was from Abbie's past experience.

"I have no idea what's goin' on," Abbie said honestly, still stunned by how lively the place had become. Some patrons were even dancing on their tables, the LED implants in their tattoos shining brightly in the darkened room. It was almost as if a switch had been flipped the moment they walked in as the calm restaurant tried to become the liveliest club in the city. Hell, even Abbie felt her inhibitions continue to lower which gave her the sudden urge to go out and get into some trouble. Good trouble if the way Kat looked at her was any indication. With a surprising amount of effort, Abbie fought these strange urges down. Call her old fashioned but Abbie didn't take people back to her place on the first date, no matter how cute they were.

"What can I say? The party doesn't start until I show up," Kat said cheekily. "Tell me about yourself. We've been talking about our likes and all that, but where are you from?" Kat asked curiously. "Like, how does a girl from down south end up here?"

"You know I'm from down south?" Abbie asked as she was positive the profile Eric had made her said that her hometown was Santa Monica. This was mainly because not even Eric knew Abbie's hometown.

"It's faint, but your accent is still there. Not to mention a name like Abigail just screams country girl, no offense," Kat said and Abbie couldn't help but laugh at that.

"None taken, I take pride in not bein' born a city slicker," Abbie said with a grin.

"So how did you end up here, if you don't mind me asking?"

"Well when I was fourteen I got accepted to New Tokyo Tech and graduated at seventeen. When I came back, I got offers to work at places all over. I could have picked somewhere back home but… irreconcilable differences with my family made me decide to take a job up north instead," Abbie answered and she did her best not to laugh at Kat's expression. Abbie's background was not exactly one someone would expect from a waitress at a diner.

"Wait, NTT? Like where the super egg-heads go to school?" Kat asked while Abbie smiled at her expression. "Not to pry, but what kind of "irreconcilable differences" makes you flee across the country?"

"I'll put it this way, they'd have a fit if they saw us right now," Abbie said and waited for the proverbial light-bulb to go off in Kat's head. "Society has changed a lot, but my family seems to be frozen in time regarding some things. It's like their values were etched in stone."

"Oh," Kat said sadly. "I get it, I know a thing or two about old mentalities getting in the way of happiness," Kat said, more to herself than Abbie who chose not to comment on it.

"Well, they didn't exactly take too kindly to it, but by that point, I had already graduated so I figured I could take care of myself. Last I checked I'm still alive and well so I guess I did somethin' right," Abbie said with a shrug to let Kat know that her question didn't bother her. "People have a habit of thinkin' that I'm sad about the way things went down back then, but honestly it was like wakin' up from a bad dream," Abbie said after a few moments and she noted the thoughtful expression on Kat's face. "You want to know how I ended up at a diner, don't you?"

"If you wouldn't mind," Kat said sheepishly. "Sorry, I've been told I'm too curious for my own good."

"Then that makes two of us," Abbie said and at Kat's confused expression she explained. "The company I worked for was big, each day was like a dream come true as I worked in R&D. One day, though, I stumbled across somethin' that didn't add up. A project I was workin' on was being repurposed for things that…let's just say I didn't approve of, and neither would the government," Abbie explained. "I blew the whistle and the entire project came down. Sadly, my promised confidentiality didn't work out so well and I've been on some sort of blacklist ever since."

"Are you serious!? But that's not right at all!"

"No, but that's the world we live in," Abbie said as she waved off Kat's concern. "I don't care so much anymore, lookin' back on it I'd do the same thing again if I had the choice," Abbie said honestly and for some reason, Kat looked a bit impressed by that. "But enough about me, what about you?"

"Me? Not much to say really. When I was eight, I was adopted along with my best friend, Jack, by our guardian. Her name's Violet but we call her Vivi.

"Vivi?"

"Yup, short for violent Violet, trust me she was not a woman you wanted to piss off. She was dangerous as hell with a belt," Kat said with a shudder as if traumatized. "We lived in Chicago where she raised us and home-schooled us herself for the last ten years. This year, Jack and I moved out west due to a job offer," Kat answered and Abbie couldn't help but smile as a happy expression crossed Kat's face as she seemed to recall memories that Abbie realized she wanted to hear one day.

"What was the job?"

"He became a bodyguard, I still laugh at it because even though he was two years older than me, he was much smaller than I was until puberty hit him like a truck," Kat said and Abbie couldn't help but wonder how strong this Jack must have been to have such a job at twenty years old. "Me? I've always been good with my hands so I've been doing odd jobs wherever I can," Kat explained. Nearly immediately after she said that, Kat grimaced. Abbie was confused until she added, "For some reason, saying that out loud sounded a lot worse than I expected."

"Hey I don't judge, gotta get paid somehow," Abbie teased.

"Shut up!" Kat said as she swatted Abbie's arm, though she couldn't help stop the giggle that escaped her. "I meant that I fix things, mainly vehicles. No one knows an engine as well as I do!"

"Oh? We'll have to see about that. I may be a computer nerd, but you know I am a car fanatic," Abbie challenged playfully.

"You're on. Still, I guess you could say that's why I ended up making a profile on that app," Kat said after a moment. "I don't have many friends here so I was getting a bit lonely. That said, I hope you understand that I definitely didn't come here tonight to just be your friend."

"Good, somethin' tells me that would have been a waste," Abbie said, grateful that Kat didn't feel like dancin' around that subject. It was then a thought occurred to Abbie. "I have to ask though, why me?"

"Uh, you sure you want to know? It's kind of stupid," Kat said sheepishly, but all that did was pique Abbie's curiosity even more.

"Try me."

"I never met anyone with eyes as gray as yours before and wanted to see them in person," Kat said and for a moment Abbie thought she was joking until she realized that Kat was being dead serious.

"Seriously?" Abbie asked laughing in disbelief.

"Yeah...see I told you I was a curious person," Kat said and Abbie had to admit, Kat definitely had her beat in that department. "Your eyes drew me in, but it was you who got me here."

"Ain't you the smooth talker?" Abbie asked as she averted her eyes with a shy expression.

"I try," Kat said before they continued on with their date. The night was young and eventually they made their way through town and stopped at various places of interest before they headed to see a movie. A bit cliché, Abbie admitted, but she ended up having one of the best nights she had in the past two years. One thing Abbie was certain of as she spent time with Kat was that she was definitely happy that she swiped right.

CHAPTER 2

......●●●●●●●●●● .....

THE MARK

Santa Monica, Eric's Apartment

Music echoed throughout the apartment as Abbie sat on a beanbag chair and bobbed her head to the smooth hip-hop beat. As she looked around the room, Abbie once more appreciated Eric's new apartment. Hell, the view alone was insane as the apartment overlooked a good portion of the city. Abbie smiled to herself as she spotted a poster that featured a very beautiful dark-skinned woman with long black hair and hazel eyes. In the poster, the woman held a crown with her right hand that was covered in a black glove that bore a golden "M" on it. The bottom of the poster had the word "Diamond" and next to that, Abbie could see the word "Goals" written in marker by Eric. Eric, himself, grinned to himself as he listened to the music before it finally came to a stop.

"So, what do you think?" Eric asked as Abbie opened her eyes after the beat ended.

"That you, my friend, might have actually found your callin'," Abbie answered. "Seriously, this is good Eric. I'm proud of you."

"Come on Abbie, don't get all sentimental on me!"

"Just tellin' it how it is, don't forget the little people," Abbie said which made Eric shake his head.

"Never forget where you came from. Besides if you and Roy hadn't hooked me up, I'm not sure if I would even be making good quality music," Eric said seriously. "I owe you, Abbie."

"Let's just say we're even, then," Abbie responded. Abbie's words confused him for a moment before a smile crept onto his face.

"Things going that well, huh?" Eric asked knowingly. Abbie averted her eyes as her cheeks reddened slightly. "Almost two months now, right? I won't lie I was a bit surprised you two actually hooked up, but y'all look good together."

"I won't lie I wasn't expectin' much myself but this is honestly the most fun I've had in a long time, Eric. She's like a breath of fresh air," Abbie explained, a fond smile gracing her lips.

"I'll say, didn't even know you could smile this much until recently, or leave that cave you call an apartment willingly," Eric said as he leaned back in his chair. "She's a free spirit that a shut-in like you definitely needed. You're even taking risks again, living life instead of going day to day like a zombie."

"It wasn't that bad, was it?" Abbie couldn't help but ask and the look Eric gave her told her that, yes, it had indeed been that bad. "Speakin' of risks, I gave Al my notice. Figured I'd go try to get some kind of job in my actual field again, even entry level pay is better than what I'm making now."

"Wait, aren't you black-listed?"

"Yeah, findin' a job in any of the big corps again is a pipe dream, but I'm sure there is some small business that would take me in. The only reason I haven't checked before was that I just…didn't care anymore, you know?" Abbie explained tiredly. "But I know for a fact I can't keep my sanity at Al's anymore."

"That bad?"

"With you gone, and no one else takin' your job, he's been workin' me to the bone. I can't take it anymore, the pay is nowhere near good enough for all the hours I'm there," Abbie said and Eric knew from his own experience that she was right.

"Well, good luck then."

"Appreciated," Abbie said before she checked the time on her phone. "I gotta go."

17

"Tell Kat I said hey."

"Will do."

*　　*　　*

Santa Monica, Arcade Nox

"Here you go," Abbie said as she placed a can on the arcade game Kat was engrossed in. She held back a laugh as she watched Kat use the fake gun to shoot down holograms of zombies.

"Thanks-oh no, no!" Kat called out before the music from the game died down as the words "Game Over" were displayed before her. "Damn it!"

"Sorry, kitten, but you'll never beat my high score," Abbie gloated before she handed Kat the can. "Here, use this to wash down the salt."

"One day I will defeat you, just watch," Kat swore before she downed the drink. "That hit the spot."

"Admit it, you just date me because I get you booze," Abbie teased.

"Babe, if that were true, I'd date someone who gives me more than a single can of beer."

"Hey, you're the one drivin'. I don't care how high you say your tolerance is, you're not gettin' me killed," Abbie said before she flicked Kat on the nose. "Or yourself for that matter."

"Aw, you do care."

"Seriously though, why don't you get a fake ID or somethin' instead of sneakin' into these places? In fact, how are you so good at doin' that?" Abbie asked as she wondered how Kat had managed to sneak into every bar and club they met up at.

"What did Jack call it? Oh yeah, the legacy of a misspent youth," Kat said cheekily. "As for why I don't get an ID, well…this is more fun. I'm 18 which means I won't get to enjoy the thrill of sneaking in to places much longer."

"You're crazy. You know that, right?" Abbie asked and in response Kat stood on the tips of her toes and kissed the taller woman on the corner of her mouth.

"For you, I might be," Kat said playfully. "Come on, let's get out of here."

"Let's," Abbie agreed as Kat looked around the arcade for a moment.

"I'll meet you outside, gonna go out the way I came," Kat said before she and Abbie went their separate ways.

*　　*　　*

"Miss me?" Kat asked as Abbie stepped out and found her waiting by her bike. Abbie just rolled her eyes at the question.

"Yes, that was the hardest two minutes of my life," Abbie joked as she went to grab her helmet. "Let's get out of here-"

"Not so fast," a voice said, turning around they saw a police officer approaching them. "I've received an anonymous tip that there was underage drinking occurring within that building."

"Uh, good for you?" Kat said awkwardly. "What's that have to do with us?"

"The tip described two individuals in great detail, individuals that matched your description to a T," the officer said pointedly which made Abbie frown before she pulled out her license.

"Well as you can see, I'm legal," Abbie pointed out making him frown before he turned to face Kat.

"What about her?"

"No, but I didn't come out of that bar either. I'm just here to pick her up," Kat lied smoothly, though the officer didn't seem convinced.

"Is that so? Then you wouldn't mind if I smelt your breath, then would you?"

"Actually, I would mind, creep," Kat said with a frown. "Who wouldn't?"

"Miss, I'm going to need you to come with me," the officer told Kat who just laughed much to Abbie's surprise.

"Babe, wanna make a run for it?" Kat asked curiously as both Abbie and the officer looked at her as if she had lost her mind.

"Kat!"

"What? It'd make a good story, promise," Kat said with a grin and to her own horror, Abbie forced back a laugh. There was nothing funny about the situation they were in but everything suddenly just seemed too surreal to take seriously. "But you're probably right, this guy seems like someone with a twitchy trigger finger. Wouldn't want you to get hurt," Kat said before raising her hands. "Cuff me but let the record show that I would have totally gotten away," Kat said, as the officer glared at her before he handcuffed her.

"Kat, wait..."

"Don't worry, trust me, I'll be fine, catch you later," Kat said only for the officer to interrupt her.

"Oh no you won't, she's coming too. My source says she got you the alcohol, didn't she? She also tried to lie about it, she's coming in as well," the officer said and Kat's eyes narrowed a bit when Abbie found herself being arrested.

*   *   *

Abbie and Kat sat in the back of a police air shuttle, their hands cuffed behind their backs as the officer flew above the city. The night lights reflected in their eyes as they stared out of the windows in silence. To say that this was not how Abbie expected the night to turn out would be an understatement. She couldn't really get mad either, legally they were in the wrong but something about the entire situation just didn't sit well with her. An uneasy feeling filled her stomach as the cruiser began to fly over the ocean.

"Wait the department isn't this way, where are we-" Abbie was cut off when she suddenly tasted apples. The words had died on Abbie's lips after Kat leant over and claimed them for her own.

"Hey what are you two doing back there!?"

"What does it look like?" Kat asked after breaking the kiss. Kat glanced back at the officer that glared at them through the rear-view mirror. With her back now toward him, she flipped him off before she continued. "Just because you interrupted our date doesn't mean it's over. Pay attention to flying before you get us killed," Kat said before she turned back to Abbie, her face so close that the officer assumed that she continued to kiss her. "Trust me," Kat whispered quietly. The officer just grumbled to himself as he looked away from them and focused on flying. With wide eyes, Abbie watched as Kat's hands had suddenly but silently freed themselves. Immediately, Kat began to work on Abbie's handcuffs. "Close your eyes until I tell you to open them, just keep calm, and trust me okay, Abbie?" Kat whispered into her ear. Abbie closed her eyes and she tensed when she felt her hands become free. Not long after that, Abbie could hear the officer exclaim loudly as the sound of the door next to her being opened entered her ears. Abbie could no longer feel the seatbelt around her as the wind blew through her hair. The officer's shouts were drowned out by the beating of Abbie's heart. Abbie felt a sense of weightlessness as a pair of arms wrapped tightly around her. "Hold your breath!" Kat's voice suddenly shouted. Abbie barely had enough time to do as Kat instructed before Kat spun them around so that Abbie's body wouldn't be the first to hit the water. Immediately when they were both submerged in the cold water, Kat maintained her hold on Abbie to make sure she didn't fall too far. When they broke the surface of the water, Abbie broke free from Kat's hold so that they could both make it to the shore. "Damn that was a rush!" Kat said as they stepped onto the beach.

"Kat, what the hell!?" Abbie asked incredulously as she looked at Kat, the both of them completely drenched.

"What?" Kat asked as with an unwavering smile. "Don't tell me you didn't see that that whole situation was wrong, right? He wasn't going to the department and he didn't even read us our rights. Can you say sketchy?" Kat said and Abbie realized she was right. "And what was that crap about smelling my breath? Why not use a scanner like every other cop?"

"So, what? You're sayin' he wasn't a cop?"

"Hell, if I know, his gear seemed legit but he sure didn't act like he knew what he was doing," Kat said as she pulled off her ever-present hoodie and tied it around her waist. "Something was wrong there so I decided to trust my gut," Kat said as she pulled out her phone. "So glad they made this thing water-proof."

"What are you doin'?"

"Texting Jack and letting him know what happened so he can grab my bike. I left the key in the ignition, just hoping nobody jacked it," Kat mused.

"Should...should we call the cops?" Abbie asked shakily. Unlike Kat who took the whole thing in stride as if it were an everyday occurrence, Abbie appeared to be on the brink of a meltdown. Abbie had no idea what to do or think about the terrifying situation they were just in.

"Something tells me if that guy was a legit officer then that would be a mistake," Kat said as she pocketed the phone.

"But we can't just do nothin', Kat! Say that guy was some sick bastard, we got lucky but what about whoever he gets next?" Abbie tried to reason.

"Whoa, whoa, relax, no one said we were doing nothing," Kat said as she placed a hand on the taller woman's shoulder. "Like I said, I texted Jack. He'll handle it," Kat said confidently. "We need to calm you down a bit," Kat said before she gestured toward a harbor in the distance. The harbor was illuminated by a rainbow of lights covering it and a massive Ferris wheel. "It's a bit of a walk but let's go and relax. When we get back we can pick you up a new phone if you need it."

"N-no...mine will be fine," Abbie said before she took a deep breath and tried in vain to calm herself. Abbie had always been an over-thinker and too many "what if" scenarios played in her head to keep her calm. Abbie expected to have a panic attack but instead she was surprised to feel her fear slowly shift into excitement. Abbie looked down at her hand and saw that Kat had grabbed it tightly. It was then Abbie was certain, she didn't care how crazy it would have made her sound, something about Kat affected her in a way that wasn't natural. Despite this, Abbie didn't question this welcome change but instead held on to Kat as if her life depended on it. Abbie's grip was strong but Kat showed no signs of discomfort. For a moment, Abbie said nothing lost in her thoughts as Kat led her away. "Thank you," Abbie said after a few minutes and though Kat hadn't looked back at her she could tell that Kat had been smiling.

"No. Thank you."

"For what?"
"Trusting me."

*   *   *

"Hey, want to talk about it? You looked very scared back there, not that you obviously shouldn't have been but uh…yeah…sorry, I'm not good at this," Kat said sheepishly as they sat in the Ferris wheel.

"I…" Abbie began but it was obvious to Kat that it was hard for her to talk about.

"You don't have to tell me, you know I'm just too curious for my own good," Kat reassured quickly.

"No, it's…it's fine, just give me a second," Abbie said as she took a deep breath. "Before you, the last person I dated died two years ago," Abbie began as Kat listened intently. "She gave me this," Abbie said as she pulled off a pale gold cross from her chest and handed it to Kat. "For our anniversary."

"This is really beautiful," Kat said as she held the pendant.

"Yeah," Abbie said quietly. "That night we were kidnapped," Abbie said and Kat's eyes widened in alarm. "I had a stalker, a researcher at Drakenova Corp. that had been fixated on me since I interned there during my senior year. I don't know why he chose that night of all nights, perhaps he just wanted to hurt me, I don't know, but he ended her life in front of me. I am pretty sure he was going to come after me next, but it's only because of Eric that I got away," Abbie explained which confused Kat. "We were supposed to meet that night and I never miss an appointment I make without lettin' someone know ahead of time. When Eric realized somethin' was off he tracked my phone and came in when the monster turned his attention to me. Eric shot him twice, it didn't kill him but it put him down long enough for the police to get him. Two in the head and he just didn't die."

"I'm…sorry I asked."

"It's fine, he's locked away now but…it's just I never thought somethin' like that would happen to me, you know?" Abbie said quietly. "You see that shit broadcasted all the time but you never really realize that it can happen to you until it's too late. Tonight… it could have happened again and I'm just sick of it, I'm sick of my terrible luck."

"Your luck isn't too bad. I mean we got together, right?" Kat asked with a smile which Abbie returned weakly. "What was his name? The monster that hurt you?"

"Alexei…" Abbie answered quietly. "…why?"

"Just curious," Kat answered as she tightened her grip on the cross. "Let's get you home."

* * *

Santa Monica, Abbie's Apartment Complex

"You sure you'll be fine?" Abbie asked when they stopped outside of her apartment.

"Definitely, though I'll be avoiding the cops for a while just in case. See you soon," Kat said as she turned away from Abbie and walked away. Abbie watched Kat for a moment longer before she turned to enter the building. It was then that an arm wrapped around her waist before a hand covered her mouth. Abbie was unable to make a sound before she was dragged away into an alley. Her eyes watered as she watched Kat's back, unable to get her attention. Soon Abbie found herself slammed into a wall with enough force to knock the wind out of her.

"Finally, after all these years, an opportunity presents itself," an all too familiar voice growled. Her face shifted into an expression of horror as she stared up at her attacker. His hand was wrapped tightly around her throat to prevent her from being able to scream.

"A-Alexei?" Abbie choked out as she found herself trapped by her past tormentor. "You're supposed to be in jail!"

"My sweet, did you honestly think that cell could hold me back?" Alexei asked as he gripped the side of her face. "There is so much about this world that you know nothing about. I was out of that excuse of a prison the very next night," Alexei revealed as the blood drained from her face. "I have friends in very high places," Alexei said with a laugh. "Since then, I've been waiting, biding my time for just one moment when you would let your guard down and it finally happened. Oh, I can't tell you how much I wanted to kill that fool you call a friend for separating us, but if I did, then you'd no doubt realize that I was free. I thought I was a patient man, but that was proven wrong once I realized you didn't learn your lesson from last time."

"L-lesson?"

"That infidelity would not be tolerated, my dear. It was bad enough you chose that whore over me the first time, but then you turn toward a thief of all people?" Alexei snarled. "Stealing from their own kind is bad enough but then they dared to steal from me!?" Alexei continued angrily as his grip tightened. With an enraged roar, he slammed his hand down on a nearby dumpster, and Abbie paled as she saw the metal warp under his might. "No, something had to be done and soon, so now here we are. I wanted that damn officer to remove your cross for me, but fortunately your little…toy…did it for me."

"What are you?" Abbie asked in morbid fascination as she watched his eyes glow red with his rage. "You really are a monster," Abbie whispered incredulously.

"You have no idea, but you will soon, I can open an entirely new world to you. All you have to do is be a good girl and accept my embrace," Alexei said as he bared his fangs. "Despite what you might think, I just want what's mine," Alexei said as tears fell from Abbie's eyes as his breath drew closer to her neck.

"Really? Because last I checked, she was with me," Alexei paused in his actions when he heard the voice before he released Abbie. Alexei turned to face a hooded Kat who stood at the end of the alley. Her lips were curled up in a faint smile that failed to reach her eyes which held nothing but contempt. Kat's green eyes were even brighter than Abbie remembered, an electric green that seemed to shine in the dark alley as Kat stared down the monster.

"Kat, run!" Abbie begged weakly, "He's-"

"-Not human, I know," Kat said as she pulled out Abbie's cross. It was then that Abbie realized that she had never gotten it back from Kat. "Sorry, but it was the only way to get him out of hiding," Kat said as she tossed the cross to Abbie. "Quick, put it on!"

"No!" Alexei roared before he whimpered in pain as it sailed over his head and landed in front of Abbie. Abbie wasted no time and quickly grabbed it. "You don't get to take her from me!"

"I took nothing, she chose me. That's the problem with you damned parasites, you never know when to keep your hands to yourself," Kat said and though her anger was clear, her smile widened. "You're brave though, you know that interfering with the Guild spells death, especially for monsters like you vampires. We've shown you mercy, but it seems you really wish for us to hunt you all to extinction," Kat said and as she approached them a black ash-like material began to spilled from beneath her hoodie and from the top of her pants. Abbie watched as the strange substances floated up into Kat's grasp. Green sparks danced around the strange substance as it merged in Kat's hand and formed a bladed metallic whip. Kat silently tightened her grip on the weapon which caused green sparks to crackle along its length. "So, you can't blame me for what happens next."

"Interfering with the Guild? I did no such thing! She does not bear your mark, she is a civilian which means she's free game," Alexei said as he glanced at Kat's whip. "If anyone is interfering it's you with my mating!"

"Who do you think will be believed?" Kat asked unphased by Alexei's claims. "You don't matter. Your people will gladly let you die to maintain the peace and you know it," Kat said as she tilted her head. "Did you even get permission to embrace her?"

"I...I love her, they'll surely understand after the fact!" Alexei said with a manic expression. "You're alone, without your band you thieves are no threat. You are clearly at a disadvantage."

"I know," and somehow Kat's grin widened even more. "That's what makes this such a rush!" Kat said before she ran at him while a green spark danced in her eyes. Kat swung her whip at him and it released a loud crack as it tore into his body. The whip left a sizeable gash in his back but to Abbie's horror, he didn't bleed even as he screamed in pain.

"Come on," Kat taunted as she kicked him in his new wound, his skin burning from the mere contact. In fact, it seemed as though Kat even being close to him caused Alexie pain. "Show me the power you gave up your humanity for," Kat said and he growled in response as his nails lengthened into two sets of dangerous looking claws. Black veins appeared over his body as it shifted and cracked while his body became more bat-like in appearance. His clothes ripped and tore as his body grew in size and Abbie found herself forced to hold back her vomit at the grotesque sight. Alexei lunged at Kat with a roar that sent chills down Abbie's spine. Abbie watched in muted horror as he attacked Kat at speeds that clearly surpassed human limitations. Still, somehow, Kat managed to react just fast enough to avoid his attacks. Kat ducked under one vicious swipe of his claws and grinned as his claw slammed into a nearby wall and got stuck. Kat giggled as she whipped him and tore into his body with her assault until he finally ripped his claw free. He clawed viciously at Kat only for her to duck under the blow and dive between his legs as the strange green energy crackled faintly across her body. Abbie watched in amazement as she saw Kat dive into the ground as if it were made out of water and become a shadow that slid toward her quickly. When Kat leapt from the shadow, she landed in front of Abbie as Alexei turned to face them. Only then did he notice that a strange golden card was stuck into the ground between his legs. "Close your eyes," Kat warned as she shielded Abbie as much as she could with her body and closed her eyes tightly. The card pulsed once like a heartbeat before it quietly exploded into a blinding flash of light that illuminated the alleyway. So bright was the light, it made Alexei recoil in agony and claw at his eyes as his body released a dark smoke as if he had been burned. While he was distracted, Kat stood up and turned around as more cards slid down from her sleeves and into her hands. Kat then began to toss them into the ground in front of Alexei and into the walls surrounding him.

"How dare you!?" Alexei shouted while his vision struggled to correct itself. Black spiked chains exploded from the cards and entangled Alexei like a web that bound him in place. Alexei screamed as the chains burned his body wherever they made contact with his skin.

"Man, this is the best you've got? I was expecting something to get my heart pumping, you really are pathetic," Kat said as the strange ash merged together above her palm and formed another gold card. "A gift," Kat said as she handed the card to Abbie who took it hesitantly. Upon closer inspection, Abbie noted that the card looked and felt as though it were made out of gold. The back of the card had what appeared to be a classic yin and yang symbol though instead of two sections, it had three. Each section had a small circle inside of it and each circle was connected together by a black triangle. When Abbie flipped the card over, she noticed the front bore the word "Crush" in black that looked like it was hastily written by Kat.

"What is this?"

"That is your life," Kat answered as she knelt down next to Abbie and gestured toward the bound form of Alexei. "This man took the person you loved away from you without a second thought. He took away your joy, your life, and now his life is in your hands. I could turn him in to people that will actually do something this time. Or…you could just end it, stop living in fear, and regain some control," Kat said matter-of-factly as Alexie struggled to break free only for the chains to tighten even further. "Getting rid of his kind is easy, use silver, pierce the heart, destroy the head, or burn them. Crush that card, and those chains will make him just a bad memory.

"Don't listen to her, my love! Look, I made a mistake then…I see now that I acted rashly," Alexei said frantically. "What would your dear Alice want? She wouldn't want you to kill me!"

"You're right, she wouldn't, she'd want you to live with the guilt, knowin' the pain you caused others," Abbie said quietly and Kat frowned a bit. Abbie felt her heart plummet as the weight of what was in her hand suddenly sunk in. "She was a beautiful soul that you took away from me," Abbie said as anger filled her voice while her hand tightened around the card that dug into her skin like a razor and drew blood. "She would want us to make peace…she was a lot of things Alexie, but careful wasn't one of them," Abbie said as her grip around the card tightened more and in response so did the chains. "And what she would want, no longer matters. You made sure of that. So, I'm going to do what I want," Abbie said as she crushed the card in her hand. Kat smiled and Abbie watched in a silent awe as the chains tore Alexie asunder.

"He's gone," Kat said quietly as Abbie wept as she realized that her tormentor was gone for good. "Come on, let's get you inside and cleaned up. I'll get rid of this mess."

*　　*　　*

"What are you?" Abbie asked quietly as she looked at her now bandaged hand, her shirt off as Kat sat behind her with her hand resting above her left shoulder. Green sparks danced across Kat's hand and melded small traces of the ash into Abbie's skin. The same emblem that was on the back of Kat's strange cards slowly appeared on Abbie's skin, which made Abbie squirm at the slight burning she felt. "And what are you doin'?"

"I'm a thief like that bastard said. As for what I'm doing, I'm giving you a mark that when taken off will make you forget the stuff you've seen," Kat explained. "You've just seen too much. Again, I'm really sorry for using you as bait, but we needed him to show himself."

"Is that the real reason you came into my life? To find him?" Abbie asked quietly making Kat frown. "Did you just use me?"

"What? Wait, hold up," Kat said after she finished the mark. Kat turned Abbie around so that the woman could see her clearly. "I didn't even know about the guy until today. You can't see the things I do but I could see clearly that the officer from earlier was under someone's control. Someone who clearly didn't know how police work. When you told me your story, I realized you were being stalked by some sort of monster which is why I took your cross. The silver in it was keeping him away, he'd never show himself as long as you had it."

"But my cross is made out of gold," Abbie said with a confused frown as she grasped the pendant gently.

"Electrum," Kat corrected. "It's an alloy of gold and silver. Trust me, I work with that metal enough to recognize it at a glance but I can see how you might make the mistake," Kat answered as Abbie looked at her in surprise. Kat then gave her a wry smile. "It doesn't take much of it to harm a monster on his level. Again, I'm sorry for the bait thing but the last two months were real. I was here for you, not him."

"Then why are you gettin' rid of my memories? Makin' me forget about you?"

"What the hell are you talking about woman? When I remove the mark, your memories of yesterday up until now will be removed. Your cognition will shift and your mind will make up its own memories to make up for it. Babe, you watch too many trashy dramas. I'm not erasing our relationship and I'm not going anywhere," Kat then kissed Abbie on her forehead. "I'll stay in your life until you kick me out."

"Oh..." Abbie said and she looked bit embarrassed by how quickly she jumped to conclusions. "Will I forget he's dead?"

"The way my boss put it is that in your case, you'll probably just think you saw on the news that he was killed in prison or something," Kat answered.

"That's...that's insane. Wait? Your boss?"

"Thieves work in bands of three and we each play a different role. There's me, Jack, and you wouldn't believe who our boss is," Kat said with a laugh. "Look you're a nerd, right?" Kat asked which made Abbie frown as she nodded. "Don't give me that look, nerds rock, but anyway you know how you have those roleplaying games? Those old ones from way back where you make a hero that goes off to face some sort of ultimate evil? That's like the formula for all of them, right?" Kat asked curiously and Abbie nodded, not knowing where she was going with this. "Well, what are the four most basic hero classes that can be found in almost all of those games?"

"Uh, the warrior, the magician, the archer, and the...thief..." Abbie trailed off as she saw where Kat was going.

"Exactly, remember, fiction is always based off of reality, at least that's what my boss says. Point is, for each of those classes there exists an organization, a faction, in our world that works to protect humanity that has been around and hidden for centuries. You have the Thieves' Guild, the Mages' Circle, the Tribe, and the Knights' Order. Together they protect the world in secret from threats the people aren't ready to know exist. Well, at least that's how it should be. The alliance between the four is gone. The Knights' Order has been destroyed. The Tribe keeps to themselves now, and the Thieves' Guild and Mages' Circle are at war," Kat said with a frown. "Because of this, you've got the monsters running around like they own the place. We've been divided."

"I have so many Goddamn questions," Abbie said quietly as she looked at Kat in morbid fascination. Kat just laughed fondly at Abbie's expression, knowing how curious of a person the woman was. "But it doesn't matter, I won't remember them anyway. Don't know why you told me this much if it's such a big deal."

"I told you because I care about you dummy," Kat said as she pointed at Abbie's head. "You won't remember it there," Kat began before she moved her finger down to Abbie's heart. "But you will remember it there, and that's what I want. I want you to feel safe when you're near me. There is a lot that you and most of the population don't know for your own good. I just want you to know in your heart that I'm always fighting for you," Kat said with a grin before she pulled out a gold flask from her hoodie. "Take a sip, the smallest sip possible, of this for me. It'll get rid of your injuries since we can't have you waking up hurt."

"What is it?"

"Not only would you not believe me, but I'd be here for hours explaining it to you," Kat said with a giggle. "Just trust me. Be careful, it's potent. Too much and you'll be drunk off your ass."

"God damn..." Abbie whispered after the liquid splashed on her tongue. "That's the greatest thing I've ever tasted," Abbie said as she looked down at the flask in awe. Eyes filled with unshed tears, Abbie didn't even seem to pay attention as her bruises and the cuts on her hand began to heal rapidly. "I...I...what?" Abbie said as she wiped her eyes, caught off guard by how much the strange drink affected her.

"Okay so this might sting a bit, but what I just gave you will definitely get rid of the headache you're about to get. I'm going to remove your mark now," Kat warned before she placed her hand on the mark, she had given Abbie. "One...two...three..." Kat said and Abbie just sat there as if she felt...nothing.

"That wasn't so bad," Abbie said before she immediately frowned as she realized her memories were still intact.

"Wait a second, what?" Kat wondered before placing a hand on Abbie's shoulder again. "One, two, three and...what the hell?" Kat asked quietly before she tried again only to get the same result. "Okay, let's try this," Kat muttered as the pendant in her collar began to spin before it stopped with a small click, with the gold section on top. Abbie could feel Kat shudder for a moment before she once more attempted to remove the mark. "Uh-oh."

"Uh-oh? What uh-oh?" Abbie asked with a frown as she watched Kat dial a number on her phone. A moment passed as Kat held the phone to her ear and looked over at Abbie with a frown.

"Hey, boss? Yeah, he was taken care of. Jack did what? Cool, glad he handled business," Kat said as Abbie watched her talk to her apparent boss. "Look...we have a problem," Kat trailed off as she looked at Abbie. Both Kat and Abbie looked just as confused as the other. "I can't get her mark off."

CHAPTER 3

· · · · · · ●●● ● ●●● · · · · · ·

BAND THIRTEEN

Santa Monica, Midas Tower

"We're here, let's see if the boss can do anything," Kat said as they entered a large apartment complex. Abbie's eyes widened as she looked around the lobby, to say the place was a bit out of her price range would be an understatement. It was clearly meant to only cater to the rich and powerful. Everyone she saw in the lobby was dressed elegantly.

"Ms. Umbra, welcome back," the doorman greeted Kat who nodded toward him as they passed.

"You've been livin' here the whole time?" Abbie asked incredulously as they entered an elevator. A part of her even felt embarrassed that she ever allowed Kat to see her own run-down apartment when the woman was apparently living a life of luxury.

"Yeah, but I'm splitting the bill with two other people so it's not that impressive."

"If you say so," Abbie said skeptically. "Where are we goin'?"

"Straight to the top," Kat said as she moved forward and pressed the button to send them to the penthouse suite. As the elevator went up, Kat released a sigh as she leaned against Abbie and placed her head on her shoulder. The two stood in silence as they looked out of the elevator and toward the illuminated city. As they watched the sunrise in the distance, Abbie realized that it had been a long day.

"Now what?" Abbie asked quietly.

"I don't know, but if anyone can figure it out it's the boss," Kat said as she looked up at Abbie. "Trust me, we'll figure this out."

"I hope you're right. Though if it's any consolation, I always wanted a tattoo but the needles scared me," Abbie said as Kat gained a thoughtful expression.

"Good to know, but you can do better than what I did. You'd be pretty hot inked up, we'll get you over that fear and get you something a bit more exotic one day," Kat said as the elevator came to a stop. "Look, the other two can be a bit...intense...but they mean well," Kat said nervously. Abbie tensed, that kind of warning never meant anything good. In fact, it reminded her of all the times meeting the parents of girls she was interested in going horribly wrong. "The only one I'm concerned about is Jack, he's the most dangerous," Kat said with a scowl before looking up at Abbie as her scowl was replaced with a pout. "Don't forget you're with me."

"Okay?" Abbie said though it sounded more like a question as they entered the penthouse. Nearly immediately a black pit-bull rushed Kat and climbed up her leg.

"Hey! Get off! Stupid dog!" Kat complained but her heart clearly wasn't into it as she grinned at the dog. "I missed you too, Sal."

"Sal?" Abbie asked looking a bit amused. Abbie was nervous when the dangerous looking dog turned to face her, but he did nothing but sit down and look up at her happily.

"Short for Salvatore. I named him after he got me out of a jam a few months ago and he has been with me ever since. He actually belonged to the boss but had run away from home when I found him, talk about a small world," Kat said as she petted him on his head.

"Salvatore...that's Latin, right? You speak it?"

"Yup, Spanish too."

"Kat? Are you finally back?" a voice asked and Abbie noted that it had an English accent. Moments later a well-dressed young man with platinum blonde hair entered the room. "Ah, you brought her as well, good," the man said as he approached them. His clear blue eyes seemed to twinkle with mischief. "Jack Frost, pleased to finally meet the lovely lady that caught Kat's attention," Jack said as he kissed the back of Abbie's hand. "Though looking at you I can't blame her, you really are quite beautiful," Jack said as he gave her a charming smile. "No idea how Kat won you over, but if you ever come to your senses, I'll be waiting," Jack said and Abbie realized quickly what Kat meant by him being dangerous. Something about him felt as though it called out to her, Jack radiated a strange feeling that was similar yet different to the feeling of excitement Kat gave off.

"Abigail Stone, nice to finally meet you. I doubt I will 'come to my senses' but if I ever need a beard, I'll call you," Abbie joked and Jack placed a hand on his chest as if visibly wounded but his smile never wavered.

"And she's got a quick wit too? Kat, I might actually need to come to you for tips, now," Jack joked as he wrapped an arm around Kat and brought her in for a quick hug.

"Yeah, yeah, I know. Just keep your hands to yourself. I swear your fingers are stickier than mine," Kat said, her annoyance clear though it soon melted away as she grinned at her long-time friend.

"That's an …interestin' name you have," Abbie said making Jack chuckle.

"What can I say, mother was a fan of fairy tales. Don't hear them much nowadays, so I guess I was her way to keep them alive," Jack said before he gestured for them to follow him. "She's in her study, won't lie she is not in a good mood," Jack said, his tone suddenly serious and Abbie saw Kat tense. "Still, you know she doesn't blame either of you but rather the situation, this does throw a wrench in our plans after all."

"I know," Kat said as Abbie looked at her in concern. When Jack opened the door to the study, Kat stepped in first. "I'm back boss. This is Abigail Stone. Abbie, this is Diamond…"

"…Midas," Abbie finished and her face did nothing to hide her shock. Of all the people she expected, the famous singer was definitely not one of them. Diamond nearly looked the same as she did on Eric's poster, from her black hair to the ever-present black glove on her right hand. The one difference Abbie noticed instantly was that Diamond's hazel eyes were now a stunning golden color that seemed to be highlighted by her black eye-liner. Altogether Abbie would say that the woman was a walking work of art.

A work of art that did not seem too pleased to see her at the moment.

"A pleasure," Diamond said as she closed the laptop in front of her before making her way toward them. "Kat's explained the mark to you right?"

"Yeah, that if you take it off, I'll forget all of this," Abbie answered.

"Exactly. Well then, let's make this as quick as possible, show me your mark," Diamond ordered and Abbie's eyes widened at the weight that suddenly seemed to fall on her shoulders. Abbie's breath hitched as she suddenly felt the need to submit to Diamond's will. It was then that Abbie's suspicions were confirmed. Whether it was feeling more adventurous with Kat, being charmed by Jack, or the dominating feeling she got from Diamond, it was obvious the mere presence of the thieves affected her greatly. Abbie did as she was told and she showed her shoulder to Diamond. "I'm going to be rough, this will hurt but we have to get this off of you for your own good," Diamond warned. "It'll be like ripping off a bandage."

Like ripping off a bandage that was fused with her skin, Abbie realized when her mind suddenly exploded with pain. It felt as though Diamond tried to rip off the very skin on her shoulder, it felt far worse than Kat's attempt.

"Diamond, stop!" Kat said as she grabbed her boss' wrist after a few moments when she heard nothing but Abbie's screams.

"This is ridiculous," Diamond muttered and Abbie felt the pain stop abruptly when Diamond removed her hand. Abbie panted tiredly as she held her shoulder in pain, her vision swam a bit. "Even I can't do it?" Diamond asked herself as she looked at her hand.

"See? I don't know what's wrong," Kat said as she moved between the women. "I tried everything. I even put a second mark in the middle of her back, but that one came off without a problem."

"Of course, it did. Each band can only mark one person at a time. Though they look identical, any later marks are ineffective,"

Diamond explained as she crossed her arms and sat on her desk. "It budged slightly but that was it. It was like trying to remove something etched in stone. Was tonight really the first time you saw something…supernatural for lack of a better term?" Diamond asked Abbie who frowned in thought. "If you saw something before that was extraordinary and didn't have that memory dealt with then, it could grow and make your mind resistant. If you ever gaze upon the secret world, truly believe it exists, then it becomes much harder to take away your memory."

"A few years ago, Alexei-the monster that attacked me earlier-he killed someone close to me, he bit their neck," Abbie explained quietly and shuddered when Diamond's scowl deepened. "He was then shot in the head twice but didn't die…I don't know I always thought he was just some psycho with a vampire fetish and that he got lucky when he didn't die."

"It's possible that deep down you knew something wasn't natural and buried that realization in your sub-conscious," Diamond mused.

"From what Kat has told us, you're very smart, love," Jack began "A strong mind mixed with that memory that was allowed to fester… it's no wonder that mark won't budge. To take that off would be the same as taking away a core of your beliefs now."

"And there is no telling what damage removing it will do to your psyche," Diamond revealed. "Not that it isn't worth the risk. The issue is what to do now? We can't afford to waste our only mark on you."

"Diamond, it's not her fault!" Kat snapped. Diamond turned to face her, her gaze unwavering.

"I know and forgive me if I seem to be taking it out on her, but look at the big picture, Katarina. The job we planned to take on is all but impossible now," Diamond said and Abbie frowned at this.

"Job? Wait, what even is the point of marks? If you're all thieves or whatever why do you need to drag regular people into this?" Abbie asked as she managed to not wilt under Diamond's intense gaze.

"In the Guild, there are three classes of thieves," Diamond said before she pointed at Kat. "The infiltrators who break into strongholds and bring down defenses," Diamond said before she gestured toward Jack. "The enforcers who defend the band and fight off enemy threats," Diamond said as she then gestured to herself. "And the assassins who eliminate the key targets and threats to you, the civilians," Diamond said as she pointed at Abbie. "Each band also has three roles," Diamond said before she once more pointed at Kat. "The pilferer, the one who focuses on and steals the objective," Diamond then pointed at Jack. "The grifter, who manipulates targets and gets us the information we need," Diamond then pointed toward herself. "And the boss, who keeps the band together, makes the plans, and tries to keep us all alive on each and every job we take. We all have our uses; our own skill sets that we bring to the table. That, however, is not always enough. Sometimes we need softer skills that we have no experience in and for that we make a contract with the civilians and get their aid."

"The mark," Abbie realized.

"Exactly," Diamond answered. "In return for their services they are paid appropriately and then forget anything that has to do with the Guild. They get paid and their mind makes up a memory to explain their sudden wealth in a way that doesn't bring suspicion to them. Like winning the lottery, for example," Diamond said as she shook her head. "We have a job coming up that will be incredibly difficult, we planned to steal from Magnus Financial Bank downtown," Diamond revealed. "Their security systems are nothing to be trifled with which is why we had planned to get us a hacker since technology does not fall in any of our areas of expertise. Unfortunately, when a job is accepted, you make a vow to complete it for better or worse so we can't fall back now."

"Those robberies on the news, was that you all?" Abbie questioned.

"Maybe two of them were, we are still new recruits to the Guild, which means we have a four-year probation period where we need to hone our skills, we've only started a few months ago. Some of the heists were us but others were just other bands from our year. Full-fledged thieves deal with jobs that rarely show up in the public due to how sensitive they are," Diamond explained. "Thirty-nine recruits made up our year, that's thirteen bands. We are the 13th band formed which, believe me, says a lot of good things about us. The fact that even I can't get your mark off means we'd have to go to a professional. Your mark budged, I felt it, so I know it's not impossible. That said, Katarina was right to stop me, if I kept going like I was I might have crippled you."

"So why not get a professional?" Abbie asked in confusion.

"Because that would mean our expulsion from the Guild," Jack answered. "Revealing ourselves to a civilian, compromising the Guild as new recruits, is not tolerated by higher-ups. Hell, we weren't even really supposed to start marking people until our second year when we gained a bit more experience," Jack revealed. "It's not against Guild rules, but it's definitely frowned upon to do it this early."

"So, I'm stuck like this then?" Abbie asked as she now understood the situation.

"Well we could always kill you," Diamond said and Kat glared at her in response as Abbie looked at her in horror.

"Diamond!"

"I'm not saying we would, just letting her know what other bands might have resorted to," Diamond said simply. "I am an assassin, Abigail, and I have a position in our society that would require me to end you right now. That said, despite all of that, I won't because to do so would hurt Katarina, and hurting her would hurt all of us," Diamond reassured Abbie. "A band isn't just three people working together. Our initiation forged a bond that's symbiotic in nature. Closer than the closest siblings and more intimate than the most passionate of lovers. Our minds and souls are separate, but our hearts are one."

"That's…that's insane," Abbie said breathlessly as she tried to comprehend that.

"Kat cares for you deeply, her feelings have become an extension of my own and Frost's as well, we wouldn't do anything that Kat wouldn't. That said, we'll leave it to her to express the more…intimate feelings," Diamond said with an eye-roll as Kat smirked at her.

"Though if you need some help, I'm more than willing to-"

"Shut up, Jack," Kat said as she punched him in the arm. Jack just chuckled as Diamond shook her head at his antics.

"Look, the job is a lost cause. We're just going to have to take that failure. We've done enough to soak up a major loss like that and still stay in the Guild," Diamond began as she glanced at the occupants of the room. "From now on we'll pick our jobs more carefully and as we improve ourselves we can see about removing the mark when we are a bit stronger," Diamond said as she faced Abbie. "You're going to be stuck with us for a while. I'm afraid we must keep an eye on you after this," Diamond said and Abbie seemed to ponder something as that reckless feeling Kat sparked in her seemed to be amplified by being so close to the rest of the band.

"These jobs you take...do they harm the innocent?" Abbie asked suddenly.

"We steal from mages, monsters, and civilians that are a threat to the general population. Those in need are under our protection," Diamond answered.

"Then...then can I help?" Abbie asked and the thieves were clearly caught off guard by her question. "If what I saw from Kat is any indication, then I can never do the things you all can do or face the things you face, but I am good with a computer," Abbie said as Kat looked at her in disbelief.

"Are...are you serious?" Kat asked as the corners of her mouth turned up a bit.

"I...appreciate the offer..." Diamond began clearly skeptical. "...but we need more than someone just good with a computer, we need the best, a hacker-preferably one of those offered by the Guild...which we don't have access to, because they are too few in number."

"Look I won't lie, I'm not sure how good your Guild hackers are, but I am no slouch either. If you give me a computer, I can show you," Abbie said firmly. "If you're gonna to be stuck with me, I might as well make myself useful. It's my own personal problem that led to this anyway, let me make it up to you. I refuse to be a burden."

"By all means, show us what you're capable of," Diamond said as she gestured toward her laptop, a bit impressed with Abbie's attitude. "Though I don't exactly have any software you could use on it," Diamond said as Abbie turned the computer around. Diamond said nothing as they looked at the login-screen, if Abbie was really any good then she figured the woman could log in herself.

"That's fine, I brought my own," Abbie said as she pulled off her cross. They watched as Abbie detached the bottom of the cross and revealed a hidden memory stick that she plugged into the laptop. Nearly immediately the login information filled itself in as Diamond's desktop appeared.

"Had no idea you were such a gamer," Abbie joked as she took a moment to notice the games Diamond had installed on her computer.

"Silence," Diamond muttered as both Jack and Kat smirked at her. It was then a program began to run on the laptop.

"Welcome back to Wonderland, Ms. Stone," a voice on the computer said as they noticed a small white rabbit that was formally dressed on the screen. The animated bunny had a gold monocle and a matching pocket watch in his hand.

"I suppose it's been awhile, let's see, first find any info on one Diamond Midas," Abbie muttered to herself as she began to type rapidly on the keyboard. Diamond frowned as she saw a picture of herself pop up. "Then find some bank info…wait, Diamond, your account is frozen?" Abbie asked with a frown as she glanced at Diamond who frowned when she saw her bank information on display. Diamond could even see her social security number, credit card statements, and her pin number around a picture she used for her ID.

"The Guild freezes accounts of new members for their probation period so that we all start on the same foot," Diamond explained, a frown on her face. "Everything we have now is due to the recent jobs we've taken up together and held in the Guild Bank."

"Seriously? Didn't you guys just start off or something and you can afford all of this? You really are good," Abbie mused before raising an eyebrow. "Still sucks that all the cash you racked up from your concerts pretty much meant nothing though," Abbie said as she whistled at the amount of money she saw frozen.

"You can say that again, love. I think Diamond ranted and raved about that for a week," Jack joked as he approached the desk, an impressed look on his face. "Can you unfreeze her account?"

"Well, whoever is in charge of doing that is good," Abbie said as she typed away. "I can see why you'd want to recruit someone offered by your Guild, but at the end of the day," Abbie trailed off before she smiled victoriously. "They still have much to learn. There, done."

"Done? What's done?" Diamond asked as Abbie smirked at her.

"I made you an account overseas at another bank and put the money there," Abbie explained. "Your account still looks like it has the money, that figure will be frozen in place there but it's actually empty," Abbie explained as Diamond pursed her lips. "I doubt I can ever do the things you all can do, but if it's just this, then no problem. Won't lie, I was expecting more than five million."

"Most of my money went to charity," Diamond explained. "After these four years are up, I'm going to come into a lot of money. Money is a tool, nothing more, so why not use it for something worthwhile?"

"And here I thought you were a diva," Abbie said with a laugh. "You all are really modern-day Robin Hoods, huh?" Abbie asked before she was taken aback by the looks of disgust all of them, even Kat, gave her. "What?"

"That guy is so overrated," Kat complained.

"You want to see a diva, you should see his descendants," Diamond said with a grimace of her own.

"Wait, hold up, you're sayin' he was real!?"

"Unfortunately. Damn, you could have at least said Umbra instead." Kat complained and in response Jack rolled his eyes.

"She's a civilian, Kat, she doesn't even know who that is."

"Who's Umbra?"

"A thief fairy tale that Kat was named after that's nearly as old as the Guild. A lone thief with the power of three that legend says still operates in the shadows till this day," Jack began but before he could continue, Diamond raised a hand to silence him as she knew how he could get when he recited his tales.

"That's a story for another day," Diamond interrupted so she could get them back on track. "For now, Abigail Stone," Diamond said as she extended a hand toward Abbie. "Welcome to Band Thirteen."

CHAPTER 4

• • • • • • • • ● • • • • • • • • •

GRAND THEFT AUTO

Santa Monica, Midas Tower

"We'll need to sit down and go over the plan since we managed to get a hacker," Diamond began as she looked at the occupants of the room. "That said, it's safe to say that this has been a long night. Get some rest and we'll talk about what to do next tomorrow. Abigail, you'll stay here tonight with Katarina. I don't feel comfortable sending you back home before the sun comes up, in case Alexei had friends. It's unlikely, he was unstable even by vampire standards, but it doesn't hurt to be safe," Diamond reassured Abbie. "While we're on the topic, Frost, what did you get from the officer?"

"Alexei was the one who enthralled him," Jack answered, a frown on his face. "The poor man had been hypnotized, his mind was too weak to resist it. I didn't get much more information since he was quickly freed after Alexei was destroyed, he had no idea where he was or why."

"Wait, you actually found that creep?"

"See? I told you Jack would handle it," Kat said proudly.

"He's lucky he was a victim as well or I would have gladly done your job for you, Diamond," Jack told his boss. "Abbie, between your cross and the mark you should be safe. That said, Diamond is right, it's late and you should rest."

"Oh well then, pardon the intrusion," Abbie said and Diamond just waved off her concerns before she went to leave.

"It's fine, you did just make me five million dollars," Diamond said matter-of-factly before she glanced back over her shoulder at Abbie. "That said, I know it's been an emotional evening for you, but I value my beauty sleep. Try to keep it down if you feel the need to thank your savior."

"Or don't, I can lend her my earplugs, they block out everything," Jack said as he wiggled his eyebrows suggestively. Diamond did not seem amused as she dragged him away and left the mortified couple alone in the study.

"Was she serious?"

"Diamond doesn't joke. Uh…can we just pretend that didn't happen?" Kat asked though it sounded more like a plea if anything.

"Gladly," Abbie said as she cleared her throat before they made their way toward the living room. Kat clapped her hands and cut the lights before she pressed a button on the sofa that made it shift into a bed. For a moment, Abbie thought that Kat set the bed up for her until she watched Kat fall back onto it.

"Hope you don't mind, but you're bunking with me," Kat said as she grinned. "It'll be like a slumber party."

"You sleep here?" Abbie asked curiously as she sat down on the bed. "How many bedrooms does this place have?"

"Three," Kat answered after a moment of thought.

"So how did you end up out here?" Abbie asked, her confusion clear, deep down wondering if Kat had managed to get screwed out of a deal by her teammates.

"Cause' I called dibs," Kat said proudly as Abbie adopted a blank expression. "Got the best entertainment system to myself, quick access to the fridge and bathroom, plus a great view of the city? Easily the best room we have," Kat said and after she thought about it, Abbie realized that Kat actually had a point in her own odd way. What was the lack of an actual bed compared to all of that? Abbie squeezed the mattress and couldn't help but laugh to herself as she noticed how comfortable it actually was.

"Don't change, kitten," Abbie said before she kissed Kat on her cheek.

"What?" Kat asked, confused by the statement as she watched Abbie kick off her shoes before she laid back on the mattress. "You're weird," Kat said before she closed her eyes.

"Kat?"

"Yeah?"

"Thank you," Abbie said quietly as she held Kat's hand. Kat just squeezed her hand in response, a small smile on her face.

"Anytime."

*   *   *

The first thing Abbie noticed before she even opened her eyes was a heavenly smell that permeated throughout the room along with a loud sizzling noise. As Abbie sat up, she shook her head before she looked toward the kitchen. There she found Diamond at the table, reading something on her phone, along with Kat. Jack just hummed to himself as he cooked something on the stove.

"Good morning," Diamond said as she kept her eyes on her phone while Kat perked up and beamed when she noticed Abbie was awake.

"Morning!"

"Mornin', what's that smell?" Abbie asked curiously.

"Bacon, love," Jack answered with a grin as he picked up the skillet and slid the meat onto a plate. He brought the plate over to the table, stepping over Sal who was eating his own food. "Come on, I made you some too," Jack said as he set a plate out for her.

"Man, haven't smelled breakfast this good since I was a kid," Abbie said with a smile as she made her way toward the table while Jack sat down. After they all filled their plates, Jack made one for Diamond as she continued focusing on her phone. "So, uh, what's the plan for today?"

"Like I mentioned last night, we're still in training so today the three of us will have to go to the Guild and, well, train," Diamond answered. "We finish early in the afternoon, so we can regroup then and come up with a more solid plan."

"Actually, I'm going to be a bit late," Jack spoke up which made Diamond raise an eyebrow.

"Again?"

"Afraid so," Jack said apologetically.

"Well, we can meet in the evening then."

"So, you guys have to go to school?" Abbie asked, not sure if she should laugh or not, as she saw how each of them looked about as enthusiastic as a regular student would be about attending classes. Well, she took that back, Diamond and Jack looked less than pleased but Kat actually looked a bit excited. "Is school for thieves that bad?"

"What? No, it's awesome!" Kat said brightly but it seemed Kat was alone in her opinion.

"Ignore her, love, she's our version of a bookworm," Jack said dryly. "It can be exciting if you're an infiltrator like her and spend the whole day in a playground on steroids. However, if you're an enforcer like me then you spend the day getting beat up as your teacher tries to teach you how to fight," Jack said dryly and Abbie winced a bit at the idea of being a punching bag for hours on end.

"What about you?" Abbie asked Diamond curiously.

"If you're an assassin or at least a first year one like I am, then you spend the day in a glorified philosophy class," Diamond said as she took a bite of her food. "I was trained from an early age in combat but I am not supposed to fight as much as Frost. I need to survive long enough to get the important kills. That's what I'm learning, how to kill. Though, before I can truly learn how to kill, I must first learn what a life means to me," Diamond said though the last part was said as if she had quoted someone. "I fell behind in my reading last night and I need to catch up before today's lessons, which is what I'm doing now," Diamond said pointedly as she gestured to her phone. Her golden eyes had never once left its screen during the entire explanation.

"That's Diamond's way of saying she was worried about you two last night," Jack piped up cheekily, which earned himself a swift kick from Diamond.

"Hey, wait, so you're all in the same year, right?" Abbie asked suddenly. "Isn't Kat younger than you two? How did that work out?"

"Your formal training starts the year you turn twenty but in Kat's case, our guardian Vivi pulled some strings to get her admitted early," Jack explained. "Unlike myself and Diamond who come from respected families, Kat's considered an outsider but she's a prodigy and Vivi didn't want that talent wasted."

"An outsider?"

"Yeah, like you would be," Kat explained. "People outside of 'the know' who were brought in. Twelve families helped found the Guild, I'm not from one of them like these two, I was like you but I learned early on that I would be joining too."

"She's the youngest in our year, but definitely one of the best," Diamond said before she glanced up at Kat with narrowed eyes. "Now if only she wasn't so reckless."

"So, you're an adrenaline junkie by even their standards?" Abbie asked as Kat looked at her in confusion.

"Adrenaline junkie?"

"Ha! I like that, that fits her perfectly, love!" Jack said as Diamond nodded. Kat pouted and focused on her food instead.

"I'm not that bad," Kat said though she was completely ignored.

"By the way, Abigail, my bank is one thing but Magnus Financial is run by the Mages' Circle. They have a habit of mixing technology with the arcane arts," Diamond explained. "They do so to keep up with the world's continuously advancing technology."

"Are you serious?"

"Always," Diamond said dryly. "As you probably know, there are three major companies in the tech industry. You have Prosperity Industries, the Drakenova Corporation, and Hattori Tech. Prosperity Industries is controlled by the Mage's Circle while the Hattori Tech is with us," Diamond explained. "Mage's incorporate magic into their devices to make them run faster, better. It's really just a simple rune hidden inside the logo."

"That...that explains so much," Abbie muttered. "It's no doubt those brands are the best in the market. The issue my friends and I have had was that Hattori Tech and the Drakenova Corp. progressed naturally, their devices evolved through innovation. Yet, P.I. managed to keep up with hardware that was pretty stale. I've jailbroken phones and other things from those brands before to make a quick buck and that always bugged me. It was like any changes in their hardware were just for show but somehow their products were harder to breach than even Hattori Tech's," Abbie said as she shook her head in wonder. "I guess now I know why," Abbie said as she frowned. "They were cheatin', though not too well, didn't they just have a scandal about their latest phone blowin' up?"

"Yes, safe to say that gave us an edge in the market," Diamond said matter-of-factly. "The main issue now is that they've secretly released a new O.S. to their allies last month and every company in bed with them has become impossible to breach, including Magnus Financial. If we had attempted the job earlier when their security was still able to be breached then it wouldn't be such an issue. Now, however, our deadline is approaching and it'll take too long for the Guild to learn how to crack it."

"That's what we get for procrastinating," Jack mused as Kat placed her face in her hands.

"It's not our fault that we couldn't find a hacker that didn't try to take a stupidly large cut," Kat complained, her voice muffled. "Seriously, one guy wanted fifty percent. Fifty! Not even Diamond gets fifty!"

"Maybe we can get an extension?" Diamond muttered and it was surreal for Abbie just how much the thieves before her treated robbing a bank as if it were a college project. It was then that it sunk in that to them, it might as well had been.

"You guys are givin' me flashbacks, I almost forgot how much I hated school," Abbie said with a laugh. "Still, that just means you have to cram. I can definitely hack it for you, the issue is that I need to get my hands on the new O.S. which will be next to impossible to find."

"Maybe not," Kat piped up as she pulled out her phone. They watched as she frantically searched for something before a smile threatened to split her face. "Here," Kat said as she raised her phone and showed them an article that detailed an upcoming showcase and press-conference by Prosperity Industries. "I saw this awhile back. They're preparing a new fleet of luxury cars, says they can switch between both land and air seamlessly. They're going to have a demonstration and everything. What are the odds that the cars they ship over have the new O.S.?"

"The odds are good if they are trying to show off," Diamond said, a dangerous gleam in her eyes that sent a chill down Abbie's spine. "We get our hands on one of those cars, then we get our hands on a key into Magnus Financial."

"Exactly," Kat said proudly while Jack chuckled.

"We're back to stealing cars? Feels like orientation week all over again," Jack said. "Regardless, this works for me."

"We'll come up with an actual plan later," Diamond said as they finished up their meal.

"Want to meet up at my place?" Abbie piped up. "There's a garage for sale near it that might be helpful if you're taking a car, plus all my gear is at my place and it would be hard to move it..." Abbie trailed off when she noticed that Diamond and Jack just looked at her with blank expressions while Kat's smile somehow managed to grow. "What?"

"So, this is what happens when you live a repressed life," Diamond wondered as Jack shook his head.

"Bloody hell, you've taken to the life of crime well, love. It's a damn shame you weren't sponsored by someone in the Guild," Jack said as Abbie just looked a bit embarrassed.

"I...I'm just tryin' to help, is it that odd?"

"Trying to help? No. Being so blatantly adept at it? A tiny bit," Diamond said as she stood up from the table with her band. "There's a story there, somewhere. That said, I never look a gift horse in the mouth. You've proven yourself not to be dead weight," Diamond said as she went to a nearby wall and pulled off a painting. On the wall behind it, Abbie saw an all too familiar mark that made her grab her own instinctively.

"That's her way of saying she likes you," Jack supplied happily as he put away the dishes.

"Frost!"

"What? Dear, you know you need a kindness translator," Jack said with a laugh as he stepped behind Diamond with Kat who glanced back at Abbie sheepishly.

"So, yeah, sorry I can't walk you to the door, but you know the way out, right?" Kat asked which made Abbie nod. "Good, I'll see you at your place then," Kat said as Diamond placed her hand on the mark. Soon the thieves' bodies were completely covered in ash before being seemingly sucked into the mark. Abbie stood alone in the penthouse for a few moments before she shook her head.

"What the actual hell did I get myself into?"

*　　*　　*

Santa Monica, Abigail's Apartment

It was that evening that Abbie heard a knock on her door. When she opened it, she smiled when she saw Kat, Diamond, and Jack on the other side. Kat carried a pizza box as Jack held the drinks.

"We come bearing gifts!" Kat said with a grin that Abbie returned as she let them into her apartment.

"Good, I'm starvin', I've been workin' all day and haven't had a bite to eat. Put it on the table," Abbie said as they walked into the apartment.

"Wait, don't you work at a diner?" Kat asked.

"Trust me, I've been in that kitchen. The last thing you want to do is eat there," Abbie explained and the thieves couldn't help but feel sorry for the woman who looked as though she were going to gag from the memories alone. "Shame because that plot of land would be perfect for any other business."

"Is that right?" Diamond asked and she looked a bit thoughtful at that last bit of information before she shook her head. "Doesn't matter, I've also gotten you something," Diamond said as she handed Abbie a black cloth. "In the off chance, you ever need to keep your identity hidden."

"A mask, huh? Do you guys have one?"

"Never leave home without it, love," Jack answered as a black mask formed out of ash over the lower half of his face, a black embroidering covering its edges. "Though ours are a bit more effective, admittedly."

"Really? Besides the design they look the same," Abbie pointed out which made Jack chuckle. Kat quickly shared a glance with Jack as she left the room before suddenly returning with the lower half of her face covered by a black cloth that bore the same pattern as Jack's but with a bright crimson color. One thing that Abbie noticed was that the woman's electric green eyes seemed to glow brightly and she found herself being unable to look from them. "What the hell..." Abbie muttered, a disgruntled expression on her face as she looked at the masked woman. Deep down she knew she should have known who stood before her. It was obvious, she had just seen the woman leave after all, yet despite everything her mind refused to make the connection. "Jack, Diamond, why don't I know who that is?" Abbie asked which made the masked woman giggle before her mask simply dissolved into ash, breaking the odd trance Abbie had slipped into. "Kat? What just happened?"

"Like Jack said, ours work differently than yours," Kat began. "Our masks are just a small part of the overall uniform that hides our identities. Even if you should know who we are, if you aren't in the Guild you won't be able to put two and two together. There are a lot of important people, famous people, that work with us so keeping our identities hidden is a must," Kat explained. "But..." Kat trailed off as the ash reappeared, green sparks dancing amongst it briefly before it formed her mask once more. Though this time Abbie could still reconcile the masked woman with Kat. "...If you actually see us putting on or taking off the mask, the effect stops working. Diamond will 'reveal' herself to you later today to make sure things go smoothly in the future."

"That's definitely a neat trick," Abbie said before she turned to Diamond. "Thanks, even if it's a regular mask, I appreciate it. I have a gift for y'all as well," Abbie continued. "I know where we can get the cars."

"Where?" Diamond asked as Abbie gestured for them to follow her. They followed her to her bedroom, where she kept her computer. When they looked at the screen, they saw that it displayed a map of Santa Monica.

"They're gonna be shipped here in a couple of days," Abbie revealed before she frowned a bit. "I guess if you can somehow intercept them before they get here, then there's your ticket into Magnus Financial," Abbie said before she sighed. "That's about as much as I can do for you, I have no experience with that kind of thing."

"That's fine, you've done enough for now," Diamond said quietly, lost in thought as she examined the map for a second. "If you wouldn't mind, could you leave me here for a few minutes? I won't mess with your computer, but I do need to think alone for a bit."

"Uh, sure I guess," Abbie said as Jack led her out of the room with Kat.

"You've helped, but don't forget we are the thieves," Jack joked. "And there is a reason Diamond is the boss."

"She'll come up with the plan in no time, your only job now is to help us with this pizza," Kat said and as if it heard her, Abbie's stomach seemed to growl in response.

"Sounds like a plan," Abbie said sheepishly as Jack laughed.

"I'll make Diamond a plate, you two just relax for now," Jack said as Abbie and Kat sat down at her table while he fixed Diamond a plate and left. When they did so, Kat noticed a picture that showed two young brunette girls playing together in a garden. Upon closer inspection, she noticed that the shorter of the two girls looked very similar to Abbie.

"Hey, Abbie, you have a sister?" Kat asked curiously which startled Abbie before she noticed the picture that caught Kat's attention. Kat blinked in surprise as she could have sworn she saw an angered expression flash across Abbie's face but it had disappeared as soon as it showed up.

"An older one by two years, her name's Haylen, we were inseparable when we were kids," Abbie said with a small smile that didn't quite reach her eyes. "She actually got me into computers."

"You never mentioned her," Kat said as she raised an eyebrow.

"I...try not to think about my family," Abbie said with a sigh. "They're an interestin' group, to say the least. They're powerful and the way they use that power can be questionable more often than not. She and I were close as kids, her protectin' me from every little thing. Now, however, she's the exact opposite of me. She's cold, efficient, and cruel," Abbie said with a frown. "You know, in many ways, Diamond actually reminds me of her," Abbie said before catching herself. "In a good way, I mean!"

"It's fine, love, Diamond's a dangerous woman and has an attitude to match," Jack said as he returned. "If you think the three of us got along when we first met you'd be mistaken."

"Really?"

"Oh yeah," Kat said with a laugh. "Jack and I were cool, we were raised together. That said, you could almost choke on his angst. He had like no emotion and talking to him was like talking to a wall," Kat said with a look of disgust on her face. "If you told me a year ago this man could smile, I'd put you in a nut house."

"I was not that bad."

"You totally were, you had to be the most emo person I've ever met," Kat said with a laugh. "I swear flowers died near you," Kat then shook her head while Abbie looked at the man in shock, he seemed like such a happy individual, a slightly older and male version of Kat at times. "Then there was Diamond, she can seem distant at times toward you but that's nothing compared to what we had to deal with. She was, without a doubt, the biggest bitch I have ever encountered in my life. Before our initiation into the Guild, we all spent a year living together at her place. Listen, Abbie, if there was just one more day added on to that? Someone would have died."

"Don't act like you didn't come with your own set of problems," Jack said and Kat stuck her tongue out at him. "This girl entered her rebellious phase and never left it, her sole reason for existing seemed to consist of pissing off everyone around her. When we were forced to live together, she and Diamond fought so much that I realized that Sartre was right, 'Hell is other people'."

"So, what happened? You three seem as thick...as...thieves..." Abbie trailed off as the irony of that statement sunk in. "Please pretend I didn't just say that."

"Not happening," Kat said with a smirk which made Abbie groan. "As for what happened? Well, we became a band. Our hearts were linked together and at that moment everything changed, I guess," Kat answered with a shrug.

"We could feel how our words and actions affected each other, we gained understanding," Jack answered before he gestured toward Kat. "Kat became more considerate when it came to her actions."

"Jack, here, got his head out of his ass and realized he wasn't the only person in the world," Kat said bluntly and though Jack looked annoyed, Abbie noted that he didn't deny it. "He learned to love," Kat said this time with a softer expression as Jack smiled a bit.

"And Diamond?" Abbie asked before tensing as she felt a hand on her shoulder.

"I stopped being alone," Diamond answered matter-of-factly as Abbie glanced up at her in surprise. "I have a plan," Diamond began. "And we're going to need your help. We know the location of the cars. The issue is that they are in a cargo container and are being shipped in with other merchandise from P.I. So that's where you come in, we need you to identify exactly where the cars are being held. Can you do that?"

"I should be able to, but you'll need this," Abbie said before pulling out her phone. "Get this next to a terminal at the docks and I can get all the information you need, the problem is that those tend to be guarded," Abbie stated with a frown only for Diamond to wave off her concerns.

"That's why we have Kat."

*   *   *

Santa Monica, Docks

A guard sat at a desk in a room that overlooked the hundreds of cargo containers found on the docks. In the distance, a blue container with the letters "P.I." could be seen being lowered from a ship. The guard, however, paid no mind to that as he watched a boxing match on the terminal.

"That's it, Rose! Bob and weave!" the guard shouted to the screen, completely ignorant to the shadow that crept toward him on the floor. A masked Kat rose from the shadow and stood silently behind him before she pulled out one of her cards. The word "Sleep" appeared on its blank side before she placed it in front of his face. The guard jumped in surprise but nearly immediately found himself falling unconscious when the card released a black smoke and dissolved within her grasp. It was then that Kat dragged his body away before she returned to the terminal and placed Abbie's phone next to the computer. Kat quickly started up an app and watched in satisfaction as a familiar white rabbit appeared on the screens of the phone and the computer.

"I'm in," Abbie's voice said from Kat's earpiece.

*   *   *

"Okay, so you can get me in, but how do you guys actually go about taking the car?" Abbie asked as Diamond gestured toward Jack.

"That's where Frost comes in. Katarina can break into and out of places, but when it comes to actually going through them that's where his skills come into play," Diamond answered as Jack smirked.

*   *   *

Kneeling over the downed guard, Kat stole his I.D. card before she handed it to Jack who had just entered the room. Jack studied the picture for a moment before he glanced down at the guard. Jack placed his right hand over his face and Kat watched as Jack's body was covered in ash, turning his form pitch black. Removing his hand, the ash seemed to fade away leaving a mirror image of the guard standing in his place.

"Alright, I found it," Abbie began. "It's at the North end of the docks, the third container and you'll run into it on the right. I'll track you through the surveillance camera and guide you if you get lost."

"Appreciated, love," Jack said, his voice not sounding like his own as Kat moved toward the window.

"I'm going to take the scenic route, meet you there," Kat said as she departed. As Jack made his way through the docks, he nodded toward

55

some of the other workers and even made a joke or two. When prompted Jack would show his ID as Abbie directed him through the docks.

"Alright, turn right and it should be right there," Abbie said and sure enough before Jack was a P.I. cargo container.

"Perfect, and I think I found our ticket out of here," Jack said as he spotted a semi-truck that was waiting to be loaded up. "Kat."

"Way ahead of you," Kat said and he saw her jump down from on top of the containers and quickly rush toward a crane. The poor driver couldn't even shout in surprise before he found himself quickly knocked out by Kat and pushed over as she took his seat. As Kat busied herself with grabbing the container, Jack made his way to the truck and gestured toward the driver.

"Hey pal, I need your help. I need you to sign off on something before your next delivery," Jack said making the driver groan. "Hey, I don't like it either, too much paperwork if you ask me."

"Amen," the driver muttered as he opened the door and nearly as soon as he got out, he found his collar grabbed tightly by Jack.

"No hard feelings, mate," Jack said before he slammed a powerful right hook into the man's face that knocked him out instantly. Jack dragged his body away and hid it in between the containers. Jack then placed a hand on the driver's face and quickly assumed his identity. As he made it back to the truck he watched as Kat loaded up the container before she hopped out of the crane. Once they made it to the container, they noticed that the container was chained shut. Thinking quickly, Jack grabbed the chains with his hands, ash covering his hands and forming what appeared to be a pair of black gloves that fit him like a second skin. On the back of his right glove, his tattoo reappeared, outlined by a bright blue crackling energy. When Jack gripped the chains, a black "I" emblem appeared on the forehead of the tattooed skull as a small circle of ice began to form on the ground around his body. Kat watched as blue sparks danced across the chains and froze them in Jack's grasp before he ripped them off and shattered them. When the doors of the container opened, they looked inside and gave each other a high five as they saw what appeared to be a car covered in a white tarp.

"Got it!" Kat said happily.

"Good now hurry, some workers are headed your way!" Abbie *warned and Kat quickly climbed into the back and closed the doors behind her while Jack climbed into the driver's seat and drove away.*

* * *

"Still, we have the issue regarding your phone. We can't just leave it there, that's the quickest way to get you locked up," Diamond said with a frown.

"I can deal with that, just let me back up my data. I have a spare phone from P.I. laying around here somewhere," Abbie said, a mischievous glint in her eyes.

* * *

Abbie's phone released smoke and sparks before it suddenly combusted, destroying itself and the terminal next to it.

* * *

"I love this phone, but you gotta appreciate the fireworks it can make," Abbie said as Diamond and Jack once more looked at her with blank expressions while Kat seemed excited by the very idea. "What?"

"Why do you know how to do that?" Diamond asked with a raised eyebrow and in response Abbie gestured around at her apartment.

"I get bored easily and phones are easy to mess with. I honestly don't get why so many people are startin' to get them implanted in their heads when regular smartphones are still liable to blow up under certain conditions no matter who manufactures them. Anyway, I'm rantin', the point is that you'd be surprised at what you can learn to do with enough free time," Abbie said as Jack just chuckled.

"You two might have been more of a match than I realized, love."

"Insanity loves company," Diamond muttered as Abbie shrugged having not gotten what the big deal was.

"The real issue is what are you going to do to get away? I mean they are bound to figure out what went down before you get very far," Abbie pointed out.

"That's fine, remember that garage you mentioned?" Diamond asked. "If we go ahead and purchase that, we'll be fine."

"How?"

"You know the mark you saw at our place?" Kat asked which made Abbie nod. "We can only put it on one person at a time. That said, there is no limit when it comes to places we own. By placing the mark in that garage, we can turn it into a safe house. If a thief goes to their safe house, pursuers of any kind are the last thing we need to worry about."

*　　*　　*

"You've got company," Abbie warned as Jack drove through the streets of Santa Monica, police sirens echoing throughout the city. Glancing through his mirror, Jack saw a group of police cars pursuing him.

"Pull the vehicle over now!" an officer ordered.

"Umbra, what's your status?" Jack questioned.

"I'm in, is it clear?"

"They're trying to flank me so go now, straight down the middle!"

"On it!" Kat said and soon Jack heard the sound of an engine roaring to life before Kat drove out of the back of the truck and in between the officers whom all frantically swerved out of her way. The black car she was driving handled far better than any vehicle she had ever driven before. "This thing is amazing! Can I keep it!?" Kat practically begged as she outmaneuvered the cars that turned to chase her down.

"Get it back to the garage and it's all yours," Diamond's voice answered. "Frost, get ready, I'm coming to extract you," Diamond said as she drove out of an alleyway on Kat's bike, the lower half of her face covered by a black and gold mask. When Diamond looked forward, she saw that there were only two cruisers pursuing Jack. Diamond extended her hand and a beautifully crafted black handgun formed from ash in

her grasp. It was faint, but the word "Roderick" could be seen engraved onto its side in a pale gold. Taking aim, Diamond quickly released two rounds that tore through the tires of the cruisers which made them crash into each other. Diamond pulled back on the bike, and drove right over the crashed cars. "Now!" Diamond ordered after she corrected her position and drove next to Jack., Jack steered the truck toward a ditch and out of the way of any civilians before he leapt out and landed on the back of the bike. It was then that Diamond turned the bike quickly to the right and away from the crashing truck and rode through the city streets.

"I lost them," Kat said as Jack placed a hand to his face and returned to his normal appearance, his mask still firmly in place. "Heading to the garage."

"We'll meet you there," Diamond said as her gun dissolved into ash.

"Boss?"

"Yes?"

"Can we never do something that reckless again?"

"No promises."

*   *   *

Santa Monica, Band Thirteen's Garage

Abbie looked up from her computer as Kat drove into the garage followed by Diamond and Jack a few minutes later. She simply shook her head in wonder as she heard the officers on the nearby police scanner completely forget what they were doing. The officers eventually blamed the wreckage on fugitives who apparently went in the exact opposite direction that the thieves had taken.

"And that, Abbie, is how we do things," Kat said proudly as she stepped out of the car.

"Well you can color me impressed, that's for sure. I've never seen anything like that, I couldn't see clearly from the cameras but did you actually change your appearance?" Abbie asked Jack who just winked in response.

"I'm good at what I do."

"I can tell," Abbie said as she walked toward the car and placed a hand on its hood before releasing an appreciative whistle. "This thing is a beauty. Four doors too? This is how you take road trips in style."

"Hell yeah," Kat agreed as her mask disappeared, revealing a bright grin. "So, what now?"

"Now I take this thing apart. There is a chip I need that will be your key into the bank," Abbie answered which made Kat look at her in horror. "Don't worry, I won't hurt it. Besides, we were going to have to take it apart anyway if we wanted to really customize this baby later on," that seemed to do the trick as Kat's horrified expression turned into one of complete and utter joy.

"When will you be done?" Diamond asked and Abbie sighed as she scratched her head in thought.

"Give me a day, two at the most. It all really depends on just how much they changed the O.S," Abbie answered.

"Then we'll take on Magnus Financial in three days. I'll come up with a plan while you deal with this," Diamond said. "Good work everyone, we'll go over the plan before the job. As for now? Let's take a quick break."

"Well," Abbie began as she got Kat's attention when they dispersed. "Guess I can scratch grand theft auto off my bucket list."

"And you did great," Kat said as she hugged Abbie. "Just wait, babe, we'll make a criminal out of you yet," Kat said with a laugh and for the life of her, Abbie could not figure out why that statement didn't terrify her as much as she knew it should have.

CHAPTER 5

• • • • • • • • ● • • • • • • • •

THE MAGNUS
FINANCIAL JOB

Santa Monica, Midas Tower

"Father, everything is under control. I know the deadline is coming up, but don't worry we just finished getting our preparations in order," Diamond explained. "I understand you're just concerned about me, and I appreciate it but you need to show a little faith. It will be done this week," Diamond reassured. "Understood, I love you too," Diamond said before she ended the call just as Kat walked into the study with Abbie and Jack.

"We're back," Kat said as she waved at her boss. "Jack and I got the info you wanted and we picked Abbie up along the way."

"Please tell me you have good news, Abigail."

"I do, it was slightly more difficult than I expected but I got in, even did a test run without any problems. I can now get in and out of their systems without a hitch," Abbie said with a smile.

"Perfect, I just got off the phone with my father. Our brash approach the other day caught him off guard and I had to reassure him that everything was fine. I'm glad that turned out to not be a lie."

"Old man was that worried, huh?" Kat asked knowingly.

"Still can't believe Roderick is in this business too," Abbie said before she shrugged. "But it makes sense if he's your dad. I love his movies, think I can get an autograph?"

"I'll make him write as many as you want if we get through this," Diamond said as Jack approached her. Abbie watched as the skin on the back of his neck suddenly turned into ash that spread apart to reveal what looked like a metallic version of her mark. Reaching back, he popped it out leaving nothing but a thin silver ring in its place as Diamond mimicked his actions. In their palms, gold and blue circuits appeared over the surface of Diamond and Jack's tokens, respectively. Soon black tendrils formed around the tokens and linked them together. "I'll review this information now," Diamond said, as they pulled their tokens apart. "We're going to do this tomorrow evening, Kat, Jack, rest up. Abbie, you're staying here today so we can go over the plan later."

"Alright, I'm fine with that."

"Good, now, like last time, please leave me to my thoughts," Diamond ordered and the three quickly left Diamond to her thoughts.

"Gotta admit, I've seen some strange tech but nothing like that," Abbie said. "Talk about a secure way to share information."

"You haven't seen anything yet, babe," Kat said with a grin. "How about we show her our gear, Jack? I think she's ready."

"I think you're right," Jack said with an expression that matched Kat's in a way that made Abbie a bit uneasy.

*   *   *

"You've already seen the masks," Jack said as they stood in his room. Abbie watched as the ash formed his and Kat's masks.

"Yeah, but why are their edges different colors, personal preference?"

"No," Jack answered "The Guild is an ancient entity, one that traces its origin centuries ago during the age of the divine. The colors each represent one of the three Goddesses that were said to have taught our founders. They gave them the foundation needed to make the Guild what it is today, including the mark you bear. When you join the Guild, you join one of their sects. Every person in a band is a member of a different sect," Jack explained. "Black means that I am a follower of Laverna, the Goddess of thievery," Jack said and Abbie watched as Kat took off her hoodie. Soon after, both her and Jack's clothes turned into ash. Green and blue sparks danced over their bodies respectively as the ash reformed into a pair of skin-tight mod-suits. "But though the masks are important, they are just a piece of our equipment."

"What the…" Abbie trailed off, startled by the sudden change.

"The Thieves' Guild's combat class mod-suits," Jack began as he clenched and unclenched his fist. "They were developed during the last world war as a way to combat the sudden increase of augmentations amongst civilians and private militaries. Physical augmentations and cybernetic implants are messy and require too much surgery in the long run if you want to upgrade. That's why we have these suits, they're symbiotic and help us change whatever we want about our bodies in an instant to serve whatever purpose. Skills and abilities that once took months or even years to learn can now be downloaded from another thief in an instant. This allows thieves to personally modify their skill-sets, hence the name. Also, it may not look it, but it's very durable and protects us against civilian blades and light gunfire. Though getting hit by either will still leave you sore," Jack explained to a fascinated Abbie. "Anything stronger, however, will tear right through it so we have to stay on our toes and keep moving. Especially, Kat," Jack said and Abbie noticed then that Jack's suit had a bit of armored plating while Kat's lacked any extra protection whatsoever.

"I can't afford to be weighed down like Jack, I'm not supposed to be fighting head on like him. In and out, that's my job, and I need to do my job fast," Kat explained. "Because of that, infiltrators and assassins lack the added protection enforcers get. Though Diamond is fortunate, she can take even more punishment than Jack, here," Kat said though she didn't elaborate further on that last piece of information. "What it lacks in defense it makes up for by increasing our strength, speed, and reflexes. You can touch it if you want."

"Whoa," Abbie whispered as she gently trailed her fingers alongside Kat's arm. The mod-suit felt like it was a second layer of skin. "What is this made out of?"

"We call it ash, one of Laverna's greatest gift to the Guild," Kat said as she grasped Abbie's hand. A shiver ran down Abbie's spine as green sparks danced from Kat's hand and over hers. Around Kat's hand, the mod-suit turned back into ash and covered Abbie's hand before reforming into a glove. "Shortly after the Guild was founded, Laverna sacrificed her body to protect the world. The Guild uses her ashes to continue her mission in her stead. Laverna's ashes can temporarily take the form of any material and allow us to manipulate shadows. The Hattori family has used it to make our weapons and clothing since the Guild was founded," Kat said as the ash formed a black cross that was identical to the one Abbie wore. A green spark danced across it before the color of the cross went from black to a pale gold. "Of all the materials it can copy, our go-to is electrum."

"Why electrum?"

"The sparks you see? Though it's not electricity it does share similar properties and electrum makes for the best conductor. We call this energy, presence. It's the power of the gods. Without it, the ash would be useless as it only responds to the power of the divine with it being the remains of a Goddess," Jack explained as he raised his hand and Abbie saw a bright blue spark of energy jump between his fingers. "Look at Kat's traps, for example," Jack said as Kat created a single pale-gold card out of ash. "Making them out of electrum helps Kat channel her presence easily."

"I use the ash to write a command, with the thought of the trap in my head," Kat began as the word "bubble" appeared on the blank side of the card. "Then my presence brings the words to life," Kat said as the card exploded into dozens of bubbles that floated throughout the room. Jack just grinned to himself as he and Kat watched Abbie look up in awe at the bubbles that surrounded her.

"What happens when you run out of ash?"

"We'll need to take a dip into a nearby shadow. Laverna had an affinity for shadows which fortunately means her ashes can mix with them and refill our supply of it. This is why we have these," Kat said before she turned around and gestured toward a token that was on the back of her neck, embedded in the suit. Abbie looked closer and could see that each of the three sections were a different color being either black, red, or gold. "This badge is proof we are members of the Guild. They used to be simple tokens that could mix the ash with shadows to make more. Then the last war happened and the Hattori family turned them into chips unique to each thief that store our mods and other important data."

"Thanks to the Hattori family and their technology, a modern thief can grow more in one year than ancient thieves could in several. The drawback is that these tools are powerful and so a thief doesn't begin their training until much later in their lives when compared to the other three factions. By being adults, we are ideally mature enough to handle the new tools." Jack explained before he cast a pointed look at Kat who just winked in response.

"Think of a badge as both a license and the 'keys' to our mod-suits. With the badge implanted into the suit, it allows it to be functional and makes the ash hold its form," Kat explained as Abbie raised her black-clad hand and looked at it in wonder. Abbie clenched her fist briefly and shook her head at how she felt her grip strength double. However, when she moved it too far away from Kat it simply dissolved and the ash returned back to Kat and covered Kat's hand once more. "We pretty much use the ash for everything, it's like a utility belt," Kat said after a moment of thought. "My teacher always tells me to use it for important things."

"Like impressing girls," Jack teased as he gestured toward a few of the lingering bubbles. Kat simply nodded in response.

"Like I said, the important things."

"What about your Goddess?" Abbie asked Kat who then gestured to her own mask.

"Black and red means that I am a follower of Discordia, the Goddess of chaos and rebellion," Kat explained. "She's the one who gave us presence."

"Fitting," Abbie said with a chuckle as Jack smirked. "You're a literal agent of chaos, kitten, let that sink in."

"Yeah, yeah, whatever," Kat said as she rolled her eyes, though she couldn't help but laugh herself. "Like Laverna, Discordia shared her power with us as well. Her Apples of Discord are what give us our presence. By eating one of her fruits, her presence flows through us and merges with us, making her power ours. This give us the ability to use the ash to do cool things like making powerful illusions, set up traps, and other neat tricks. This is how I was able to fight Alexei like I did and what separates a thief from a civilian."

"So, if I ate one, I could do what you all can?"

"Pretty much, but the apples are poisonous," Kat said after a moment of thought. "Only those worthy of being a thief can eat one and live. Not to mention you'd still be missing the tools to actually draw out your presence. We were lucky," Kat began and her smile waned slightly. "We were the first year in a long time that had all thirty-nine of the recruits survive initiation," Kat explained as Abbie looked at her in horror. "An Apple of Discord can be very dangerous in the wrong hands so Discordia created artificial life, servants called Dolls to protect them and serve the needs of thieves. Each Doll is given an apple to keep safe in the event something happens to Discordia's garden where she grows them. In return the apples give the Dolls life, so this task is a fair trade for that."

"Lastly, there's Diamond's Goddess, Juventas," Jack said as he held up a familiar golden flask. "The Goddess of life and youth who is represented by the colors black and gold. She gave us what's in these flasks. We call it nectar. We consume a little bit every month to keep ourselves in perfect health. It heals severe injuries quickly, keeps us young, and makes it so monsters can't corrupt or consume us."

"What exactly is nectar?" Abbie asked with a frown as she remembered the heavenly taste that had taken away all of her pain.

"Despite everything you have seen and heard, trust me, you wouldn't believe us, so just call it nectar," Jack said which made her pout as he basically gave her the same answer Kat did. Still, she didn't push and decided to ask Kat a question that had bugged her for a while.

"So does that collar of yours have any significance? It reminds me of your badge."

"It's her treasure," Jack said as Kat gestured toward the pendant. "Our bodies constantly produce presence so you can think of treasures as batteries that store our presence so that we don't endanger those near us."

"Batteries, huh? What happens when you overload them?"

"Not sure, but something tells me it'll be worse than blowing up a phone," Jack joked. "That might be worth testing one day. Anyway, a treasure can be an object forged from Laverna's ashes or a brand that seals an ancient artifact from Laverna's personal collection of stolen goods. Outsiders tend to get the former while members of the founding families get the latter," Jack said as he gestured to the tattoo on the back of his right hand. "There is only one exception that doesn't fit this mold but it isn't relevant at the moment. What all treasures have in common is the ability to store a vast amount of power. This is why they are so vital to us but as you can expect, something this valuable isn't given for free. They are exchanged for something we hold dear and as a result, these treasures can develop different abilities, unique to its thief, over time."

"In my case, I was always extremely lucky," Kat began as she got Abbie's attention. "I can't begin to tell you how many times I almost died before joining the Guild, but I never did. So, I gave up that luck and got my treasure in return. It's called the Change of Fate," Kat said with a smirk as she tapped her collar. "The pendant spins and randomly lands on the gold or green section. This can create extremely good luck for myself, ridiculous even, or I can supposedly give bad luck to everyone around me."

"Supposedly?"

"I've never done it," Kat said with a shrug. "I've been very lucky with this treasure so far and hope to keep it up."

"That's...that's amazin', did you use this on Alexei?" Abbie asked only for Kat to shake her head.

"I try not to use it that much to tell you the truth. The possibility of giving everyone bad luck scares me," Kat said honestly. "If I used it and it failed, you both would have gotten bad luck and I didn't want to test to see how that would end up. You could have gotten killed in the crossfire," Kat said and a chill went down Abbie's spine as she thought about the possibilities.

"Oh, good call," Abbie said as she understood Kat's hesitance. If Kat were working alone it would be no problem, but the last thing Kat needed to do was to bring misfortune upon her allies as well as her enemies. "Still that's incredible, Kat." Abbie praised. "What about you, Jack?"

"Not much to say about mine, it's a brand called Arondight," Jack answered. "It lets me absorb energy and turn it into presence."

"Arondight...where have I-" Abbie trailed off before her eyes widened as she realized where she heard that name before. "Wait, as in Sir Lancelot's sword? That Arondight?"

"You know of it?"

"My mom was like yours I guess, she was a die-hard fan of those legends."

"Oh no, you're multiplying," Kat complained.

"Interesting, but yes, the very same," Jack said, a fond smile on his face. "That very sword is sealed within me by this brand which allows me to draw on its power. The brand has nine levels, nine 'circles', that give me access to more of its power. By the time I graduate I should be able to wield the blade itself but until then I'll have to make do."

"Anyway, there's a bit more, I guess, but you'd have to ask Diamond," Kat said with a shrug. "Not because we don't trust you, of course, but she's better at explaining these things."

"Relax Kat, I understand," Abbie reassured Kat with a small smile at how nervous Kat seemed. "I'm honestly grateful you guys trust me this much."

"Sorry it's just, you know how you jump to conclusions," Kat teased. Abbie's cheeks reddened at that while Jack raised an eyebrow.

"Oh?"

"Yeah Jack, you should have heard this drama queen when I first tried to take the mark off-" Kat was cut off as she was forced to avoid Abbie who did her best to shut Kat up as Jack looked on in amusement.

*   *   *

"Alright, first things first, Abbie is that car drivable?" Diamond asked as they stood in the study, a holographic image of Magnus Financial appearing on her desk.

"Yeah, I put it back together after I got the chip."

"Good, we'll need a way to get to and from the bank," Diamond said making Abbie look at her in surprise. "What?"

"Nothing just…I did see you all disappear into thin air before, didn't realize you all actually needed cars. I figured Kat just rode a bike because it was fun or somethin'," Abbie explained making Diamond shake her head.

"We can travel between our safe houses and the Guild. If we have a lot of safe houses scattered around the world, we can use the Guild as a shortcut to and from each one, but that's it. As thieves, we can use shadows to quickly change our immediate position but crossing even a few blocks like that is tiring," Diamond said as she crossed her arms. "Only a mage can teleport which is why we need a good getaway car."

"Well then, thank P.I. for trying to be flashy because that is definitely a good car," Abbie said with a smile.

"Good, now back to the situation at hand," Diamond began as she regained their attention. They watched as the image focused on the bank's lower levels. "The lower levels are where they keep the money and safety deposit boxes of the civilians. The mages, however, keep their belongings at the top of the bank and that's where our target is," Diamond said before zooming in on a room full of safety deposit boxes that had one in particular high-lighted. "This is our objective, this one is owned by the Arch-Mage August. Of course, this isn't where he keeps anything important. Probably just a few jewels, but there is a reason this is the hardest first-year job offered. Even now no band has completed it," Diamond said as she placed the picture down. "In fact, I got a decent amount of this information from Band Twenty-Twenty."

"Really? What did you trade for that?" Jack asked sounding a bit surprised.

"Band Twenty-Twenty?" Abbie asked curiously.

"Think of them as our upperclassmen, top band of the current second years. They were what we are now as the top band of our year," Diamond explained. "As for what they wanted in return? The usual, they wanted to gain favor with me, something I approve of as a close relationship with them will be invaluable in the future. They came the closest to completing this job, their failure almost ruined their standing but they persevered and recovered. To be honest, I think the real reason they gave us this is because their pride is hurt and they want someone to finally put this job to rest."

"Still, they're no slouches. They're already as skilled as full-fledged thieves, on track to being fully initiated early. Do you think we can do this?" Jack asked with a small frown.

"We have no choice, too late to turn back. Plus, we have something they didn't," Diamond said as she gestured toward Abbie. "Between her and an advantage of information, we can pull this off. We know exactly where and how to strike. Abigail, you will take down the surveillance and the rest of the security systems. While that's being done, Kat, you will scale the outside of the bank and reach the required floor. With the systems down, breaking in through a window shouldn't alert anyone," Diamond said making Kat nod. "While that's being done, Jack and I will go in through the side-entrances and deal with any guards."

"Wait, if I'm going in through the top, undetected, why do you two need to go in at all?" Kat asked with a frown.

"Because this is where Band Twenty-Twenty failed," Diamond said before a purple dome surrounded their objective on the map. "They bypassed the technological security but they forgot about the arcane defenses set up by the mages. There is a barrier blocking that room, and last time I checked you can't just hack magic. Jack and I need to find the catalyst that's keeping it up. Once we do that, you can take the objective and we can return here and officially put an end to this job once and for all."

"Sounds simple enough," Kat said making Jack frown.

"And that's a problem, it's never simple with us," Jack muttered making Diamond nod.

"Exactly," Diamond said before showing them another image. "Which is why we'll go through with this plan, but we have to treat this as if anything that could go wrong will. We need to be able to escape if a mage like Xavier shows up."

"Who is that?" Abbie asked with a frown that deepened when she saw the scowls on Jack and Kat's faces. Diamond pursed her lips, not looking very fond of the man herself before explaining.

"Xavier is a young mage, a year older than us, who has recently completed his training. Since we've started, he's stumbled his way into a couple of our jobs, we barely managed to escape each time. You can say he has a…fascination…with our band that he developed after unmasking Frost and deciding to spare our lives. This fascination is one we could very well do without," Diamond explained. "If you see him and he starts speaking Italian, run. When a mage speaks in their native tongue, chances are they are going to cast a spell of some sort on you. Something about their native language being the closest to their soul or some nonsense."

"Noted," Abbie said, looking a bit pale at the thought. "So, he's like a rival?"

"An enemy," Jack corrected his voice firm. "We are at war, love, you have to remember that."

"It hurts my pride to admit it, but we are weak. As a first-year, you're barely even considered a rookie in the Guild. We're good for what we are, but who we are now and who we will be next year is as different as night and day. That's how intense our training is. If we were stronger, believe me, I would have killed that man by now," Diamond said, her voice cold and Abbie shuddered as she saw a dark glint in Diamond's eyes. "I have a vendetta against him that can only be paid with his blood, but only when we are all at our best. I need an honorable victory, getting lucky won't cut it," Diamond said with a small frown. "Enough about him. We must get ready."

* * *

That evening a masked Kat scaled the side of the bank as the night sky cloaked her body from sight. The fingers of her mod-suit had transformed into sharp talons which sunk easily into the side of the building. Once Kat reached the third highest floor, she used her talons to cut into the glass of the window.

"Umbra, what's your status?" Diamond's voice asked through her ear-piece.

"Made it in, boss."

"Good, Stone, was she spotted?"

"Nope, she's in the clear and you will be as well in a minute. Get ready to go in…"

* * *

"…now." Abbie said as she disarmed the alarms and watched over the thieves from her apartment.

* * *

"Clear the floor," Diamond ordered Jack once they made it inside, her voice muffled slightly by her mask. Nodding, Jack proceeded to do that as she made her way to a shadowy corner. "I'll find the catalyst."

"There are five armed guards on the floor, be careful they're armed to the teeth," Abbie warned. *"Doubt I have to say it but stealth is definitely advised, there are more guards in the upper floors so try not to alert them."*

"Understood," Jack said as he quietly made his way toward one of the guards. Once he was positioned behind the armed man, the first circle shone on Arondight as the brand began to shine brightly as his presence coursed through his body. It was then that Jack drew his right fist back before he rammed it through the man's back. Jack's hand exited through the guard's chest while blue sparks crackled over his fist. The armed man couldn't even yell before his body was suddenly encased in ice. The frozen form of the guard shattered around Jack's fist before he drew it back.

"Frost! What the hell!?"

"It was a golem, artificial soldiers created by the Mage's Circle," Jack explained as he raised a crimson crystal that he had ripped from the guard's body toward a nearby camera. "They look human but are just moving pieces of earth and clay. Feel no sympathy, love, these things have no true sentience, they're just glorified rocks."

"I...I see," Abbie said as Jack went on to systematically remove the golems from the floor.

"Guys I made it to the barrier..."

*　*　*

"...but it's like we thought, I can't think of a way to breach this thing. I haven't even seen any guards on this floor but that doesn't mean security isn't tight," Kat said as she stood at the end of a corridor, her objective right in front of her. However, in between Kat and her goal was a purple wall of energy, a magical barrier that protected the room from intruders. In addition to the barrier, there was a laser-grid security system that filled the room as well. "Stone, can you at least do something about these lasers?"

"Lasers? Perhaps, but I can't even see into that room, are there even cameras in there?"

"There are but they luckily aren't facing me," Kat said with a small frown.

"That's strange...where you should be, I just see a void for lack of a better term. Something is blocking me and it's not something I can breach."

"Must be the magic," Kat realized. "Well then, it's all up to you, boss. Can you spot the catalyst?"

*　*　*

"Yes, but there is a problem," Diamond muttered as she stared up at a large golden statue. The statue depicted a knight on the back of a mighty steed that was raised back on its hind-legs. The knight held out his sword in front of him as if he commanded an invisible army to charge. One thing that was peculiar was that the knight had no head, instead, he held a helmet in his free hand.

"Problem?" Diamond could hear Jack ask as he made it back to her. "Oh…yeah, that's a problem."

"The catalyst is in the helmet."

"Yeah, but this is obviously a trap, right?"

"Yes," Diamond said and though half of his face was covered, Jack's grimace was still clearly visible.

"We're going to spring it anyway, aren't we?"

"Yes," Diamond said as two black handguns formed in her hands, the names Roderick and Isabelle each etched into one of the weapons in gold.

"Are you two about to have fun without me?"

"You know what they say, Kat, three's a crowd," Jack joked as he stood in front of Diamond and made his way toward the statue as she backed away. "Just stay put, hopefully, this won't be much of a problem. Boss, you know this is going to be loud."

"Yes, but the golems will fall if we take out the catalyst. If we're quick we won't have to worry about getting outnumbered," Diamond explained.

"Understood," Jack said before he charged forward with his fist cocked back. However, before he could land the blow the statue suddenly lunged out of the way as a crimson light began to shine from behind the visors of the helmet.

"Seriously!? I've seen it all now."

"Love, this is just the beginning," Jack said as he cracked his neck. "It's has been a long time since I've seen August's servant," Jack mused. "If it's the Dullahan, its weak spot is likely beneath the helmet."

"Then get me a shot," Diamond ordered before she stepped backward and disappeared into the shadows of the room. The Dullahan's horse dug its hoof into the ground and charged Jack who simply raised his fists in response. Once the servant was close enough, Jack moved to the side and slammed his right fist into the horse's front leg with enough force to make it recoil back onto its hind legs and release a pained roar. The knight swung at Jack with his blade but as soon as the blade made contact, the sword found itself stuck inside of a statue of ice that was shaped like Jack. Jack stood unscathed behind his frozen copy which was nearly immediately shattered by the enraged servant. The servant released a roar that shook the very floor of the building and raised its helmet high into air. The light behind the helmet's visor increased in intensity before a beam of pure energy exploded from it and shot toward Jack.

"Damn," Jack said before he raised his right hand as if to catch the beam. Arondight crackled with presence as the crimson energy was absorbed into the brand, filling the line that connected the first and second circles. The power of the attack slowly but surely pushed Jack back across the floor until his back was planted firmly against the wall. Jack gripped his wrist tightly and braced himself as he continued to absorb the energy while ice appeared on the wall behind him. When the light died down, Jack pried himself from the wall with an audible crack. A biting mist escaped his mask and surrounded his body as he cracked his neck. Jack seemed to carry himself differently as he strode toward the servant. With each step a small circle of ice constantly reformed on the ground around him.

"Frost, can you take another one of those?" Diamond asked from some unseen location.

"At my current level, no, but he's given me more than enough power to use my second circle," Jack said calmly as Arondight's second circle began to shine. At that moment the ring of ice on the ground around him doubled in size as small blue circuits appeared around Jack's brand on his mod-suit and spread to the top of his wrist. "I'll get you that opening."

"Don't push yourself," Diamond said as the Dullahan rose his helmet. Just before he could fire a second blast, however, Diamond shot up from Jack's shadow and knocked him to the side. Diamond immediately opened fire at the servant and the horse released a pained noise as the bullets chipped away at it. Immediately, the servant switched its attention to Diamond. "Now!" Diamond ordered and Jack shot toward the Dullahan. Jack slammed his fists together and froze them before he broke them apart. Both fists covered in ice, Jack slammed a devastating right into the horse. Upon impact, Jack's fist exploded into what looked like a storm of ice and lightning. After the horse was frozen in place, Jack slammed his left fist into the knight's chest plate with enough force to dent it and knock the knight off of the horse. In one last-ditch effort to stop the thieves, the knight threw its helmet high into the air, the entirety of it glowing red as it prepared to take the two thieves down with it. "Frost," was all Diamond said before Jack suddenly seized the knight's sword from its body and threw it up into the air behind the helmet. Diamond stared up at the helmet and waited for her chance to get a good shot at the catalyst within it. Diamond quickly turned around and released a bullet toward a shadowy corner of the room. Once the bullet disappeared into the shadows, it reappeared from a shadow on the ceiling that was cast by the helmet's light coming into contact with the airborne blade. The bullet grazed the edge of the blade before it slammed into the underside of the helmet and destroyed a large crimson crystal. Immediately the light died down as a few of the golems that stormed into the area began to break down into dust after the source of their power was destroyed.

*   *   *

"Alright, it's down!" Kat cheered as she watched the purple wall dissipate.

"And I can see. Hold on a second, kitten," Abbie said as she brought down the laser grids and took over the security cameras. *"You're in the clear."*

"Awesome," Kat said as she proceeded to take the objective.

*   *   *

"Gotta say, your trick shots have gotten a lot better," Jack praised.

"Yes, but that took way longer than it should have," Diamond muttered as she looked down at her gloved hand. "I should have been able to end that in one shot."

76

"Baby steps, you'll get there eventually. We're just lucky I was able to understand what you wanted," Jack said as he stretched his arms.

"A perk of our bond," Diamond said as she faced him.

"Which one?" Jack asked curiously. The question made Diamond's eyes widen ever so slightly but before she could respond, a sharp intake of breath caught their attention.

"Wait, I'm pickin' somethin' up. I think someone's..." Abbie's voice trailed off as the sound of footsteps echoed throughout the room.

"Well, what is this? Someone actually managed to break in here," a voice said as they turned just in time to see a young man with black hair and blue eyes walk into the room. The man was garbed in a gray suit and he looked more amused than anything as he spotted the thieves. "Though if it's you all, that's to be expected, you never cease to amaze me. With each encounter, you rookies seem to grow by leaps and bounds."

"Xavier..." Diamond trailed off as anger filled her golden eyes.

CHAPTER 6

· · · · · · · ● ● ● ● ● ● ● ● ● · · · · ·

XAVIER ROMERO MAGNUS

Santa Monica, Magnus Financial Bank

"Xavier? Please tell me you didn't just say Xavier," Kat pleaded as she took the safety deposit box. "Guys! I'm on my way, try to keep him talking!" Kat said frantically as she ran out of the room with the box under her arm. A feeling of dread filled Abbie as she had never heard Kat sound remotely scared before. Abbie began to type frantically as she explored the systems in the building and tried to see if there was anything she could do to help from her end.

"Kitten, listen to me. I'll direct you through the fastest route," Abbie said as she looked at the bank's layout.

*   *   *

"It was cute before, but now you are disrupting family business. I'll have to take you down. I, Xavier Romero Magnus, son of the late Arch-Mage Romero Magnus and head of House Magnus shall face you," Xavier said with a dramatic bow. Xavier frowned as he did a quick head count. "You're missing someone, or has her stealth just improved that much?" Xavier wondered before he looked over at the destroyed servant. "Either seems possible seeing what you've done to August's servant, that's the enforcer's job right? Defeating servants?" Xavier asked as his eyes landed upon Jack. "You're getting strong, brother."

"I am a lot of things, Magnus," Jack began calmly. "But don't you ever call me that," Jack said before he shot forward and released a punch at Xavier who caught it effortlessly. A blue light that surrounded Xavier's body flashed ever so slightly as the mage looked at Jack with visible disdain.

"I actually felt that against my shield," Xavier praised before he slammed a quick blow into Jack's stomach that made Jack double over in pain. "But you're still too slow," Xavier said before he unleashed a barrage of rapid punches into Jack. Each blow knocked Jack back until Xavier ended his onslaught with a vicious right hook that knocked Jack onto his back. As Jack quickly recovered and climbed to his feet, the sound of gunfire echoed throughout the area as Diamond released three shots at Xavier. The blue light flickered around Xavier's body as each shot bounced harmlessly off of him. "I was wondering when you were going to step in your highness. Shame there are only two of you, I was hoping today would be the day you all could actually make me use my staff, I'm curious to see your growth."

"Did he just shrug off gunfire!?"

"It's his shield, I need to get to them so I can take it down!" Kat explained.

"You're almost there. Boss, Frost, hang on just a little bit longer!"

"Okay, let's try that again," Jack said as he rolled his shoulders. For a moment, the two men just sized each other up before they quickly rushed each other. Jack remained emotionless while Xavier grinned at him as they rained blow after blow down upon each other. Though Jack's attacks didn't faze Xavier, Jack never let up his assault as he powered through the pain. While Jack kept the mage at bay, Diamond aimed one of her guns at the back of Jack's head.

"Frost," Diamond called out which made Jack duck. Golden presence sparked briefly down the barrel of the gun just as she pulled the trigger. Xavier grunted when the bullet slammed into his head and knocked him back.

"Good shot," Xavier said just as Jack slammed a vicious left hook into his face. Xavier gritted his teeth as he glared at Jack. "I almost felt that. A shame, you could have been one of the greatest mages," Xavier began as a ball of fire suddenly roared to life in the palm of his hand. "But instead you chose to stand alongside those who murdered our father!" Xavier shouted as he swung the ball toward Jack who in turn slammed an ice-covered fist into the inferno. The resulting explosion from the two attacks blasted the brothers away from each other. Diamond used Xavier's distraction to quickly vanish into the shadows so that she could find a new vantage point.

"He was no father of mine," Jack said as a blade of ash formed in his hand before Arondight released presence along its edge, encasing the blade in ice. "And you reap what you sow. Want me to feel bad for him, do you? Sod off," Jack said as he charged Xavier who released fireballs at Jack who cut through each of them with his make-shift blade. Each fireball ire dispersing as soon as they collided with his ice and their fading flames were consumed by Arondight. "He started this war, the least I can do as someone cursed with his blood is help the right-side end it. That's the honorable thing to do," Jack said as he swung his blade at Xavier only to be knocked back when a pulse of magic erupted from the mage's body.

"Honor? You outnumber your opponents, fight from the shadows, and steal the belongings of others and you try to lecture me about honor?" Xavier questioned with a sneer. Soon a bright twelve-pointed star appeared beneath his feet. A blue ring appeared around the star, bearing an emblem for each of the zodiac signs which appeared above each of the star's points. "You still have much to learn about this world, allow me to teach you," Xavier muttered, his blue eyes shining brightly. "*Sorgere, Eva!*" Xavier chanted and almost immediately what appeared to be a young woman appeared behind him that floated effortlessly in the air. The newcomer had tanned skin, black hair, and glowing blue eyes that seemed to pierce through the souls of the thieves. What stood out the most about her, however, was that she seemed to be clothed only in what appeared to be a black straitjacket that stopped above her knees. Blue chains of magic wrapped around her and floated in the air surrounding her.

"Bring them to their knees, Eve," Xavier ordered as the sound of gunfire suddenly rang out. Xavier didn't even bat an eye as bullets were blocked by the chains that surrounded Eve. Eve's eyes shone a bit brighter as the bullets were reduced to dust before they looked up to find Diamond crouched on one of the rafters, her weapons aimed down at them. Eve's chains quickly wrapped around the rafter and Diamond flipped off of them just in time as they were reduced to rubble. The chains retracted and floated above Diamond ominously. Diamond dove to the side and fell into a shadow just in time to avoid being caught by them before she reappeared from Jack's shadow. Instantly, Diamond took aim at Xavier and Eve and unloaded her weapons as Ever blocked them all until Diamond heard two unsatisfying clicks.

"Amusing, you really are desperate when you're not all together aren't you?" Xavier mused as large chunks of the floor and nearby tables and desks began to float above Diamond and Jack. They cursed as Eve's telekinesis seemed to extend far beyond her chains which suddenly shot forward and bound them in place. "A shame, Eve take them down."

"Yes Master," Eve said quietly but before her attack could land, golden cards sailed through the air and stabbed into the debris. The cards all pulsed for a moment before they exploded and destroyed both the debris and Eve's concentration. With Eve distracted, Jack and Diamond wasted no time and broke free. "What!?" Xavier exclaimed as a shadow slipped between his legs and left a single gold card stabbed into the ground. Like the others, the card exploded and blasted Xavier away as Kat sprung out from the shadow and landed in front of her band. "Eve, get her!"

"As you wish," Eve said before she flew toward Kat, her body covered in Xavier's magic. A card formed in Kat's palm before she threw it at Eve who made it stop in mid-air only for it to erupt in a bright light that sent her recoiling backward as she found herself blinded.

"Looks like I made it in time," Kat said with a laugh. "This looks interesting,"

"The box, did you get it?" Diamond asked making Kat nod.

"Yup, had to take a moment to put it somewhere safe. That's why it took me so long, the objective comes first, right?" Kat asked cheekily which made Diamond nod. When Kat turned to face Xavier, her eyes were filled with mischief as her whip formed itself in her hand. "How about we even up the odds a bit, boss?"

"Gladly," Diamond said before her body was covered with her presence, gold sparks coursed around it while the whites of her eyes turned pitch black. Jack and Kat trembled as they felt a powerful thunder build up inside of them as they found themselves filled with Diamond's presence. The bright golden storm of energy ripped itself from their bodies as the whites of Jack and Kat's eyes turned black while their irises were filled with an electric gold which was mirrored in Diamond's eyes. The tiles of the floor beneath them cracked as Diamond's will and presence overtook them.

"So, you're taking control of my brother? Don't want him to fight his own battles?" Xavier taunted when he saw the change. In response, Diamond just scoffed.

"Please, he's a member of my band. His battles are my battles," Diamond said as she felt her band submit to her. Like their hearts, their minds were now one as well. "Stone, think you can shut down the power? Do that much and we can get out of here."

"Yeah, but it'll take a couple of minutes."

"That's fine," Diamond said as she tossed her guns to the side. Her weapons turned into ash and reformed in her grasp, fully loaded. Diamond backed up as Jack suddenly rushed toward Xavier while Kat dashed to the side. Eve charged forward to intercept Jack only for Kat's whip to suddenly wrap around her ankle. Eve's eyes widened slightly as she found herself slammed into the ground. Jumping over Eve, Kat rushed to aid Jack against Xavier.

"Master…" Eve grunted before she floated up into the air. Diamond glared up at her as she realized she needed to take down the servant quickly. Eve fired a chain at her which Diamond caught before she wrapped it around her right arm and pulled the surprised servant toward her. Diamond quickly fired a shot at Eve that the servant managed to stop cold in mid-air before she sent it back toward Diamond. Diamond's head was knocked back when the bullet slammed into her forehead. Diamond stumbled back as Eve landed before her but she didn't fall. Diamond glared at the servant as the flattened bullet fell from her forehead harmlessly. Diamond then delivered a vicious head butt that knocked Eve down onto the ground as Diamond released the chain. Eve recovered quickly and knocked Diamond back with a telekinetic push. Diamond realized then that being quick wasn't enough, she'd have to end her battle soon.

"Here goes nothing," Diamond muttered as she continued to fight Eve. As they battled, Diamond slowly but surely led Eve away from her band and Xavier. "Give up, if I learned anything from our previous battles it's that your reach only goes as far as your chains extend."

"This is true, but irrelevant for you," Eve said as Diamond backed herself into a wall. Eve's chains rose menacingly and shot toward the trapped Diamond only to miss when she suddenly fell into her shadow. From the shadows of the ceiling, Diamond emerged and landed on the back of the now startled Eve. Eve struggled for a moment as Diamond bit the finger of her ever-present glove and pulled it off. The fight between Xavier, Jack, and Kat paused when they all saw a flash of gold light on the opposite side of the battlefield. By the time they could turn to see what had happened, Diamond had already reequipped her glove. Gone was the servant and in her place was a golden statue of Eve. Eve's stunned expression frozen on her face before the statue exploded into a golden dust that left nothing behind except a crimson orb covered in intricate gold sigils. Diamond panted tiredly as she walked forward and picked up the orb.

"Eve!" Xavier shouted as he felt a large amount of power return to his body. His magic erupted from his body in a bright explosion that forced Jack off of him. Jack recovered quickly and landed on his feet before he stomped the ground which made a wall of ice appear in front of him just in time to block a torrent of lightning which had erupted from Xavier's palms. The enraged mage's eyes turned pitch-black before countless small lights appeared inside them that made his eyes appear as though they were windows into space itself.

Jack turned around and cupped his hands together as Kat ran toward him. Kat's treasure began to spin as she ran to Jack and placed her foot into his hands. Using all of his strength, Jack launched her up into the air and over the wall. Xavier glared at her as he stopped his spell before two balls of fire appeared in his hands just as the pendant stopped with its golden section on top. At that moment, Kat giggled as large amounts of golden presence coursed sporadically over her body which began to release a faint golden glow. As Kat fell down toward Xavier, she grinned as each of his fireballs missed her. Kat flipped forward and slammed both of her feet into his face. Kat jumped back off of him, an act that made Xavier stumble back as Kat threw two cards at him that both exploded as soon as they were close. The power of the explosions was enough to lift Xavier into the air. Jack then appeared above him with both of his fists frozen together before he slammed them down upon Xavier. The ice shattered as more ice exploded from his fists upon contact and froze the young mage against the floor. Gold sparks danced across the ice as Xavier grunted in pain. Soon Xavier's entire body shone blue before the light exploded into countless particles as his shield shattered. Xavier glared at them as he felt even more of his power return to him.

"Boss, I'm in," Abbie said as Diamond strode toward her band.

"I see, wait for my signal," Diamond ordered as she stopped in front of Xavier. "Ah-ah, I wouldn't do that," Diamond said as she saw the ice begin to crack. Diamond held up the orb Eve left behind and watched in satisfaction as Xavier attempted to escape. Xavier's eyes returned to normal as he looked up at Diamond wearily. "Good, you are quite fond of your servant, aren't you?" Diamond asked as she tossed the orb to Kat who caught it with ease. Diamond took a knee and gazed down into Xavier's eyes as her eyes and those of her band returned to normal. "Do you know why you lost? After all, even I know we aren't strong enough to best you yet here we are," Diamond mused and Xavier said nothing as he glared at her. "You lost because you let your guard down and didn't take us seriously. Even a snake can be killed by a mouse under the right circumstances. That's what I want, to kill you, but not like this. If I ended you like this my mother would roll over in her grave. No, when I bring you down, I want there to be no mistake on your part that my band is superior to you. After all, that's why you let us live last time, right? You want to see us grow so you showed mercy, this is me returning the favor and bringing an end to our life-debt. We're even now and our honor is restored," Diamond said as she stood up. "Next time we meet will be the last," Diamond said before she stood up and began to walk away with her band. Diamond then stopped and glanced back at the downed Xavier. "Consider this your lesson in honor," Diamond added before she glanced toward a camera and gave a subtle nod. It was then that the power of the bank suddenly shut down which darkened the entirety of the building. After a short while, the power returned to the building and Xavier found himself alone in the lobby with nothing but the red and gold orb resting on the ground before him.

*   *   *

"Are you sure you did the right thing?" Jack asked Diamond as Kat drove them back to their safe house.

"Not at all, but I had no choice," Diamond mused. "We are bound by honor and there is no honor in killing one that spared you. To do so would be to act without honor, and without honor, there is no difference between us and the dirt beneath our feet. At least that is what my mother claimed."

"A lot of assassins would call you insane for what you just did, you know," Kat pointed out as she glanced back at her boss through the rear-view mirror.

"Guess that just proves I still have much to learn. That said, I'm leaving this confrontation out of my report. The last thing I need is for this momentary lapse in judgment to make it back to the headmistress' ears. I don't want or need another lecture," Diamond said with a frown. "We have yet to take a life, whether that's good or bad I do not know. What I do know is that Kat, you prefer unnecessary bloodshed. Also, Jack, as much as you try to deny it, you have yet to truly sort out your feelings about your brother. I won't even get started on my issues. It hurts my pride as an assassin, but as a boss I know we are not ready to cross that line yet. Our bond is still fresh and vulnerable. I refuse to cause further unnecessary damage to it than I already have. I won't do things you both don't approve of. I'm your leader but I'm not, nor ever will I be, a tyrant," Diamond said resolutely.

"Well," Jack suddenly began as his mask disappeared. "I just hope we can go a bit longer this time without another family reunion."

"You can say that again," Kat said as her mask disappeared as well. "Now let's hurry up and get home, you already know Abbie's worried to death."

"What? I am not!"

"So, this perfect traffic is a coincidence? You're not hacking the streetlights?" Kat asked knowingly with a grin. "Don't think we've had a red light yet now that I think about it."

"...Shut up." Abbie responded and despite herself, Diamond shook her head a bit as Kat parked in front of Midas Towers.

"Well, it's official," Diamond began as her mask vanished and revealed a small smirk. "We can officially consider the Magnus Financial job, complete."

CHAPTER 7

· · · · · · ●●● ● ●●● · · · · · ·

PAY DAY

San Diego, Magnus Manor

The taste of defeat was bitter in Xavier's mouth as he stood before an older blond man and brunette woman. The battle replayed over and over in his mind as he tried to figure out just when he had lost the upper hand.

"I'm just happy you're okay," the woman said as she hugged him tightly. "But you should have handled things better. I'll leave it to my brother to lecture you. Unfortunately, I have a project that needs my attention immediately. I will see you when I have more free time. Until then, August, make sure you lecture the boy properly."

"Of course, June," August said before his sister disappeared in a blue flash of light. "Honestly, my boy, I understand that you're eager to begin life as an official member of the Circle, but the least you could have done is come home first instead of checking on your father's old properties," August said as he looked down at Xavier with disappointment clear in his dark green eyes. "We haven't seen you in years and the first thing you do is almost get yourself killed?"

"I'm sorry uncle August, but once I felt the wards my father cast around his business break, I knew I had to at least see what was going on," Xavier said as he bowed, frustrated by his failure. "The band there was one I encountered before, rookies still in training. I thought I knew what to expect."

"Pride is more often than not the cause of the downfall of even the strongest of men," August said sagely as he led Xavier throughout the manor. "Like me, you have the heart of a lion! Brimming with pride! That said, I had always hoped you would be better than me. Never let your guard down around a thief, even the youngest of them know how to exploit a moment of weakness," August lectured. "And you say you recognized them? Just how many times have you ran into this particular band?" August questioned which made Xavier grimace.

"About three or four times?"

"Are you asking or are you telling me?" August asked dryly. "Any particular reason why you didn't put an end to them when you had a chance?"

"They're just beginners, uncle."

"Beginners who've bested you," August said bluntly. "The deadliest thing about a thief is their ability to adapt, my boy. Every encounter will only serve to make them stronger if you don't bring them down when you have the chance. I understand your hesitancy, you are new after all, but remember that this is war. Do you not remember the incident that started this war? How one of their so-called Dolls slaughtered dozens of our women and children without mercy?" August questioned making Xavier clench his fists at the thought.

"No, uncle, I remember."

"Then why have you not dealt with this particular band?"

"Because it's my brother's band," Xavier revealed and August paused for a moment as he took in the new information. "The first time I encountered them I removed his mask and was unable to finish them so I spared them. I tried to limit Jack's band by trapping them in a life-debt and since then I've monitored their growth a couple of times to ensure they would be no threat. And they weren't...until tonight when they somehow managed to get even with me. If it was anyone else, I would have gladly ended them by now. However, my father's blood still runs through Jack's veins and I can't help but wonder whether or not my father would approve of me bringing harm upon him. Yes, this is war, but you know how my father was. His one rule was to never turn your back on *la famiglia.*"

"Romero was a great man, even now I wonder if I am doing his station as the Arch-Mage of August any justice. That said you must understand that this is war. He was hopelessly optimistic and that lead to his downfall," August said seriously. "His bastard must be at least twenty years of age by now. Not only that but Romero, even to my surprise, didn't take the necessary precautions to ensure his child with that whore would be born female. That makes that bastard even more of a threat to you personally as you have yet to take a bride and have a son. Should you fall, some of the most valuable assets of the Circle will go to him, to the thieves, is that really what you want? Especially in these volatile times?"

"No, of course not, uncle!"

"Then remember what the thieves have taken from you when you see that band again. Your father and my brother, in all but blood, was destroyed for seeking justice. Our beloved Regina, your mother and my sister, was assassinated by the demon that seduced her husband and poisoned your youngest sister to the point where she could never hope to join our ranks," August said and Xavier felt his blood boil with every word. "Your…brother… is too far gone. Ending him now would be an act of mercy so that you can bring an end to his evil. Focus on the pain you feel now and never again lose sight of your allegiance. Do you understand my boy?"

"Yes, uncle August."

"Good," August said before he held his nephew in a fatherly embrace. "Now, welcome back, you've grown to be strong. Even Arch-Mage Enero said that you surpassed his expectations when he taught you," August praised.

"Yes, but I clearly have much to learn. I'm sorry for being unable to protect your belongings," Xavier apologized.

"Don't worry just some old tools and some notes I can easily replicate with some time in my study," August said as he dismissed Xavier's worries. "Now let me be on my way I have a call to make,"

August said as he pulled out his cell phone which made Xavier frown a bit when he noticed the model.

"You know, you should really get an upgrade. You do know your model is faulty, right?" Xavier asked with an obvious concern for August's well-being.

"Please, Xavier, I've barely used it as is, but it has served me well for the past year. As long as it works there is no need to change. Enero may fool these civilians into buying the same thing every year, but I know better," August said dismissively. "Now go reunite with your sisters, they've missed you," August said before he departed.

"Well, I wouldn't say we both missed you," a new voice said and Xavier turned around to find a blonde woman who appeared less than happy to see him. She gave Xavier a once over and Xavier could see nothing but contempt in her bright green eyes. "But Faith hasn't been quiet since she heard you were returning. Follow me, I'll show you where she is."

"Lilia," Xavier began with a look of disdain as he followed her. "Charming as always, and here I thought you would have grown out of your petty dislike of me."

"Funny, here I was wondering if you've grown up enough to realize just why I dislike you," Lilia said with a humorless smile. "Poor little brother, a boy trapped in a world of men. Why-oh-why couldn't Jack be the heir?" Lilia wondered as Xavier clenched his fist tightly. "Perhaps one day you'll fill father's shoes, but that day is not today," Lilia said and Xavier just glared at her. "Now enough pleasantries," Lilia said sarcastically. "Force a smile on your face and hurry up, the last thing I want to deal with is poor little Faith knowing that we still get along just as well as we always have," Lilia said before they both entered a room. However, as soon as they did, their fake smiles dropped when they saw Faith asleep in her wheel chair. "Hm, she must have fallen asleep waiting on you," Lilia mused as Xavier frowned. "Here we thought you could return for her sixteenth birthday, but of course you had your own thing to do," Lilia drawled as she moved to help her sister as Xavier looked at her in horror.

"Damn it, that was today, wasn't it?" Xavier asked before he moved to help Lilia who brushed a lock of black hair from Faith's face.

"Yes, but disappointing your family is nothing new for you, now is it?" Lilia asked rhetorically. "Leave us, I'll handle it. She has at least one sibling she can depend on, after all, must be nice," Lilia said pointedly and Xavier clenched his fists tightly before he turned and left the room.

*   *   *

Santa Monica, Midas Tower

The next morning after the successful heist, Abbie went to the safe house to meet up with the thieves to figure out their next course of action.

"Come in, you came at a good time," Diamond said as she let Abbie inside the penthouse. "I was just on my way to run some errands, you will be coming with me."

"Oh okay, where are the others?"

"Training with their mentors, mine gave me the day off so I could settle matters regarding the heist and officially bring it to a close. We won't be doing anything too serious, just some paperwork," Diamond reassured Abbie. "I want you to come with me because it will prove to be an invaluable experience for you."

"Where are we headed?" Abbie asked as Diamond led her to the kitchen.

"To the bank."

"Which one? We're not headin' back to Magnus Financial, are we?"

"No," Diamond began as she removed the picture from the wall. "We're headed to the Guild bank," Diamond revealed as she placed a hand on Abbie's shoulder before using her free one to tap the mark. Abbie yelped when she felt her stomach churn as her surroundings became distorted. The time of day seemed to shift from day to night in a matter of moments. Diamond released Abbie quickly as she stumbled back and covered her mouth with both of her hands. Diamond lazily pointed to a nearby trash can and waited patiently as Abbie emptied the contents of her stomach into it.

* * *

"Take a sip, it'll settle your stomach," Diamond said as she handed her flask to Abbie who proceeded to do just that. Abbie shuddered when the liquid splashed against her taste-buds.

"Seriously, what is that stuff?"

"You're too inquisitive, we'll never get to the bank if I tried to explain it. It's nectar which is all you need to know," Diamond said as they stepped out onto the roof of the safe house. Abbie realized then that the safe house must have been sound proofed when they were immediately bombarded by music that seemed to echo throughout the realm. "Welcome to the Thieves' Guild's capital, Dorado." Abbie's eyes widened as she took in the beautiful city. The streets were literally paved with gold as lights of a myriad of colors came from the buildings that were constructed from a black stone. "In the distance, you can see the ancestral homes of the founding families. From the Frost family's home of Niflheim," Diamond began as she gestured toward a large frozen manor that floated above the city that was engulfed in a blue light. "To the home of the Ardent family, Belinos," Diamond said as she gestured to a large mansion opposite of Niflheim that was engulfed in a perpetual fire. The lights of the realm reflected in the awe-struck Abbie's eyes as she looked around the realm and noted the different shapes and sizes of nine other houses between Niflheim and Belinos. What drew her attention the most, however, was the solid gold castle that rested in the center of the capital.

"Amazing," Abbie whispered. "Who owns the castle?" Abbie questioned but before she could get a response her hair began to blow wildly. With a frown, Abbie looked up to find an air-shuttle begin to lower itself on to the roof.

"Come, our ride is here," Diamond said and when the air-shuttle landed, the two climbed into it and took off toward the capital.

"This place is incredible," Abbie said as she placed her hands against the glass of the shuttle's window and looked down at the illuminated city. Abbie watched in awe as a much larger version of the thieves' mark etched itself into what appeared to be a vacant piece plot of land. Soon, a torrent of ash swarmed toward it and formed a large building. "Wait I've seen that building before, it's an old apartment complex Eric used to live in."

"Someone must have turned it into a safe house," Diamond mused. "To the bank please," Diamond instructed the pilot.

"Right away, Your Highness!" the pilot answered before he veered off to the right.

"Your Highness?" Abbie repeated as she raised an eye-brow.

"You asked who owned the castle? That belongs to the royal family that runs the Guild, the Midas family," Diamond revealed as Abbie looked at her as if she had grown two heads.

"Wow," Abbie said after a moment as she looked at Diamond in a new light. "Can't say I ever thought I'd be talkin' to a Princess. Should I start calling you Your Highness and start bowin'?" Abbie asked. "Because, no offense, but I don't bow. It's just not in my blood."

"Good, between you and me, I hate when people do that," Diamond said with a barely noticeable smile, a bit impressed by Abbie's bravado. "Don't call me Your Highness either, Diamond is fine and boss while on the job."

"I see," Abbie said as she looked down at the streets of the capital. Everywhere she looked she could see thieves. Some thieves donned their mod-suits and others didn't but they all seemed to enjoy themselves. "Everyone's so happy."

"An eternal party. It's said to be the Goddess Juventas' idea. It makes the Guild a place where our members can be free and relax. This party being interrupted is never a good sign. What tends to follow is the announcement of a war or the death of someone of the royal line," Diamond explained though the last bit was said a bit more

93

quietly. "Fortunately, all my predecessors had an heir before passing on, allowing the royal treasure to continue being passed down."

"What is your treasure, by the way?" Abbie asked as she realized that Diamond's treasure was still a mystery. "Your glove?" Abbie guessed and Diamond shook her head. Though Diamond's face remained as impassive as ever, Abbie could see a hint of pain in Diamond's eyes. This was enough for Abbie to realize that Diamond's glove was a topic that was in her best interest to avoid. For a moment, Diamond said nothing as if she were silently debating something in her head before she nodded to herself. Forming one of her guns Diamond quickly pressed the barrel of the weapon into her bare palm. Abbie jumped when Diamond pulled the trigger and continued to look on incredulously as Diamond removed the weapon and revealed a flattened bullet. "My treasure is my very blood. It is Royal Blood and Royal Blood must never spill," Diamond said as if reciting something she had heard countless times.

"You're indestructible..." Abbie trailed off as she understood what Kat meant when she said that Diamond was more durable than Jack.

"Only my skin and bones, it's why I am able to handle the recoil of my weapons so well. My durability is more for everyone else's protection than my own. Should my blood spill...the consequences will be devastating from what I have been told. I try to keep myself as healthy as possible. I drink nectar on a strict schedule to prevent the chance of any unnecessary bloodshed," Diamond explained before she took a sip from her flask. "That being said, I am not immortal. I can be both hurt and killed, my enemies just have to be a bit more creative."

"But that's still insane! You can probably pull off some crazy things with that."

"It has definitely been helpful. This is the only treasure not forged from ash but instead carried down through my family from parent to child," Diamond said and soon they felt the shuttle land. "Come on we're here," Diamond said as they stepped out in front of a large building. Abbie instinctively reached for her own mark as she looked at the large one carved on the bank's surface. It looked like a large thief badge only the inner three circles were no longer empty. Inside the smaller circles in the black, red, and gold sections was a hand, an apple, and a wine glass carved in them respectively.

"How the hell did I hack you?" Abbie whispered in confusion when an opening formed for them in the front of the bank when its stone-like exterior dissolved into ash and allowed them passage.

"A lot of resources aren't exactly spent on freezing a recruit's assets. They used modern civilian tech. Don't be too amazed by what you see here though, the only people who know how it works are the Hattori family. Where the Mages' Circle focused on the arcane arts, the Guild preserved the knowledge lost in the dark ages and left it to the Hattori family to further develop it. Eventually, we ended up centuries ahead of what you see in the outside world. At the end of the day, however, we just read the manuals the Hattori family sends us. You're probably closer to understanding it than myself at this point," Diamond explained as they made their way inside. However, before they could make it to a teller, they ran into an older man.

"Ah, if it isn't the young Midas."

"Councilor Ardent," Diamond greeted, her voice colder than Abbie had ever heard it.

"I hear you were successful in your latest heist, I suppose congratulations are in order but do not get overconfident because of one success. You have much to do before you even come close to being seen as a worthy heir," the man said before his hard gaze moved to Abbie. "And who is this?"

"Someone I contracted."

"So, you needed help from a civilian?" the councilor questioned with a visible sneer that made Diamond clench her fists tightly. Abbie decided right then that she didn't like the man before her.

"I did what I needed to do to succeed."

"Careful with your words, your grandfather had the same mentality before your mother brought him down. Don't want others to think we have another 'Mad King' on our hands," the man said as Diamond's eyes widened in anger.

"Sorry, but don't you have somewhere to be? We are busy," Abbie interrupted and Diamond used that moment to force back her emotions.

"Indeed, we are. As much as I would love to continue this conversation, we must go," Diamond informed the councilor.

"I see, well don't let me stop you. Just make sure to unmark the civilian, would you? You're in a sensitive position, you can't afford any mistakes," the councilor warned before he left.

"Thank you," Diamond said after he left.

"Don't mention it. You got mad and it looked like somethin' bad was gonna happen. He just wanted to get a reaction out of you. Don't give him the satisfaction," Abbie said as Diamond released a long breath and calmed her nerves. "Who was that prick anyway?"

"Heathcliff Ardent, current head of the Ardent family and Vivi's father."

"Vivi? Where have I heard-wait-as in Kat and Jack's guardian!?"

"The very same. Congrats, you just met the closest thing Katarina has to a grandfather. She adores him by the way, so try to stay off his bad side," Diamond said matter-of-factly as Abbie looked at her in blatant horror. Abbie then scowled when she saw the amusement that shined in Diamond's eyes. "I'm kidding, Vivi and her father do not get along and Katarina barely knows him, they aren't close at all."

"Not funny."

"On the contrary, it was hysterical," Diamond said bluntly as her face didn't betray the amusement Abbie knew Diamond felt at her expense. "Come on, let's finish up this visit."

*   *   *

"Without a doubt, you delivered the safety deposit box owned by Arch-Mage August," A well-dressed woman said from behind a counter. "Congratulations, Your Highness, you've succeeded where dozens of first-years failed before you," the woman said before she placed a black briefcase on the counter. "I will take this to my superiors and mark this job as complete. In addition to your payment, the Guild will award your band five hundred honor each. With your current amount, your treasures are now worth enough in the Guild's eyes for you to begin creating a business in an industry of your choice. Good work as always, Your Highness," the woman said before she turned to Abbie, "The same goes to your band and the contracted as well."

"Er, thanks," Abbie said bashfully before she glanced at Diamond. "Honor?"

"It's how we gauge our reputation, the higher the honor, the more resources become available to you," Diamond said as she opened the briefcase. Now Abbie wasn't sure what she expected to see in that case, part of her thought it would be just filled with wads of cash just like in all of the old movies. Instead, to her complete and utter shock, she found that the case was filled with gold coins. The coins were placed in stacks of ten, five rows and ten columns inside of the case. "Five-hundred, perfect."

"Is that pure gold!?" Abbie asked, her face filled with shock as Diamond nodded. Abbie did the math quickly in her head before she stared at the gold in wonder. "That's over half a mil, easy, and for what? Notes and trinkets?"

"A job is a job," Diamond said with a shrug. "This was valued highly, why, I do not know or care because we have just gotten paid," Diamond said and then turned to face the teller. "Thirty-five percent into my account, and twenty-five to both Jack Frost and Katarina Umbra," Diamond said before turning to Abbie. "Give her your information so that she can give you the remaining fifteen percent."

"H-hold up! I'm gettin' paid too!?"

"Yes?" Diamond said before realization hit her. "Please don't tell me you did this for free…"

"Uh…"

"Juventas, give me strength," Diamond whispered. "What kind of life did you lead that you'd rob a bank for free? Regardless of the circumstances?" Diamond questioned as she rubbed the bridge of her nose. "Give her your information. Even a Doll can only be built with so much patience."

"I have as much patience as is required of me, Your Highness," the thoroughly amused bank teller said. Her amusement only grew when she noticed how the civilian looked at her. "In fact, this part of the job is my favorite. Civilians who have never met Dolls before always make the best expressions. Though after all the decades I've been doing this, this one may be my favorite. Would you like it in USD or Global Coin?"

"GC, it'll make my purchases a lot easier. There is so much I wanna say…but I'm tired," Abbie said as she rubbed her temples to fight off an impending migraine. Abbie just gave the teller her information and watched as the Doll left to deposit the gold. "I couldn't even tell the difference."

"You're not supposed to," Diamond pointed out. "They are meant to be indistinguishable in every way. The pilot was one too."

"You know, it's weird, normally I'd be freakin' out a lot more about this but…I just can't," Abbie muttered.

"That…may be our fault."

"How?"

"Tell me, Abigail, since meeting Katarina, have you ever felt foreign emotions filling you? The urge to do things you never once even fantasized about?" Diamond asked curiously.

"Oh…yeah…" Abbie said dryly, though there was a look of fondness on her face as she thought about all the risks she had taken since meeting Kat.

"The reason that happens is a side-effect of being near us. As a thief, our presence is projected outwards and can change another's very cognition which helps us with sneaking into places. However, how exactly it affects people's cognition depends on the thief. Katarina makes you feel rebellious and free of inhibitions. Frost can seduce and charm others, their personal preferences be damned," Diamond said as Abbie finally understood the strange feeling Jack radiated. "My presence? It dominates, makes people submit to my will and be happy doing so. In fact, my mother who shared my presence could paralyze people with only a look when angry. Unfortunately, there is no real off switch for this but its effects are least potent when we are not actively trying to use it. Because of this, allow me to be the first to apologize."

"For what?"

"Unfortunately for you the three of us have presences that when combined make it very hard for a civilian like you to uphold their inhibitions. The fact that you will be in constant contact with all three of us…I am truly sorry. I can't say you will stay the same person you are now," Diamond stated and her expression softened ever so slightly as the weight of her words registered with Abbie.

"I'm changin'," Abbie said simply but it wasn't a question like Diamond expected but more like a statement, a realization of something she had long since suspected. Abbie wasn't a fool, she knew the slight changes in her behavior weren't exactly normal but she didn't want to pay it any mind, because it didn't hurt her. On the contrary, Abbie liked the feeling they gave her. A feeling of freedom from the incredibly reserved person she had always been.

"I'm sorry."

"Don't be," Abbie said firmly. "I…I think I like who I'm becomin'. It's scary, of course, to know that no matter what happens I am going to change as a person. But that's life though, isn't it? We're always changing. Who I'll be next year was always going to be different than who I am now. The difference now is that I can see that being a good change for once."

"You…are something else. It seems Katarina has chosen wisely," Diamond said after a moment and Abbie smiled a bit when she realized that at some point, she had earned the boss' approval.

"So, what's next on your agenda?"

"Now, as the boss, I have to plan for our future," Diamond answered. "The first semester requires one thousand points of honor and each semester continuously raises the quota by five hundred. With this heist done, we each effectively have twenty-five hundred points of honor. We need twenty-two thousand to graduate."

"So, you have a really long way to go."

"Yes, and right now I'll need you by my side for our next endeavor."

"What?" Abbie asked, clearly caught off-guard. "If you need me to hack somethin', you got it. Well, as long as it's ethical."

"No, actually I don't need a hacker for this. Now that we have met the honor requirements, I'm going to start a business. What I need now is an assistant," Diamond revealed. "That is unless you prefer working at the diner?"

"Let's talk benefits," Abbie began without preamble and her face bore the most serious expression Diamond had ever seen from the hacker. Abbie's feelings for Kat and newfound hunger for adventure aside, Abbie had just made six years of her current salary in a week. There was no way she was about to turn down Diamond's offer.

CHAPTER 8

•••••••••●•••••••••

POWER MOVES

Santa Monica, Eric's Apartment

It had been a few weeks since Abbie started her new impromptu job as Diamond's assistant and to say it was a step up would have been an understatement. The work wasn't overly difficult and the pay was good. All she really had to do was help Diamond schedule her days and look into properties for the band's first business venture. Diamond had surprised Abbie when she took her input seriously and shaped strategies around Abbie's advice. Despite the change in pace, a small part of Abbie couldn't wait until the next time they accepted a job. The previous job had given Abbie a thrill and awakened a part of her that she had long since thought she had buried. Abbie tried to distract herself in her free time, something she had a lot more of since her career change. During this time, she would either spend it with Kat, Eric, or alone as she used it to keep her skills sharp. Currently, she was with Eric as she acted as a practice audience for the music he created. As Abbie listened to the music, she noted that another poster had joined Diamond's. This one showing three young women of Korean descent. They appeared to be triplets though each had their own unique style. On the poster, there was simply one word, "Hindsight".

"Yeah! How's this one?" Eric asked as he nodded his head to the beat.

"It's actually better than the last one. I can't believe it, you're actually good at this," Abbie said with a laugh. With a grin Eric brought the music to an end before he turned to face his friend. "See you added a new poster. I didn't know you were a fan of K-pop."

"Me either," Eric said as he glanced at the poster. "But I heard rumors that Roderick Midas was thinking of adding them to his label in order to make up for Diamond's disappearance. I figured I'd learn from his example, broaden my horizons and get a taste of all sorts of music. Now I see what' I've been missing! They're good, Abbie. If they get the right people backing them, they can blow up here in the West," Eric explained. "But enough about my taste in music, what's up? I thought you and Kat had something planned today?" Eric asked and Abbie could see he was a bit concerned. "Everything alright between you two?"

"Huh? Yeah, we're doin' great. Gonna see her in a few," Abbie reassured Eric. "I'm actually here on business. My boss is gonna host an event soon and music is needed. So, I'm here to offer you a chance to make a quick buck, that is if you're interested?"

"Am I interested!? Of course, I can't believe you got me a gig!" Eric said jovially. "Thanks! I appreciate it but you know my music ain't really good for cocktail parties or anything. Who are you even working for? Don't think you ever told me."

"Just someone in the entertainment industry. Figured you two could help each other a bit. I want you to network and get your foot in the door." Abbie explained. "I'll send you the details later since I actually have to get goin' now. Just come prepared to play the music you always have, be the DJ you've always been. Feel the atmosphere and work accordingly," Abbie said as she made her way to the door. "I know you work best under pressure so I'll add this, mess up and both of our career plans are shot," Abbie said seriously which made him look at her with a mix of confusion and horror. "Good luck."

* * *

Santa Monica, Garage

Abbie hummed to herself as she looked online on her tablet for different car parts while Kat worked on the vehicle she had stolen.

"So, what's our budget?"

"Budget?" Kat asked as if confused. "Babe, I'm splurging. The price doesn't matter, we'll make it back eventually. Honestly, no matter how much we spend it'll be a profit because I was saving up to buy this car eventually." Kat explained. "Seeing how we had that good five-finger discount, I have enough cash to trick this baby out to my heart's content. We just need this thing ready to make one hell of a statement. We have to show up to the grand opening of our first business in style, after all."

"I'm just surprised we managed to set up a nightclub so quickly, the paperwork alone should have taken way longer," Abbie mused as Kat grabbed a wrench.

"Between the Guild being able to forge any document you could ever need, and renting a few Dolls for some quick construction, you'd be surprised at what you can get done," Kat said before she slid from underneath the car. Oil stains covered Kat's face as she looked at her current project with a grin.

"I see," Abbie said before she frowned. "Wait, how come you never got a fake ID?"

"Like I said, where's the fun in that?"

"You're crazy," Abbie said but even she couldn't help the small smile that appeared on her lips. "Then again, I suppose that makes me crazy too, to some extent anyway. Come here, I need your opinion on somethin'."

"What's up?" Kat asked as she made her way over to Abbie. Once there she saw what appeared to be a 3-D model of their car, only this one had a far sleeker appearance. "Whoa."

"With the parts, we picked out so far I managed to build what our car should look like when we finalize the purchases. What do you think?"

"Looks great though despite blue being my favorite color, I say we keep it black," Kat suggested. Abbie nodded and quickly changed the color of the car. "Much better, I love it."

"The car will have all the power you want without losin' any of the beauty," Abbie said with a grin. "That baby's gonna be a beast, think you can handle it, kitten?"

"Oh, you have no idea," Kat said smugly. "I can probably get back into the street racing scene with this beauty, make a few bucks on the side, you know?"

"You need more money?" Abbie asked with a laugh while Kat simply beamed at her.

"Can never have too much coin. I might even test out this baby's flight feature."

"Just make sure to do it when I'm not in the car," Abbie said firmly and Kat snickered at the expression on Abbie's face. Abbie's newfound recklessness still had its limits it seemed.

"Aw, okay," Kat said with mock sadness. Suddenly, Kat snapped her fingers as she remembered something important. "Oh, we forgot to mention, we've invited some other thieves-in-training to stop by."

"What!?"

"Yeah, it's kind of a tradition when a band opens up their first business. Look, not every band from our year is coming, but for sure Band 11 and our sister band, Band 12, will show up."

"Sister band?"

"Yeah, like I would say rivals but it's all in good spirit, we're all good friends no matter how much Diamond tries to deny it," Kat explained. "The point is if Diamond being a thief has taught you anything it's that some of us are very famous. So, try not to freak out if you see a couple of celebrities."

"That shouldn't be a problem, never been much of a fan girl," Abbie said with a small frown. "I think I handled meetin' Diamond well enough."

"True," Kat mused. "You were also scared shitless, though," Kat pointed out and in response Abbie stuck her tongue out at her. "Just wanted to give you a heads up because they're all very perceptive and we can't exactly risk them knowing the truth about you. Like, it's okay to be surprised to meet them, they'll expect it, just try not to let on that you know too much."

"Should I stay home instead then? That seems like a safer bet," Abbie suggested only for Kat to shake her head.

"Babe, we've hung out, and got a bit closer," Kat said and she smirked when she saw Abbie blush. "But I don't think we've had a legit date since the Alexei incident. I want you there tonight, we all do, we wouldn't even have this club if it wasn't for you," Kat said firmly. "Tonight, there's going to be a lot of networking and deals being made. Things Diamond and Jack deal with. Me? It's my night off and we're going to have some fun. Besides, Band 12 will be expecting you."

"What? Why?"

"I'm being taught alongside their boss who's a close friend, and I might have let it slip to her that I was seeing someone," Kat said nervously. "Big mistake on my part, forgot she was an even bigger die-hard romantic than Jack. Point is, she wants to meet you but she doesn't know you know as much as you know, you know?" Kat said quickly and Abbie just frowned as she tried to dissect that last sentence Kat had rambled off.

"I'm not sure what you just said but it sounded concernin'."

"The point is we don't need 'Abbie the gifted hacker' to show up. You get to rest and relax for once. We need Abbie my hot older girlfriend to show up, get it?" Kat said as Abbie just raised an eyebrow.

"So just act like I know nothin' Guild-wise?" Abbie simplified which made Kat pause.

"Well...yeah?"

"Alright," Abbie said with a shrug. "Just to be safe though, can we find a way to limit our contact with the other thieves?"

"No problem, you're going to be with me practically the whole night anyway," Kat said as she wrapped her arms around Abbie.

"Yeah, yeah, come on you're gettin' me dirty, kitten," Abbie said though her heart was clearly not in it as Kat sat on her lap. "Now help me look through some more parts."

* * *

105

Santa Monica, Duskhaven

"That's loud," Diamond said from the back seat as the newly customized car pulled up in front of the club which had a golden under glow.

"Just means the DJ is having fun," Jack said before he glanced out of the backseat window and whistled at the size of the line that was outside of the club. "Almost looks like you might get your investment back in one night."

"So far, the feedback has been great. Seems like buyin' Al's lot from him was a good idea," Abbie said as she looked at her phone. "The club's trendin' and you haven't even shown up yet."

"Let's fix that," Kat said as she stopped the car.

"Let's," Diamond said as Jack got out of the car and held the door open for her while Abbie and Kat climbed out. As soon as she stepped out, the gathered crowd began to cheer, the camera flashes almost blinded Abbie though the others didn't seem fazed at all. Kat slid across the hood of the car and tossed the keys to the valet. Kat warned him not to scratch it as she slid an arm around Abbie's waist.

"You know for someone so against receiving gifts, that dress looks amazing on you," Kat said as she admired the black dress Abbie wore. "Good job, Diamond."

"Thank you, though getting her in a dress was almost as impossible as getting you in one. Which is why instead of a gift we'll call it a business expense. That was the only way I could get her to accept it," Diamond said as Abbie rolled her eyes in response.

"Still don't know why you were so gung-ho about dressin' me up."

"Because if you are to be my assistant, you must look the part," Diamond explained.

"Translation, Kat never let Diamond dress her up so now she's taking it out on you," Jack explained.

"For once, Frost, could you humor me?" Diamond asked dryly which made him laugh as they entered the club. Nearly as soon as they made it inside, they were bombarded with loud music, bright lights, and the sight of dozens upon dozens of clubbers who danced the night away.

"Yeah! That's right, Santa Monica! Let's turn it up!" Eric's voice boomed and the clubbers cheered loudly before the music somehow found a way to be amped up even more.

"Hell yeah!" Kat cheered loudly before she turned to the other three. "Yo, this is crazy! I haven't even shown up yet and it's already like this!?" Kat said, a bright grin on her face as both Diamond and Jack looked on with varying degrees of surprise at how the club turned out. "I didn't know he was this good, Abbie!"

"He's amazin', just don't let him know. Keep him humble," Abbie said before she gestured to the back of the club where they could see a door. "V.I.P. room is right there as requested. Saw some messages about a few celebrities spotted here earlier, your friends?"

"More than likely, come on," Diamond said as they followed her.

*   *   *

"Welcome Diamond," a feminine voice laced with a French accent said as soon as the door opened. When the door opened up fully to reveal Diamond and her entourage, Diamond didn't seem amused as she looked over at the source of the voice. It was a blonde woman with fair skin that looked at Diamond with mischief shining in her blue eyes. Abbie's heart clenched painfully for only the briefest of moments as she swore that she saw her ex. However, she quickly reminded herself that the woman before her was someone completely different.

"Dominique," Diamond greeted and turned to the blonde's companions which were a young Japanese man and a red-haired woman. "Rose, Akira-san."

"Greetings, Midas-sama," Akira said as Rose nodded toward her. It was then Diamond raised an eyebrow as she looked at the fourth and final person.

"Michael? You're alone?" Diamond asked as she looked at the timid man that had messy black hair, brown eyes, and a thick pair of glasses.

"Huh? Oh no," Michael said quietly. "Robyn's on the dance floor," Michael answered and Abbie noticed that all of the strangers looked a bit annoyed, even Dominique who somehow managed to keep her smile. In fact, Band 13 seemed annoyed as well.

"And Alexander?" Diamond asked and Michael started to respond but stopped when he glanced at Abbie. Michael looked back at Diamond as if they exchanged a silent conversation. "Well I suppose he's always off doing his own thing, regardless," Diamond said dismissively.

"Now, who do we have here, *ma chérie*?" Dominique asked politely as she eyed Abbie. Despite her kind demeanor, Abbie couldn't help tense as she felt as though the woman stared through her very being. Something about Dominique reminded Abbie of her first encounter with Diamond. This consequently shattered any lingering thoughts Abbie might have had about Dominique being similar to her ex in any way. Though Abbie couldn't make heads or tails of to whom the various new presences she experienced belonged, she was positive that the sense of overwhelming freedom she felt came from the French woman.

"This is Abigail Stone, Katarina's plus one," Diamond introduced Abbie before she gestured toward the occupants of the room. "Abigail this is Dominique Victoire, you've probably seen her in some movies or modeling here and there. Next, you have Rose Ardent, she was last year's lightweight boxing champion. Her older sister is actually the one that raised Jack and Kat," Diamond explained and Rose gave Abbie a quick two-fingered salute. "The man next to her is…"

"…Hattori, Akira," Abbie finished for Diamond as her eyes glittered like stars. "Can I have your autograph!?" Abbie asked quickly. Only when she saw Akira's look of surprise did she notice the attention on her. Abbie's face flushed in embarrassment as Kat snorted.

"Not a fan girl, huh?" Kat teased as Abbie's face reddened even more.

"Sorry, just a huge fan of your family. Your father is a genius," Abbie said sheepishly while Jack chuckled as Kat burst out in laughter, even Diamond seemed a bit amused.

"Seriously? That's the one you recognize?" Kat asked incredulously. "You're such a nerd!"

"Shut up," Abbie said quietly as she wished the floor could swallow her whole. "Uh...sorry."

"No, don't be Stone-san, I am honored by the request," Akira said with a smile. "I'll make sure one gets to you," Akira said which lifted Abbie's mood. Diamond cleared her throat before she gestured to Michael.

"And lastly, this is Michael Insegnare," Diamond introduced and there was absolutely no recognition in Abbie's eyes. "He's heir to a large construction company," Diamond explained and Abbie noted that she didn't go into detail about which construction company and decided not to push the issue.

"Wow. I won't lie, when I went out with you, I wasn't expecting you to have friends like these," Abbie told Kat.

"What can I say? I'm full of surprises, babe," Kat said before she grabbed Abbie's hand. "Now that introductions are done, let's go party," Kat said as she started for the door.

"Wait, where are you going?" Dominique questioned and Kat froze. "You cannot just leave like that! I want details, *ma chérie.*"

"Good luck," Jack said with a sigh as he looked like a kicked puppy. "I've been barking up that tree for months now," Jack said which made Dominque pout as Abbie looked at him skeptically.

"I think there's a big difference between the details you want and the ones she wants, Jack," Abbie said but to her surprise, Kat was the one that shook her head.

"No, there's not. She's just as bad as he is," Kat said dryly as Dominique put a hand on her chest as if offended.

"Excusez-moi!?"

"Seriously?" Abbie asked with a perturbed expression.

"Uh, should I be offended, love?" Jack asked Abbie only to be ignored.

"We have things to discuss that would be far too boring for Abigail," Diamond interrupted them. "Katarina, go enjoy your date. The faster we do this, the faster you can interrogate them later, Dominique."

"All work and no play," Dominique said with a sigh. "What happened to the little girl that used to follow me everywhere when she would visit *la France?*"

"She grew up," Diamond said dryly. "Go have fun," Diamond told Kat and Abbie once more, though it almost sounded like an order. Kat quickly left with Abbie as Diamond took a seat. Jack just leaned against the wall behind Diamond. "Let's make this quick."

"Agreed," Jack said before smirking. "Shame Alexander is out, but make no mistake Akira, Michael, tonight the boys will play!" Jack declared with a fist-pump as Rose, in particular, looked annoyed while the men just smiled in response.

"Frost, Victoire, Ardent, Insegnare, and Hattori, with you all at my side that makes five of the twelve families willing to work alongside me when I ascend," Diamond began before she turned to face Michael. "What about your band?"

"Robyn and Alexander said that they are fine with following whatever decision I make," Michael said a bit nervously.

"So that makes Hood and Grimm with me as well, that gives me the support of seven families then," Diamond said sounding a bit pleased at the news.

"Yes, but remember, we have far more outsiders than we have members of the twelve families. The outsider seat has the power of three of our seats. Since it's an elected position, that also makes it a wild card," Dominique reminded Diamond. "Excluding the royal Midas family, there are eleven seats for the ancient families and three for the outsiders. Fourteen votes of which you have control of only seven. Not to mention it will take some time before you can reestablish the Frost family's position which brings you back down to six in the worst-case scenario. If you want to have a smooth reign, Diamond, I suggest you try to get at least one more seat on your side."

"She's right," Jack spoke up as he glanced at his boss.

"Indeed, but I've already taken that into consideration. If tonight goes smoothly, then I will have one more seat locked down," Diamond revealed which surprised all of the occupants of the room except Dominique whom just laughed.

"So that's why you took on that impossible heist, yes?" Dominique asked. "*Ma chérie,* I almost can't wait for these four years to go by so that we can see what you're made of."

"I'll try not to disappoint," Diamond said before she released a long sigh. Diamond's expression genuinely softened for once as she looked at the occupants of the room. "Now, before we continue, let me just say that I cannot thank you all enough for your support. I can't promise I'll be as successful as my mother, or hell even my father, but with your support, I'll try to run the Guild the best I can."

"Diamond, I think I speak for us all when I say we don't want you to be like them. We want you to be better, to be you," Jack said firmly and Diamond could see that the others shared his sentiment.

"Seeing how hard you're trying now, years before you ascend, gives us our faith in you because it shows you're trying," Dominique said before she grabbed Diamond's gloved hand. "Which says a lot because your family gave up the ability to fully express their emotions for the sake of the Guild. So, for you to show as much emotion as you do is a testament to how you really feel."

"Well said," Michael said with a smile.

"Thank you," Diamond said before her expression hardened once more. "Now let's get down to business."

*   *   *

After the meeting the thieves dispersed and decided to enjoy themselves at the party. Rose made her way towards the bar while the men left to mingle with some of the clubbers. Diamond decided to find a place to relax and opted to rest for a moment on a couch that overlooked the dance floor. She leaned back in her seat and relaxed as she spotted Kat and Abbie conversing with Eric about something as he continued to play music. Her eyes rolled in annoyance as she saw a brunette woman cheer loudly as she crowd-surfed.

"Damn Hoods," Diamond muttered as she shook her head at the sight of Robyn who had decided to ditch the meeting. Deep down she wondered if Michael ever truly would get a handle on his band. That said, that was his burden, not hers.

"So, she's your secret weapon?" Dominique questioned as she sat next to Diamond.

"What are you going on about now?"

"Abigail, of course, she's more than Kat's lover," Dominique said knowingly. "I won't lie, she's a good actress but she's no Frost," Dominique said with a laugh. "Don't feel too bad, you know as well as I do how hard it is to keep secrets from a member of the Victoire family. I wonder, just how much does she know?" Dominique wondered. "You know, if I were hiding a civilian no one would know until I wanted them to. You need to keep your cards closer to your chest. Then again, I always was the better thief, no?"

"Then why aren't you leading Band 13?"

"Because you're stronger," Dominique admitted easily. "Strength and skill are two very different things."

"What do you want?" Diamond asked Dominique whose smile dropped.

"Advice," Dominique answered. "We're almost at the half-way point for our first year, and my band is still having problems with shadow synch. You wouldn't mind helping your friend out, would you?"

"What happened to having more skill?"

"As a thief? Yes. As a boss? Debatable."

"I'm surprised," Diamond said honestly. "Being Band 12, I figured you'd have it down by now."

"We can do it, but making it last for extended periods is, how do you say, a bit of a challenge for us," Dominique explained. "You all make it seem as easy as breathing."

"Which it is," Diamond said before she turned to face Dominique fully. "The secret is faith," Diamond said simply. "When you fill them with your presence, don't be scared. You won't hurt them, be firm and take over. You have to drown them out and trust yourself with their lives as much as they trust you with them. Our band runs as one unit, one being if you will. I'm the mind, I make our decisions. Katarina is the heart, we leave the burden of dealing with our emotions to her. Jack is the body, the face that represents us both on and off the battlefield. We fit together, which makes it easier for us to use shadow synch."

"I see," Dominique said to herself. "And it has nothing to do with your...connection to Frost?" Dominique questioned as she gestured toward the opposite side of the club where Jack, Akira, and Michael talked to a group of women. From what they could see it looked as though Jack and Akira had managed to get Michael a date for the evening, much to the shy man's embarrassment.

"That has nothing to do with it," Diamond said coldly making Dominique frown. "And you will do well to keep such thoughts to yourself."

"Jack is a marvelous actor, I could almost believe he is half as promiscuous as he lets on."

"You don't?"

"I did," Dominique admitted. "Then I learned the truth when I made it clear that the hearts of those that I care for were not toys."

"You threatened my band?" Diamond asked dryly though she didn't seem surprised.

"We came to an understanding," Dominique corrected. "Frosts fear nothing, to threaten them is a fool's errand."

"So is not minding your own business," Diamond said pointedly, her voice tight.

"It's a new time, Diamond, the only ones that even care about the old rules will be gone in three years," Dominique said with an eye-roll, her own annoyance clear as she spotted Rose drinking alone at the bar. Rose looked irritated as the boys continued to flirt with the women. "And it's my business as the boss of Band 12. Stopping Rose from pinning after Jack will be a plus for both my band and yours."

"Drop it."

"As you wish, Your Highness. Just know that I'm in your corner whenever you get your head out of your ass, *ma chérie*," Dominique said dryly. "So, how does our civilian friend fit in this?" Dominique asked as she changed the subject. "I'm guessing she's the reason you were able to bypass the bank's security system, yes? How long will she be bearing your mark?"

"Indefinitely."

"A mark isn't supposed to be held that long," Dominique reminded Diamond who just glanced at her. Diamond's eyes narrowed ever so slightly and Dominque suppressed a shudder before she decided not to push the issue. "Your actions affect more people in more ways than you know. I hope you know what you're doing."

"So, do I," Diamond said before cheers could be heard at the entrance. Diamond stretched a bit as she stood up and glanced down at Dominique. "I still have some work to do, enjoy yourself."

"I will," Dominique said as Diamond left. Dominique glanced around the club and her eyes landed on the sight of Kat, Abbie, and Eric. Dominique's eyes seemed to twinkle a bit as she looked at them, or more specifically at Eric. "I will indeed."

*   *   *

"You and I are going to have a long talk about full-disclosure," Eric said seriously as Abbie laughed at him. "Seriously? You're working for Diamond of all people? And you didn't tell me? That's messed up."

"It's about to get worse too," Kat mused as she nodded toward the club entrance. Eric felt his jaw drop as he saw all three members of the group Hindsight enter the building.

"Seriously!?" Eric asked as Abbie raised her hands defensively.

"Hey, I'm just as lost as you," Abbie said as she gave Kat a pointed look. Kat only laughed nervously in response before she pointed to the bar.

"Get yourself something to drink, I'll be over there in a few," Kat said as Abbie figured this more than likely had something to do with the Guild. "Sorry," Kat continued. "I know what I said but I think I should be there for this."

"It's fine, just know that you're mine for the rest of the night," Abbie said and Kat pecked Abbie on her lips before she went off to see the newcomers. From the corner of her eye, Abbie could see that both Diamond and Jack had made their way there as well. Diamond talked to them for a moment before she gestured for them to follow her into the V.I.P. room.

"You know, you're tall," Eric said suddenly.

"Uh…thanks?" Abbie said, obviously confused by the random statement. Seeing her confusion, Eric decided to explain.

"No, I mean, you've always been slouched over, keeping to yourself, so I never noticed. Your posture has changed recently, looks good on you," Eric said with a small smile.

"You know? I think so too. Hey, want somethin' to drink?"

"Nah, I'll grab something when the time is right but I'm still in the zone," Eric answered as he focused on his current task.

"Suit yourself," Abbie said as she headed for the bar.

"What can I get you?" the bartender asked as Abbie sat down. The bartender was a kind looking young woman with dark skin, hazel eyes, and black hair that had blonde highlights. The glitter on her face seemed to shine from the lights in the club. Abbie gave her order and was about to check her phone when, out of the corner of her eye, she noticed the bartender pull out an all too familiar flask before she poured a splash of the golden liquid into her drink. Stirring it quickly, the bartender placed the drink in front of Abbie with a wink.

"Here you go, made it special for those in the know, you know?" the bartender's words shocked Abbie to her core.

"What?"

"It's fine, you don't have to pretend if you have a mark. Not like I care one way or the other, we're here to have fun tonight," the bartender said with a grin. "Look, you don't become the best bartender in the world and not learn how to read people. Diamond's an old friend and she hired me so I'm going to do my job, alright? Here, it's on the house."

"Uh…thanks, Crystal?" Abbie said hesitantly as she read the nametag.

"It's fine, just tell your boss to find me whenever she needs a drink, alright?" Crystal said before she walked away to tend to the other people at the bar.

"Miss me?" Kat said as she eventually reappeared at Abbie's side.

"Didn't get a chance to, that was quick," Abbie said as she raised an eyebrow at her.

"They couldn't stay for long, they just wanted to congratulate us and show their support for Diamond," Kat explained. "They're triplets from the Song family, Areum, Ha-Neul, and Seul-ki. They actually helped us out with the information needed."

"They're the 'upperclassmen' you talked about?"

"Yup. Hey come with me, there's something I need to tell you. You need to hear this if we want to take whatever it is that we have any further," Kat said softly. This made Abbie frown a bit as she had never seen Kat look even remotely as nervous as she did at that moment.

"Lead the way."

* * *

"Should we be out here?"

"Why not? It's our roof," Kat pointed out and Abbie realized that she had a point. "I wanted to show you something, look around," Kat said as she gestured around them. Doing as instructed, Abbie's eyes widened as she found herself surrounded by a sea of lights that came from the illuminated city. "Pretty right? I love sights like these, beautiful cities at night. I want to see every beautiful city and their lights and I want to see them with you. Before that can happen though you need to understand your importance to not just me but also the band," Kat said as she looked up at Abbie, gazing right into her eyes. "You remember what I said about why I chose to ask you out?"

"You said something about my eyes?" Abbie answered. "That you never saw someone with gray eyes before?"

"Yeah, and that was true, but what I didn't tell you was the real reason why I was looking for a date," Kat said quietly. Kat had claimed she was lonely in a new city, but that was clearly just a cover story when Abbie thought about it. Something Kat said to hide her life as a thief. "Tell me, what do you think about Jack and Diamond?"

"They're good people, good friends."

"Yeah, but what do you think about them together? Like as a couple?"

"Wait, you mean they're together?" Abbie asked, caught off guard by the information. "I mean I had my suspicions but…" Abbie trailed off awkwardly. Suddenly the irony of Jack's treasure made sense to her.

"No, they aren't. You see, the Guild...is an old group, we've been around for centuries. As a result, you have some old rules in place. One of which the Guild is most adamant against is the idea of intra-band relationships. There is a belief that they can only lead to misfortune for the band, no exceptions," Kat revealed with a frown. "In fact, it's because of this that Diamond's dad's band is broken with Jack's mother missing. Roderick and Vivi are trying to make it work but it's hard for two people to do the work of three especially with them being unable to use shadow synch with her gone."

"But what does that have to do with us?"

"Being a part of one of the twelve families is more than just having a name. There are certain traits...curses...that get passed down through each bloodline. For the Frost family, they are born with the inability to feel emotion, their hearts are frozen solid. For the Midas family, they feel ten times more than a regular civilian, especially when it comes to greed and pleasure. That, along with the curse that upon puberty whatever they touch with their right-hand turns to gold, makes them a danger to everyone around them."

"Wait...so that's why Diamond wears that glove?" Abbie asked. "The legend of King Midas was real?"

"In a way...fiction is always..."

"...based off of reality," Abbie finished for her.

"Anyway, by sealing off their golden touch, they also seal their hearts as the curse is linked to their emotions. This doesn't mean they don't feel, but it means it's hard for them to express what it is they really feel. Their emotions are so powerful, that in the time it takes the average person to make an acquaintance, they could have fallen in love or made an arch-enemy," Kat said quietly. "We don't like to speak of Diamond's curse, things happened with it that you just don't need to know. Things she can't talk about."

"Then should you be tellin' me this? She made it clear she wanted it to be unknown," Abbie said cautiously.

"She can't talk about it but it doesn't mean she doesn't want to, she wants to explain it to you because it directly involves you.

She wants to tell you so much it hurts, I know because I have to feel it every day," Kat said and Abbie remembered that the band did share a pool of emotions. "Still I'll only tell you what you need to know, not the whole thing regarding that issue," Kat said as she gave Abbie a nervous smile. "When we became a band, to say emotions ran high would be an understatement. Jack, who until that point was an emotionless, rational, being suddenly found himself feeling things he never had before because of Diamond's emotions. They forged a bond after that. Jack has been devoted to her and the Guild ever since because they gave him what he was missing for the first twenty years of his life, the ability to feel," Kat said before her nervous smile turned sad. "They love each other, deeply, but they aren't together."

"Because of the Guild rules?"

"Exactly, it's not just old superstition. There is science behind it that Guild researchers discovered. Think of a band as one heart, three bodies. When two members of the same band fall in love, it does something. Messes with the chemicals in their head. That love for all intents and purposes becomes like a drug. A dangerous one. A kiss alone can be addicting. Anything further? I'll leave to your imagination. Without very strict care, moderation, their love could lead to self-destruction," Kat said firmly as Abbie looked at her incredulously at the revelation. "The last thing Diamond needs is a scandal before she can reach the throne. People are trying to discredit her claim to it and we can't have that...which brings us to why I asked you out," Kat began as she bit her lip. "The plan was simple, we split our duties into three parts. Diamond's the brains, Jack's the body, and I deal with our emotions. Problem is, the love Diamond and Jack have is a lot to deal with and it was building up quickly. They are like a ticking time-bomb. Their feelings needed a release."

"And that's where I come in. You dated me so that all of that built up emotion had somewhere to go," Abbie said with a frown, not sure how to take this revelation. "I...I don't know how to feel about that," Abbie said honestly. "You lied to me when I asked if you used me. It may not have been for the reason I thought but make no mistake you did use me and you lied about that." Kat said nothing as she averted her eyes. What was worse was that Abbie didn't sound angry, just disappointed and for some reason that hurt Kat even more. Abbie bit her lip, unsure of what to say, what she had heard hurt but what was worse was that she understood. From a logical standpoint, she could at least see why they tried such a desperate plan, but that didn't make the taste in her mouth any less bitter. "Did it at least work?" Abbie asked and her question made Kat's shoulders sag in relief.

"Not exactly," Kat said as though she sounded almost relieved by that. "I'm so glad you let me get this far. Yes, it worked perfectly at the beginning. They could focus more and the tension decreased a lot. But...we made a mistake. One large, and unfortunately very cliché, miscalculation," Kat said with a smile as Abbie looked at her in confusion. "See, I never cared about romance. I just wanted to have fun and see the lights like I told you. At first, being with you was my responsibility," Kat said before she shook her head. To say that out loud, hurt both of them and made the betrayal that much more real. Somehow Kat felt worse than she already had. "I didn't plan on actually falling as hard for you as I did," Kat admitted. "But I did, and now my own feelings are being added to the mix so in the end, we're kind of back at square one. Jack sees you as a friend, Diamond sees you as a sister, and I see you as a lover. At least, that's how it should be. There are a lot of emotions going around now so lines get a bit blurred every now and then so I apologize now for any screw-ups. That is if you're willing to give me a chance to mess up again. I believe we can still work out because there's a thunder inside us, a storm of emotions that threatens to consume us. However, it's one storm I wouldn't mind getting lost in as long as I'm with you."

"You could have kept this all to yourself and I would have never known. You realize that, right?" Abbie asked quietly.

"Yeah, I do," Kat answered as she reached up and gently grasped the side of Abbie's face. "But there's no honor in that. That's not fair to you. You need to know what's going on if it involves you, the others have only just now realized what I'm doing right now. They're...scared...but they understand," Kat revealed. "There's just so many secrets, not just including the ones you try so hard to hide," Kat said quietly and Abbie tensed. "I don't want things to go back to how they were before this, I want them to be better. We all have secrets and for good reasons. The ability to lie is one of a thief's greatest assets but in a band, lies cause more harm than good. As far as I am concerned you are part of this band until you no longer want to be."

"You could have messed up whatever it is we had," Abbie said pointedly.

"But did I?" Kat asked as a nervous smile grew on her lips.

"No, like you said there's so much about me that you all don't know," Abbie began only to be silenced when Kat placed a finger on her lips.

"Then tell us when you're ready like I did. I clearly took my time telling you the truth. We already felt there was more to you than you let on. You're brilliant, Abigail, if you have secrets then it's for a good reason. I didn't come clean just to make you do the same," Kat said as she moved her finger.

"So, what do we do now?" Abbie asked and she once more felt that strange rush that filled her body whenever she was near Kat.

"We could go back to the party?"

"Or?"

"We could try something new?" Kat offered shyly. "Something a bit more intimate?"

"One more," Abbie began as she embraced Kat. "One more chance, but this doesn't happen again. As many secrets as you claim I have, none of them involve you like this. Please don't do this again."

"I won't," Kat swore before she kissed Abbie, who savored the apple flavored lips of the thief.

* * *

"The Song Family is on my side now since we were successful in the heist. Though they said not to risk ourselves like that again, we still have to perform well enough for them to all keep their allegiance with me," Diamond said as she turned to face Jack. "They respect me now, but if I stagnate that faith may waver."

"True, but I suppose we could worry about that another time," Jack mused before he grasped Diamond's hand. "Care for a dance? Don't think I've seen you on the dance floor all night."

"Frost," Diamond said her voice filled with warning but he just smiled wider in response.

"Come now Diamond, no one will think twice about two friends dancing together. A good Queen knows when to both work and play," Jack pointed out. Before Diamond could respond, both she and Jack almost stumbled when they felt a wave of emotion wash over them. The feeling nearly drowned them both with its intensity. Briefly they were confused as the wave hadn't come from either of them. Neither of them had been prepared for this unprecedented amount of passion to come from Kat of all people. "Besides it looks like our 'heart' is a bit...preoccupied elsewhere." Diamond just looked at him for a few moments and then wordlessly accepted his hand. Though what he said was true, they both still felt a spark of passion course through them when their hands touched.

"Wipe that look from your face, Frost," Diamond muttered as she led him away toward the dance floor.

"I have no idea what you mean," Jack said as he began to dance with Diamond. All in all, he felt it had been a productive night. Everyone seemed to have made power moves in one way or another, and Jack couldn't help but wonder just what the future had in store for them.

CHAPTER 9

• • • • • • • • ● • • • • • • • •

ELDERS

Santa Monica, Abbie's Apartment

Abbie woke up the next morning in a daze. Her body ached as she attempted to recall the previous night's activities. Only when she felt a pair of arms tighten around her did she realize that she was not alone in her bed. Abbie smiled tiredly when she spotted Kat snuggled into her side, and she enjoyed how the heat from Kat's body kept her warm. Abbie's phone vibrated on her nightstand and she quickly grabbed it to see who texted her.

Eric: Last night was crazy, yo!

Eric: I got to play for Diamond and got another job offer from a model.

Eric: Things really looking up for ya boy! Text me when you get the chance!

Abbie held back a laugh at how excited Eric seemed, she was happy for him and hoped things continued to work out for her friend. As Abbie scrolled through her messages, she raised an eyebrow when she saw one from Jack.

Jack: Uh, you guys realize we drove here together right, love?

A look of horror appeared on her face as memories from the previous night came back to her and she realized that she and Kat had ditched Jack and Diamond at the club.

Jack: I tried Kat but she's not answering either.

Jack: Wait…she's probably too busy with you, never mind, love.

Jack: You probably have your hands full too then. I'll get us home, you two have fun~

Abbie felt mortified and only hoped that Diamond was as understanding about the situation as Jack. As Abbie began to type a reply, she received another message from a number that made her scowl.

"Ugh, what time is it?" Kat asked as Abbie locked her phone.

"Nine."

"Really? Feels like it's later," Kat said as she picked her hoodie up from the floor. Kat grabbed her phone from its pocket and quickly checked her messages. "Damn, I have to head to Hollywood, Diamond's pops wanted to see us."

"Roderick? He's your King, right? Somethin' important?"

"No idea, it could be or he could just want to see his daughter again, they're really close," Kat said as she stood up and stretched. "Either way, it just means Jack and I get to see Vivi, so it's a plus. Mind looking out for Sal until we get back tonight? I'll give you my key."

"No problem, but mind droppin' me off somewhere first? I'll head to your place a bit later…" Abbie trailed off as she finally got a good look at Kat and realized that her foggy memories of the previous night did not do her lover justice.

"Sure," Kat agreed and she smirked when she saw Abbie's eyes drift lower, away from her face. "But first, how about we hit the shower?"

"Please, lead the way."

*   *   *

Santa Monica, Lux Cafe

Abbie walked briskly into the building and scanned the room until she found her target. In a booth off in the corner, sat an intimidating woman with long black hair that gazed down intently at her tablet. The woman's cold gray eyes never once looked up as Abbie made her way towards her.

"What do you want, Haylen?" Abbie asked without preamble as she sat across from the woman.

"Is that any way to treat family, Abigail?" Haylen questioned with a southern drawl. "And after I came all this way to see you?"

"Please, I doubt I'm your main reason for comin' this far. What brings you to California, let alone Santa Monica?" Abbie asked dryly as Haylen continued to work on something on her tablet. After a few moments, Haylen put her device down and finally gave her sister her full attention.

"I've gotten a contract with Prosperity Industries," Haylen said as Abbie looked at her in surprise. "Apparently one of their associates', Magnus Financial, was broken into recently. They had a security system in place that should have been impenetrable for quite some time but it seems that wasn't the case."

"So, they hired you and your team?"

"Yes, funny cause' they turned my offer down once before," Haylen said before she sipped her coffee. "My team is number one for the private security of all types of businesses, so it won't be long before we deal with this issue."

"So why contact me? Needed to see a familiar face in this city?" Abbie asked skeptically.

"No," Haylen denied. "Needless to say, after our last…encounter… you made it very clear you didn't want to see me again. That said, one of us is still a firm believer in family so I figured I'd warn you."

"Excuse me?"

"See when I looked over the security breach, it was somethin' I hadn't seen in a long time," Haylen said pointedly. "It was precise, efficient, and almost left no trace that the system was even hacked. I haven't seen somethin' like that since the days those cyber terrorists, Wonderland, waged war against corporate America."

"Well you disbanded them, didn't you? Was a decent sized group, can't be surprised if a few of the members that got away found jobs elsewhere," Abbie pointed out.

"You're right, which is why I called you here today. You know, as a member that got away and found employment...elsewhere," Haylen said as she slid her tablet toward Abbie. When Abbie looked at its screen her eyes widened as she saw an article about Diamond and the grand opening of Duskhaven. In the pictures presented with the articles, she saw herself and Band 13. "You've landed a good job, she says she hired you as her personal assistant. Shame I had to find out through an article and not from you. If I had known a bit earlier I'd have invited you somewhere else to eat."

"Well seein' how the last time I told you about my life it ended up with me kicked out of my own family, I decided you might not be the best person to tell things too," Abbie said sarcastically and Haylen narrowed her eyes at her sister.

"You weren't kicked out, you left."

"Whatever helps you sleep better at night, I'm over it," Abbie said dismissively. "Yes, I'm her assistant, a job I only have because of a mutual connection we share," Abbie explained. "It's called networkin'."

"And who exactly is this connection?"

"Not that you need to know, but it's my girlfriend," Abbie answered which made her sister grimace. "I'm not playin' this game with you, Haylen. Spit it out, what do you want?"

"I want to make sure you're not involved in somethin' stupid. Might be hard for you, I know," Haylen said sarcastically. "You got a bad habit of gettin' seduced into situations that are bad for you."

"Bad for me? Or bad for you and our family's oh so important image?" Abbie asked knowingly. "I've been a good girl, is that what you want to hear? You put me in my place once and I've been on my best behavior ever since."

"Put you in your place? Please, we both know if that tramp you got mixed up with didn't die you'd still be doin' who knows what," Haylen said before Abbie rose abruptly and grabbed her by her collar. Abbie brought them face to face as she ignored the surprised patrons of the cafe.

"Are we gonna have a problem, sis?" Abbie asked as she glared at Haylen. "Disrespect her again and I'll put my boot up your ass."

Haylen's eyes widened at the sudden show of aggression but soon she gave Abbie a glare of her own.

"Please," Haylen scoffed as she pried Abbie's hand off of her. "You're makin' a scene. Look I called you out here with good intentions. Advice from sister to sister, that on the off chance you are involved, you should think about gettin' out of whatever situation you're in now before it goes up in flames."

"Haylen," Abbie began with a laugh that had no humor at all in it. "The only thing that ever goes up in flames is my happiness whenever you get remotely close to my life."

"Please cut the dramatics," Haylen said as she straightened out her shirt. "There was once a time you sought solace in me."

"Haylen the only solace I can get from you is the fact that you're older," Abbie began. "Because that means there's a chance that I'll get a few years without you when you finally drop dead," Abbie said as Haylen looked at her in shock. Hurt briefly flashed across Haylen's face though Abbie paid it no mind. "Look, I hear your warnin' loud and clear but whatever you're lookin' for ain't got shit to do with me," Abbie said as she turned away. "Goodbye, Haylen."

"For your sake, I hope you're right," Haylen said as she watched her sister leave. "I can't save you from daddy again."

*   *   *

Hollywood, Midas Manor

"Home sweet home," Kat said with a grin as they were led through the manor by an older well-dressed gentleman.

"Indeed Ms. Umbra, the Master has been awaiting your arrival all day, he said it was a matter of the utmost importance," the man said as Diamond raised an eyebrow.

"Sebastian, to him, forgetting to call him would be a matter of utmost importance," Diamond pointed out.

"Yes, but to be fair, when have you ever forgotten to call him?" Sebastian asked "I'd be worried too!"

"Touché, Sebastian, touché," Diamond muttered as Jack looked toward the older man curiously.

"How's Vivi, you two still at each other's throats?" Jack asked which made Sebastian grimace.

"My boy, besides the Master, is she not at everyone's throats?"

"I'll take that as a yes then," Jack said as they stopped before a large study.

"Lady Midas, the Master will see you now," Sebastian said before he turned to the other two. "Come, I'll take you to see Vivi, despite what she may say she does miss you two."

"Aw, I knew she cared!" Kat said though Jack looked highly skeptical.

"If you say so," Jack said as he and Kat continued to follow Sebastian.

Opening the door Diamond stepped into the massive study where she could find her father behind his desk. Roderick Midas was a dark-skinned man with a shaved head and a well-trimmed beard. On his neck was a black "M" tattoo that was similar to the emblem on Diamond's glove. Roderick was a youthful looking man who didn't seem much older than Diamond herself. That said, his hazel eyes betrayed the decades of wisdom he possessed. Diamond glanced briefly at a large golden ring he wore, it bore a purple gem in its center and there was a pale gold lightning emblem embedded in the gem. His expression was an intimidating one as he worked but, when he noticed his daughter, his expression shifted into one of kindness and joy.

"Hey baby girl, I haven't seen you in months," Roderick said as he rose from his chair. Quickly he enveloped her in a powerful embrace that she returned. Roderick stepped back and looked at his daughter. "Seems the outside world is treating you well, you look stronger than I remember."

"I've had no choice but to get stronger," Diamond said as she shook her head. "When you told me that being a boss wouldn't be easy, I didn't realize how right you were. The task is hard and taxing…"

"But?"

"Nothing I have ever done has felt more rewarding," Diamond said honestly which made Roderick grin. "Those two complete me in a way I never thought possible and for that alone I want to do right by them."

"A feeling I know all too well," Roderick said as he glanced toward one of the many portraits that hung in his study. One in particular showed Roderick as he sat in an old antique looking chair with an intimidating smirk gracing his lips. On his right stood a red-haired woman who, like him, was wearing a black suit though her tie was red while his was gold. On his left, a gorgeous blonde woman wore a black evening gown. The blonde had a pair of blue eyes that seemed to be filled with mischief. "Advice from one boss to another, don't let your guard down like I did. One mistake is all that is needed to ruin that bond you care about so much. Be better than me."

"No pressure, then," Diamond said sarcastically which made him laugh loudly as he wrapped an arm around her.

"Relax, you're my baby girl, you can handle it," Roderick said reassuringly. "Since when do diamonds crack under pressure? You can handle any situation that comes your way, just like your mother," Roderick said making her smile slightly. "Now sit, we have much to discuss," Roderick said and Diamond realized then that this wasn't a social visit. "It's about your last job, great work. Pulled it off even though you had me worried with you cutting it that close to the deadline," Roderick said as he reached into the drawer of his desk and pulled out a black USB stick. "Here, this was found in the safety-deposit box you stole. What we found on it was...unsettling, to say the least."

"What did you find on it?"

"Plans. Plans August had to end this war," Roderick began, his expression grim. "He's been looking for a way to resurrect the Knights' Order under his own command. If he were to be successful, we'd have to deal with a lot more than mages."

"He could end the war," Diamond muttered. "But how could he resurrect them? The Order was destroyed completely from what I heard."

"He's trying to find the holy sword, Excalibur. With it, he'll have the key to resurrecting the Order. With that blade, he could make his own knights. I sent word to a contact in the Tribe, told them to keep a lookout but they are staying clear of this. They aren't quite fond of the Guild or the Mage's Circle at the moment, and I can't really blame them. This war has gotten out of hand."

"So, what are you going to do?" Diamond asked. "Surely you and the council realize something needs to be done about this."

"Oh, believe me, I brought this to their attention, but they are still too busy trying to fight over your throne," Roderick said tiredly and Diamond could swear she saw her father age before her eyes. It was almost as if the nectar had suddenly been drained from his veins. "The few families in my corner agreed that something needed to be done but the outsiders and the other families blocked any action. If I were to send even one band to do anything, we'd have a civil war on our hands."

"Even though the survivability of the Guild itself is at stake?" Diamond asked incredulously. "Are those old fools really that dumb?"

"Yes, words cannot describe how fast I want these next few years to go by so this toxic excuse for a council can be disbanded but the Guild may not survive that long. These aren't the days of your grandfather when the King's word was absolute. The only way to overrule them now would be a direct order from the Goddesses."

"But they're missing," Diamond said darkly. "Why? Why are they gone when we so obviously need them the most? Why did they leave us as soon as this war started? Do you think they've forsaken us?"

"I don't know Diamond, I honestly don't. But that's the thing about faith, you never actually know, you just have to believe they are there for us," Roderick said as he looked toward another painting. This one showed Roderick embrace a shorter caramel skinned woman in his arms. She was wearing a white wedding dress that was in complete contrast to her pitch-black hair. The woman's beauty seemed to illuminate the entirety of the portrait as Roderick met her warm golden gaze. "You know, before Isabelle fell, she said something to me. It was a joke, but your mother was a person that whenever she spoke it had a purpose. She said that as long as the Guild had nectar to fill their flasks, there was always at least one Goddess in their corner. I'll tell you this, Diamond, even when the Goddesses vanished, we have had no shortage of nectar. So, at the very least, one hasn't forsaken us. However, the fact still remains that my hands are tied," Roderick said. "Which is why, even though it pains my heart, I must bring this issue to you. You're in training and therefore you're technically not yet a true band of the Guild," Roderick revealed which made Diamond's eyes widen ever so slightly. "I'm not asking you to deal with this, you stand no chance against an Arch-Mage, but I am asking you to look for more information. You found this, maybe you can find more. Enough information for me to sway the opinions of the council. For them to realize this issue should take precedence over their petty fighting for a seat that doesn't belong to them in the first place."

"I'll do what I can," Diamond swore and Roderick released a sad sigh in response.

"I won't lie, baby, a part of me was hoping you'd refuse," Roderick said honestly. "I'm torn between the duties of a King, a husband, and a father. The King in me wants to protect the Guild, the husband in me knows your mother would expect nothing less from you, but the father in me wants you as far away from this as possible. Still, I can't baby you anymore. You're a grown woman, and I'd be a hypocrite considering the things my band did for the Guild while we were in training. Just be safe, do what you believe is necessary to get this done. If it becomes too much, get out. Do you understand me?"

"Yes, father."

"Good, now I suppose it's time to tell you just how the Knights' Order fell. I was waiting until your second year to tell you the truth behind the last World War but I suppose if you're going to help me with this, you need to know now," Roderick began as Diamond's frown deepened. "As you know there was an alliance between the four unions, but have you ever thought about what exactly we were allied against?"

"I thought we aligned because we all wanted to help humanity."

"That common understanding was a side-effect of the alliance and why it remained for as long as it did. No, the alliance was born out of necessity," Roderick explained. "Monsters and demons aren't as unorganized as one would assume. Though they are split into countless factions now, there was a period when they were all unified beneath one banner. The Legion of the Black Moon is what they called themselves. Morgana, the mother of ruin, formed it after betraying Merlin and the Mage's Circle. That woman brought death in the millions, pitting civilians against each other in an attempt to wipe them all out. She single-handedly instigated the third world war and countless wars before that," Roderick revealed. "She had a weapon that single handedly wiped out the Knight's Order in 2032. When the war came to an end and she fell at the hands of Merlin himself, the alliance placed four anchors to seal her weapon away deep inside of the planet. Merlin was as powerful as our Goddesses but not even he could come out unscathed, it's why he's missing now. He sealed himself away to fight off Morgana's corruption and heal from his injuries."

"But why tell me this? She's dead right?" Diamond questioned as a feeling of dread formed in the pit of her stomach. "Right?"

"Officially, though I have my suspicions that she might have escaped her fate. She was a mage, yes, but she was as crafty as a thief," Roderick said darkly. "We fought her for a long time, Diamond. To even mention that she may be around would cause an untold amount of panic. Without proof, I fear my mental health will be called into question which could cost you the throne. I have to act carefully, but as of now you, Vivi, and a few choice contacts I have are the only ones aware of this possibility. You are to take my place soon, so I can no longer hide such things from you for soon they will be your responsibility."

"What was Romero thinking!? Killing my mother when the biggest threat wasn't even dealt with properly!?" Diamond asked fiercely as Roderick closed his eyes, a solemn expression on his face.

"I ask myself that every day. Romero was a close ally, yet single-handedly destroyed our only chance at victory if my suspicions are true. He and Julia have done a lot of damage to the alliance. Fortunately, the Black Moon is still in shambles, I just pray for the sake of you all that it stays that way," Roderick said seriously. "Now let's move on. Fortunately, you filled this year's honor quota so spend your time training and doing what you can about this issue. I've informed your teacher about this, she says if you need to take a day off just let her know. Headmistress Corday has always been a close confidant," Roderick explained. "Now, enough of all that, catch me up on how you've been," Roderick said with a fatherly smile.

∗   ∗   ∗

"I see, thanks for bringing this to my attention, I'll speak to the lad," a woman with short red hair said, her voice thick with an Irish accent. She grabbed the training robot she fought and slammed it into the ground with enough force to make it shut down immediately.

"That's all I wish, he has potential, I hate to see it wasted simply because of a lack of patience," an older gentleman of Asian descent said with a frown as a much younger woman stood politely behind him. At that moment the door to the gym opened before Sebastian led Jack and Kat into the gym before he left them. As soon as Jack noticed the individuals in the room he paused in his greeting.

"Ah, well, perfect timing," the older man said stroking his beard thoughtfully as he and his companion began to leave the gym. "Come, Meifeng, this is a family matter."

"Yes, father," Meifeng said respectfully as they left. Meifeng's polite expression shifted into one of pure sympathy as she glanced at Jack and simply shook her head sadly. This sent a chill down his spine as he looked back at his former guardian who looked less than pleased to see him.

"Lad," was all Vivi said as she stalked toward them.

"Jack, what the hell did you do!?" Kat asked fearfully.

"Now, Vivi, I can explain," Jack began only to be ignored when the woman grabbed him by his collar and trapped him with her vice-like grip.

"Lass, leave," Vivi ordered and Kat didn't need to be told twice. All thoughts of a heartfelt reunion thrown out of the window as she realized that self-preservation came first. Jack shuddered as he watched black wisps of smoke spill from Vivi's lips while the hand so close to his neck began to increase in temperature. The green had left

132

Vivi's eyes and in its place was an electric orange that shone brightly as she glared at him. Despite being a few inches taller than her, Jack felt incredibly small when face to face with the powerful woman. "What's this I hear from Master Li about you ditching his lessons… for months," Vivi asked once Kat left.

"It…it just wasn't a good fit," Jack tried to explain as the woman gritted her teeth.

"A good fit? He's the greatest teacher for enforcers the Guild has to offer! He trained me from the ground up, and you're going to disrespect that man by not even showing up after he offers to teach you!?" Vivi asked angrily. "In addition, you've been doing jobs without training? Do you have a death wish, lad? Tell me why I shouldn't shove my foot up your ass!"

"Because I'm still here?"

"Explain."

"Look, Vivi, I'm not knocking the man, I can see clearly that Master Li is a great teacher. It's just his methods don't work for me. He refuses to teach you how to defend yourself until you achieve 'balance' through meditation, whatever the hell that is," Jack said dryly as Vivi released him. "According to him, it took you a week to do it."

"As it should have taken you."

"Yeah, well, it didn't. Rose, on the other hand, actually beat your record," Jack said and he wasn't sure if Vivi was surprised by the news or not, she had no reaction at all to her sister's progress. "Meanwhile, I'm sitting on my ass for a month twiddling my thumbs like a bloody idiot waiting to achieve something that personally I don't even believe exists. I'm forced to watch your sister improve by leaps and bounds and be bombarded with praise about you when you were his student. I also have to deal with the emotions of Kat and Diamond as they feel pride from their own record-breaking growth while my progress is stagnant. I'm many things, Vivi, but you know I'm not one for inaction. I see something about myself I don't like? I change it," Jack said firmly and Vivi's expression softened ever-so-slightly. "I don't sit around looking like a fool and wait for change to come to me. You gave me one hell of a foundation on how to protect myself, Vivi, I honestly wish you could be the one training me."

"I can't do that lad, I barely have enough time to maintain my own strength with all the shit I have to deal with because of the council," Vivi said as she rubbed the bridge of her nose in frustration. Vivi took deep breaths as she tried to calm herself. Soon the smoke that poured from her mouth dissipated.

"I understand that," Jack said reassuringly. "That's why I'm taking my growth into my own hands, finding ways to improve myself. The council may be full of idiots but the Guild as a whole isn't, you'd be surprised at how many thieves are willing to sell a mod for the right price."

"A mod lets you use skills, that's it. You still have to master them, lad! Do you think just buying another's skill is enough to keep you up to par?" Vivi asked incredulously. "You need a teacher!"

"I'm still here," Jack pointed out. "I'll find my way. The founders didn't have teachers and they became legends. Besides the way the quota system works, actually learning from your teachers is optional, isn't it?" Jack asked which made Vivi frown. "The only thing that matters is filling the honor quota for the next four years. You don't get honor or gold from going to lessons. They just exist to make filling the quota easier."

"The founders may not have had teachers, but they had the Goddesses. You don't. You can't complete all four years like this," Vivi said as she willed herself to remain calm. "The first year is a joke compared to the following three. Without balance, you can never succeed as an enforcer and draw out your true strength. The only way to get balance is through a teacher, and you're trying to turn down the best teacher."

"The best teacher for you," Jack countered. "His methods may work for you and everyone else seeing how the other teachers adopted his ways. But come on, Vivi, you've raised me for how long? You of all people know I'm not exactly the same as others."

"You're serious about this," Vivi said and the fight left her when she saw Jack's resolve.

"I am."

"Fine, no matter what I say or do you'll just do what you want to anyway. Just like your damn mother in that regard," Vivi said and

Jack was surprised that Vivi backed off. "That said, be better than Julia. I raised you long enough. You're my brat, if anyone can figure this out it's you."

"Did you just praise me?" Jack asked cheekily.

"Don't push your luck," Vivi warned reminding him that he was not in the clear just yet. "The world hasn't been as dangerous as it is now since I was your age and that was in 1960," Vivi said as she wrapped an arm around him and pulled him into a strong embrace. "Just know that the world is a harsh place. Watch yourself out there, alright lad?"

"Of course, Vivi."

"Come on, let's go find the lass. Unlike you, she's actually making me proud."

"I wouldn't get so happy with her either," Jack said with a smirk. "After all, she's been dating for a few months, did she let you know?" Jack asked curiously and within no time, Vivi's enraged expression returned.

"Katarina!" Vivi boomed and within moments, Kat poked her head out from behind the door. Kat was obviously both startled and confused by the yell. Between the enraged form of Vivi that stomped her way toward her and an amused Jack in the background, Kat realized she had been thrown under the bus.

"What the hell did you do?" Kat asked Jack in horror though this time it was in concern for herself rather than Jack. She would get her answer soon as she found herself interrogated by her overly protective former guardian.

* * *

San Diego, Magnus Manor

"How is Eve?" Faith asked, her concern for her brother's servant evident as they ate lunch in their backyard and caught up with each other.

"She'll be fine, her core wasn't damaged. That said, I can use this time to make some much-needed improvements, so she will be out of action for a few months," Xavier answered.

"What!? Will you be fine? She is your Mastercraft after all, the one feat you have that proves your right to be a mage," Faith said worriedly. "I don't want you to get hurt with so many thieves after you!"

"Calm down, *sorellina*," Xavier said as he ruffled his little sister's hair affectionately. "She's very important to my strength, yes, but I wouldn't be me if I didn't have my fair share of spells hidden up my sleeves, I'll be fine until she's finished."

"Really?"

"Really."

"Fine, then I will try not to worry," Faith said as she decided to have faith in Xavier's skills. "Can you show me some of those spells?" Faith asked hopefully.

"Faith…"

"Come on brother, can't you show me just one spell?" Faith pleaded with Xavier. Xavier just looked at his younger sister with a raised eyebrow.

"Faith, you know magic isn't a toy, spells need to be used responsibly," Xavier chided.

"I know, but you cannot blame me for being amazed by the things you can do," Faith said apologetically. "I'm a bit envious, truth be told. You can do all of these miraculous things and I'm just stuck here bound to this chair watching holovids to pass the time. All the power in the world and the Circle still can't fix me," Faith said before she forced a smile back on her face. "I apologize, I don't mean to mope."

"Faith, you know I'm still finding a way to undo what that monster did to you. Just give me a bit more time, I'll heal you," Xavier swore.

"I know you'll try," Faith said which made Xavier's heart clench. "Though, now that you're here, perhaps you can answer this question that has been pestering me."

"What is it?" Xavier asked with a confused frown.

"The woman that did this to me, Julia," Faith began as she gestured to herself and her chair. "Is she really a monster? As evil as everyone says?"

136

"How can you even ask that!?" Xavier asked incredulously as he believed the answer was obvious. "I…I'm sorry, continue," Xavier apologized as he noticed that his exclamation startled Faith.

"It's just I hear all of these stories about how great a man father was, and my memories of him are nothing but fond," Faith began, clearly troubled. "So, if that's true, how could he be involved with someone like her? There must have been some good in her for him to fall in love with her."

"Faith, listen to me, what that thief and what our father had was not love," Xavier began patiently as he tried to keep his own emotions in check. "Our father was a great man but he was still just human, he made a mistake, a big one. The Thieves' Guild, they specialize in preying on the weakness of others, and that's what she did to him for she would never be able to face him down in combat. This is why you can't trust them, especially with this war going on. They have to be stopped at any cost."

"Even our brother?" Faith asked quietly.

"Who told you about that…er…him?" Xavier asked, his voice just as quiet but there was an undeniable edge in it.

"Lilia," Faith answered and Xavier scowled. "Memories of before the incident have slowly been returning to me and I remember him. I even remember a run in or two with Julia and she seemed… nice. Lilia said that I wasn't a child anymore and as a rightful heiress in the family, I needed to be aware of our family's current state of affairs. Especially seeing how I won't be wedded off anytime soon," Faith said and at his confused expression, she explained. "A bride on death's door makes for a very weak link in aligning families," Faith said ruefully. "I am not exactly attracting many suitors for House Magnus. Even if I was cured, it's too late for me to use magic which has many fearful of weak heirs."

"I'm sorry, I had no idea you were dealing with such pressures," Xavier said quietly which made Faith giggle a bit before she grabbed his hand reassuringly. The smile she gave him made him feel ashamed as an older sibling as he found himself being comforted by her despite not being faced with nearly as many problems.

"It's fine, I'm stronger than I look," Faith said confidently. "But back to my question, is brother evil? I have few memories of him. He was…cold but he was the only one to get Lilia to smile, even now she smiles thinking about him."

"Jack is complicated. He doesn't care about anything, even when father made his mother-that monster-bring him over to visit he just spent most of his time waiting for her to pick him back up," Xavier explained with an uncomfortable expression on his face before he sighed. "We never got along, but he did entertain whatever you or Lilia wanted to do no matter how rudely. You were also the first person he gave a nickname to, he called you little bird," Xavier said before he shook his head to clear it of the memories and despite everything, he smirked. "Even when you wanted to play dress up. But enough about him, those days have long since gone," Xavier said before he looked back and forward as if searching for someone, which confused Faith greatly. Xavier winked at her before he cupped his hands together and Faith looked at him in amazement as she saw a bright blue energy shining from between the cracks of his fingers. When Xavier opened his hands, Faith gasped when a dove with a blue flame-like appearance flew from his hands. She laughed as she watched the bird fly around her head for a bit, warmly nuzzling her cheek, before it faded from existence.

"That was amazing! But I thought spells needed to be used responsibly," Faith teased.

"We call that a rule, Faith. Lilia is…right," Xavier said and Faith giggled at the look of disgust he had on his face after he said those last three words. "You aren't a child anymore, so you're old enough to learn that there are times rules need to be bent."

"An important lesson," a voice said that startled them before they turned to find an amused August.

"Lilia and I have finished our work for the day, come we must hurry or we will be late for the meeting we are to have with that security team Enero hired," August informed Xavier who grimaced at the thought.

"I have no idea why he enlisted civilians, surely the Circle is more than capable enough to handle a security breach?" Xavier asked skeptically.

"You know how it is, no one loves civilians like Enero Prospero," August said with a chuckle. "Though I must admit, in an age-dependent on their technologies more than ever, never before have they been so useful…or profitable."

"Now you sound like a thief, Uncle," Xavier said dryly and Faith giggled at the offended look on August's face.

"Come now, my boy is that any way to treat your elders?"

CHAPTER 10

• • • • • • •●• • • • • • •

THE GLADIUS
GALLERY JOB

Santa Monica, California

"Hey baby, wanna come have the time of your life?"

"Hey! I got some shit that will blow your mind, twenty bucks!"

"Come on, boy," Abbie said as she tugged on Sal's leash. Abbie ignored the streetwalker and drug dealer as she made her way through the slums of Santa Monica. A simple walk through the city was exactly what she needed to clear her mind. Abbie desperately tried to figure out how to deal with not only Haylen's reappearance in her life but also her employment by Mage's Circle. Unlike her, Haylen knew nothing about her employer's true nature. It was in this fact alone that Abbie found solace. This gave her a much-needed advantage in terms of information which Abbie would sorely need in order to handle Haylen.

"Quick! Heed my warning my children! Forsake your false gods before it's too late!" a voice shouted hysterically. Abbie looked over and found a homeless man at the end of the street she and Sal were on. "The Black Moon is coming and it will drown out the light along with the heretics!" the man screamed as many people tried to ignore and walk around him. Abbie tried to ignore him as well but unfortunately, the crazed man seemed to have a particular interest in her. "You, my daughter, it's not too late!" the man said as he grabbed her roughly by her shoulders. The action scared Abbie as others shouted in protest at the sight. Sal snarled and barked viciously at the man before he bit him on his leg. The crazed man screamed as a passerby pulled him away from Abbie. "You are marked by heathens! The Black Moon will eclipse you with its darkness girl! Calamity is coming soon and you will lose everything!" the man screamed as Abbie looked at him, visibly shaken by his sudden attack. "You can't resist! Your light will be snuffed out!"

"Someone, call the cops!" a bystander shouted as Sal roughly tugged on his leash as he attempted to pull Abbie away from the scene. Abbie followed Sal and attempted to put as much distance between herself and that lunatic as possible. As Abbie and Sal walked, she felt her phone vibrate. Abbie pulled it out quickly and read the message from Diamond.

Diamond: Come back to our place, we need to discuss our next move.

"Come on, boy," Abbie said as she looked down at Sal. "Duty calls."

*   *   *

Midas Tower, Santa Monica

"I'm back," Abbie called out as she walked into the penthouse "How was the trip?"

"Enlightening," Diamond answered from the couch as she and Kat watched the news.

"Exhausting," Kat answered tiredly. "Vivi wants to meet you but that's neither here nor there. We'll worry about that later."

"Isn't putting things like this off what got you into this mess in the first place?" Diamond asked skeptically only to get a dirty look from Kat in return.

"Don't you start."

"Anyway, we have much to discuss, come on, we need to figure out what we're doing next," Diamond said before the three went to the study.

"Wait, where's Jack?"

"Going to be six feet under when I see him again," Kat muttered. Diamond rolled her eyes at Kat's attitude.

"He went to deal with something regarding his lessons. He didn't feel as though he performed well against Xavier and is going to see his teacher about his training," Diamond answered as she sat behind the desk. "Fortunately, we won't need him for this discussion."

"Okay, so what's wrong?" Abbie asked curiously.

"Inside the safety-deposit box we stole, the Guild found plans made by August to resurrect the Knights' Order," Diamond said as she handed Abbie a memory stick.

"And that's bad?" Abbie asked with a frown. "I thought they were your allies?"

"They were but August seeks to rebuild them from the ground up under his command and add their strength to the Mage's Circle. Should that happen, we will lose this war," Diamond explained. "The Knights' Order was the very heart of the old alliance, its foundation. Their destruction is part of the reason the alliance collapsed so badly. We need to do what we can to get more information on this and, if possible, ensure that a revived Knights' Order is on our side or at the very least impartial to this war like the Tribe. They hold too much power to allow them to become an enemy."

"So, what do we do?" Kat asked Diamond, unable to see how they could help.

"We need to get the Knights' grimoire."

"Grimoire?"

"It's a contingency," Kat told Abbie. "The Guild, Circle, Tribe, and the Order all have one. They're supposedly indestructible objects that contain the information needed to recreate each faction in case they're destroyed."

"Should August get his hands on their grimoire, he will have access to their secrets and will know where to get all the materials needed for their resurrection," Diamond continued with a scowl.

"We cannot let this happen, which is why we need to get it first. Look through that information, perhaps you can find something that can point us in the right direction."

"I'll try, but I can't make any promises, somethin' like that sounds like it would be heavily guarded or well hidden," Abbie pointed out.

"I understand, we're all a bit out of our depth here. I'm just asking for an attempt. The rest of us will poke around and try to find out what we can but this is top secret, not even other thieves can know what we're doing," Diamond said firmly. "One thing August stated in his notes from what I've seen is that the Knights' Order cared for civilians even more than the Guild which is saying something. August claimed that if their grimoire would be hidden anywhere it would be amongst them," Diamond informed Abbie. "It's not much but hopefully that can help you."

"Better than nothing," Abbie said with a shrug. "I'll see what I can dig up."

"Good, you have a week, we'll reconvene afterward. Try to also figure out what's going on with a folder in there, labeled 'P.A.' It looks empty but something we can't find might be hidden in it as well, so give it a once-over. Also, we'll be meeting at your place as I'm having this room refurbished," Diamond informed Abbie who nodded. Abbie noticed how tense Diamond and Kat seemed and she could understand. Unlike the first job which was for the band's benefit, this one seemed as though it would affect the entirety of the Guild, they couldn't afford to mess this up.

*　　*　　*

As the others planned how they were to go about their roles in the war, Jack was outside behind the building preparing for the future in his own way. Jack pulled out a small black bag of gold coins and tossed it up and down in his hand.

"This should be enough, right?" Jack asked and tossed the sack into the shadows. "One coin per lesson."

"That is the fee," Meifeng said as she stepped out of the shadows. "Still, with this amount...you really do plan on studying under me for quite some time. You know it would be safer and cheaper for you to train with my father instead."

"If his teachings worked for me, you'd be right," Jack said dryly. "Personally, I don't feel like sitting down while my band tries to compensate for my lack of skill. Besides you taught me each day after the lessons ended before, this shouldn't be too bad."

"I taught you because leaving the head of the Frost family defenseless is irresponsible," Meifeng said matter-of-factly. "Teaching you a few moves while you tried to achieve balance wasn't going to hurt anyone. That said, I added this ridiculous fee to my lessons in order to persuade you to go back to him," Meifeng said with a troubled expression. "I never pictured you to be crazy enough to actually pay me. Something about selling my father's teachings like this seems wrong."

"Well if you want, I could always take my money elsewhere," Jack pointed out.

"Now don't get ahead of yourself, I never said I would not teach you." Meifeng said as she pocketed the gold. "I am a woman of my word and cannot turn down someone so obviously eager to learn from me. To do so would be to act without honor and without honor we have nothing," Meifeng said wisely. "That said, we must keep this a secret. I am but my father's assistant. My father is the head of all enforcers, including their trainers. Until I get his approval as a Master, I cannot officially teach anyone within the Guild. Do you understand? We are breaking important rules, nothing good awaits us if we are discovered."

"I hear you loud and clear, but rest assured, secrets are my specialty."

"As expected of a member of the Frost family, the only thieves that can keep secrets even from their own band," Meifeng mused. "Your training begins tomorrow. I will give you access to one of my safe houses as you have done for me, I'll message you the details later," Meifeng said before she stepped back into the shadows and left Jack alone behind the building. Heading back inside, Jack could only hope this paid off in the end so that he could better help his band. He couldn't explain it, but he had a feeling that things were going to get a lot tougher for them soon and he could only hope that he was ready.

$$* \quad * \quad *$$

Santa Monica, Clair de Lune

"That took a bit longer than anticipated, Mr. Gladius, but I believe we are on the same page now," Haylen said as she sat across from August and Xavier. "Mr. Prospero paid for my services, not just for Prosperity Industries, but for a number of its associates which includes both you and Mr. Magnus. Now, you say this wasn't an isolated incident but rather the start of attacks on all of your associates?"

"Yes, instead of money, what was stolen from my nephew's bank is confidential information," August explained. "That leads me to believe there will soon be another attack that will be targeted on my gallery downtown, quite possibly within the next week or two."

"That's oddly specific, mind tellin' me how you came up with that?"

"Unfortunately, that is confidential so I am going to have to ask you to take my word on it," August answered with an apologetic smile.

"Sir, you have to give me somethin' so that I can better prepare."

"There is a piece of...art, that I've recently purchased from a museum in England that I wish to have displayed in my gallery. The Stone Shield," August said which made Haylen look at him in surprise. "Perhaps you've heard of it?"

"Heard of it? My family was the one that sold it to that museum in the first place," Haylen informed them.

"I see, so it wasn't a coincidence, you are part of the Stone family," August said making her nod while Xavier looked lost.

"The Stone family, Uncle?"

"Yes, an old family, very wealthy that came over here from England back when this country was founded. I do believe they've dabbled in a bit of every business at this point, am I correct?"

"More or less," Haylen answered before sipping her drink. "We had a lot of things like that floatin' around before my father started sellin' them off a few years after the war. The last I heard of the particular piece you bought, we sold it for quite the price. If you bought it then it'll probably be one of the most expensive pieces you'll have on display."

"The most expensive," August confirmed. "I made quite the investment on it, so you can see why I am a bit nervous about it being targeted by thieves."

"Well then, I'll get my team ready to ensure its safe transfer to your gallery," Haylen said with a small smile. "We haven't failed a task yet, and afterward I can begin updatin' the security on Prosperity Industries and its associates. Mr. Prospero said that we will be workin' together for a bit, so I hope we can get along."

"As do I," August said politely while Xavier smiled.

"Agreed."

∗   ∗   ∗

Santa Monica, Abigail's Apartment

For the next seven days, Band 13 and Abbie discussed and plotted their next course of action to no avail. Though Roderick had not given a specific time-frame, Diamond couldn't help but feel restless. The pressure slowly but surely got to her and though she hid it well, her band and even Abbie were able to tell that the boss' patience was almost gone. Fortunately, on the seventh day luck finally seemed to be on their side as Abbie stumbled across a news article.

"Got it!" Abbie said victoriously as she turned her laptop toward them. "Guess who just made the headlines?" Abbie said as they saw an article about a recent purchase that August made from a museum in England. "I'm not sure what the grimoires you mentioned look like, but what are the odds this is it?"

"Very likely, I haven't seen the Thieves Guild's grimoire but from what I've been told they tend to be old artifacts that a civilian probably wouldn't look at twice. It could definitely pass off as old art," Diamond said as she looked closer at the Stone Shield. "Yes, this is it, look," Diamond said as she showed them an image of the artifact. On its front, they could see what appeared to be the image of a shield that was surrounded by thirteen swords. "Everyone gets so enthralled by the image on the front, few mention the strange writing on the other side," Diamond said as she showed them an image of the opposite side of the artifact where they saw illegible writing and symbols carved into it. "This is a code, one the Order probably used. If I had to guess this has the information August needs to resurrect the Knights' Order. How long do we have?"

"At least another week before it shows up at the gallery," Abbie answered. "Also, I did what I could to that P.A. folder but believe it or not, it's just an empty folder."

"I see, then it doesn't matter. We have our target. Kat, look around for all the entrances and exits of the gallery. Frost, infiltrate the employees and find out as much as you can about this. We need a time-frame and a location of where we can intercept the grimoire. Understood?"

"Gotcha!" Kat said with a grin as Jack nodded.

"Interesting, we're stealing art now? Bout time we got to steal something with a little bit of class," Jack said before frowning a bit when he noticed a confused expression on Abbie's face. "What's wrong, love?"

"It says that this thing used to be owned by…the Stone family," Abbie said as she read the background of the Stone Shield. All of Band 13 looked surprised at this and their confusion was obvious in the glances they shared amongst each other. "Why would my family have this? Actually, wait," Abbie muttered as she rubbed her temples as if being overcome with a sudden headache. "I think…I think I remember this. Like I think it used to be in my house before it disappeared one day."

"Well that's not concerning at all, love," Jack said sarcastically, though he was clearly concerned for Abbie.

"Abbie, are you alright?" Kat asked in concern.

"Yeah, just a headache, remembering something from a childhood I'd rather forget tends to do that to me," Abbie said quietly before she shook her head to clear it. "Still, why would my family have that?"

"It's not uncommon for civilians to pick up supernatural artifacts, believing them to just be sculptures or art," Diamond explained. "But to think a grimoire? You know, your resistance to having your mark removed is something we blamed solely on Alexei. However, if you had something like that in your house as a child, that definitely added to it," Diamond pointed out. "But we'll have to worry about that later seeing how we are now pressed for time."

"Agreed, but while we're on the topic of family, there is somethin' I need to warn you about that I put off for too long," Abbie said as she got their undivided attention. "It's about my sister, she's been put on the Circle's payroll."

"By that, I hope you mean like a secretary or something at P.I.," Kat said nervously as her bandmates looked at Abbie with varying degrees of shock.

"Sorry kitten," Abbie denied apologetically. "They hired her team as security after we were able to breach their system. I would have told you last week but when I was attacked while walkin' Sal, it completely slipped my mind."

"Wait, what, you were attacked!?" Kat asked incredulously. "What the fuck!? Are you alright!?"

"She's clearly alright," Diamond said dryly as she rubbed the bridge of her nose. "After this, we're going to have a long talk about full disclosure, but fortunately you told us early enough before I could begin planning," Diamond said and Abbie had the decency to look embarrassed about her lapse in memory. "How good is your sister?"

"She's the one who gave me my foundation," Abbie admitted,

"Perfect," Diamond said sarcastically. "We're probably going to have to tone down our abilities for this job then. We cannot risk exposure, especially with our mark unavailable for use. If Abbie cannot guarantee those cameras stay down, we cannot risk getting discovered by her or her team."

"You sure you're not thinking too far ahead? P.I. hired her, didn't they? What are the odds she'll be doing business with August

Gladius, of all people, and his gallery?" Kat asked Diamond but it was Jack who answered.

"Think, Kat, if we took the information regarding August's plan then he knows we know what his target is. The whole Circle is probably expecting us to go after the grimoire and thanks to the news we now know where it is," Jack explained.

"This is probably why he hired your sister to begin with," Diamond told Abbie. "Dealing with civilians is one thing but dealing with skilled civilians is another. He did this to avoid fighting himself because that would cause too much of scene when he destroys whoever the Guild sends after him."

"Is he that powerful?" Abbie asked suddenly terrified of August's apparent power. Abbie's fear only grew when she noted that Diamond seemed certain that whoever challenged him from the Guild would fall. "No one in the Guild can deal with him?"

"An Arch-Mage's power is nothing to scoff at, they could destroy entire cities at a time if they wanted to," Diamond explained and the blood drained from Abbie's face at the thought. "Our highest skilled bands could take them on and even win, but August is the exception. His shield has been officially deemed to be unbreakable, making him invincible on the battlefield. Every Mage's shield has a weak spot and can be worn down after taking enough damage but August's is the exception. I hear his shield is the reason he was allowed to become a mage and it allowed him to rise through the ranks quickly."

"If Julia wasn't M.I.A, then perhaps Roderick's band could take him down but that is not the case. The only thing thieves can do when faced with him is flee on sight," Jack muttered, a scowl on his face as he thought about his mother.

"Frost," Diamond began before she stopped herself and faced Abbie. "Anyway, that power of his is a double-edged sword. Being too powerful means that he has to pick and choose his battles carefully or risk exposure, fortunately for us he chose not to partake in this one it seems."

"Lucky us," Abbie said as she shuddered at the thought of August's apparent power. "Look while Kat and Jack are out, I'll gather all the information I can about my sister's team."

"Good, I'll go call up my father and let him know we have a lead, we'll reconvene in a few days," Diamond said before they all left for their assigned tasks. The situation was far more intense than the last job yet Abbie couldn't ignore that particular rush she began to crave from flowing through her. Dealing with her sister would not be easy but unlike any other time she challenged Haylen, she had the support of her new friends. That alone made Abbie feel far more optimistic about this job than she normally would have been.

* * *

San Diego, Magnus Manor

August made his way toward his study when he saw Lilia approach him. With a smile, he greeted his niece who returned the gesture though it was obvious that it was more for formality if anything.

"Uncle, how was the meeting with the civilians?"

"Enlightening, it seems that despite their lack of magic, they still have their uses. Your uncle Enero was right all along," August mused. "Tell me, my girl, how goes that…task…I've assigned you?" August questioned which made Lilia frown briefly before she quickly schooled her expression.

"It remains a difficult one, but each day it becomes easier and easier to extract the information you seek. Honestly, at this rate, you won't even need that blasted grimoire nor need to involve my foolish brother any further," Lilia said confidently.

"I see, well, a little insurance wouldn't hurt after all. At my age, you learn quickly to prepare for all possible outcomes and claim as much control over your surroundings as possible no matter what the cost," August said knowingly. "Should we lose the grimoire, our plans will be set back a bit, but I'm sure you will be able to succeed on your end and get the information required. You have simply far too much invested in this endeavor to fail."

"Our plans?" Lilia repeated incredulously as August strolled past her.

"Yes, after all, you got us this far did you not, my girl? Whatever the future holds will be on both of us," August said as he walked away. Not once did he notice or care about the dark look Lilia shot him. Fortunately for the indestructible mage, looks were not enough to kill.

CHAPTER 11

• • • • • • • • ● • • • • • • • • •

LINES CROSSED

Santa Monica, Midas Towers

It would be three days later when Abbie and the thieves regrouped to go over their findings. Fortunately for them, now that they knew exactly what their target was, their progress moved much more smoothly.

"So, what are we dealing with?" Diamond asked the three and Jack opted to go first with his findings.

"I spent the last three days working with the gallery's security team, I infiltrated them by taking the place of a guard they believed was on vacation. Luckily, I was a good judge of character. The guard I replaced kept to himself, the others didn't even seem to know he wasn't supposed to be in," Jack said and chuckled at the memory. "What I've learned is that in three days, the grimoire is being shipped into the same bay as the car we stole. Problem is security over there has increased since our last visit."

"So, going back there is out of the question, especially if we are going to try to keep this simple," Diamond muttered.

"Should we go for it when they are delivering it?" Kat asked.

"Yes, but we can't do it too early. Between the traffic and witnesses, attacking the delivery truck in the streets and attempting to get away will be next to impossible," Diamond explained. "We're going to have to wait until they unload the grimoire at the gallery. We'll be out of the public's eye, plus we'll be only a few blocks from Abbie's apartment which we can turn into a safe house. Kat, how many entrances and vantage points could you find?"

"Too many, emergency exits, roof entries, windows, you name it. A lot of ways to break in but they're all blocked by security cameras. I won't lie though, they aren't exactly placed well," Kat said perturbed. "It's almost like they're for show like he just put them there with the thought that just having them there will scare off intruders. He was either super confident or he didn't have a firm grasp on what he was doing."

"We'll go with the former, he's an Arch-Mage so we're going to have to treat this as if anything that could go wrong, will."

"Gotcha, boss. All I need is a minute at most and I'm in," Kat said and Diamond turned to Abbie.

"Can you get her that minute?"

"Yes, breakin' into the system isn't the issue, it's stayin' in once Haylen notices me," Abbie explained. "I'll be able to do whatever you need me to, but for drastically reduced periods of time when she starts fightin' me off."

"Then we'll have to use your skills smartly, you've told us about your sister but what about the rest of her team?" Diamond asked curiously while Abbie typed something on her laptop, after a moment she turned it around and showed them three profiles she had pulled up."

"Together, they're a four-man group," Abbie began before pointing to a large bearded man who seemed to be in his late forties. He had tanned weathered skin and black hair that was peppered with gray. "First up is Jebediah Ford, he was our bodyguard when we were younger before Haylen bought his contract. He's almost more machine than man given the number of military-grade augments he was given during the war. The most noteworthy of his augments are the subdermal titanium nanites that both protect him and increase his strength. The safest bet would be to avoid him completely if you can."

"He looks like he's flowing with old man strength," Jack joked. "But, I think I can take him."

"You're going to have to. We can't have him lurking around, you need to find him and keep him busy. If we're going to be forced to fight more like civilians then it's out of the question for either Kat or me to try to deal with him," Diamond said as her eyes landed on a second profile. "Especially when it seems as though I'll be needed elsewhere."

"Jezebel Adams, a mercenary that's been workin' with my sister for years. She was a decorated sniper in the army before she left. She ain't afraid to get her hands dirty. I've only met her a couple of times but believe me, she is messed up in the head. It's only because of Haylen that she's allowed to roam free," Abbie said with a visible shudder. "Her implants in her eyes help her hit whatever she's lookin' at. You all need to keep your heads down or she'll take em'."

"I'll keep her eyes off of the others then," Diamond said before she noticed that Abbie looked as though she still had something she wanted to say. "What is it?"

"It's just…look, you're an assassin, right?" Abbie asked and Diamond nodded. Abbie seemed to be troubled by something before she finally spoke. "While I personally don't approve of killin' anyone, I won't blame you in this instance because you might have to."

"Abbie?" Kat asked startled by Abbie's words.

"I know Jezebel, the way she thinks ain't right. I'm not tellin' you to kill her," Abbie clarified. "I'm just warnin' you that you might have to if only to keep them and yourself alive," Abbie said before she turned to Kat. "I can't lose you," Abbie said firmly. "I've lost enough people to her," Abbie continued quietly and the thieves chose not ask what she meant and put it on the list of mysteries that surrounded Abbie.

"I see, I'll heed your warning," Diamond said before she looked at the last profile. This one showed a man in his late twenties that had a fair complexion, and dark brown hair that was slicked back.

"Last we have Samuel Pala, a smuggler my sister hired after traveling around down south. When it comes to escorting people and goods from point A to point B, he's the one in charge," Abbie said. "So, if you want to get at the Shield, he'll probably be nearby."

"So, I just have to get past him," Kat muttered. "Shouldn't be that hard."

"Be careful, he's the only one besides my sister without augments but he is very skilled," Abbie warned. Kat smirked and pulled out her treasure.

"He may be skilled, but I got more than enough luck to make up for it."

"You sure that's a good idea?" Abbie questioned. "You kind of light up like a Christmas tree when you use that, kitten, can't pass that off as an augment."

"Civilians can't see her glow or presence," Diamond told Abbie. "The only reason you can see it is because you bear our mark. Kat and I can use our treasures without immediately risking the Guild's exposure. Frost on the other hand..." Diamond trailed off as the man sighed in dismay.

"...Is shit out of luck," Jack finished. "Cryo-based technology isn't advanced enough to explain my abilities."

"We also need to watch how we use the ash," Diamond warned. "It's almost time to act. Use this time to make the preparations you need," Diamond said before she departed to go gather her thoughts and left the three to discuss what they needed to do amongst themselves.

* * *

Santa Monica, Gladius Gallery

Haylen frowned to herself as she stood in the gallery's surveillance room with Xavier, watching the screens for signs of any suspicious activity. As she watched, she saw the guards make their rounds and patrol the grounds of the Gallery.

"Still quiet, you sure you needed to call us out for this Stone?" Haylen heard Jezebel ask through her earpiece. Haylen looked at a screen where she could see Jezebel set up shop on top of a nearby building. *"I'm actually getting bored."*

"You're complaining about easy money for once? Lola, we need to talk about your priorities," Samuel joked as a large truck pulled up behind the building.

"I told you to stop calling me that!"

"I'll take this over our usual contracts any day," Samuel continued as he ignored her.

"Agreed," Jebediah said as Haylen watched him and Samuel exit the truck.

"Pussies, am I right, Haylen?" Jezebel asked as Jebediah unloaded the Shield from the truck and gave it to Samuel who held the stone slab under his arm.

"Focus, all of you," Haylen ordered as she eyed the cameras. One thing she idly noted was that Xavier seemed just as focused as she was as if he too waited for something.

"Lively bunch," Xavier said clearly amused by the banter.

"Forgive them, despite their attitudes they are quite capable."

"Of that, I have no doubt. I've learned by now that the most eccentric tend to be the ones you need to watch out for," Xavier said as his eyes scanned over the monitors.

"What has your panties in a bunch, Stone?" Jezebel questioned as she aimed her rifle at the building. The windows of the gallery gave Jezebel a good shot of each floor. If someone suspicious were to even pass by one of the windows she was ready to take them out.

"Need I remind you that the system breach was nearly identical to methods used by Wonderland?" Haylen questioned curiously. "We cannot take this lightly."

"Whatever. Destroyed them once, we'll do it again."

"Wonderland?" Xavier repeated as he rubbed his chin in thought. "That's a name I haven't heard in a long time, nearly ruined my family's businesses, you're the group Uncle Enero hired?" Xavier asked and he sounded a bit impressed. "You have my gratitude, you stopped them before they could do irreparable damage."

"Think nothin' of it, as crude as she is, Jezebel is right. If it's them, we'll handle it. They were dangerous but too naïve to stand on their own feet when their leader fell," Haylen muttered. "Their second in command, who was a much bigger threat, in my opinion, couldn't deal with the grief and as a result, the organization fell as a whole. We were just fortunate to be there at the right time to take advantage of that."

"An impressive feat nonetheless," Xavier said but stopped talking when Haylen held up a hand to silence him. Xavier could see that she was suddenly completely focused on the task at hand as she began to type rapidly on her keyboard. "What's wrong?"

"The camera flickered," Haylen muttered and Xavier noticed through the monitors that her team all seemed to tense up at this.

"Well, they are quite outdated-"

"-No," Haylen interrupted with a shake of her head. "They're in," Haylen said simply. "Jebediah, Samuel, protect that artifact with your life. Jezebel, look for any sign of them and watch the entrances. Xavier, get your guards to scour the floor!" Haylen ordered and Xavier immediately put the guards on alert. "Now...where are you?" Haylen muttered as she worked on her computer.

*   *   *

As Samuel and Jebediah made their way into the gallery, Kat dropped down from beneath the truck where she had hung from since they picked up the Shield at the docks. She stayed under the truck and kept an eye on the security camera looking over the rear entrance.

"*Quick, go! She's noticed me!*" Abbie said and Kat immediately moved from under the truck and darted toward the entrance. "*Good, stay close to them but be careful, those two need to be separated,*" Abbie instructed as Kat silently trailed behind the two men. Kat conjured up as much skill as she could muster to avoid detection as they made their way through the gallery. As Kat followed them, she kept an eye on each upcoming security camera and stopped her pursuit just before it could detect her. "*Go,*" Abbie said after she took control of the camera. As if he sensed someone behind him, Samuel stopped and glanced back only to find no one there.

"What's wrong?" Jebediah questioned.

"Nothing must be my imagination," Samuel said as they continued onward. Neither noticed Kat step out from a pillar she had barely managed to hide behind before she followed them.

✶   ✶   ✶

"Somethin' is definitely wrong," Haylen muttered as she lost control over each camera every time Samuel and Jebediah moved by them. Patterns were a thing Haylen never took lightly, and in no-time, she realized what was going on. "Jebediah, Samuel, act natural you're being followed," Haylen ordered. "Stop at the next camera," Haylen said as she took control over the camera. "Not this time," Haylen murmured as she fought off Abigail's attempt to take it over. After gaining control over it, she forced the camera to quickly move and look behind the men but to her ire, she saw nothing.

✶   ✶   ✶

Kat hid behind a display case just barely out of the camera's line of sight and watched it and the men with wide-eyes. That was entirely too close for her comfort but thanks to her incredibly high reaction speed she managed to avoid detection.

"That was close but they're focused on you now just like the boss said, which means we can move on to phase two," Abbie said before alarms began to ring throughout the building.

"There you are, hurry, there was an attack in the east wing!" a guard shouted frantically to Jebediah and Samuel. "It happened near the Renaissance exhibit, come on!"

✶   ✶   ✶

"What?" Haylen muttered before she looked at the exhibit's camera to find six guards unconscious in the area. One in particular who must have sounded the alarm collapsed before her very eyes. She had been tricked, that much was obvious. Haylen had been tricked to focus on the Shield's security and failed to watch over the cameras in the

158

east wing of the building. With them hacked without her notice, there was nothing to stop the intruders' attack on the guards. This threw Haylen for a loop for Abbie was incredibly intelligent but nowhere near that devious. "Who am I dealin' with?" Haylen muttered. "Jebediah go with them, Samuel keep your eye on that artifact, go!"

*   *   *

"Jebediah's far enough away now, Umbra, go!" Abbie said as the Change of Fate began to spin. When it stopped, Kat grinned when she felt a surge of luck fill her body. Kat soon darted from behind her cover and charged Samuel. Startled, Samuel backed up in surprise at her sudden appearance and tripped over himself which made him fall onto his back.

"I'll take this," Kat said as she snatched the artifact from his grasp and ran away with it under her arm. "Hey, this thing got some weight to it," Kat said as she ran with the Shield. "It's slowing me down."

"Hang on tight and go for the exit like the boss said, right now the grimoire is the priority," Abbie said as Kat ran through a corridor.

*   *   *

"Stone, the Shield!" Haylen heard Samuel shout before she looked toward his position and saw him chase after a masked woman whom now had the Shield in her grasp.

"God damn it!" Haylen cursed as she realized she had been outplayed again.

"Focus on the one that took the Shield, anything else will be a distraction," Xavier said as if he spoke from experience. "Remove them from the equation and this whole plan goes down."

"Jezebel west wing corridor, you should see one of the intruders approachin' it soon with Samuel in pursuit. Neutralize them," Haylen ordered as she glared at the screen.

*   *   *

"Gladly," Jezebel said with a smirk as a holographic visor appeared in front of her eyes. Within no time she found the corridor just as Kat ran into it. The crosshairs on the visor locked on to Kat before Jezebel held her breath and took aim. Locked on to Kat's head she pulled the trigger and the bullet ripped from her weapon immediately and blasted through the window. To her surprise, however, the shot simply missed the masked woman by mere inches. Kat seemed completely caught off guard by the sudden attack but did not slow her movements as she continued to run. Irritated, Jezebel took aim again and fired shot after shot into the corridor. Jezebel grew increasingly irritated by her inability to eliminate the intruder. "Are you serious!?" Jezebel growled as Kat comically dodged each attempt on her life before she left the sniper's line of sight.

"Did you just miss every shot!?" Samuel asked incredulously as he continued his pursuit. Before Jezebel could respond she suddenly found herself snatched backward courtesy of Diamond who put the woman in a powerful chokehold.

*　　*　　*

"How did she miss? She never misses!" Haylen said as she slammed her fist down on the desk while Xavier rubbed his chin in thought.

"That thief seems to be incredibly…lucky," Xavier trailed off and his eyes widened as realization sunk in. "Really the rookies?" Xavier muttered to himself quietly before he turned to face Haylen. "Your team won't stop them," Xavier said matter-of-factly and Haylen could tell he hadn't dismissed her team's ability but rather it was as if he had praised the abilities of the intruders. "They're the same people that robbed my bank, the moment they catch you by surprise it's too late."

"Like hell, Jezebel what's your status!?"

*　　*　　*

"A bit…preoccupied…" Jezebel forced out as she tried to fight off her attacker to no avail. Quickly Jezebel reached to the side of her leg and unsheathed a hunting knife before she stabbed backward at Diamond. Diamond immediately released Jezebel in order to avoid being stabbed in the eye. "You should have killed me when you had the chance, you won't get the drop on me twice," Jezebel said as she drew a side-arm.

"We'll see," Diamond said, a handgun held tightly in her grasp. Jezebel's eyes widened ever so slightly when she noted the golden "M" on the back of Diamond's glove though she said nothing. A tense silence passed between them before Jezebel threw the blade at Diamond.

*   *   *

"Whoa!" Kat exclaimed as she ducked just in time to avoid a knife that lodged into the wall next to her, burying itself up to its hilt. "This guy's not playing!" Kat said as she ran with Samuel hot on her trail who pulled his blade from the wall as he ran past it. Samuel took aim at the thief once more and threw the blade again only for it to miss when Kat lost her balance next to a "wet floor" sign.

"Seriously!?" Samuel asked before he too lost his balance and crashed into the floor. Frustrated beyond belief, Samuel scrambled to his feet while Kat did the same. Kat took her whip and swung it toward a display case, which made it wrap around its leg tightly. Kat then pulled the display between herself and Samuel. Samuel cursed when he crashed into it and fell down to the ground once more as Kat collected the Shield and continued on with her escape.

*   *   *

"Over here," the guard told Jebediah as they entered the exhibit. Soon a fist slammed into the guard's jaw and knocked him out instantly. Jebediah turned to face the culprit who was the seemingly downed guard who had pulled the alarm. Before Jebediah could get a good look at the attacker, Jack returned his face to normal while his suit maintained its disguised appearance with the exception of his mask.

"How did you get in here?"

"You don't really expect me to answer that do you?" Jack asked skeptically before he released a devastating right hook at the man whom quickly blocked it. Jebediah grimaced a bit as he felt the sting of the blow and his arm trembled from its unexpected weight.

"Nice punch," Jebediah said and then, to Jack's confusion, the skin on his hand turned silver. A malleable metal tore through his sleeves and coated his arms before he slammed a powerful blow into Jack's stomach that knocked Jack back a bit. Jack grunted from the force of the blow and glared at Jebediah. The power from the attack was felt even through his mod-suit.

"Back at you," Jack said as he shrugged off the pain before the two immediately found themselves locked in hand-to-hand combat. Much to Jack's frustration wherever he would land a blow would just get covered by the strange metal and protect Jebediah from harm.

* * *

"Where did he come from!?" Haylen questioned as the cameras showed Jebediah and Jack rain blow after blow upon each other. The way the two attacked each other was reminiscent of a boxing match with the way they bobbed and weaved around one another's attacks.

"Like I said, it's too late," Xavier said which made Haylen glare at him.

"Fine, since you seem to be an expert on what's goin' on, what do you propose we do?" Haylen asked angrily. Xavier hummed in thought as he took in the current situation.

"First things first, cut off the alarm and send the authorities away, if anything they're going to be a hindrance to us," Xavier instructed. "Those thieves are going to use them to protect themselves and escape in the confusion."

"Protect themselves? Protect themselves from what?"

"Me," Xavier said as a smirk graced his lips. "I'll be damned, they even took my own pride into account," Xavier mused as he realized just why his brother pulled the alarm. The thieves had figured there was a high chance that he wouldn't take his previous defeat lying down and prepared countermeasures in case he had decided to intervene anyway.

"You? What can you do?" Haylen asked as she went to shut down the alarm.

"I wonder," Xavier said as he gave her a wink. Without Eve, he was at a disadvantage and he knew it, that said, he figured he stood a better chance than the civilians and also deep down wanted to know just what his limits were without his servant. "Next, we wait for your team to tire them out a bit more, we need them separated for as long as possible. Don't worry they don't kill, that's not how they operate."

"I wasn't worried about that."

"Is that so?" Xavier asked skeptically which made Haylen scowl at him. "Just figured I'd let you know."

"Just what are we dealin' with, Magnus?"

"Exactly what you think, thieves," Xavier answered. "Just of a different breed than you're used to."

* * *

"Oh, come on, you're a better shot than that! Your last ones proved that!" Jezebel taunted after a bullet shot past her head. "I have an eye for talent and I know when someone is messing around and missing shots on purpose," Jezebel said as she took a shot at Diamond that forced the thief to dodge. The action caused Jezebel's second shot to hit her gun and knock it from her hand. Diamond cursed before she dove behind a vent on the roof and used it as cover while another handgun formed in her palm. Diamond hated being forced to dodge Jezebel's shots but she knew she was unable to simply shrug off gunfire in front of a civilian. Diamond had to be creative in how she approached this situation. "See, just like that, you must have a good pair of eyes to dodge that. Probably even better than mine, you could be someone amazing if you learned to stop hesitating."

"You're actually lecturing me about hesitating?" Diamond asked with a scoff. "Pray tell, what would you call what you're doing now?" Diamond asked before she took two shots at Jezebel which forced the sniper to take cover.

"This? This is a personal project," Jezebel said with a laugh that sent a shiver down Diamond's spine. "You got the drop on me, that's something that hasn't happened before. Seems you made the mistake of gaining my interest!"

"Well I don't want it, take it back."

"You're not that lucky," Jezebel called out as she reloaded her gun. "Your hesitation betrays your youth, you know? I used to be like you, back when I was younger. Thought I knew what I was doing with a gun, robbing people to get by."

"What's this, an intervention?" Diamond asked which earned a laugh from Jezebel.

"On the contrary, I want you to be better. See, I got the drop on the wrong person and paid dearly for it. When I came to, I was branded, forced to be a servant for her. At least that's what I thought. She trained me, showed me what I needed to become if I wanted to keep using a gun. It was the best and most hellish year of my life, I was broken and made into something stronger, better, deadlier," Jezebel said as she rolled up her sleeve, finding a small black "M" tattooed on the other side of her wrist that was identical to the one on Diamond's glove. "For that year she gave me a home, of course not one near her family, but she gave me a start and the price for it all was simple. She said to pay it forward, that it was the honorable thing to do."

"And what do you know about honor?"

"More than you know, girl, more than you know," Jezebel said as her heart thundered in her chest. Jezebel glanced to the side toward the gallery and she could see Jack and Jebediah fight. As she watched them, she noticed that Jack managed to get the upper hand when he tripped up Jebediah and slammed him down into the floor. "Without honor, there's no difference between us and the dirt beneath our feet," Jezebel said just loud enough for Diamond to hear. The words made Diamond freeze as Jezebel smirked knowingly. "You remind of the woman who taught me that, but your gaze is too soft."

"What are-" Diamond was interrupted when Jezebel suddenly leapt from her cover and rushed toward her sniper rifle. She took two shots at Diamond with her handgun to force Diamond back behind cover before she discarded it. Jezebel picked up her rifle and aimed at the building. When she focused on Jack, the crosshairs in her eyes locked on to him before she pulled the trigger.

*　*　*

Having enough of being chased, Kat stopped suddenly before she spun around. The action caught Samuel off guard and left him helpless as she slammed the Shield into his face. The force of the blow knocked him out and sent him down onto the floor. Kat smirked at her work and ran to the ancient civilization exhibit. To Kat's surprise, she found Jack and Jebediah already inside.

"Seriously, you're not done?" Kat joked however before Jack could respond with something witty as usual his mind suddenly exploded with pain. Thanks to the suppressor, Jezebel's shot was practically silent except for when the bullet passed through the now shattered window. Silent, however, was not a word that could be used to describe Jack's pained shout when the bullet tore through his left shoulder. The armor piercing round ripped through his suit with ease and Kat could do nothing but watch Jack fall. "No!"

"Jack!" Abbie exclaimed as she watched their enforcer fall to the ground.

*　*　*

Diamond's heart clenched as she heard the screams of Kat and Abbie before it was filled with Kat's fear and sadness. Those emotions, however, were quickly drowned out by a surge of pure anger that consumed Diamond's powerful heart and flooded the emotional link between Band 13. Her heartbeat was loud as her Royal Blood pumped through her body.

"Whatever your line of work is, if it involves weapons, you better be prepared to use them. Your hesitation could end up getting your allies killed," Jezebel advised as she glanced over at Diamond and smirked at the pure hate she saw in her eyes. "Now you look like her," Jezebel said before she raised the rifle at Diamond and pulled the trigger. Jezebel's eyes widened a bit, as the bullet slammed into Diamond's shoulder and made her stumble back a step. The shoulder of Diamond's suit was torn but her skin remained unscathed as the bullet fell to the ground. Jezebel took aim again but was too late when a bullet ripped through her visor and shot through her eye. Diamond remained silent as she popped her shoulder back in place and gazed down at the bloodied sniper.

* * *

"Jack!"

"Jezebel!" came the shouts from Xavier and Haylen who both looked at two different screens. Xavier himself couldn't believe how fast the situation went south and Haylen was stunned as she looked at the screen. Xavier had not expected both Jack and Jezebel to find themselves gunned down. He realized that it was now that he'd have to interfere before things got even worse. With a grimace Xavier glanced at the horrified face of Haylen before he grabbed her shoulder.

"Stay put, I'll deal with this. Whatever you see, just stay calm, I'll explain it later," Xavier said urgently and Haylen stumbled back in shock when the man suddenly disappeared before her very eyes in a blue flash of light.

* * *

Xavier appeared on the roof right between Diamond and Jezebel's body. Xavier was startled when, without hesitation, Diamond shot him three times only for his shield to stop each of the bullets. Xavier conjured a fireball in his palm threw it at Diamond which forced her off of the roof when it exploded into a large inferno. Diamond allowed herself to fall into the dark alley and disappeared in the shadows of the buildings. Diamond reappeared from a shadow on the roof of the gallery as both of her hand guns formed in her hands.

* * *

"Kat, stay back," Jack gasped out as he weakly looked at Kat who had rushed toward his side, her eyes filled with tears. Jack weakly reached into his pocket and pulled out his flask and sipped from it. Jack shivered as he felt his wound stitch itself together before he punched the ground with his right hand. Diamond's anger flooded his veins as he forced himself back to his feet. "Don't interfere," Jack instructed as he pocketed his flask and turned to face Jebediah who looked surprised to see the younger man apparently shrug off a shot from a sniper.

"You can't fight in this condition," Kat said as Jebediah grimaced.

"Kid, ain't no amount of money worth your life," Jebediah said. "Put the artifact down and leave."

"Like hell, mate," Jack said as he raised his right hand. Jack clenched his fingers in a way that made his hand resemble a claw while his left arm hung limply at his side, seemingly useless. "This is about more than money, it's about honor," Jack told Kat. "Get out."

"I'm not leaving you here in that condition!" Kat said angrily.

"Then don't interfere, this fight is mine," Jack said before he charged at Jebediah who did the same.

* * *

Santa Monica, One-week prior

"Vivi gave you a solid foundation, but it's time for you to learn a style more suited for you," Meifeng said before she straightened her posture and turned her body toward Jack. Her right hand raised before her, her fingers clenched in a way that made her hand look like a claw while her left arm hung at her side. "Mimic my stance, I will begin teaching you the first lesson of Hēishŏu."

"Hēishŏu?"

"Black hand," Meifeng translated. "It's a style I created from my father's teachings that's based around misdirection," Meifeng continued as Jack mimicked her stance. "Your dominant hand and your legs are your main tools. Through each blow you land, you will use your presence

to siphon the strength of your enemy. You should be very familiar with how to do this given your treasure," Meifeng said as she circled Jack while she maintained her stance as she did so. "And then, when you've gathered enough strength and effectively distracted your opponent..." Jack blinked and suddenly found Meifeng's left fist directly in front of his face. Jack had watched her movements so closely and followed her words, that he completely forgot about her other hand. "You take them down using all the power you gathered in the unseen hand, the black hand," Meifeng explained before she tapped a stunned Jack on his nose. "This is Hēishǒu."

* * *

Jebediah released blow after blow at Jack whom simply slapped the blows away and deflected them from his body. Jebediah noted that Jack had gone on the defensive and realized that the younger man was far nimbler than he let on. Kat watched apprehensively, not sure what Jack had planned as she had never seen him fight this way before. It was only after the next blow which failed to connect that Jebediah realized his attacks had become weaker. Unfortunately for him, it was just after this realization that Jack went on the offensive. Like Jebediah did at the start of their encounter, Jack slid inside his guard and slammed his fist into the older man's stomach. The metal moved to protects his stomach and absorb most of the damage. Jebediah glowered and looked up only for Jack to kick him back into a wall. Startled by the sudden increase in Jack's strength, Jebediah was forced to defend as Jack released a barrage of expertly executed punches. The metal above Jebediah's skin moved to ward off each blow. Distracted by Jack's attacks, Jebediah never noticed the fingers on Jack's left hand begin to clench. Before Jebediah could realize what happened and move the nanites in his body, a devastating left hook slammed into his jaw with an audible crunch. Jack gritted his teeth through the pain of the bullet still lodged in his shoulder. The force of the blow made Jebediah's body spin around before he collapsed and lost consciousness as Jack stood victoriously behind him.

"What was that?" Kat asked in surprise as she had never seen Jack dominate an opponent like he had just done. Before Jack could respond, Xavier teleported into the exhibit while Diamond dove down from a shadow on the ceiling and released shot after shot at Xavier. His body repeatedly flashed blue as his shield deflected each of the bullets.

"Jack?" Xavier asked in surprise at seeing Jack already back on his feet.

"You want to play for keeps? Fine then, it is war after all," Diamond said as she gently landed down on a display. Diamond hopped off of it and walked in between Kat and Jack. The whites of their eyes turned black as a storm of golden presence erupted from Diamond's body and consumed her bandmates. Kat and Jack shuddered as they felt the full brunt of Diamond's anger. The golden presence coursed over their bodies menacingly as three pairs of electric gold eyes glared at Xavier. Diamond stepped back and raised her weapons while Kat placed the Shield down. Quickly, Kat moved to flank Xavier while Jack rushed forward. Gauntlets formed from ash around Jack's hands as Arondight shone brightly with a "II" emblem inside of it. Xavier's hand erupted with fire before he released a fireball at Jack whose body became encased in ice right before it slammed into him. The force of the spell shattered the ice around his body instantly but he remained unharmed. Before Xavier could figure out what to do next, he felt his leg get snatched from beneath him after Kat wrapped her whip around it and pulled back. As he fell, Diamond shot him twice and weakened his shield even further before Jack slammed a devastating blow into Xavier that knocked him back into a pillar. Xavier's head slammed back against the pillar with enough force to crack it. Before Xavier could react, Jack moved forward and pinned him in place with his hand wrapped tightly around the mage's neck. Jack gritted his teeth as he pulled back his right fist. Gold presence released from Arondight's eyes as a blue light began to fill the light between Arondight's second and third circles.

"Damn it," Xavier cursed, caught off guard by the unprecedented show of power from Jack. Xavier attempted to conjure another fireball but before he could, Jack slammed his fist into Xavier's face. Upon impact, a torrent of ice erupted from the blow with enough force to shatter Xavier's shield and freeze him against the pillar.

"You're trembling Xavier," Diamond said darkly as Xavier felt the full force of the biting cold from the ice produced by his brother for the first time. Xavier shivered from the cold as golden sparks danced across the frozen crystals. The power of his fallen shield made Xavier's eyes blacken as they became filled with stars. Yet, before he could use his increased power, he felt it being drained by Arondight. Xavier's attempts to break free were stopped when Diamond approached them. The handgun in her right hand turned gold as she took aim at Xavier. It was then that Xavier realized that he was going to die.

"Brother-"

"He can't hear you," Diamond interrupted coldly. "You went too far this time," Diamond continued as she prepared to end him, however before she could finish him, Abbie's voice stopped her.

"*Stop!*" Abbie shouted loudly. Abbie's hoarse voice cut through Diamond's rage-filled mind, and Diamond could only wonder how long Abbie had tried to get her attention. "*I know you hate him, but unfortunately he's the only one that can erase the memories of Haylen's team since I have your mark. You can't kill him, no matter how much you believe he deserves it,*" Abbie said, her voice measured as she tried to get Diamond to see reason. Diamond gritted her teeth when she realized that Abbie was right. As long as the threat of exposure was there, she couldn't afford to kill the mage.

"By the Goddesses, you have no idea how lucky you are," Diamond muttered before she forced herself to lower her weapon. "We've done our job," Diamond said as Kat picked up the Shield. "Now you do yours and deal with the civilians," Diamond ordered as she lowered her gun. "This is on you and the Circle, don't blame me for whatever happens the next time we meet. You won't be saved again," Diamond muttered as Jack released his brother who was still frozen to the pillar. "Let's go," Diamond said before the lights of the gallery were shut down. When they turned back on, Xavier once more found himself defeated and alone. It was just like in their last encounter but this time he had a feeling he hadn't believed he'd ever have toward Band 13.

Fear.

CHAPTER 12

· · · · · · ● ● ● ● ● ● ● ● ● ● · · · ·

CHANGES

Santa Monica, Abigail's Apartment

"Ouch, easy back there Kat!" Jack complained as Kat used a knife to cut into his back. "Bloody hell," Jack muttered as Kat seemed to be even rougher in her attempts to remove all traces of a bullet from his shoulder.

"Oh man up, you're the one who decided to take nectar with a bullet still lodged in your body. I have to reopen the wound to get it out!" Kat snapped as she continued to work on Jack, her hands now soaked with his blood. "What the hell were you thinking!? We're a band for a reason, we fight together, don't tell me to stand back on the battlefield!"

"It was just a civilian, I thought I could handle it."

"Bullshit. Don't act like he was normal. His augments aside, something about him was off. I felt it, so I know for a fact that you did!" Kat shouted which made Jack grimace as he realized she was right. Jebediah was practically a living weapon with how strong his body was. It took everything Jack had and then some to hurt the older man. "We could have handled it faster, together," Kat said as she removed the last piece of the bullet from Jack's body. "We're thieves, Jack, our priority is always the objective. I know you're new to the whole having emotions thing, but there is no place for pride in our line of work. You know this," Kat said before biting her lip as she tried to search through the storm of emotions that filled her heart in an attempt to sort out Jack's. "You're our enforcer," Kat said as she felt his heart within her own, understanding dawning on her as she could feel the fears and insecurities that he possessed but dared not disclose to any of them. "You don't need to prove a damn thing to us, we know how strong you are," Kat said softly as she rested her forehead on his back and closed her eyes. Jack tensed as he felt the fear and sadness that Kat had when he was shot down. "I can't lose you."

"Don't worry, Kat. I'm still here," Jack reassured her as he reached for his flask only to have her snatch it away from him. "Kat!?"

"Not this time, consider this your punishment. You want to act like a civilian? You're going to heal like a civilian, now be still as I stitch you up," Kat said firmly.

"You can't be serious!"

"Oh, I am, or should I call Vivi instead?" Kat challenged and Jack felt the blood drain from his face. "That's what I thought, though I should, seeing how you sold me out last time. Consider this payback."

"I apologize."

"Little late for that," Kat said dryly. "Doesn't matter, just stay still and let me work," Kat muttered as she continued to work on Jack. Abbie, who was on her way into the room decided to turn around and leave the two alone. Abbie made her way into her bedroom where she found Diamond. Diamond stared silently out of Abbie's window as she tried to gather her thoughts.

"You know, I never thought I'd see Kat that angry, remind me to not get on her bad side," Abbie joked in an attempt to lighten the mood. Once they had made it back to Abbie's apartment, Kat snapped at Jack immediately and Abbie worried that she would get noise complaints from her neighbors.

"It is not a pretty sight," Diamond mused. "Jack and Kat were raised together. For all intents and purposes, they are siblings so I'll let her vent for the both of us. Though it doesn't change the fact his injury is my fault," Diamond said tiredly, clearly frustrated. "Goddesses, I swear it seems like Kat is the only one who doesn't screw up in this band. It's like she was made for this life which is saying something seeing how I was literally born into it."

"Hey now, don't be too hard on yourself. I can't imagine taking a life is ever easy, even if they are someone as messed up as Jezebel," Abbie said in an attempt to make Diamond feel better. However, instead, Diamond's face just showed an even more pained expression. "Want to talk about it?"

"Not much to talk about, I went to subdue her, it failed. After that, I had multiple attempts to bring her down as she clearly posed a threat. Time after time, I didn't take the shot I knew I could have. Because of that Jack nearly lost his life and that's on me," Diamond said as she turned to face Abbie. "The anger I felt wasn't toward Jezebel or Xavier, no, that anger was directed toward myself. There are no replacements for bandmates. Once one of them is gone, the entire band ceases to be operational. If Jack had died, my claim to the throne would have been forfeited," Diamond revealed. "Who would follow a Queen that can't even keep her own band alive? For my mother, it was simple, her bandmates perished long after she claimed the throne and long after she had proven herself. My Father? His band is alive but broken, that alone has caused many to question his ability despite his band being the strongest in the Guild. Frost and Katarina are more valuable to me than any reward a job could possibly offer and yet my hesitation almost cost me everything. We succeeded tonight, but now I realize we still have much to learn," Diamond said before she glanced at the Shield that rested on Abbie's bed. "We got the grimoire, now we let the fully trained thieves handle this."

"Stop while we're ahead, that's a plan I can get behind," Abbie mused. "But will you be alright?"

"She was my first intentional kill," Diamond said quietly. "She will not be the last, either. According to my teacher, it doesn't get easier but you do get better at it."

"That's fuckin' scary."

"Right?" Diamond said with a small smile. "Thank you," Diamond said suddenly. "For stopping me," Diamond clarified. "You were right, if I killed him and left those memories with the civilians then everything that I worked for would have been lost. I would have never forgiven myself if a moment of tunnel vision made me lose everything. Once Kat finishes working on Jack, we will get out of your hair. We have imposed enough. Hopefully, the next job we deal with involves less blood."

"Amen."

"By the way, tomorrow, come to our penthouse. We want to discuss some changes with you concerning our current arrangement," Diamond said before she rolled her eyes when she saw the concerned and slightly fearful expression on Abbie's face. "Kat wasn't kidding, you do jump to the worst conclusions first. Believe me, it's completely beneficial for all of us. This makes the second time you've gotten us out of a jam. You've more than proven yourself to be an asset to me, so I have a proposition I want to make you after a good night's rest." Diamond explained. "But we will deal with that tomorrow, get some rest, Abigail."

*   *   *

San Diego, Magnus Manor

"Really great job you did there, brother, glad to see you made such a difference," Lilia said sarcastically as she held a long golden rod. At the end of the rod was what appeared to be a golden flower that had a green crystal embedded in its center. From the crystal came a green beam of energy that was currently focused on the downed form of Jezebel who bled profusely over the bed. On the floor were the unconscious forms of Samuel and Jebediah. Never had Haylen seen her allies in such a state. "The first day off I have in months, and of course, you screw it up," Lilia muttered as she concentrated on the task of healing Jezebel. "Let's not forget the fact you were bested by rookies again. Are you the heir of House Magnus or a fool?"

"It's not his fault, I watched the recordings, this situation could have been handled if Jezebel hadn't gone AWOL," Haylen said as she gazed down at her fallen teammate. "I've never seen this woman miss or screw around on the job, this behavior of hers was unprecedented and when she wakes up, I will find out why."

"She's branded, nothing more than the property of thief royalty. In this instance, she was never on our side, just a tool of the Midas family. Curse my bleeding heart, I should just let her perish," Lilia muttered as she glared at Haylen. Soon that glare shifted to Xavier. "Not that it matters to you, you're going to forget what happened here as soon as possible. The footage she speaks of, did you destroy it?"

"All of it," Xavier said exasperatedly. "Don't treat me like a novice, I know protocol."

"You know protocol?" Lilia asked and the beam of light disappeared when Jezebel's bleeding stopped. "You could have fooled me!" Lilia snapped while the golden petals at the end of her staff closed around the green crystal. Lilia slammed the bottom of the rod on the ground right before her brother and Haylen's eyes widened slightly at the loud thundering sound that echoed throughout the room. "If you knew protocol I wouldn't have a smart-ass civilian talking to me right now. If you knew protocol, you wouldn't have been bested by the same rookies two times in a row!" Lilia roared as her eyes turned into twin black voids that were filled with stars. Lilia practically growled as she gestured toward the rod. "Tell me, what is this?"

"Your staff," Xavier answered with a grimace.

"And what does it do?"

"Allows a mage to control their magic to its full potential."

"And without it, not just myself but all mages are restricted to the most basic of spells. When a mage's servant and shield are destroyed, that power returns to them to make them stronger. Without your staff to capitalize on this, to draw out the most of this newfound strength, that power is utterly worthless!" Lilia snapped. "You sit there, do something as risky as fighting thieves of all things, without your staff, and expect me to believe you know protocol? Where the hell is your staff!?"

"I'm…making changes to it at the moment so I can't use it just yet," Xavier answered and his sister trembled with barely restrained rage.

"And you still decided to go out to fight? To nearly get yourself killed!? Do you not realize that the bloodline ends with you if you die now?" Lilia asked through gritted teeth. "Enero is wrong, you are too prideful and too foolish to be the Head of House Magnus. You're ill-fit for your position."

"And who would be a better fit? A bastard like you?" Xavier asked with an angered expression. Silence rang out through the room, as Lilia's eyes returned to normal instantly at that remark. For Xavier, it was as if his mind had finally caught up to his mouth and his expression went from one of anger to horror at his own words. "Lilia…"

"Stop," Lilia said quietly as she narrowed her eyes at her brother. "Don't even try to apologize because you meant that," Lilia said as she strolled toward the door. "But know this, I'd rather be the twisted bastard that I am than the failure of a son you turned out to be," Lilia said coldly, "No wonder father tried again," Lilia said with a scoff before she opened the door. Lilia was surprised to see August on the other side.

"Am I interrupting something?" August questioned with a frown.

"No, I'm done here, excuse me while I get back to work on our project," Lilia said as she strolled past August.

"Uncle, about the Shield-" Xavier began only to be stopped when August raised a hand to silence him.

"What matters is that you are okay," August said simply. "Losing the Shield was, well, it was the expected outcome in the end I suppose. In your current state, you make very little difference, Magnus or not," August said and his audible disappointment seemed to hurt Xavier more than any injury he had sustained that evening. "We can only look toward the future. Your failure is in the past, a lesson to be learned from. What matters most now is our civilian friend here."

"Oh, am I allowed to break up this little family moment?" Haylen asked sarcastically. "What the fuck is goin' on here?" Haylen snapped. "What did I witness tonight and will my team be okay?"

"A spit-fire this one is," August said with a chuckle. "My boy, why have you not erased her memories? And what of her companions?"

176

August questioned. The sheer ease in which August made messing with her mind sound, along with everything she saw that night, proved to be more than enough to strike fear even into Haylen's cold heart.

"They were all taken down before anything too unnatural was shown to them. With the exception of the big one, Jebediah. I had to alter his memory of Ja-er-I mean the Frost heir recovering from his nectar. She saw the most but the memory alteration spell isn't working on her," Xavier explained to August who stroked his beard in thought.

"Well perhaps that's the case for you, she is an intelligent woman," August said before raising a shining palm at Haylen. "But allow me to try," August said as he went to move his hand toward Haylen who stepped back apprehensively only to find herself pressed against a wall. Just as he touched her forehead, August's eyes widened as he felt his spell blocked before it dispersed into harmless white particles of light. "What?"

"Like I said it isn't working," Xavier said with a frown which August mirrored as he gazed down upon the confused woman.

"This poses a problem, did the relic play a part with its time in her family's possession?" August wondered to himself. "Doesn't matter, since we can't safely remove her from this secret world of ours now, we'll have to come clean and get her cooperation until I can bring this to the inner circle."

"What are you talkin' about!?" Haylen asked. "Please, just give me my team and let us leave," Haylen pleaded and she cursed how weak her voice sounded.

"In due time but first let me ask my girl, do you believe in magic?" August asked curiously as his eyes glimmered with amusement.

*　　*　　*

Santa Monica, Midas Tower

"So, what did you want to talk to me about?" Abbie asked after Kat met her inside the safe house. Abbie knelt down and pet

Sal on his head after he happily rushed her. "Missed you too, boy," Abbie said as the dog licked her cheek. A whistle from Diamond was enough to get the dog to stop and sit down quietly.

"Kat, this is your job," Diamond said as she made her way to the kitchen where Jack poured her some coffee. Abbie noted that Jack favored his right arm as she figured his left one was still sore from the previous night's events.

"Huh?"

"You're dating her, not us," Jack pointed out. The smirk on his face was infuriating to Kat as she noticed that he was paying her back.

"Oh, come on, you can't get back at me for getting back at you! The cycle will never end!" Kat complained only to be completely ignored by Jack.

"Want some coffee, love?"

"No, I'm fine, had a cup before I came," Abbie said as her suspicious gaze never left the now nervous Kat. "What's all this about?"

"Okay, well, wasn't expecting to be put on the spot like this but uh, move in with us?" Kat said though it sounded more like a question as she handed Abbie a key to the penthouse.

"Smooth," Jack teased while Diamond shook her head in disappointment.

"This is why she's not the grifter," Diamond said with a sigh.

"I don't know, I think she'd do a great job. What woman couldn't say yes to that?" Jack questioned, doing his best not to laugh.

"Okay, can the peanut gallery please shut up? Thanks," Kat said dryly before she turned back to an amused Abbie. "So, what do you say?"

"Well I wouldn't mind, I suppose I could bunk with you but where would I put my equipment?" Abbie asked while Kat looked like something exploded in front of her.

"Wait, you would have slept with me?" Kat asked incredulously. "Quick! Put her bed back!"

"Excuse me?" Abbie asked sounding confused as Jack downed his coffee.

"Alright," Jack said as he started to leave only to get held back by Diamond.

"Stay put, if anything, this is the only way to get her out of the front room and give us our couch back," Diamond muttered before she gestured for them to follow her. "I told you I was refurbishing my study," Diamond said as she opened the door to her study. "What do you think?" Diamond asked as Abbie gasped at the sight. The already beautiful study had been turned into a bedroom with a bed where the desk used to be. The desk had been moved near a window and had multiple monitors resting on it with a computer beneath it. The shelves were filled with books on coding and it had equipment that Abbie realized could come in handy for hacking that ranged from a personal drone to spare hard drives.

"Wait a second," Abbie said as she looked at the contents of the room. Abbie pursed her lips for a moment before she turned to the three thieves that did their best not to make eye contact. "Is this my shit? How did it get here!?"

"Kat," Diamond said as Jack chuckled nervously.

"This is your job."

"Oh, screw you two, don't act like you didn't help!" Kat complained as Abbie's eyes narrowed further.

"Kitten."

"Okay, look, we may have robbed your apartment," Kat said as she put emphasis on the word 'we'. Kat noticed that Abbie didn't look amused.

"How!? It was all there this mornin' when I left!" Abbie said incredulously. "You're tellin' me between the time I left and made it here, you robbed me and set all this up!?"

"We're really good at what we do, love," Jack piped up. "Though thanks for agreeing to stay with us, would have been awkward moving this back."

"You're all unbelievable," Abbie said as she rubbed her temples and fought off a headache. Still, despite her irritation about being robbed, she couldn't help but laugh at the absurdity of the situation. "Well I guess this makes movin' easier," Abbie joked which put the other three at ease. "Still, how did you all manage to set my stuff up correctly?"

"Katarina instructed us," Diamond answered.

"I picked up a thing or two from our dates, you love talking about new tech," Kat said sheepishly which made Abbie's expression soften. "It would be bad if I couldn't do this much by now. We didn't move everything obviously, just the heavy stuff so we'll have to head back to your place and get the rest."

"Still it's a good thing you agreed, now we can move on to something a bit more pressing. Everyone in the band has a job and a role as you know," Diamond began as she gestured to Abbie. "Though you're a civilian if I had to come up with a job for you, it's clearly being a hacker," Diamond explained. "What we want to discuss now, is your role."

"My role?" Abbie asked curiously. "I'm your assistant, ain't I?"

"Yes, and you've performed marvelously which is why it's time for a promotion. From now on you'll be my advisor, my second opinion if you will," Diamond revealed and Abbie was stunned. "You've proven yourself useful and even stopped me from making a very big mistake. Unlike Frost and Kat, in tense situations, you aren't completely affected by my will as they are. The world has changed a lot since either of my parents first became thieves, a boss alone is not viable any longer in my opinion," Diamond explained. "You will be my advisor, which is why I need you here, close, in case something occurs. So, what do you say?"

"I, well, I just hope I don't disappoint you all," Abbie said as Diamond extended her hand. Abbie accepted it with a grin before they shook on it, prepared to continue to work together with a new and strange dynamic to the traditional band system.

"Good, now before we have to go deliver the Shield to my father, we need to talk about your routine," Diamond said. "You lack the abilities we have and that will never change, but as you saw last night these jobs will only get more difficult. There may come a time when you may actually need to be boots on the ground with us," Diamond revealed. "You need to be able to fend for yourself to some degree, at least against other civilians. Kat and Jack will help you work on your body and teach you how to defend yourself, respectively. You will use the private gym in this tower and work with them after we finish our lessons. Understood?"

"Uh, sure?" Abbie said as she figured a little physical conditioning might be good for a worst-case scenario. "A little workout never hurt anybody, right?" Abbie said but soon she shuddered at the mischievous glint in Jack and Kat's eyes.

$$* \quad * \quad *$$

San Diego, Blessings Medical Clinic

"Her injuries were the most severe, so she will have to stay here for a bit longer to recuperate," Lilia, now garbed in a white lab-coat, explained to Haylen's team and Xavier. "It was touch and go for a while but she did manage to pull through, she is definitely a strong woman."

"That's my Lola for you, always crawling her way back up from *al borde de la muerte*," Samuel said softly as he and Jebediah looked down at Jezebel, who had a bloodied bandage over her right eye. "I swear I will get whoever did this."

"Agreed," Jebediah said before he turned to Lilia. "Thank you, doctor."

"Don't mention it, I'll give you all a moment," Lilia said as she made her way to leave the room. However, before Lilia could leave, she stopped when she felt a hand on her shoulder and glanced back to find Haylen.

"Thank you," Haylen said seriously.

"Don't mention it," Lilia said before she departed.

"Jebediah, Samuel, head home. You're off of this job," Haylen said without preamble.

"What? You can't expect us to leave after this!" Samuel said as he gestured to Jezebel.

"I can and you will. Do not forget who is in charge here," Haylen said calmly though her gaze was as hard as stone. "You're both filled with a need for revenge and are no longer thinkin' objectively. Go home, rest, and forget about this. I will finish the contract, all I need to do is set up some security systems as originally planned."

"But-"

"Haylen, be reasonable," Jebediah interrupted Samuel. "I've watched over you since you were but a girl and you want me to leave you alone after some punks did this to Jezebel?"

"Yes, that is exactly what I want and what you will do so long as you're under my employ," Haylen said matter-of-factly. "Mr. Magnus and I will finish this and once things have simmered down, I'll head back down south and pick you all up."

"Really? And what can this rich kid do that we can't?" Samuel challenged as he glared at Xavier who simply raised an eyebrow in response. Xavier had no idea what he did to upset the smuggler.

"He has more power, resources, and influence than the both of you combined," Haylen said dryly. "This is not the time to start a dick measuring contest you won't win. Need I remind you it is because of him that you all made it to this hospital in one piece? Before you snap at the man who saved Jezebel, show some respect," Haylen said coldly before she headed toward the door. "Mr. Magnus, we need to discuss the next step."

"Agreed," Xavier said as he left with her. Once they exited the room, they heard a loud bang which more than likely meant one of the men had punched a wall. "Are you sure you want to keep them out of this? Unlike you, I can deal with their memories with ease."

"Yes, but like I said in there, their minds aren't in the right place, they'll do more harm to themselves than good for us," Haylen explained.

"You care about your subordinates."

"I'm simply protectin' my assets," Haylen said and Xavier rolled his eyes as he knew the concern that she had shown the previous night told an entirely different story. "Good idea, movin' them to this clinic, by the way. It stopped a lot of unnecessary questions. Does your sister actually work here or was that some act?"

"She doesn't just work here, she owns this place. Despite her... charming...demeanor, she means it when she says she has a bleeding heart. She can't stand the sight of someone in pain," Xavier said softly and Haylen could tell that he was lost in some memory or another. "Speaking of her, I apologize that you had to see that...altercation...

last night. I was stressed and didn't have the patience I normally have available when dealing with her."

"Stop, I couldn't care less about your family problems, especially when it seems I have my own to deal with once again," Haylen muttered as they found a more remote place in the clinic where they could speak freely. "It's about that group's fourth member."

"What!? Fourth?" Xavier asked completely thrown off by Haylen's statement. "What do you mean fourth?"

"Are you an idiot? Think, if all three of them were busy with my team, then who the hell was attackin' our systems?" Haylen questioned and Xavier paused as he realized she had a point. In fact, the more he thought about it, the more the heist at his own business made sense.

"Thieves' are known for their willingness to hire civilians for jobs."

"Yes, and the way I was attacked was similar, too similar, to the work of my wayward sister," Haylen explained. "She's younger than me and has a record of being rebellious and hanging with the wrong crowds. How someone so brilliant can be so stupid, I'll never know," Haylen said with a scoff. "What I do know, is that she bit off more than she can chew this time. If they're willin' to kill for what they want, then that makes them far more dangerous than that last rag-tag group of people she worked with. What you've told me about this… Thieves' Guild, only proves it."

"I see, if you're right then this does pose a more immediate issue," Xavier said, his voice deathly serious. "The mark of the thief is only supposed to be borne for short amounts of time, long enough for one job. If she's been wearing it for as long as I believe then she is in danger of having her entire identity changed when they remove it," Xavier revealed to a now startled Haylen. "Once removed, it gives the civilian false memories that cover the day prior to when it was placed up until the moment of removal. A week or two of false memories is one thing, but months? Her mind could break from that," Xavier explained with a grimace. "Band 13, are you truly that cruel or just clueless?"

"Forget about that, how do we remove it?" Haylen asked immediately. "We need to get rid of it before it does too much damage."

"It may already be too late, if it gets removed now, there is a good chance she could become a vegetable," Xavier said before he suddenly found himself held tightly by his collar by an irate Haylen.

"You mean to tell me you don't have a spell or whatever that can save her?" Haylen asked angrily while Xavier just gave her a sad look as he shook his head. "Don't fuck with me, Magnus!"

"It is not my attention to do so, I'm simply telling you the truth!" Xavier said honestly. "Even the memory alteration spell is warded off by the mark. It's a divine tool, a weak one, but divine nonetheless which means it can't be tampered with by just any magic," gray eyes mixed with blue as Haylen tried in vain to find any semblance of deceit. When Haylen found none, she simply released the Mage with a curse.

"God damn it!"

"I am sorry," Xavier said sincerely as he felt true sorrow for the woman before him. "You really love her, don't you?" Xavier asked and he noted how she didn't even try to hide her pain as she did with her team earlier.

"She hates me with every fiber of her being and I won't lie, I despise her at times myself," Haylen said quietly as she looked up at Xavier. Haylen's eyes shone with tears that her pride refused to let fall. "But we're family, and a Stone never turns their back on family."

"I see," Xavier said quietly as he thought about his father and his love for family. "Then let me promise you this, I'll do everything I can to find a way to fix this. My younger brother is on that band, by blood his sins are my sins and I will do my best to cleanse them," Xavier swore. "I'll wait for you outside and give you a moment to collect your thoughts," Xavier said quietly as he left the woman alone in the corridor. After a few moments of silence, she collected herself and started to follow him only to stop when she heard someone behind her. When she turned around, she spotted August behind her.

"That boy is a passionate one, too much like his father without the skill to back it up," August said with a sigh. "Forgive my nephew, he did not mean to give you false information, he is simply too young to know how this secret world of ours operates."

"What are you talkin' about?" Haylen questioned as she looked at the large man suspiciously.

"The mark of the thief that your sister bears," August clarified. "It can be removed easily, that is, if the band who placed it upon her is destroyed."

"But about her mind? Won't that break it?"

"No, she will retain her memories, a fail-safe that was placed on the mark. This way if a band was destroyed or in danger of it, they could send a civilian back to the Guild to explain what happened. If this band is destroyed, your sister's mark will vanish and her memories will still be intact. And with the mark's disappearance..." August trailed off as realization began to dawn on Haylen.

"...Then your spell won't be warded off and you can fix her memories safely," Haylen whispered. "No," Haylen said suddenly as she shook her head. "If your spell doesn't work on me, it won't work on her either then. We lived with that relic for a while."

"My girl, that spell didn't work but that doesn't mean I don't have stronger ones that will," August said with a boisterous laugh. "They just require a bit more time to prepare."

"Destroy the band...that means, the three of them will have to die, right?"

"No, because the greatest weakness of a band is their greatest strength," August said as he walked toward her. "If you destroy one member of the band, the entire thing collapses like a house of cards. This works in our favor seeing how one of them has a lot of popularity amongst the civilians so losing her may draw too much attention. Xavier's brother can also be freed from the insidious grasp of the thieves and return to House Magnus where he belongs. Only the least important one has to fall, the no name," August said with a dark glint in his eyes. "Get rid of her, and you save your sister. One life, for your sister's, a small sacrifice if I do say so myself."

"How do we even know that they haven't removed it already?" Haylen questioned quietly as the idea began to appeal more and more to her.

"Trust me, those monsters will need her skill for at least one more job," August said and there was no doubt in his words. "What do you say? Want to help me out and save your family?"

"Tell me more," Haylen said as a dark resolve overcame her.

"That's my girl," August said as he placed a hand on her shoulder. As they talked, neither noticed Lilia at the end of the hall nor the look of anger that quickly appeared on her face.

CHAPTER 13

· · · · · · ●●●●●●●●● · · · · ·

SOLSTICE

Santa Monica, Midas Tower

"You could hold back a little, you know?" Abbie said sarcastically as she held the side of her face. Jack chuckled as he helped Abbie up to her feet before they both moved to their sides of the ring. It had been a very painful month for Abbie since she moved in with the thieves. Kat and Jack had not taken it easy on Abbie as they trained her to her absolute limits on a daily basis. Abbie was positive that she had somehow awoken a sadistic side to Kat who was surprisingly merciless in how she trained Abbie almost to the point of cardiac arrest. "Tough love" is what Kat called it one day after Abbie woke up after she passed out in the middle of an intense session. It didn't help Abbie that Kat and Jack were more than willing to share their nectar with her which meant they could push her far beyond what civilians were capable of. Abbie wanted to quit, but she couldn't because despite the pain and agony, she began to show positive results.

"I am holding back, love," Jack informed Abbie. "But our enemies won't. I'm trying to go at your pace but you need to help me help you," Jack said as he watched her raise her fists. "Want to get a sip of nectar or keep going? Believe it or not, you are getting better."

"Right, because you totally didn't just lay me out with one punch."

"Well, he did," Kat piped up from the sidelines. "But you lasted way longer this time, thirty seconds at least."

"That's thirty times longer than her first session," Jack said with a grin. "Baby steps, love," Jack said before they began to spar once more. Jack went on the offensive and rained down blow after blow upon Abbie whose arms trembled from each impact as she attempted to block his attacks. Abbie realized that she couldn't keep this up forever and managed to side-step his next punch. Abbie conjured up a month's worth of frustration and punched Jack in his jaw with all her might. Unfortunately for her, all her might wasn't enough to do more than make his head move to the side slightly. Jack grinned before he slammed a punch into Abbie and knocked her back down onto her rear. "See, baby steps," Jack said as he offered her a hand while Kat cheered.

"Yeah! See, you actually hit him!" Kat said as Abbie looked at her own hand in shock before she let Jack pull her up to her feet.

"How about we take five, love?"

"Sounds good," Abbie said tiredly as Kat walked over and handed Abbie her flask. Abbie shuddered as she felt the healing effects of the nectar course through her body and replenish her stamina.

"By the way, Jack, Christmas is coming up soon, right? What do you want for your birthday?" Kat asked curiously.

"Your birthday's comin' up?" Abbie questioned curiously.

"Yes, sorry, did I forget to mention it? Happens all the time with it being on the holiday, it's a bad habit," Jack said apologetically. "Honestly, a nice dinner with you, Diamond, and Abbie along with Roderick and Vivi would be perfect. I want to experience what it is like to be all together for it."

"Do you all not normally spend your birthday or holidays together?"

"Oh, we do, but my curse stopped me from truly appreciating it. This is why this year it will be my first time actually experiencing the so-called warmth that comes from a family," Jack explained and that was quite possibly the saddest thing Abbie had ever heard from him. Even Kat, though she knew Jacks feelings on the matter, looked a bit moved by his simple want for a gift. Abbie was just touched he considered her important enough to be present.

"Sounds easy enough," Kat said after a moment. "I'll talk to Diamond about it when she gets back from her old man's place."

"Hope she isn't there because of somethin' bad," Abbie said only for Kat to wave off her concerns.

"Nah, he probably just wanted a visit from her, that's all," Kat reassured her. "Alright, that's it for today Jack. I need to work on her flexibility," Kat said and Abbie shuddered when she saw the sadistic glint in Kat's eyes.

*   *   *

Hollywood, Midas Manor

"Any luck on deciphering the grimoire?" Diamond asked Roderick as they sat in the garden.

"Unfortunately, no, the Knights' Order seemed to make sure that its secrets remained just that, secret. Even when we contract civilians, the grimoire reacts to their mark which renders their efforts useless. Only unmarked civilians have a chance at deciphering it and even then, if the grimoire would deem them unworthy, they too will be turned away. Such an enchantment is expected of their Lady."

"Their Lady?"

"We have our Goddesses who formed our Guild, the Knights have their Lady who constructed their Order. The Lady was the one who made their grimoire, knew all the Order's secrets and she would protect them as much as she could. Being unable to crack her code should honestly be expected. I had half a mind to give the grimoire over to a contact within the Tribe. At least with them neutral, we wouldn't have to worry about a new Knights' Order helping the Circle. Unfortunately, an act like that would no doubt cost you the throne so I've decided to lock it away. Perhaps when you ascend you can help a new Order form, but enough of that, I did not call you here to talk about things that no longer matter to you."

"Then, what did you need to see me for? You made it sound serious."

"It is," a new voice, thick with a French accent, spoke up sending a chill down Diamond's spine. Diamond turned and saw an elderly woman behind them garbed in a black gown with a matching black lace collar around her neck. Her gray hair was worn up and her cold blue gaze seemed to pin Diamond in place.

"Headmistress Corday?"

"Your Highness, we need to speak about your...performance lately," Corday said as she took a seat across from them. "When I took you under my wing, you were on track to be my best student along with young Akira. You two have the potential to surpass even the likes of Julia and Isabelle, yet while Akira is still continuing on strong, you are falling behind. You've become distracted, and today I wish to know why," Corday said as she cut straight to the point. "I understand you took on a private task for your father about a month ago, it was then that your decline began. Tell me, what is it that has knocked you off track? You may be royalty, but that is irrelevant until you sit on that throne. I will cut you from the program and focus my time solely on Akira if you continue to waste my time. I demand excellence and have no time to spare for those who do not give it their all."

"Diamond?" Roderick asked with a frown. "I had a feeling something was off, but I wanted to step back and let you handle it. Did something happen on that job?"

"There...was an altercation," Diamond finally answered as she looked up at them. "There was a civilian sniper I failed to subdue that shot down Frost. I didn't handle it well and killed her," Diamond explained. Corday frowned to herself while Roderick looked at his daughter in shock. He was surprised that she would keep her first intentional kill away from him.

"I see," Corday said after a moment. "It is always a rough time when an assassin gets their first kill, especially for a first-year."

"But it's not my first kill, you all know that," Diamond said quietly which made both her father and her mentor look at her sadly.

"Diamond, what happened on your birthday was not your fault," Roderick began carefully. "No one expected your curse to activate so early. You had at least another year before you would have even been fitted for your glove. Those deaths are not on you."

"Tell that to their families who think they were lost in a terrorist attack," Diamond said with a scoff. "They don't even know the truth."

"My King, if you could give us a moment," Corday asked and Roderick looked unsure for the briefest of moments before he rose from his seat. If anyone could help his daughter with this it would be her mentor, unlike her, he was not an assassin.

"I leave her in your care," Roderick said before he left.

"Your Highness, I cannot cast judgment upon you, I am no Goddess. I can't tell you whether you were right or wrong with your recent kill or if you are guilty for what happened on your birthday," Corday began as she held Diamond's gaze. Those golden eyes held a storm of emotions that Diamond's face refused to show. "However, you will be Queen one day. You need to be able to do all of your jobs without error. Killing will never get easier but you will get better at it, an unfortunate truth in our line of work," Corday explained. "So, let me ask you the same thing I asked your mother when she dealt with this. What does the throne mean to you?"

"Everything," Diamond said without hesitation.

"And it's something you cannot achieve without your band," Corday explained. "Now let me ask you this, what is the duty of those who sit upon that throne?"

"To protect the Guild."

"And what is the duty of the Guild?"

"To protect the world."

"Exactly, and the Guild can't do that without a Queen and you cannot become Queen without your band. Yes, you killed someone but you also did your duty as heir to the throne," Corday said reassuringly. "I'll give you the same warning I gave your mother. If you think you can become Queen, especially as an assassin, without getting blood on your hands then you better give up now before it's too late."

"I will die before I give up my throne," Diamond said firmly as Corday stood up.

"Then you better get ready to do your job," Corday said as she looked down at her student. "Each kill is a lesson. Learn from your opponent. Take this experience and turn it into power," Corday advised. "Answer me this, honor or glory?"

"Excuse me?"

"Which do you live your life for, honor or glory?" Corday asked. "What kind of person you'll be depends on how you answer that question. One who lives for glory will only find despair, but one who lives for honor will lead a life of true fulfillment. The weak choose glory, but the strong choose honor. I asked your mother that and it paved the way for the rest of her reign. I want you to think on it, and decide not just what kind of Queen you wish to be but also what kind of person," Corday instructed before she left Diamond alone with her thoughts.

*   *   *

Santa Monica, Midas Tower

When Diamond made it back to the safe house she was greeted by the sight of Kat, Jack, and Abbie watching a holovid while Sal rolled around on the floor. They all gave their greetings when they saw her making her way toward them.

"So, how was it?" Kat asked as she handed Diamond a bowl of popcorn.

"Enlightening," Diamond said before she looked at the projection skeptically. "What the hell are you all watching?"

"Some movie Abbie picked out," Kat answered while Jack chuckled a bit.

"You were right Kat, she does watch too many trashy romance movies," Jack joked as he grabbed some of the popcorn.

"Oh, shut up, it's a classic," Abbie defended as she nudged him.

"Yeah, classic trash," Jack joked. "Did Roderick have any luck on cracking the grimoire yet?"

"No, and he's done as well," Diamond answered. "He too knows when to stop. We stopped the mages from getting their hands on it which is good enough."

"Yeah, but it's so weird, like why go through the trouble of getting the damn thing if it can't be read? If you want to stare at an unreadable code, you might as well look at a picture of it online or something," Kat complained. It was then that both Diamond and Abbie froze while Jack frowned in thought. "What?" Kat asked hesitantly as she saw the looks on her friends' faces. "Did I say something weird?"

"No, but you brought up a valid point," Diamond said as she stood up and began to pace. "Why go through all that trouble for something he didn't even need? Better yet, how did he even know that the Shield was the grimoire, to begin with?" Diamond asked as she narrowed her eyes. "What exactly was the source of his information that even got this plan of his started to begin with? Not only that but this was no small plan, this was a game changer, why would he hire civilians for something this big?"

"I thought it was to force thieves to hold back," Abbie said only for Diamond to shake her head.

"But that doesn't make sense, you need to understand August isn't his name, it's his title," Diamond revealed. "He's one of the twelve Arch-Mages that makes up the mages' inner circle, their governing force. For mages, your birth date isn't something to take lightly, it truly does define who you are. With each seat corresponding to one of the twelve months, you only have a chance at the seat that corresponds with the month you were born in."

"But what are you gettin' at?" Abbie questioned. "That he wouldn't hire civilians because he was born in August?"

"Exactly, he's a Leo which means he's prideful to a fault. It's how we knew Xavier would be lurking around at the gallery," Jack explained. "August has no history of ever being fond of civilians, this plan would have given him no small amount of prestige. For him to trust your sister's team with something this vital, in hindsight, it really doesn't add up."

"Personally, I don't get why they believe in astrology so much. Maybe it has something to do with their magic. I mean Vivi told me that I'm a Gemini, but I'm anything but two-faced," Kat said with a shrug, though Abbie gave her a pointed look that made her wilt slightly. "Most of the time," Kat amended sheepishly. "Still, what do you think he needed the grimoire for?"

"A likely scenario would be that the grimoire would have made his plans easier," Jack began. "But whatever his current source of information is, it is more than enough to get him what he needs."

"So why bother with it at all?" Kat asked still confused.

"Wait," Abbie began as she got their attention. "Let's assume this source of information he has is a person, like a former Knights' Order member or someone close enough. Say he has them hostage and is prying them for the info, which adds up with what you're saying. The last bit of information he needed wasn't given to him so he searched for the grimoire instead."

"Likely, no, very likely," Diamond muttered. "The Order is destroyed but surely there are at least some survivors. If he wants to resurrect the Order, he would definitely go to them first before looking for their grimoire. Still, if he couldn't get this last bit of information out of whoever it is, why give up the grimoire so easily?"

"Like Kat said, he doesn't need it. He just needs a picture online. The code has always been available to him," Jack explained. "What he needs, I'm assuming, is something to crack it."

"Holy shit," Abbie said as she suddenly shot up from her seat. "I'm so fuckin' stupid!" Abbie exclaimed before she rushed to her room and left three worried thieves in her wake. They quickly followed after her and watched her search through files on her computer. "When lookin' through August's notes, he had a folder labeled P.A.," Abbie said as she brought up the folder. "But I ignored it because it was empty."

"So what use is it?" Diamond questioned with a frown not sure why an empty folder was so important.

"It just occurred to me that there is a good chance he made this folder beforehand, he didn't have a chance to fill it with what he wanted," Abbie said as she bit her lip nervously, obviously frightened by the thought of whatever could have been planned to go in that folder. "P.A., or should I say Project Athena," Abbie said before she faced the thieves. "It was a minor project really, little more than an app that would be used as a universal translator for P.I.'s smartphones to give them an edge over Hattori Tech in the market. However, Hattori Tech beat them to the market with their next generation of phones that came with an advanced artificial intelligence. At least that's what they said but it wasn't real A.I. It was just a complex voice command system," Abbie explained. "P.I. responded by attempting to make their own true A.I. that would come with the universal translating properties of the app and an anti-virus software to help protect the owner's privacy. An A.I. made with each phone that would break down the barriers of language both spoken and written in real-time. That's all it was supposed to be."

"What happened?" Diamond questioned as Abbie grimaced.

"People," Abbie said dryly. "The head of the R&D department realized he could make a pretty penny off of it if he could get it to some buyers before limitations could be placed on the A.I. You see, the thing about Athena was that it worked too well. It wasn't just language, it was patterns, code, you name it. Not only that but whenever Athena's defenses were attacked, it would fend off the attack before changing its own code so that the same method never worked twice. It got to the point where it could only be breached directly through its servers. What started off as a way to bring people together became one of the biggest threats to them. If it was allowed to fall into the wrong hands, the destruction would be immeasurable. Imagine, nuclear launch codes available on a whim. Anyone's private information given to you..." Abbie trailed off before she snapped her fingers. "...just like that. A whistle was blown on the project and when the head of P.I., Enero Prospero, found out he shut down the project and removed the R&D team," Abbie said as she rubbed her temples. "Maybe when the grimoire was made, only certain civilians could read it but times have changed. If anything can crack that code, it's Athena."

"How do you know so much about this?" Diamond asked suspiciously. "This doesn't sound like anything made public or something you could just stumble upon even as a hacker."

"I know so much because I'm the idiot who made it," Abbie revealed. "Fresh out of college I got a job with them, my dream job I thought. I made Project Athena to help people but my superior had other ideas."

"So, you blew the whistle and got blacklisted," Kat said quietly which made Abbie nod.

"Yeah, my ass of a superior didn't take kindly to me cuttin' his payday short so he along with some of my so-called colleagues got me blacklisted as if gettin' fired by Enero wasn't bad enough," Abbie said sarcastically. "It wasn't all bad, nearly immediately after, I met Alice. She was the leader of a group of hackers that were just trying to do right by the people. She stumbled across what happened and offered me a place to be me and use my talents for good."

"Wonderland," Diamond realized. "We all know you were affiliated with them in some way, that program around your neck is incriminating enough. If your ex was the leader, be honest now, just how high up the ladder were you? It's obvious that your past affects all of us now."

"Second in command," Abbie said with a sad smile. Diamond frowned as Abbie's uncanny ability to adapt to a life of crime suddenly made sense. Abbie had already been a criminal, she practically led a group of cyber terrorists. Kat and Jack just looked at Abbie in surprise. "She saved me from a dark place, she was my beacon, my reason for existing. I loved her so much despite all of her secrets which each probably had a dozen secrets of their own. Even now I reckon Alice wasn't even her real name and I was as close to her as you could get," Abbie said with a pitiful laugh. "I rose through their ranks quickly, believing in their cause. The third world war in 2032 wasn't caused by countries, it was caused by corporations. Privatized militaries ran amok, a few small countries completely erased, and for what? Increased stock prices and access to raw materials they had no right to. Even now, a country's banner is just for show. True power and loyalty fall under a brand logo."

"Abbie…" Kat said softly, caught off guard by the fire in Abbie's eyes. Genuine anger was an emotion they had yet to see on Abbie. Gone was their civilian tag-along and in her place was a woman that fought and sacrificed for a cause she still believed in.

"Look at the world now after the war," Abbie continued with visible disgust on her face. "The middle-class was nearly destroyed and you either have or have not. In response, most countries put most of their military spending into healthcare, subsidizing it to the point where people across the economic spectrum can get life-altering surgery on a whim. Crime rates have dropped drastically, but only because half the shit that used to be illegal no longer is."

"They're distracting the world with pleasure," Jack murmured.

"Exactly. Governments don't want the people to pay attention to the fact it's the corporations with the power and not them. People today can change whatever they dislike about themselves on a whim. Recreational drugs? Sex? On average a five to ten-minute walk to get either and I'm pretty sure both have coupons now. Instant gratification stops people from looking at the big picture, from seeing how fucked up our survival as a species is and corporations know this. Corporations that aren't limited to the same rules and regulations as the governments are on a global scale. Corporations that don't care because by the time it matters, they believe they'll already be dead. Do not get me wrong, there are good ones like Hattori Tech who use this power for good, but there are many more like the Drakenova Corp. that don't and that's what Wonderland fought against. Those who even after the Great War, still continue to make the same mistakes."

"And you succeeded to a certain degree anyway," Diamond said after a while. "I remember many a night I'd overhear my father complaining that you were doing the Guild's work for them when it concerned corrupt civilians."

"Glad to hear that," Abbie said softly before she wiped her eyes. "We did so much, tried so hard, because a fourth world war will be the last. The small countries are gone which only leaves the big ones and the world can't survive that. We were in the middle of exposing unethical human testing of military-grade augments by the Drakenova Corp. when Alexei got fixated on me. When he killed Alice, that was the start of Wonderland's fall," Abbie said as a dark expression crossed her face. "The Drakenova Corp. hired Haylen and her team shortly after. That bitch destroyed it all, she tore my new family apart and had the nerve to tell me to be grateful that she didn't get me arrested," Abbie spit out as she clenched her fists until her knuckles turned white. "She destroys all I hold dear, and almost did it again in that last job," Abbie said as Jack reflexively rubbed his shoulder. "We beat her last time but that woman is sinister, especially when driven. You killin' Jezebel ain't somethin' she will let slide," Abbie told Diamond. "But enough of all that right now. To get back on topic, we know what he needs now, he needs Athena which should still be held up in the P.I. headquarters in Silicon Valley."

"Then it's already too late, love, there is no way he hasn't gotten it by now."

"I wouldn't be so sure, Frost," Diamond said, a thoughtful expression on her face. "We all know that the council is a mess at the moment, they get nothing done and it's a miracle we haven't been destroyed yet. Have you ever wondered why we haven't been beaten if we're so disorganized?"

"It's because the Circle is just as screwed up as we are!" Kat realized.

"Exactly, this is probably why he let us take the grimoire in the end," Diamond said which made Abbie frown as she put the pieces together.

"Fear is a powerful incentive, thanks to us stealin' the grimoire he has a reason to scare the Circle into givin' him whatever he needs to stop us, includin' Athena," Abbie said quietly. "That bastard played us."

"Still, it's been a month so like I said, shouldn't they have it already?" Jack asked with a frown.

"No," Diamond answered confidently. "According to my father, the inner circle only gathers four times a year. Once per season, during a solstice or an equinox when magic is most potent. It's tradition, and mages will never break tradition. Whether that's because of arrogance or a crippling need to believe they have order, I don't know. What I do know is that we have until the winter solstice to stop August. The only way to do that is to steal Project Athena."

"I thought we were pulling out," Jack said with a frown.

"We were, but we have no choice now. We are too short on time," Diamond said before Abbie raised her phone and showed them the date.

"She's right," Abbie said with a grim expression on her face. "Today is the solstice, the meeting could be goin' on right now for all we know," Abbie said and Jack cursed. "We have no preparation at all, you really want to do this?" Abbie asked Diamond whose expression betrayed a rare moment of hesitation. Soon, Diamond's expression hardened when she recalled Corday's words from earlier.

"I-no-we have to do our duty," Diamond told her band. "We have to go, Abbie watch our backs," Diamond ordered before she and Jack left the room, Kat right behind them.

"Kitten," Abbie said, not sure why a feeling of dread began to fill up inside of her as Kat stopped at the doorway. "Be safe and come back to me."

"I will," Kat said with a smile and for a brief moment, Abbie saw Alice standing where Kat did. "Just trust me, everything will work out in the end," Kat continued before she left to catch up with her band. Despite Kat's reassurance, Abbie could not shake the feeling that something bad was going to happen.

*   *   *

San Diego, Magnus Manor

"Yes, don't worry, everything is going as you said it would. There is a slight delay on my end but that will be dealt with after the meeting," August said as he spoke on his smartphone. "I will see you there, June," August said before he hung up. August then shook his head pitifully at the sight of a blonde woman chained against a wall. Her body was covered in scars as she glared up at him weakly with blue eyes that seemed as deep as the ocean. Even while blood spilled from her porcelain skin, the woman showed no fear. "Now, now, my Lady. This would be much easier and less painful if you just worked with me and told me where the sword is. We've been at this for months and I'm starting to lose my patience."

"I will not yield!" the Lady shouted before she spit blood on his face. August sighed and felt his irritation grow as he wiped it off. "Heir of Mordred and Morgana, your twisted bloodline just doesn't know when to stop!" the Lady said as she glared at him viciously. "I will die a thousand deaths before I ever let you rebuild my Order!"

"Well, that may be tested sooner than you think. Now stop yelling. You know no one can hear you scream in here thanks to my enchantments," August said before he glanced back toward the door when he heard it open. August smiled as he saw an emotionless Lilia enter the room. "Ah, great, you're here. Try to get some more information from our guest here, will you? If you don't get me any results, well, you're probably used to the routine by now. I'll do to you what has been done to her, ten-fold," August said with a bright smile while Lilia tried and failed to suppress her fear.

"You're a monster," the Lady sneered.

"Sticks and stones my Lady, sticks and stones, now if you excuse me, tonight is going to be an eventful evening," August said happily. "Tonight will be the night, I finally win!" August said before he disappeared in a blue flash. Silence echoed throughout the study as Lilia approached the Lady, her staff already in hand. Tears fell from the Lady's eyes as Lilia raised her staff toward her. Just knowing what Lilia planned to do seemed to cause her visible pain.

"Stop," the Lady pleaded as Lilia began to heal her wounds. "If he finds out you're helping me again he'll do far worse than last time."

"It's fine, healing is my specialty. Once his torture is over, I'll patch myself up again," Lilia tried to say nonchalantly even as she choked back a sob of her own. *"Curse my bleeding heart,"* Lilia chanted quietly. *"The things I would give to care as little as he. Yet until then, let your pain be mine."* The effects of Lilia's spell were instant as wounds vanished from the Lady's body and reappeared on her own. "I've heard about you, you know. They say you see eons into the future. Some say you are as great as Merlin, as strong as the Goddesses of the thieves combined."

"And you wish to know how August captured me?" the Lady asked knowingly.

"I wish to know why you let him," Lilia corrected. "But you knew that."

"I just wanted to hear you say it," the Lady admitted as her blue eyes shone brightly. "The big picture, I am cursed to see it for all of eternity. This moment of suffering pales in comparison to the bliss it will lead to. He can do to me what he wishes because it will all lead to his downfall and the downfall of his treacherous allies."

"Is this really the best way? Is this pain worth it?"

"Yes, but this pain serves to humble me and help me relate to the pain of you mortals," the Lady answered. "We are so vastly different after all, though you may be the one mortal that is the most similar to myself. A question of my own. Why do you use that spell in particular, surely a skilled healer like you can mend wounds in a less barbaric way?"

"It's a spell an old friend of mine helped me develop, something that is truly mine after so much has been stolen from me," Lilia explained with a faraway look in her eyes. "It's also my way to pay for my sins, I suppose. I have to hurt those I love to protect them, in a way this helps me understand the pain I cause them."

"Hurting yourself is not the answer, girl," the Lady said quietly. "This will not give you back the control over your life you seek."

"Then what will?"

"Redemption."

"There is no redeeming the things I've done or the things I've had done to me!" Lilia snapped and the Lady only continued to look at her with eyes filled with sorrow. Lilia took a moment to calm herself and began to heal her new wounds after the Lady was healthy once more. "Answer me one question, how will he die?"

"Torn apart by a Cerberus," the Lady answered which made Lilia chuckle bitterly.

"If you wish not to tell me, so be it," Lilia said with a sneer. "Just don't take me for a fool, your Order killed the only Cerberus."

"I know, which makes his end that much more ironic," the Lady said as her eyes twinkled with mischief. "Imagine me, saved by the thing I had killed!" the Lady said with a laugh that made Lilia snort. "This Cerberus is different, this one will be born from that fool's mistakes. I'll also tell you one more thing for free," the Lady began as her expression softened while her eyes burned with a fire Lilia found herself hypnotized by. "You will be great, redemption is not lost to you. I know because I have been waiting a very long time to meet you. So, persevere a bit longer because tonight a Cerberus will be born."

CHAPTER 14

· · · · · ·●●●●●●●●●● · · · · ·

THE BROKEN DOLL

Mages' Circle, Central Chamber

The innermost chamber of the Mage's Circle was a cold and empty snow-filled room made of stone. The chamber was illuminated by moonlight that shone through a massive open skylight. The moonlight intensified as the time passed and melted the snow which revealed a massive twelve-pointed star of the Mage's Circle. In each point of the star there was a different colored crystal that each began to shine. The moonlight began to focus on a transparent orb embedded in the middle of the star. This created a beam of pure moonlight that washed away the shadows of the chamber. One by one each of the twelve crystals surrounding the beam of light began to glow until twelve ethereal figures appeared above them, each figure the color of their respective crystal. With his image forged from a golden light, August stood proudly as he swept his gaze over the other eleven Arch-Mages. It was with a friendly smile, that August spoke first.

"Greetings my comrades, we have much to discuss," August began as his eyes focused on a male figure that was forged from a blue light. "Especially us, Enero."

*   *   *

Silicon Valley, Prosperity Industries Headquarters

"Something feels...wrong," Kat said quietly as they walked through the surprisingly vacant building that was apparently in the middle of reconstruction. "This all seems too easy."

"You feel it too then?" Jack asked with a frown. "Not sure about you, but my 'it's-a-trap' senses are tingling."

"Same here but we can't leave here without Project Athena," Diamond said with a frown. "Stone, where is it?"

"It should still be shackled down in the R&D department which is directly below your current position," Abbie informed them. *"Just hurry, somethin' about this is rubbin' me the wrong way."*

"Yeah," Kat agreed. "Come on, the faster we do this, the faster we get out of here," Kat said before they went off to make their way toward the R&D department of the massive building.

*   *   *

China, Hong Kong

Meifeng smiled to herself as she poured herself a cup of tea inside of a luxurious apartment that she shared with her father. Meifeng looked up from her task when she saw her father enter the room.

"I am going to train Rose and Jack if he shows up, are you okay on your own?" Master Li questioned which made her giggle.

"Yes, father, I'm a big girl," Meifeng joked.

"Yes, but I still worry," Master Li admitted before he narrowed his eyes at one of the five guards he had placed in the apartment. "Watch over her with your lives," Master Li said in a way that sent a chill down their spines.

"You're running late," Meifeng reminded him with a small smile. Master Li quickly bid her a farewell before he departed for the Guild. Once he was gone, one of the guards waited until the others were out of sight before they made their way to Meifeng. The guard whispered something to her quietly which made her smile fall. "I see, well it's a good thing I made this then," Meifeng said as she picked up her cup and made her way to her room. "I'm feeling a bit unwell, I will be in my room for a bit," Meifeng told her guards before she went into her room and locked the door behind her. Meifeng knelt down on her mat and she looked at a small statue of a hooded woman that was in the front of her room. With practiced ease, Meifeng pulled up a nearby floorboard and grasped a ceremonial dagger that was hidden beneath it. Meifeng reached inside of her sleeve and she pulled out a golden flask. She quickly poured a sip of it into the cup of tea and placed it down. Without hesitation, Meifeng used the blade to slice her left palm swiftly. She stared at the wound for a moment before she raised her injured hand over the cup. As the dark red liquid fell from her hand to her cup, black pooled into the whites of her eyes. Meifeng gazed at the statue as she pushed the cup toward it while her irises turned an electric purple. "Laverna, darkest of the divine triumvirate, I present to you an offering forged from blood and nectar and plead that you'll hear my humble request," Meifeng prayed as she bowed before the cup even as her wound continued to bleed. "Send someone to watch over and keep my only student alive. As payment, I give you all that I am," Meifeng said quietly. A moment passed before the contents of the cup drained from inside of it and vanished into thin air. "Thank you, my Goddess. Your divine presence humbles me."

* * *

San Diego, Magnus Manor

As Xavier and Faith talked happily in her room, both siblings found themselves startled when Lilia abruptly entered the room. Lilia's face was exhausted and her clothes were stained by her blood.

"*Sleep,*" Lilia chanted as she waved a hand toward Faith. A small blast of gold magic fired from her hand and pelted Faith in her chest.

Immediately Faith was rendered unconscious as gold dust floated in the air from the impact.

"Lilia!? What-" Xavier stopped when he took in his sister's state. "What's wrong?" Xavier asked as he quickly made his way toward her.

"You need to save him!"

"What? Save who?" Xavier questioned as he held her in his arms.

"Jack," Lilia said as she held him tightly by his collar. "I can't do it anymore, I'm not strong enough to protect you all by myself any longer," Lilia said as tears fell from her eyes. "You're stronger than me now, right? You have to go and save him, August is going to kill him!"

"What!? Uncle!? He-"

"He's not what you think! It's just an act, he's a monster, Xavier!" Lilia exclaimed. "I know because he's my father!" Xavier looked at her in horror. The implications of that sentence alone ran rampant in his head and made his stomach churn. "Our mother…was not the saint you think she was, Xavier."

"You're lying!"

"What would I gain!?" Lilia snapped and Xavier tensed as he realized that she would gain nothing from this. "Romero's blood absolved you and Faith from our mother's sins but I am not so lucky," Lilia said as she ruefully stared down at her own hands, her face filled with disgust. "The three of them, August, June, and our mother Regina. All three of them, descendants of Morgana."

"But our father-"

"Knew. He knew but you know how he was, how he always saw the best in people. He believed that they could be better than what their blood implied, and they used that," Lilia said darkly. "I was there, you know? The night Jack's mother killed ours. Faith was never her target," Lilia said quietly with a haunted expression. "When our mother was poisoned, she made a last-ditch attempt at saving herself. She used dark magic, a blood ritual, to try to force her soul into Faith's body and overwrite her soul. She never saw Faith as a daughter, just a spare body. She contaminated Faith and that's why she was poisoned," Lilia revealed and Xavier slowly shook his head unable to believe what he had heard. Yet try as he might, he could not find any sign of deceit. "August made it very clear that if I told anyone, he'd kill not just me but you two and even get to Jack as well. So, I stayed quiet. I can't any longer though, he's going to kill Jack and his band tonight. Many innocent lives have been lost because of my silence. Please don't let our brother be another one. I can't live with that, Xavier. I can't. Get your staff and teleport to him. I can't because August's magic is keeping Faith alive and I need to replace it with mine."

"I...I can't...my staff is still broken," Xavier said, his fists clenched tightly as he cursed his own inability to help. Lilia stared at him quietly as tears slid down her face. However, there wasn't hate in her expression for his weakness, not even disappointment. Just a cruel acceptance.

"Then he's dead."

*   *   *

Santa Monica, Duskhaven

As the club music boomed and the clubbers danced to their heart's content, Crystal continued to serve drinks till a sharp pain stopped her. Crystal winced slightly as she felt the pain spread from her head and down to her heart. Eventually the pain subsided and Crystal picked up the drink she had just poured and downed it in one go.

"Hey!"

"Oh, be quiet, I'll make you another one. I need this more than you do," Crystal muttered before she made another drink while a troubled expression made its way onto her face.

*   *   *

Silicon Valley, Prosperity Industries

"What the hell is all of this?" Kat asked incredulously as they made their way through an unexpectedly massive department. No matter where they went, they only found various pieces of technology, prototypes for inventions and augmentations they wouldn't expect to show up for years, maybe even decades to come. "The Circle's tech was a bit more advanced than we thought."

"It was impressive but never like this. They changed it this much in a couple of years?" Abbie asked unable to believe her eyes as she followed them through the cameras.

"No, if anything, they probably had you charmed. Something tells me it was always like this," Diamond said with a frown before they made it to another door. "Stone."

"Got it."

Once the door opened, the thieves collectively took a step back. Despite their masks they were clearly horrified by the sight they saw. In in the room was what appeared to be a black marionette doll that was only a bit bigger than Kat with its chest ripped open.

"Oh no," Kat said as she quickly rushed toward the table as Diamond held onto Jack for support. Jack looked more than a bit disgusted at the sight before him.

"What the hell is that!?"

"A Doll, remember when I told you about them? Beneath their artificial skin, this is what they are," Diamond answered quietly before she made her way toward the Doll with Jack. "They are our faithful servants, Discordia's gift to us and beings deserving nothing but the utmost respect...not...this," Diamond whispered. "The color is off as well, Dolls are supposed to be gray, aren't they?"

"Extraordinary...my mother once told many stories about the Dolls," Jack began as he placed a hand on the table. "There are many myths about black Dolls, but they are supposed to be just that, myths," Jack stated before he glanced at Kat who dug her hands into the Doll's chest. "Can the Doll be salvaged?"

"Possibly, I just need its apple," Kat said quickly as she went to search around the room. "The Doll hasn't self-destructed which means it's failsafe hasn't been triggered. The apple must be in this room," Kat said before she spotted a safe in the corner of the room.

"Can Kat fix it?"

"No idea, but Kat always had a knack for repairing things for as long as I can remember," Jack said as he watched Kat who was so focused on her task, that she didn't even pay the conversation any mind. Tears in her eyes, Kat broke into the safe and found what appeared to be a golden apple. Kat grabbed it quickly before she returned to the Doll and shoved the divine fruit violently inside of its chest. A spark erupted from the apple and the entirety of the Doll's body jerked up as if convulsing. Suddenly, its black hand gripped Kat's wrist tightly as a red light shone in its eyes.

"D-Destroy...me..." said the Doll with a mechanical yet feminine voice. The words made Kat glare at it before she shoved it back down on to the table and pulled out her flask.

"Like hell, come on drink this," Kat ordered as she poured the flask into the Dolls mouth. "A black Doll...Discordia would torture us for an eternity if we harmed you," Kat said quietly as she stroked the side of the Doll's face. "Keep that with you, we're going to come back for you," Kat said before she turned to her band as the damage to the Doll began to repair little by little. "Let's find that damn thing already so we can get out of here. I knew war made people do some fucked up shit, but I thought the Mage's Circle was better than this," Kat said as she wiped her eyes while Jack wrapped an arm around her to comfort her.

"Stone, how close are we?" Diamond asked as they left the room.

"The signal I'm tracking from it says it should be coming up now, first room on your right!" Abbie said as the door opened and revealed a large vault that was filled with safes. *"This is where we kept our important prototypes, but I didn't expect it to be this big. Just how many mind tricks did they play on me?"* Abbie questioned but before they could respond, August appeared before them in a blue flash.

"Well, well, what do we have here?" August wondered as their blood ran cold. The feeling of dread only increased when they heard the massive doors shut behind them. Nearly immediately a bullet slammed into his shield which made it flicker a bit, but ultimately it left him unscathed. It was almost an after-thought when Diamond looked down at her weapon in surprise as if her body moved on its own. "Such a warm welcome, Your Highness, and here I was hoping we could be a bit…diplomatic and talk this out."

"I have nothing to discuss with you!"

"Oh, but you see, that's where you're wrong. I need to keep the Circle distracted as I rebuild the Order. Killing you would be far too dangerous. What's the saying, 'Royal Blood must never spill for once it does the results are ill'?" August mocked as Diamond glowered at him. "Hurting you too much would put my own life in danger, I am no fool. That said, your band has a bad habit of interfering with my business, so I will have to destroy it. Don't bother looking at the door, my enchantments can stop even a thief from being able to slip through it," August said with a cruel smile that enraged the thieves. Band 13's shadow synch activated without so much as an order from Diamond. Three pairs of black and electric gold eyes glared at the mage as Band 13 prepared for the worst.

"No, no, no, I can't get into the system! I can't open the door!".

*   *   *

Prosperity Industries, Top Floor

"Sorry Abbie, this is for your own good," Haylen said as she forced her sister out of their systems. "Maybe we should test out your creation?"

*   *   *

Prosperity Industries, Vault

"What? Waiting on your little hacker friend to save you all?" August asked before he smiled up at one of the cameras. "Abigail Stone, was it? You and your sister continue to impress me with your talents, so much so in fact, that I hired her again," August revealed with a boisterous laugh. "That signal, or whatever you civilians call it, that you were tracking? False, one she made for me to trap you."

"Shit! G-Guys I-I-"

Abbie's static-filled voice was cut off instantly which sent a chill down the spines of the thieves' as they realized that they were trapped with the Arch-Mage.

∗   ∗   ∗

Santa Monica, Midas Tower

"God damn it, no!" Abbie shouted as she was finally forced out of the system. Abbie cursed as she went to work. Abbie found herself forced to fend off an insidious attack on her computer that could have only come from Haylen. Soon, her monitor froze before a gold "A" appeared on it. "What did you do?" Abbie asked in horror as she realized that Haylen had used Athena to keep her out.

∗   ∗   ∗

Silicon Valley, Prosperity Industries

"We have to get out of here," Diamond said as she gripped her weapon tightly.

"I'm afraid after all of your interfering, I can't let your band leave, at least, not in one piece," August said. "You all were so close too, but unfortunately for you, I had her come to pick up Project Athena just before you got here. Enero was more than willing to let me use it since the thieves found and stole the Order's grimoire. After all, who knows what they plan to do with it," August said before he gestured to Jack and Kat. "Well since you won't make a decision, I will. In honor of your father's memory, I'll let you live, boy. However, that thing right there," August trailed off as he pointed at Kat. "It and I have some unfinished business."

"What business could you possibly have with her?" Diamond questioned angrily.

"Don't play innocent! Not with the blood of countless innocent victims on her hands!" August boomed, his voice filled with righteous fury. "She betrayed the alliance! Sided with the Black Moon and killed dozens of women and unborn children under my protection! She doesn't get to play innocent no matter what form she takes!" August said as Kat looked at him, confusion evident in her eyes. At that moment, Kat's eyes flickered between gold and green as her heart began to waver.

"What are you talking about?" Diamond asked coldly as she forced back Kat's fear and regained control.

"Back when the alliance…" August scoffed at the last word. "…was at war with the Black Moon. The Thieves' Guild had a Doll that went rogue and destroyed a nursery for the Circle that was under my care. That monster smiled at the deaths it caused. I fought it off, causing it what I believed to be irreparable damage but it escaped. Then when the war was over, your Bandit Queen had the nerve to pardon it as if it were some person that deserved redemption!" August snarled as Kat's hands trembled. "The Bandit Queen kept that monster under her care and everyone chose to act as though it were justifiable! It made no sense! One day, after my grieving, I knew I had to do something. I had to change this world that let monsters roam free while the innocent died. I wasn't a part of the inner circle, however, so I couldn't just demand an audience with the Bandit Queen and that Doll she was hiding," August snarled before a sickening expression crossed his face. "I couldn't, but Romero could," August said as Diamond felt her heart skip a beat. "Illusions, potions, charms, you name it. Changing one's physical appearance is child's play for an adept mage, especially with how many options we have," August said dismissively. "I just wanted information on the Doll's location, that's it, but she was just…so…stubborn. Things escalated and I forgot how weak she truly was without her band, she lacked the will to even cast her fabled illusion, Dominion," August said and had the gall to give Diamond an apologetic expression. "Believe me, I did not mean to kill your Queen and consequently my brother in all but blood. When the lightning spell I cast in a moment of frustration stopped her heart, I knew I had passed the point of no return. She was not meant to die, and you were not meant to see it. For that, I am sorry. I did not mean to kill her or start a war, but that is life I suppose. Exceedingly unpredictable," August said before he focused his attention on Kat. "But here we are, after all these years, I've finally found you. I've unmasked you. For once, no matter what form you take you can't hide from me."

"I...I..." Kat found herself speechless as she stepped back and tried to put as much distance between herself and August as possible. Diamond cursed as she felt her control over Kat and Jack slip. Kat wanted to deny everything the man claimed, that his accusation was entirely false. Yet, between the large unexplained gap in her memories and a sick feeling in her stomach that began to grow, she found herself unsure.

"Impossible. I've seen her age, I've seen her cry. She is human," Diamond denied.

"Please," August said with a scoff. "We both know Dolls are made to imitate humans flawlessly. It's so easy for them that they can do it subconsciously. I'll admit I was expecting her to be faster and stronger than she is now. I suppose the damage I caused to her apple had more of an effect than I imagined," August said before he raised his hand toward Kat. A golden staff appeared in his hand in a flash of blue light. The end of the golden staff had a lion's head biting down on a crimson crystal. "Your only chance for redemption is through your destruction."

"Everything...everything is your fault," Diamond said incredulously. "All of this damage, this war, shattering the alliance, and for what? Revenge!?"

"A child like you wouldn't understand," August said as his eyes never left Kat. "Now, I know you can hear me. Die peacefully or put up a fight and risk endangering the other two, the choice is yours."

"No. The choice is mine!" Diamond snapped as she glared at August. Due to their shadow synch, Jack and Kat found themselves drowned both mentally and emotionally by Diamond's anger and despair. "And I choose to make you pay for what you've done!"

"Then so be it," August said dismissively as he stood still and let the thieves attack him. He did not bat an eye and his body refused to budge even as the three thieves attacked him with everything they had. "Truly tragic that it's come to this, you really are just first years, aren't you?" August mused, unaffected by their assault which only served to anger Diamond further. "Now I know why my nephew spared you. You're strong for what you are, but strength is irrelevant for a thief, but you know that don't you Umbra?" August asked Kat who remained silent though he could see her eyes flicker between gold and green. "I thought I knew the limits to your cruelty. Yet, you would let your own band go against me in this state?"

"Shut up!" Diamond snapped angrily as Jack slammed a frozen blade into August only for it to shatter upon impact. August slammed his staff into Jack's stomach and without a single word, encased Jack in a block of ice of his own creation. The ease at which he stopped Jack struck fear into Diamond's heart as she began to see how outclassed they truly were.

"You should be angry with her, not me, Your Highness! She's the reason you are even in this situation to begin with! You didn't even know did you?" August questioned knowingly. "A relic of the past, a weapon, snuck on to your band without your knowledge and no one told you. Not even your father? And now that weapon is willing to let you all die to keep up her act. Such disrespect for who should be the most respected member of your faction. It makes me wonder if the rumors are true, that your station is just for show," August mused. Diamond wanted to shut him up, to silence him once and for all but nothing she tried even fazed him. "You should join me. By rebuilding the Knights' Order, I will gain enough favor to take that fool Enero's position. That will be half of the alliance under my command and with that I can help you take what is rightfully yours. Give you the respect you deserve. With your help we will take the Tribe as well and with the entire alliance we can shape this world as we see fit. No longer forced to serve the powerless civilians, no, we can make them serve us. The way it is meant to be.

"Do you hear yourself!?" Diamond asked. "Why would I ever side with you!? You murdered my mother!"

"The same mother that abandoned you," August said simply and his words made Diamond and Kat still. "She chose an object, a weapon, over you. She chose to leave you unprepared to rule a kingdom she fractured instead of turning in a Doll that betrayed us all. Your mother pandered to her subordinates, she killed her own father for being able to do what she was too weak to. They called him mad for how he slaughtered anything he considered 'dark', I called him a genius. He knew that the Black Moon would rise again if the monsters were allowed to live but your mother showed them mercy and killed him. And what happened? Just over twenty years ago the Black Moon rose once more and tried to kill us all," August said as Diamond trembled. "They are still lurking even now, and you know that, don't you? Of course you do and it terrifies you to know that you will be forced to fight a war you didn't start. An unprepared Queen led like a lamb to the slaughter by those she is supposed to trust," August sneered. "Your father, a liar. Your mother, a coward. Your band, a lie. Your Goddesses, gone. The loyalty of your people, only there until you make a single mistake. You are alone and have nothing. The only one that even remotely understands the pressures you were forced to withstand is me."

"Diamond..." Kat began, startled by how she felt Diamond's presence leave her. Kat's now green eyes looked at her boss in concern "...you can't listen to him, he's just trying to get into your head!"

"Says the one that continues to lie to her," August said, visibly disgusted by the sight of Kat. "The Black Moon is coming and I am the world's best chance at stopping it. I am the Champion of Light. Everyone wants to pretend they are gone for good but they've contacted me, even assisted in some of my research into the Order. They think I will help them, but as soon as I get that blade, I will drive it through Morgana's heart myself."

"Honor or glory?" Diamond asked quietly which confused August. "Are you resisting the Black Moon because it's the honorable thing to do or because of the prestige it will bring you?"

"Does it matter?" August asked with a scoff. "As long as it gets done. Who cares if I get the glory? I'd deserve it."

"Then let's stop these talks of an alliance between you and I," Diamond said with a newfound resolve as August realized his answer was the wrong one. "You are wrong, I have at least one thing even if

I have nothing else. My honor. One who fights for glory instead of honor will only find tragedy."

"Nonsense, what good is honor when you're dead?"

"Without honor, I might as well be dead regardless," Diamond countered and Kat felt relief wash over her as Diamond once more prepared to fight. "Umbra, I don't know what you are or even who. I don't care either, just bring him down."

"Right…" Kat said softly.

"As if you could," August said before he heard a loud crack. August turned back in time to see Jack break free from his prison.

"You will be stopped," Diamond said as Jack's entire body seemed to gain a faint glow. Ice appeared on Jack's arms, chest and legs like armor. The surge of his power was felt by them all as Arondight shone brightly when a blue light was released from Arondight's third circle.

"You brat, you stole my power," August said though he looked more amused than anything. "A thief that can steal magic, Romero did love his experiments even if they put the Circle at risk," August mused as he saw a large circle of ice form on the floor around Jack. "Tell me child, have you ever had that much power course through your body before? Feels amazing, doesn't it? To taste even a glimpse of my might."

"I wouldn't know how it feels, I don't feel much of anything right now," Jack said as his curse overtook him and froze his heart. Two blades formed in his hands that were soon encased in ice. The circle of ice constantly reformed around him with every step he took as he rushed toward August. Jack slammed one of his blades into August's right side and, like before, it shattered upon impact. This time, however, the ice stuck to August's arm. August grimaced when he felt the ice on his arm drain his power a bit more as Jack seemed to shine brighter as his blade re-formed. When Jack slammed his second blade into August, Jack froze the Arch-Mage's other arm. After that, Jack continued to make and break blades as he assaulted August's shield with everything he could muster. As Jack attacked, he felt the ice on his body continue to spread as he stole more and more of

August's power. However, before he could proceed any further, the ice that engulfed August shattered.

"Enough!" August roared his eyes filled with stars as the force of his power knocked everyone else back into the walls of the vault. "Too close," August muttered to himself. His hands trembled as he saw his shield flicker for a moment. "I was going to let you live, but I see now that you are a threat if left unchecked, even more so than that blasted Doll," August said as he focused his attention on Jack who shakily rose to his feet. However, before they could continue fighting, Diamond fired more shots. Each bullet was charged with her presence and more powerful than the previous.

"Why won't you just die!?" Diamond shouted as she shot at August to no avail. Diamond was exhausted but she stood ready to fight as she continued to shoot at August.

"It must be frustrating, to have a skillset as dangerous as yours yet be pitted against the one person it doesn't affect," August said, his shield deflected anything she could do to him. "You could always take off that glove. Though if you did that, you'd end up doing my job for me and kill them, wouldn't you?" August mused. "That's why your mother died, isn't it? She could have stopped me sooner but she hesitated because you were too close," August mocked as Band 13 became blinded with anger. Diamond's presence flooded their bodies as she reestablished their connection. Jack lunged forward and slammed another blow into the Arch-Mage that made August slide back a few feet. Jack charged forward to attack August once more but found his movements hindered greatly by the ice that continued to spread over his body. "I see, I was so used to dealing with older members of your family that I forgot the children aren't adept at handling the cold," August said with a laugh. "To think for a second, I almost felt a thrill from this," August raised his staff high as his magic formed around it and transformed it into a spear of light. Holding it like a javelin, August took aim at the frozen form of Jack. "I'll end you, rightly," August said before he threw the weapon at Jack. Before it could connect, Diamond jumped in front of him and took the brunt of the attack. The resulting explosion shook the vault and blew apart a good portion of her mod-suit. The pain they felt was enough to break their shadow synch once more.

"I can see. What happened!?" Abbie's voice came through their earpieces *"Guys, stay calm. I don't know what he just did but it knocked something loose in the server room,"* Abbie said as Kat crawled onto her hands and feet. *"It distracted Athena and my sister long enough to sneak back in. I need to be discreet or they'll kick me out. I need three minutes, hold on for that long and I can pry that door open. Please, just give me three minutes."*

As Kat climbed to her feet, she glanced down at the frozen shivering form of Jack, she realized that he was currently incapacitated, his body simply could not longer handle the cold. Kat watched as Diamond forced herself to her feet. Diamond's body trembled as she struggled to drink some nectar from her flask. Though the outside of her body was fine, Kat shuddered at the internal damage that Diamond probably sustained after being hit by that powerful spell. "Stay back," Kat told Diamond as she moved toward August and pulled out her treasure. Kat and August stared each other down for a brief moment as she held her treasure. This was the single most important gamble she had made with her treasure to date. When her pendant spun Kat shook her head, a horrified expression on her face when its green section landed on top with a small click.

"No," Kat whispered before she held her head in pain as she collapsed to her knees. A storm of green presence ripped from her body and surrounded everyone around her. Kat screamed as her mind felt as though it were being split apart. The pupils of her eyes became slits while her hair darkened from brown to black. Diamond and Jack watched as green sparks danced across their bodies. Everyone but August looked down in confusion at the presence that surrounded them. The feeling of despair it produced felt as though it were eating at their very souls.

"What's goin' on!?"

"Katarina!" Diamond shouted, confused by the sight before her.

"I knew it, this feeling of helplessness, pain," August said impassively. "It really is you, Umbra," August said as Kat's screams stopped. Slowly, the hooded woman climbed to her feet and to her band it was as if Kat were replaced with an entirely different person.

"Where am I?" Umbra asked with a frown as she glanced around. Umbra's green cat-like eyes shifted a bit as they scanned the individuals around her. "What am I wearing?" Umbra muttered before she tore the tattered garment from her body and assessed the situation. "One Arch-Mage…they're…recognized as hostiles now?" Umbra asked as her eyes narrowed. Soon her mind was filled with new data about the current world state. "Two thieves…my…band?" Umbra wondered. Umbra frowned when she glanced down at Diamond and took note of her golden eyes. "Royal Blood, I see," Umbra said to herself as she strode toward August. "You've grown," Umbra told August. Umbra shot at August at speeds that made her appears as nothing more than a bolt of green lightning. August transformed his staff into a spear of light and stabbed toward her as she threw a card at him which sailed past his head and stabbed into the wall behind him. Umbra jumped and flipped over him and his attack as the cards pulsed once before they formed a handle that flew toward Umbra. Umbra grabbed it and pulled her whip free, unlike Kat's her whip appeared to be a pitch-black chain that was covered in spikes. "Just not in any way that mattered. Mod-suit, limit bypass, code: Umbra." Umbra spoke before a golden light emitted from her chest, beneath her treasure, while green circuits appeared across her badge and suit.

"Drawing power from that apple of yours won't help you, I've damaged it far too much in our last fight!" August declared before conjuring massive fireballs that took the form of roaring lion heads. To Diamond and Jack, the spells shot at Umbra at blinding speeds, but to Umbra they appeared to move in slow motion. Umbra swung her whip at them before they could get too close which made the fireballs explode upon contact. "You're just making my job easier! You'll break down before you make a difference."

"The Royal Blood must be protected, anything else is expendable. Any means to ensure this? Permitted," Umbra stated matter-of-factly as she pushed her body to its limit and swung her whip through any and all of August's spells. August threw a spear of light at her but before it could travel even half way, Umbra had already made it behind him, leaving a trail of presence in her wake. Diamond moved to help only for a card to stab into the ground in front of her. Startled, Diamond looked up toward Umbra. "Don't interfere! Don't move or even hope for my victory. If I am out then anything you do will be turned against you!" Umbra warned before she swung her whip at August and wrapped it around his body.

"So, you bring misfortunate even upon your allies?" August forced out as the chain around him tightened while Umbra tried to pull him toward her.

"The only misfortune you need to worry about is yours!" Umbra hissed out. The light in her chest shone brighter before she threw four more cards at him that exploded upon impact. Despite the force of her attacks, she knew they hadn't harmed August, no, what she wanted was to keep all of his attention. When August flew up high above the room and released a barrage of spells of varying elements and sizes at her, Umbra knew she succeeded. Though a few stray spells managed to hit her, Diamond was able to fight through the pain as she helped Jack drink from his flask.

"You will pay for what you've done," August said as he transformed his staff into a spear of light. August raised it high into the air only for it to get stuck into the ceiling. August cursed his luck and Umbra used his moment of distraction to leap up toward him. Umbra wrapped her whips around his leg and flipped forward before she slammed him into the ground. August recovered quickly and glared at Umbra. A dark expression crossed his face when he noticed her body tremble. August raised his staff once more and grinned as hundreds of small orbs of light appeared behind him, each the size of a marble. "I wonder, just how damaged are you? Let's perform a little stress test," August said before the orbs began to shoot at her rapidly. Immediately, Umbra dodged the barrage of attacks, and though she held out for an impressive amount of time, the onslaught eventually became too much for her. Each projectile clipped her body as a burning sensation could be felt in her chest. It felt as though her insides were on fire, and her vision became clouded and unfocused while her joints began to feel stiffer and stiffer. Eventually, when the barrage ended, she fell to her knees. Umbra's body smoked as she felt it overheat. Smoke came from her mouth as warnings of a critical malfunction appeared in her eyes.

"Is this my limit?" Umbra wondered to herself. So weak, she couldn't even attempt to use her treasure again as she desperately tried to regain some control over her limbs. The green presence that covered the others as a result of her treasure quickly dissipated as its effects ran out.

"Oh, how the mighty have fallen, over twenty years, that's how long I've waited for this moment," August said as he descended upon the weakened Umbra but before he could begin to cast another spell, Jack tackled him from the side. "Down, boy!" August snapped before he slammed the younger man down onto the ground. "Fine I'll deal with you first," August said with a near growl. Once more August turned his staff into a spear of pure light. As August raised the spear menacingly, the door to the vault finally opened which shattered the enchantments in the process. Abbie screamed herself hoarse for the thieves to find a way out of the room. Bullet after bullet slammed into August's back as Diamond desperately tried to get him to move but thanks to his shield, he didn't even pay her any mind. "Goodbye," August said before he brought his spear down upon Jack.

"No!" Abbie screamed as Jack looked up in horror. Cracks formed on his icy heart as Diamond dropped her gun. August was surprised for a moment before he released a booming laugh as his spear found itself lodged into Umbra's chest. Umbra's body hung off it limply after she took the mortal blow for Jack.

"Why...why did I move? How...did I move?" Umbra wondered to herself as she grabbed at the spear weakly while her mask dissolved. Her mod-suit struggled to maintain its form as a golden liquid poured from her wound and onto Jack like blood. Umbra's very skin began to burn due to the heat she was releasing which revealed a fleshy black substance beneath it. "Leave," Umbra ordered Jack weakly as August lifted the spear up, with her still on it as she continued to grab at the spear in her chest. With a laugh, August flung her to the side of the vault. August stalked over toward her and completely forgot about Jack, as he saw the object of his hate grab weakly at the hole in her chest. To her credit, Umbra didn't scream even once as he continued to repeatedly stab down at her with his spear. With each attack, August vented decades worth of anger and frustration. The sight was horrific, and for a moment neither of the thieves could even move. Eventually, Jack remembered what Umbra said and quickly got up and made his way toward Diamond quietly. Jack did his best to block out the sickening noise August's spear made when it tore its way into Umbra. Jack attempted to drag the frozen form of Diamond out of the room. A biting mist escaped not just his mouth but every wound on his body as he willed his curse to help him block out what was happening.

*   *   *

Santa Monica, Midas Tower

A mortified Abbie, sobbed loudly when she saw her lover destroyed before her very eyes. Those sobs, however, turned into screams of pain as her mark began to burn, making it feel as though lava had been poured on her shoulder.

*   *   *

Prosperity Industries, Vault

"Where do you think you're going, child?" August asked coldly as he saw Jack make his way out of the vault. With a sigh Jack stopped and placed Diamond down on the ground before he cracked his neck.

"Can't blame me for trying," Jack mused. "Leave, Diamond," Jack told Diamond who managed to snap out of her stupor.

"I won't leave you-"

"You have no choice!" Jack shouted. "The Guild must live on. He doesn't want you, so do your job as heir to the throne and leave! Do your duty and I'll do mine as both a man and your enforcer," Jack said as he slammed his right fist into his palm, not once looking back at his boss.

"I'm almost moved," August said sarcastically. "Let me help you," August said before he aimed his staff at Diamond. Diamond immediately found herself engulfed by a blue light.

"What are you doing to her!?" Jack asked angrily as August simply waved off his concerns.

"Like I said, I need your Guild to stay around a bit longer. So, I'm teleporting her away," August explained. "Who knows, maybe now that she's truly alone she will see reason. Consider it an act of mercy, I am a man of honor and virtue after all. She doesn't need to see what I'm going to do to you," August stated which made Jack close his eyes as he resigned himself to his fate. For better or worse, Jack realized that this was his final fight. There was so much he still wanted to do that he would be unable to accomplish but he knew one thing.

"I'm going to take you out with me," Jack swore as Diamond disappeared just after she screamed Jack's name. "Don't laugh, thanks to you, I don't have to worry about collateral damage. Alright Abbie, time to test a theory," Jack said which made August's eyes widen as a pillar of blinding light erupted from the inside of a circle of ice that surrounded both of them. The temperature plummeted drastically as Jack raised his right fist high into the air. Arondight shone brightly and presence crackled along the brand as a torrent of blue presence ripped free from Jack's body. In an instant, Arondight released a powerful explosion as Jack's ice-cold presence quickly filled the room and threatened to freeze everything in sight. "Huh, so this is what happens when you overload it," Jack said quietly. Jack's tears froze on his face as his vision darkened. Soon, Jack's body succumbed to the freezing power of the beautiful yet terrifying blizzard he left in his wake. The last thing he heard was the sound of Abbie's cries.

CHAPTER 15

· · · · · · ●●● ● ●●● · · · · ·

ALICE

Hollywood, Crimson Rose Cemetery

Vivi's shoulders shook as she looked down at the graves of Kat and Jack. The rain that poured down around her wasn't enough to extinguish the flame of anger that burned inside of her. As she stood there, she didn't even look back when Heathcliff stepped up next to her.

"What do you want Heathcliff?"

"Look, Violet, it's no secret we dislike each other," Heathcliff began. "You will always be a failure that was unfit to take over the Ardent Family, no matter how much praise you get from the Guild."

"And you'll always be a failure of a father, a relic of the past that should have been lost years ago," Vivi said, not even fazed by his comments which made his lips quirk upward a bit. "A jealous little man that will never accomplish the things I have. You and the council blocked Roderick and me at every turn as if we weren't all on the same side. It's your fault I'm even here right now, so it better be good or I'll end you myself," Vivi said and it wasn't anger that filled her voice, but a deathly resolve. "Why are you here?"

"To tell you this. I saw the way you looked at these kids, they were your own. They might as well had been your own flesh and blood," Heathcliff said as he gestured toward the graves. "Despite

224

our relationship, know that this is something I would have never wished upon you ever, lass," Heathcliff said as his daughter looked up at him. "It was never meant to go this far. The Circle will pay for this slight against you."

"Of course, I'm just waiting for the order from Roderick. I will burn the Mage's Circle to the ground," Vivi swore as a black smoke spilled from her lips while her eyes burned an electric orange.

"I had a feeling you'd say that. Just know this, you've been a stubborn thorn in my side for decades, lass," Heathcliff said as he turned away from Vivi. "After everything you've put me through? No one gets to extinguish your flame, but me."

"As if you could," Vivi scoffed as her father left. "Old fool," Vivi said as she shook her head. A small, nearly unnoticeable smile on her face as she looked down at the graves. "Don't worry brats, mom will avenge you. If it's the last thing I do," Vivi said as she looked up at the cloudy sky and allowed the rain to wash away her tears.

∗   ∗   ∗

France, Paris

Dominique found herself alone at the top of the Eiffel tower. Even the beauty that was the city of lights could not stop the pain in her heart.

"So, this is where you've been hiding!" a loud voice declared dramatically. Dominique turned to find her teacher behind her. He was a proud man known only as the Phantom Thief by the Guild. Many knew him as the single best infiltrator the Guild had to offer. Though from his fashion sense one would find that hard to believe. The Phantom Thief could always be found garbed in a bright white suit that had a matching porcelain mask and large top hat. "You've missed our lesson again, you know? Were you attempting to practice on your stealth today? Good attempt, but alas it was no use against me, the Phantom Thief!" the man said with a dramatic bow.

"Not, now *Monsieur* Phantom," Dominique said quietly as she brought her knees to her chest. "I am not in the mood."

"Oh?" the Phantom Thief asked curiously as he twirled his cane. "And why is that?" the masked man questioned only for Dominique to look at him as if he had asked one of the dumbest questions she had ever heard. "It has been a month and what happened to young Katarina and her band was a tragic occurrence. That said, you all knew this life was dangerous when you agreed to be a part of it."

"Of course, I know it's dangerous but does that mean I am not allowed to grieve!?"

"Of course not! Do you think I am not saddened by the loss of one of my two favorite pupils?" Phantom questioned. "Just because you can't see them behind this mask, my tears are as real as yours I assure you. Every day for the past month, I've questioned every decision I have made. Wondering where I went wrong, what I didn't teach her to give her the advantage she must have so sorely needed in her final hour. The thing is, that while I do this, my body is still moving forward. I am still living life," Phantom said as he raised his hands dramatically and gestured to the world around them. "This rain will eventually subside, these lights will turn off, and the sun will rise once more in the horizon as it always does. Time will always move forward no matter who lives or who dies despite how much we would prefer it didn't. The loss of Katarina's life should not stop you from living yours. You must continue to learn, to improve, so that you can be the best thief you can be! The Guild is moving forward and a decision has been made by the council. The decision was made that the next family to sit on that throne will be the Victoire Family."

"What!?" Dominique asked as she climbed to her feet. "No! That seat belongs to Diamond and her only, I refuse to sit upon that throne!" Dominique said angrily.

"I'm afraid you have no choice. With the destruction of Band 13, Diamond cannot ascend."

"Why not? Her mother ruled for years after her band fell!"

"Yes, but Isabelle also had the entire council's unwavering support, Diamond does not. I am sure you are aware of this, given how divided the council has been since her father took over," Phantom said patiently. "He will keep the seat until you finish your training, after which he will step down and you will be our next Bandit Queen."

"And what of Diamond? What becomes of her!? Does she even know?" Dominque questioned.

"It was her idea," that alone froze Dominique in place as her teacher continued. "She refused to ever bear an heir and suggested your family take over. Juventas cherished your family nearly as much as she did Diamond's. Diamond decided you would be more than just a substitute, but rather an upgrade. I'll be honest, the way she commanded the council and swayed them into listening to her was so much like her mother that it made my heart clench. It broke, however, when I realized that she was using her obvious potential to escape her legacy. Diamond is done with the Guild, Dominique, and with her and young Frost gone we lose both the Midas Family and the Frost Family. There is an obvious need for reconstruction but that will be dealt with later once the Guild has become unified. This slight against them has them all calling for blood," Phantom said before he shook his head solemnly. "There will be a lot of death in the upcoming months. The Guild has decided on a full-on assault on the Mage's Circle."

"Why are we even still at war? August admitted to his crimes!"

"Yes, but the only thing to back that up is Diamond's word which barely carries weight to the Guild, let alone the Circle," Phantom explained. "Not to mention she insisted that an old enemy, the Black Moon, was involved which ruined her credibility. Even if she had told the truth, no one would want to believe such a claim without proof. For better or worse, Queen Isabelle made her family's position little more than figureheads. The war will continue and you need to be kept safe at all costs. Your band will be taught at the Guild and then you will be escorted directly to and from your safe house. Your required quotas will be waived, you all can no longer be out like this."

"That's imprisonment," Dominique said with a sneer.

"That's protection," Phantom countered. "Do you think it brings me joy to tell you this? You were blessed with the 'Wings of Victory' as your treasure, the ultimate form of freedom. You have no idea how much it pains me to watch you be caged. That said, this all will begin starting this time tomorrow, which gives you twenty-four hours of freedom, use them wisely," Phantom advised and he barely had enough time to finish that sentence before Dominique took that moment to dive off of the tower. Sky-blue markings shone through the back of her mod-suit and took the form of a pair of wings that were branded into her body. Blue sparks danced across the marking as a sense of weightlessness overcame her before she flew down into the shadows cast by the large monument.

"She only has that time because you promised to be with her, you know?" Master Li said as he stepped from the shadows with Headmistress Corday.

"This is my fault, I should have been harder on Diamond," Corday said quietly.

"We all should have handled that band differently," Master Li said with a grim expression. "They will be known as the first true failure of us, the Three Masters. But like all failures, we must learn from them. We need to make sure Band 12 becomes ready to uphold the Guild. Those three are going to ascend into a world nearly as hostile as the one Isabelle ascended into."

"Not sure about you, but I have had far more than one failure in my days," Phantom pointed out which made Master Li scoff.

"You know what I meant."

"I always do, old friend," Phantom said with a laugh. "Now if you'll excuse me, I must go take my own advice and move forward as well," the masked man said before he stepped back and simply vanished into thin air.

* * *

Santa Monica, Midas Tower

"Unfortunately, paramedics were unable to reach him in time before he perished from cardiac arrest. This makes him the third major CEO to die in the last two weeks alone! With the explosion at the

Prosperity Industries' headquarters last month, many conspiracy theorists are wondering if there is more going on than we know."

Abbie watched the news with a blank expression as she was lost in her thoughts.

* * *

Santa Monica, Midas Tower, Three Weeks earlier

"Oh my God, Diamond thank God you're okay!" Abbie said as she grabbed the woman in a bone-crushing hug. Tears of relief fell from her eyes at the fact that at least one of the thieves survived. *"I looked everywhere for you, I'm so sorry! This is all my fault!"* Abbie said as she choked back a sob. *"They died because of me."*

"They did," Diamond agreed wholeheartedly as she separated herself from Abbie. Diamond made sure she still had the hacker's attention as gold eyes bore into gray ones. *"At least that's what I wrongfully thought at the time. However, I am the only one guilty. In my grief, it took me a while to understand that. Fortunately, August teleported me home. A mage can only use teleportation to places they've been to so it was more of a final taunt, to show me that he was the one responsible for everything,"* Diamond explained with a calmness that put Abbie on edge. *"Still, as cruel as his intentions were, it gave me time to think,"* Diamond said, her expression as neutral as it normally was yet there was a sense of loss and despair that Abbie could feel from the woman. *"My emotions are strong, Abigail, very strong. If I had seen you after…after…what happened, you may have died and that's not something Katarina or Frost would approve of ever,"* Diamond said honestly. *"I am no longer fit to be part of the Guild, much less its Queen so I need you to listen closely because I cannot protect you anymore. The money you unfroze from my account when we first met along with this penthouse are now yours. They are an apology from me for failing your loved one. Please use some of that money to get that mark covered up. It'll keep away monsters but other thieves may ask questions,"* Diamond said easily as if she had talked about the weather. Abbie looked at her sadly as she could feel the distance Diamond had

placed between them. "There is a funeral for them in a couple of weeks, I will text you the address. For your safety, I suggest going to the graves a few days after that, again to avoid questions. If you do go to the graves and see a red-haired woman, leave. If you want to keep your life, leave. Again, you are not to blame, but loss makes even the best of us irrational."

"Wait, what happens now?" Abbie asked with a frown.

"Now? We go our separate ways," Diamond said simply. "With Katarina and Frost gone, their emotions, left with them. Any feelings of camaraderie we had were due to them, I'm afraid."

"Bullshit," Abbie denied but Diamond's expression never wavered.

"I apologize if it sounds harsh, but our relationship never extended past employer and employee," Diamond said evenly before she made her way to the door. She paused for a moment before she glanced back at Abbie. "I apologize once more for your loss, and thank you for your service."

*   *   *

Santa Monica, Midas Tower, Present

Abbie had looked at her phone and dropped it when she saw her wallpaper which consisted of an impromptu selfie Kat had taken of them on one of their dates. The sight of her former lover sent a pain through her chest. The pain was worse than what she felt when Alice had died and it affected Abbie differently as well. Instead of a crippling sadness, she felt an overwhelming sense of anger. Anger at herself for her inability to do more, for not being better. Abbie also felt hatred toward her sister who once again aided in the loss of something that gave her life meaning. It was then that she took a good look at her surroundings. Abbie had a great place to live and more money than she thought she'd ever have. Yet just like before she met Kat, she was drinking away her sorrows and drifting lifelessly from one day to the next. With this thought, Abbie picked her phone back up and bit her lip as she went through her messages. As Abbie scrolled through a countless number of unread messages from Eric, and a few from Roy, she found a message that her sister had sent the night she lost everything.

Bitch: I did it for you, I know you don't understand, but it was for your own good.

To anyone else, it would have seemed like a cruel text that was poorly timed to say the least. However, Abbie knew the truth and that alone disgusted her more than anything. Once more her sister genuinely thought she had acted in her best interests and once more it cost Abbie everything. Any attempt Abbie made to be herself, to become a better person, and help the world around her was perceived as some sort of rebellious streak. It had been like that since they were kids, and finally, it happened. Haylen finally pushed Abbie too far. Abbie started a new group message and added both Roy and Eric.

Abbie: Let's meet up at the Mad Hatter, it's time to bring back Wonderland.

Abbie hesitated to press send, but as she heard the news that continued to worsen, she knew what had to be done. The fear and anger she felt were quickly drowned out by that rebellious feeling which returned to her full force and threatened to consume her with its intensity. Abbie pressed send and pulled herself up to her feet and got ready to leave the penthouse. The next few months were about to be very busy for her.

*   *   *

Santa Monica, The Mad Hatter

The Phantom thief walked into the shop and placed his hat on the counter, he tensed for a moment when he felt his phone vibrate. When Phantom removed his mask, it was Roy that looked down at the message.

Abbie: Let's meet up at the Mad Hatter, it's time to bring back Wonderland.

"Interesting," Roy mused to himself quietly as he read the text.

$*$ $*$ $*$

San Diego, Magnus Manor

When Lilia entered August's study, she made her way toward the bound forms of the Lady and Haylen. Lilia didn't bother to spare the civilian a glance as she held Eve's core in front of the Lady.

"How's this?" Lilia questioned quietly as the Lady weakly rose her head and inspected the gold and red orb.

$*$ $*$ $*$

San Diego, Magnus Manor, One month prior

"Strange," Haylen muttered as she inspected the Shield as a disheveled August stood next to her.

"What?"

"The Shield…I can read it," Haylen said as she watched the code being decrypted by Athena. "That said, this isn't directions to the sword but rather a list," Haylen explained which made him frown. "A list of…vessels?"

"Vessels?" August repeated with a perturbed expression on his face. Haylen nodded as she continued to read.

"Arthur Pendragon, Excalibur was bound to his blood," Haylen read off of the screen of her monitor as the Shield was scanned. "However, the only heir he had, even though illegitimate, was his treacherous son Mordred. His mother, Morgana, and their descendants have been after it for centuries. The Lady would find vessels to house the sword in their bodies so that a relative of the vessel in the Knights' Order could wield the blade should they be chosen to lead."

"She would go that far? To bind the blade to others just so Mordred's heirs couldn't wield what was rightfully theirs?" August asked, his voice filled with barely restrained fury.

"That does seem kind of far-fetched," Haylen whispered, confused by the sick feeling she had in her stomach. *"Here, the last name etched on this Shield is…"* Haylen trailed off and her eyes widened as the blood from her face drained.

"Well? Spit it out, girl!" August demanded as she looked up at him in confusion.

"Mine."

*   *   *

San Diego, Magnus Manor, Present

"The top and bottom sigils are off by a millimeter, they need to be moved right to be truly centered. Use a banishing crystal to erase them, a spell will just leave traces of his magic," the Lady advised quietly which made Lilia nod before she pocketed the core and pulled out an apple. Lilia knelt down and held it in front of Haylen for her to eat. For a moment, the proud woman refused to eat it, but Lilia was patient and waited. When Haylen's stomach finally growled she gave in and ate it with Lilia's aid. Lilia tensed when she felt August's magic and pulled the apple back. Lilia began to eat it herself as he entered the room.

"And here I thought you didn't have a cruel streak, eating in front of the starving civilian," August joked as he placed a hand on her shoulder. "Though I suppose it doesn't matter, it is not like she even needs to eat anyway," August said which earned him weak glares from both the Lady and Haylen. "It still blows my mind, you know, to think you were telling the truth," August said to the Lady. "That the sword was in Stone, literally hidden inside their bloodline. Just what kind of dark sorcery did you use to pull this off?" August wondered as he stepped forward and raised Haylen's head. August inspected her with an almost childish wonder as she glared fiercely at him. When August reached down and raised her shirt a bit, he smirked as he placed his hand over her abdomen. August's hand began to burn with his magic as a red sword shaped emblem appeared on her skin.

"Still as impressive as it is, I need a sword, not a woman, I can get my choice of them afterward," August said as he released her shirt. "You will be returning to your true form during the Spring Equinox, so enjoy your last few moments of humanity," August said before he snatched the apple from Lilia and bit into it as he left the room.

"You know it's alright to cry, girl. You are still more human than blade," the Lady said which made Haylen sneer, even as her eyes glistened with unshed tears. "As an old acquaintance of mine once told me, sometimes it's best to just let the healing waters flow."

"A Stone woman doesn't cry, we get even," Haylen swore. "Somehow, some way, my sister will get me out of this. She's more than capable of doin' that much."

"The civilian?" Lilia asked skeptically. "The civilian whose lover you got murdered? You think she's going to save you?"

"No, like I said we get even," Haylen said quietly. "We're more alike than she cares to admit, she's not gonna let anyone rob her of her chance to get revenge on me."

"And when it's time for her to get revenge?"

"I'll deal with that then. I'd rather she kills me than give that monster the satisfaction," Haylen said quietly. "Look, I get that in this world of magic and monsters, the regular folk don't seem so important. But believe me when I say that you've never seen that woman when she's motivated. That will remain the only thing that brings me fear," Haylen said as she looked up at Lilia firmly. "So, let him plot, let him think he won. This is far from over. For better or worse, Abigail is still daddy's little girl."

* * *

Santa Monica, The Mad Hatter

"Bring back Wonderland? Why?" Eric questioned as he stood around a table in the back room with Abbie and Roy.

"Look around, Eric, you've seen the news," Abbie said which made Eric frown.

"A bunch of celebrity and CEO deaths, it's been a bad year or do you believe those conspiracies?" Eric asked. "That something bigger is going on?"

"I know so, it's the reason Kat was killed," Abbie said and Eric looked at her in horror as Roy narrowed his eyes slightly.

"I thought it was a climbing accident?"

"You had to think that, look I can't and won't go into detail. At the end of the day, all I have is my word, and that's somethin' I'll never compromise. Just know that things ain't what they appear," Abbie said firmly as Roy's expression softened. "Look, the people at the top? The ones we're aimin' for? They're powerful but they're terrible when it comes to technology. Mistakes, paper trails, documents that should have been deleted that show how they abuse their power to keep the people fundin' their questionable deals, there's an abundance of all of that. Enough evidence for us to take any one of them down but not for long," Abbie said as she placed her tablet on the table and showed them an article about Prosperity Industries' plans to roll out a new app with their next generation of phones. "They've dug Project Athena back up from the grave and are going to roll it out in March. If they succeed, all of that evidence becomes untouchable. Not to mention whatever else goes wrong with releasing an unstable A.I. to the public."

"Holy shit," Eric said incredulously as he grabbed the tablet. "You've told me about this thing, do they not know what can go wrong? Especially now with people implanting computers into their very bodies?"

"Like I said, they're bad with technology. Look, I brought it into this world and I can take it out, but it'll take time."

"And money," Roy spoke up. "Let's ignore the fact that most of the leaders are M.I.A like Shiva or the twins. This will all still take money, money we don't have. Alice had connections, people, secret backers that believed in her cause. You don't have that."

"Well, I wouldn't say that. Besides, I have a few million dollars to work with, not enough to fund everything, but it's a start," Abbie said which made both men look at her in surprise.

"A few million...where the hell did you get that cash?" Eric asked incredulously.

"Lottery," Abbie said with a shrug while Eric narrowed his eyes. "Look I can get us capital, and I can get Alice's backers on our side if we start showin' some results. What we need, however, is manpower. We can't depend on the rest of our inner circle to show up, you know how they are. If we show results, they might contact us again. What we need is numbers. I know at least half of the old members around the world have been waitin' to be recalled, but if what happened with Haylen's team proved anything we're going to need muscle."

"I can see if any of my old gang want a quick come-up, but none of them are like Haylen's team. That was some black ops shit they had," Eric said with a frown.

"I can invest in findin' mercenaries, not to use but rather teach," Abbie said after a moment of thought. "Even Haylen's team had to start from somewhere, you get us people, I'll get us trainers and together we get soldiers."

"Soldiers, huh? You know Alice wouldn't approve of such a militant approach," Roy pointed out knowingly.

"Yeah, well Alice ain't here now, is she?"

"Actually, I think she is. You're going to need to take up that mantle," Roy responded which surprised Abbie for a moment.

"Well fuck me, it was an alias," Abbie muttered to herself. "I really knew nothin' about her."

"Don't take it personally, she was a woman that held many secrets. Alice is a rank," Roy explained. "She led people, like you, down the rabbit hole and showed them a world they didn't know existed. She needed an alias, to be someone better. The day she took charge, Alice was born and Elizabeth Drake..." Roy trailed off as he gave Abbie a moment to process the true name of her first love. "...died," Roy explained. "She saw a world that needed changing. Elizabeth didn't rise to power by making people believe in her, but by making them believe in themselves. It won't be easy, you need to boss a lot of people around and take charge of even the worst of situations. Do you have any experience in that? In being in charge? In being a boss?"

"No, in fact, last time it was my turn to lead I failed spectacularly," Abbie said honestly before memories of her time with the thieves flashed through her mind. Abbie thought of moments where she saw Diamond take charge of a situation whether it was for a heist or to run their club. "But I may have picked up a thing or two since then."

"Good enough for me," Eric said with a shrug.

"Well, like you said, everyone starts from somewhere, I guess. So, what's the first move, Alice?" Roy questioned as he and Eric faced her.

"That's going to take some getting used to," the newly dubbed Alice said to herself. "First things first, do either of you know a good tattoo artist?"

CHAPTER 16

· · · · · · · ●● ● ●● · · · · · · ·

DIVINE INTERVENTION

Santa Monica, Duskhaven

"You know, when I said I wanted to drink with you, I was hoping it would be a bit less depressing," Crystal said with a concerned frown as she watched Diamond down her shot of tequila. At this point, even Crystal had lost count of how many Diamond had. For a while, Diamond said nothing as she simply eyed a sheathed knife that rested on the counter. When she looked up at Crystal, it was as if Diamond had just registered that she had been spoken to. "Think you might have had enough."

"What? Color me surprised, normally you would be trying to get me to drink more," Diamond said with a slur as she placed a self-deprecating smile on her face.

"Yeah, but that's when you're being too tense for your own good and need to loosen up," Crystal said as she gestured at the empty club. "Also, the sun tends to be down and there is a party going on. This? This is just sad to look at, girlfriend," Crystal said before raising an eyebrow. "Also, what's with the knife?"

* * *

Hollywood, Midas Manor one week prior

"How long are you going to keep pestering me?" Diamond asked as she gazed at a fuming Dominique. Diamond didn't look annoyed by the seemingly never-ending rant from her self-proclaimed best friend but rather tired. Whether she was tired of the conversation or just everything in general, Dominique couldn't tell and that alone made her heart break. Idly, Diamond noted she could count on one hand how many times she had ever seen Dominique truly angry, and not once did she ever see the French woman this livid.

"How long?" Dominique repeated incredulously before she released a quick string of curses that Diamond didn't even bother to translate. "Until I get some sense into that thick skull of yours! The throne is yours, not mine, it has been your dream since we were little girls!"

"You're correct," Diamond said and for a moment Dominique had hope that she finally got through to Diamond. That hope, however, was crushed when Diamond continued. "It was a dream, and this is reality. I cannot ascend without my... I cannot ascend alone," Diamond corrected unable to even utter the word that had plagued her nightmares for the last month.

"Your mother ruled for years without her band!"

"I am not my mother!" Diamond shouted which made Dominique flinch, startled by Diamond's show of emotion. "I could never be that strong," Diamond continued quietly. Diamond's voice shook as she glanced at a portrait of her mother that hung in the hallway. "My mother was a fluke, a ruler that comes possibly once in an eternity. She did things I could never dream of, powerful enough to shrug off the loss of her band and still rule with an iron fist. So please, stop comparing me to her. If I was even remotely anything like her, my...they would still be here. To think I could ever escape a shadow as massive as hers was a pipe dream," Diamond said and turned back to face Dominique with glistening eyes. "The Midas family has produced rulers that ranged from tyrants to saviors, it was only a matter of time before a failure was born. Fortunately, there are enough of their good traits in me to know when to step down, to give the Guild a chance with a Queen they deserve," Diamond said firmly. "You're strong Dominique, a better thief than I have ever been. If you have truly ever seen me as your Queen as you claim, then act like it and respect my decision."

"*C'est des conneries,*" Diamond heard Dominique mutter and paused when she heard the sound of a blade being drawn. Diamond's eyes widened slightly when she saw Dominique holding a knife that bore a black blade. "*Do you remember this? This knife belonged to your mother, her graduation gift from Corday. She gave it to you for your own protection. She said that as long as you had it you would be protected, your prized possession,*" Dominique said as angry tears fell freely. "*You gave this to me years ago when my family's curse started manifesting. I couldn't stop the nightmares that came from the hellish visions I saw, cursed to see the outcomes of every decision I made. I was positive that I would fail as a thief, and especially as a boss no matter what I did. Every outcome of every decision I made seemed to end in failure. Yet you came to me, despite just losing your mother before your very eyes leaving you wrought with nightmares. You told me the same thing your mother told you, that no matter what happened I would be protected. That was the last time I saw you smile to your heart's content before you were forced to wear that cursed glove and trap your emotions inside of you. My pain couldn't ever be compared to yours yet you still went out of your way, sacrificing more on top of what you'd lost already, just to make me find my own strength. Do those really sound like the actions of a failure of a Queen?*" Dominique asked rhetorically as she sheathed the blade. "*I will always obey your orders, for you are my closest friend and will always be my Queen. That said, I'll never respect this one. You don't get to walk away from the Guild, not like this. Because of you, I am strong now, the nightmares are gone. You need this more than I do,*" Dominique said before she tossed the blade to Diamond who barely caught it. "*Au revoir, Your Highness,*" Dominique said sarcastically with a half-assed bow before she left Diamond alone in the empty manor.

* * *

Santa Monica, Duskhaven

"It's just a knife, nothing more, nothing less," Diamond answered. "As for why I'm here, I need an honest opinion on something. There aren't many people left I can go to, I'm afraid. Not on a matter like this."

"Something you can't even ask Dominique? Wouldn't she be better? I mean I'm just a Guild server, never did the whole thief thing," Crystal said as she mixed another drink.

"No, she would simply tell me what needed to be said to get a positive response out of me," Diamond explained. "You have always been real with me ever since we were kids."

"I see, well what do you need advice on?"

"If it's even worth it anymore."

"Is what worth it?"

"Life," Diamond answered which made Crystal pause. "I, like many thieves, was born for a purpose. Born and bred to take on the most crucial job the Guild had to offer, and in an instant, it was gone. I'm not like a civilian who goes day in and day out wondering what their purpose in life is. I don't have that luxury. I've known what my purpose was since the day I was born and I failed it. So, should I just quit? End it all, and pray Juventas is merciful enough to let me into Elysium so I can once more be with those I let down?"

"That's...that's a hard question. A good friend would tell you not to give up, but in the end, your life is yours, isn't it? You have to make that decision," Crystal said with a heartbroken expression as she saw just how much Diamond had fallen. It was then Crystal frowned when she caught on to something Diamond had said. "Why would Juventas even have to be merciful? She would welcome you with open arms, and I'm positive your mom wouldn't think you let her down."

"Please, look around you. I know you servers are her personal agents but isn't it obvious that Juventas and her sisters have forsaken us? I don't know what we did, but we've pissed them off and they have abandoned us. They're supposed to always be with us, guiding us, yet they let Kat and Jack die! Fuck!" Diamond cursed as she wiped her eyes. "Now they've gotten me acting like a civilian."

"So much emotion, just how much are you hurting, girlfriend?" Crystal wondered. "Do you hate them?"

"I don't even know at this point, I just want answers. They were there for my mother but abandoned me? Did they detest the idea of her loving an outsider that much? Is that it? I didn't even do anything! It's…it's just not fair," Diamond finally said and for a moment neither of the women said anything as a tense silence set in between them. Eventually, Crystal took Diamond's shot glass and drunk it herself. Diamond watched in confusion as Crystal pulled out a flask and filled up the shot glass with an all too familiar golden liquid. After that, Crystal pulled out what appeared to be a small black pill bottle. Diamond remained silent as Crystal poured what looked like a single black seed from the bottle into her palm.

"Do you know what this is?"

"No."

"It's a seed from an Apple of Discord," Crystal informed her. "You thieves eat the fruit but never the seeds for it would mean certain death," Crystal said before the seed plopped into the shot glass. Diamond watched, perturbed, as the golden liquid seemed to corrode into a bright green color as the seed dissolved before her very eyes.

"Why do you even have something like that?"

"You said it yourself, I'm a server, one of Juventas' personal missionaries," Crystal explained. "Everyone needs a drink, people of all types, and when someone Juventas deems a threat to humanity appears for a drink, one seed is enough to take them out. Odorless, tasteless, completely undetectable. The seed only reacts this way when it's in contact with Juventas' nectar."

"Why show me this?" Diamond asked only for Crystal to slide the glass toward her.

"Even with Juventas' nectar present, this mix will still kill anyone. Royal Blood is the only thing powerful enough to withstand this concentrated poison," Crystal informed Diamond. "You see your mom as the perfect Queen yet none of you, not even your father, knows what she had to go through before reaching that point. The emotional turmoil of losing a band is life-threatening to any Midas, herself included. In her grief-like you- she wasn't even sure she was fit for the throne. So, a server issued your mom a challenge. That if she could drink this and live, she would see for herself that she was a rightful heir. If not, well, the Guild wouldn't have to worry about an imposter on the throne. It was a gambit, to see how far she would go for her peace of mind. Girlfriend, after all these years we've known each other? You have no idea how much it hurts my heart to stand before you and watch history repeat itself like this," Crystal said solemnly. "Your father is a great man. His blood mixing with Royal Blood would only make it stronger. If I can see that, so can the Goddesses. You think that they have abandoned you even though you sit here and drink Juventas' nectar? Even as Discordia placed her favorite Doll in your band?" Crystal asked and her voice continued to rise with each statement as Diamond looked at her in surprise. "Laverna even put a Frost in your band! A family of thieves bound solely to her! Do you have any idea how stupid you sound?" Crystal asked with narrowed eyes. "If you want to know so badly, to see if they have abandoned you then drink. If they have, you can die with the satisfaction of having gained truth, but if you live, then I hope you're ready to bow your head, girlfriend," Crystal said as Diamond looked between her and the glass. "You asked if you should end it and I said the choice was yours, whether or not you succeed is a different story altogether," Crystal said as Diamond picked up the glass. She hesitated a bit and her hand trembled as she realized what she was about to do. However, it was that hesitation that made her heart break as she remembered how her hesitation resulted in harm to her band. Diamond took a deep breath and downed the shot. Her vision darkened as the corrosive liquid slid down her throat like burning glass.

* * *

Santa Monica, Tartarus Tattoo

"You sure this guy is good?"

"Have I ever steered you wrong?" Eric questioned only for his friend to give him a look that pretty much said that yes, he had, a lot.

However, Eric just smirked in response and shook his head. "No, I've only steered Abbie wrong, most of the time by accident, sometimes just for the laughs," Eric admitted as he wrapped an arm around her. "But hey, new beginnings, right Alice?" Eric asked as he led her into a tattoo parlor. "Hey, Leo! We're here!"

"I'm in the back, brah!" a voice answered as the two made their way through the parlor. Alice's nose wrinkled as she could smell what she decided must have been some drug or another. Immediately, Alice began to wonder if she had made a mistake.

"I swear to God if this man is stoned," Alice muttered as Eric laughed nervously.

"It's fine, trust me, he works better like this."

"Eric…"

"Eric, my main man, how's it been!?" Leo questioned as he made his appearance. He was a young man with sun-kissed skin and brown dreadlocks that he kept tied behind his head. His brown eyes were kind but unfocused due to whatever drugs Alice decided he was on. "And you must be the lovely lady, pleased to meet ya!"

"Nice to meet you too," Alice said, though Eric wasn't sure if that could have sounded more forced if she tried.

"So, my main man Eric here tells me you need something covered up. A bad tattoo?" Leo guessed. "Should have told her to come to me if she wanted to get inked!"

"Hey, I was surprised too, I knew she wanted one but I never thought she'd do it," Eric said as he raised his hands defensively. "Where did you get it done, anyway?"

"Kat did it," Alice said quietly and Eric winced as he realized that he might have stepped on a proverbial land mine.

"Kat? Never heard of an artist by that name in the city," Leo said before Eric pulled him to the side.

"She was her girlfriend, she passed away recently," Eric explained quietly. Leo looked at him in surprise and glance over at Alice who idly took note of some of the pictures of his work.

"Bummer…" Leo said quietly. "…must have really loved her to let her ink her body. Trust me brah, nothing is more intimate than that."

"Yeah well look, this is the second time in two years this has happened to her. So, hook her up for me, will you?" Eric pleaded.

"Of course, but first I need to see what I'm working with. Look at my canvas, you know?" Leo said before he called out to Alice. "Mind if I see what I'm covering up?"

"Uh, no problem," Alice said before she pulled off her jacket so he could see the mark on her shoulder. Eric's eyes widened when he saw the mark while Leo let out a whistle of appreciation.

"I won't lie to you, this is not bad, not bad at all. Got a mystical feel to it, ya know? And these circles, Kat must have had one hell of a pair of hands on her," Leo said as he walked toward her and placed a hand on her shoulder. "May I?"

"Go ahead," Alice said as he adjusted the strap of her tank top to get a better look.

"Yeah, I can work with this, the question is, are you sure about this? I don't know why but this feels special."

"Yeah, I'm sure, I like it too but it causes me more pain than joy when I look at it now, you know?"

"I feel you. Well look around, show me what you want and we can get started," Leo said and she and Eric began to search through the possible tattoos. As time passed, they asked Leo questions about a few of his more interesting ones and bounced ideas off of each other. Alice had to admit, despite her first impressions it was clear that he was good at what he did, very good. Eventually she saw one design in particular that caught her eye. It was a sketch more than anything that was almost hidden away.

"What's this?"

"This, is my best sleeve to date, that came to me in a dream," Leo said as he pulled the sketch out. "It's Cerberus guarding the gates of hell."

"Hell? It's surrounded by roses, though."

"All flowers have a meaning, a red rose signifies enduring passion," Leo explained. "If you ask me, it takes a lot of passion to guard the gates of hell alone for an eternity. Though when you think about it, it's never really alone is it?" Leo mused as Alice looked at the image thoughtfully. "God, you have no idea how much I want to tat that on someone."

"So, why don't you?"

"People don't want it. It either rubs them the wrong way, too big, or they want to make alterations. When it comes to ideas customers want to be tattooed on them, I have no problem. That said, I'll never alter my own visions."

"I can respect that," Alice murmured as she took in the image. "How big is it?"

"The whole scene? Well on you to depict everything right it'll be your whole arm up to your shoulder and maybe even a bit down the side of your torso, why?" Leo asked curiously before his eyes widened as he finally caught on. "Wait, like, are you serious!?"

"If it covers up this tattoo, I'll take it," Alice said with a small smirk. "How much?"

"If you're serious about this then it's on the house," Leo said with a grin. "I'll even set you up with an LED implant! As an artist, you're doing me the favor here. Just tell people where you got it when they ask."

"Deal."

"Okay, you sit right there and take off your shirt so we can get started. If you have to use the bathroom go, because we'll be here for a while," Leo advised as he turned on the T.V. while Alice got situated. "Here put on something so you don't die of boredom." Leo said before he left to get his tools. Alice flipped through the channels only stopping when a breaking news report caught her eye.

"Though Diamond has been escorted to the hospital in time, reports say that she is currently in a coma. No one is quite sure about what could have possibly driven the young singer to attempt suicide but…"

Alice felt herself become light-headed as the news anchor's voice was drowned out by her own thoughts.

"Are you fucking serious?" Eric asked incredulously as Leo came back into the room.

"Is everything okay?"

"No," Alice said quietly as she wiped her eyes. "But let's focus on this right now." With a shrug, Leo began to set up his equipment and began to work on Alice. Alice was so lost in her thoughts, that the needle that dug into her didn't faze her hardly as much as she knew it should have.

*   *   *

China, Hong Kong

Meifeng sat quietly on a log in front of a fire out in the forest on the outskirts of the bustling city. Suddenly a loud crack echoed throughout the area. When she realized the source of the sound, Meifeng gazed upon a large chunk of ice that continued to crack and thaw. After a few more moments, a gloved hand ripped free as the ice shattered and an exhausted Jack appeared.

"Welcome back," Meifeng greeted as she watched Jack curl into himself as he shouted in pain. Meifeng couldn't blame him either when she noticed that he now had one less arm than she remembered. That said, Meifeng soon realized that it was not his missing arm that caused his pain. "I suggest invoking your curse and freezing your heart," Meifeng said calmly. "Spare yourself your boss' pain so you can concentrate," Meifeng instructed as she approached him. Soon a cold fog escaped from his body as he shut away his heart and emotions which left an exhausted Jack on the forest floor.

*   *   *

Silicon Valley, Prosperity Industries, One Month Prior

"Filthy abomination!" August shouted after he broke free from the ice. As he glanced around the vault which had become a frozen wasteland, it wasn't long before he found Jack, in a block of ice both unconscious and frozen in place thanks to his last desperate attack.

"Impressive gambit, I'll give you that. Not even I could shrug that off," August muttered before he aimed his staff at Jack. Before he could

end jack's life, a heavenly scent filled his nose and permeated throughout the room.

"Bloody hell, were you always this pathetic, Gladius?" a feminine voice said, thick with an English accent. August glared as he saw a hooded woman stand next to the frozen form of Jack. When she turned to face him, August saw a person he hated even more than Umbra. "This much trouble against first-years? How in Laverna's name did a coward like you ever take Romero's place as the Arch-Mage of August?"

"Julia, I knew I recognized that damnable perfume of yours, such an insidious treasure," August all but growled out as his body exploded with a bright blue light. Julia's ruby lips curved up into a smile, more amused by his display of power than anything. August's eyes narrowed as he stared at the pale gold necklace around her neck, its pendant being a small vial of a mysterious blue liquid that seemed to glow. Julia remained unfazed by the power that poured off of August even as it tousled her hair and shattered some of the surrounding ice. "Today is my lucky day, I get revenge on that Doll and now I can get revenge on the woman who killed Romero and my dearest Regina."

"Funny, last time I checked they died because of you. I just played my part in the script you wrote," Julia said and though her smile never wavered, there was an unmistakable edge to her voice. "Settle down," Julia said coldly, her eyes like twin glaciers. "I'm not here to fight."

"You won't have a choice," August said which only made Julia laugh.

"No, it's you who doesn't have a choice," Julia mused. "The moment you smelled my aroma, this conversation was already over." August cursed when Julia and Jack then vanished into thin air and left him alone in the vault.

*   *   *

China, Hong Kong, Present

"And then according to her, she brought you here since I was the one who issued the contract to protect you. I couldn't have my father knowing about this and kept you hidden out here," Meifeng said as Jack did his best to warm up by the fire. "I must admit, I'm impressed that you broke out of your first cryostasis in a month," Meifeng praised. "Normally when a young member of your family first pushes themselves too far it takes months but you did it in one. Must be a perk of being head of the family."

"I see," Jack muttered his emotions still frozen away in an attempt to protect himself from Diamond's pain. "What about your guards? You said your father was overprotective of you."

"Just as you said, they're my guards," Meifeng said mischievously. "Not his, though I don't think he realizes that just yet. They listen to me and act as though they listen to him."

"Diamond and Kat, what happened to them?"

"Your infiltrator's body was nowhere to be found," Meifeng revealed which made him raise an eyebrow. "Your guess is as good as mine. As for the Princess, well former Princess, she stepped down and chose to end the Midas line. Her grief seems to have consumed her. Last I heard she tried to take her own life, currently, she's in a coma."

"I see, then I need to be by her side," Jack said as he rose to his feet.

"And do what? Fail her again?" Meifeng said skeptically. "I was told you Frosts were to be rational without your emotions distracting you."

"What is more rational than being by my boss' side in her darkest moments?" Jack asked making Meifeng laugh softly.

"How about becoming strong enough to make sure she never feels that pain again?" Meifeng asked and Jack paused. "How about becoming a thief worthy of your family name?"

"Impossible, my treasure is gone," Jack said as he gestured to his stub with his left hand.

"A thief and their treasure are inseparable. One cannot exist without the other," Meifeng scoffed. "You can't see it but you can feel it, can't you? Arondight's power? If it were truly gone, your presence would have torn your body asunder by now." Meifeng's expression then softened. "Stay and let me teach you, show you the path to true power the likes of which not even your precious Vivi has seen."

"You know I can't pay you right now, right?"

"Fool," Meifeng said as she walked to a nearby tree and placed her hand over a thief mark that was etched into the wood. Soon shadows surrounded them both as Jack felt a twisting sensation over his body. Within moments the darkness disappeared and Jack found himself on a mountain with a full moon shining brightly behind him.

"What the hell!?" Jack exclaimed before his eyes widened. His curse was no longer active but he still felt no pain. "Where are we?"

"My legacy, this temple is where I plan to have my school. I had it made in secret, hidden in the black desert surrounding the Guild," Meifeng said making him turn around to find her standing on the steps of a temple. However, though he knew she was Meifeng, he couldn't believe it. Instead of her white robes, Meifeng now wore a silky black robe as her hair now fell freely. Her robe hung off her shoulders which revealed part of a black butterfly shaped brand that seemed to take up a majority of her back. Her electric violet eyes shone even brighter as she made her way toward him. Gone was her kind, almost shy, demeanor and in its place was a quiet ferocity that seemed to keep an overwhelming darkness at bay. "A place where I can be who I really am. I am Li Meifeng, master in all but name. It is with your help that I plan to remedy that."

"What do you mean?"

"The way thieves are taught is dictated by those given the title of Master. Of those Masters, there are three that are ranked the highest and are given the ability to dictate who can and cannot become a Master and open their own school within the Guild. For assassins they have Headmistress Corday, for infiltrators, it's the Phantom Thief, and for enforcers, that honor is given to my father," Meifeng said with a sneer. "Their ways are too old and will get future thieves killed. They refuse to change, to adapt to times even as our enemies do. Their mentality is crippling us and the only way to stop it before it's too late is to get true masters who understand how this world works to teach future thieves. My methods may seem too…dark… for my father's liking and he will never approve, despite my obvious skill. This is one of the reasons I chose to help you, for I could see myself in your frustration, your anger," Meifeng said as she strode toward him. "Tell me, between The Three Masters, did any of them teach a single member of your band about the changes the mages have done to their spells?"

"Changes?" Jack asked with a frown.

"They've begun weaponizing the element of light from the sun and moon, says it helps them defeat monsters easier. However, that extends to thieves as well as they weaken the power of our shadows with their light," Meifeng said as Jack recalled how August turned his staff into a spear of light. "By adding light to their shields, they reduce the power our skills have on them, a technique based off of tactics used by the Knights' Order. I imagine someone like August, in particular, would find such an ability useful. For poor unsuspecting first years, it could be the difference between life and death."

"What are you getting at?"

"What if I told you there was a way to counter this method? A way that I told my father and he ignored in his foolish attempt to maintain traditions?" Meifeng questioned curiously.

"Why would he ignore it?"

"Fear, fear to do what needs to be done. If the Mages' Circle begins to use more light, then should we not counter it with darkness?" Meifeng questioned. "You are a Frost born into darkness. My father's idea of balance is but a pipe dream for you. However, you have me and I will make sure you succeed by any means necessary."

"You are risking a lot just for me to succeed, why?"

"Laverna came to me in a dream, she saw how much I was training you and gave me a chance to become a Master, to prove my theories," Meifeng explained. "If I can make you an enforcer that she deems acceptable, she will give me the rank of Master herself. From there I can build a school that surpasses father's and bring an end to the old ways of the Three Masters. I could save the Guild's future initiates before it's too late. Before they end up band-less like me... like you almost were..." Meifeng said quietly. "So? What do you say? Not even nectar can regrow your arm but let me truly train you. I can give you back everything you've lost with interest as well as give others like us a chance to truly thrive."

"Meifeng," Jack said quietly as he fell to his knees and bowed while she gazed down upon him. "Teach me."

"Teach you what?"

"Everything."

CHAPTER 17

• • • • • • • • • ● • • • • • • • • •

HEALING

Elysium

When Diamond came to, she grimaced as her eyes had to adjust to the bright scenery that surrounded her. Diamond was confused when she felt soft blades of grass beneath her fingertips and looked around to find herself in an incredibly beautiful forest. After she forced herself to her feet, Diamond began to walk around the strange realm in wonder.

"Beautiful, ain't it?" a voice asked making Diamond turn to find herself face to face with Crystal. "Come on, follow me, there's something you need to see," Crystal said as she grabbed Diamond by her gloved hand and practically dragged her through the forest.

"Crystal, where are we?"

"Elysium of course!" Crystal said with a grin as Diamond looked at her in shock. "Come on, you said you wanted to know if the Goddesses abandoned you? Let's find out. Just remember what I said, be prepared to bow if they haven't," Crystal said before they came upon a large clearing. Diamond gasped, eyes wide, as she saw a massive ivory throne that rested in the middle of the clearing, separated from them by a stream of water.

"It's...empty..." Diamond said and her heart plummeted when she saw that the abandoned throne was covered with vines and moss.

"Of course, it is, no one has sat in it in ten years," Crystal said as she walked to the river.

"Then doesn't that mean they…left…us," Diamond trailed off as she watched in confusion as Crystal undressed. "What are you doing?"

"Taking a bath, it's been a long day," Crystal said as she glanced back at Diamond before she dipped a toe into the water and shivered at how cold it was. "Easy does it," Crystal muttered as she slowly climbed into the river and slowly submerged herself. Confused by Crystal's actions, Diamond sat down and took a moment to just think. Think about life and just where everything went wrong. Before Diamond could come up with an answer, she heard a splash and saw Crystal climb up out of the water on the opposite side of the river. "That's better," Crystal said, her eyes closed as she ran her fingers through her hair. Diamond began to say something only to stop when she noticed that Crystal's gold highlights seemed to grow and spread throughout her hair. Diamond rubbed her eyes and looked again only to see that Crystal's hair color had really began to change. Crystal's dark skin seemed to glitter even more than usual only Diamond was positive that it wasn't make-up. This was only reaffirmed when it looked as if Crystal had the very stars themselves branded on to her back. A glowing blue constellation soon formed on Crystal's skin. Crystal hummed to herself as she rung the water from her hair while an elegant white transparent toga formed around her body. Diamond could only watch when Crystal strode toward the throne as her body drastically grew in size. With a wave of her hand, Crystal removed the vines and moss disappeared before she sat upon the throne. A golden diadem appeared on Crystal's head before she crossed her legs and gazed down upon Diamond with now bright golden eyes. As she rested her cheek in her hand, the divine being smiled down upon the incredulous form of Diamond. "Now, tell me again how I abandoned you?"

"Juventas," Diamond whispered in shock. To say there was a lot she wanted to say, to ask, would have been an understatement. That said, it didn't take long for Diamond to realize what she had to do. The former Princess had to do something she had never done before.

Juventas watched in amusement as Diamond simply fell to her knees and kneeled before her.

"We have much to discuss," Juventas said as Diamond bowed her head.

* * *

Hollywood, Midas Manor

"Roderick...I'm so sorry," Vivi said quietly as she rested a hand on her boss' shoulder while he gazed down upon the unconscious form of his daughter who barely clung to life. "What the hell did she take that even nectar can't wake her up?"

"Is it my fault?" Roderick questioned with a frown. "I tried hard to be both father and King. She was always so strong, my little gem, unbreakable just like her name," Roderick said as he gently grasped the side of his daughter's face. "It's hard to know when a Midas needs help, but I tried so hard just like I tried for her mother. Yet like before, here I am failing to be there when they need me most of all."

"It's not your fault," Vivi tried to reassure him. "Diamonds are durable, yeah, but they can shatter if hit in the right spot. You couldn't have known someone would hit that spot, don't blame yourself."

"You're wrong. If you're a parent and your child is in this situation...an attempt on their life by their own hand? You've messed up somewhere," Roderick muttered before he kissed Diamond on her forehead. "Let's get to work, Vivi, they've taken our children. So, from them we'll take everything."

* * *

China, Hong Kong

"Again!" Meifeng ordered as Jack forced himself to his feet." Come on, I thought you wanted power."

"I do, but I am at a bit of a disadvantage if you hadn't noticed," Jack said as he gestured to his stub.

"A disadvantage of your own choosing. Your mother's blood is in your veins, her darkness is yours," Meifeng said coldly as she went on the offensive. Jack grimaced as his body trembled from the force of her blows. Use that power to regain what you've lost!" Meifeng shouted as she grabbed his wrist and with quick fluid motion, snapped his left arm. The pain almost blinded Jack but it was drowned out by a rush of fear when Meifeng kicked him in his chest and knocked him off of the mountain.

*   *   *

Jack was confused. One moment he was falling off of a cliff, the next he found himself standing in the middle of a frozen wasteland as a blizzard raged around him. However, before he could question what was happening, he noticed that nine massive circles were etched into the ground, each one inside another. From each circle, a frozen chain extended toward the center of the realm and wrapped around a large beautifully crafted blade that was thrust inside the innermost circle. The blade was identical to the brand on Jack's arm and just like it, the sword had nine circles etched into it, all connected by a single line that ran from the tip of the blade to its hilt. Behind the blade, Jack saw a demonic suit of armor that seemed to have been sculpted from black ice. The gauntlets of the armor resembled a pair of claws, and its talons were light blue and crackled with a blue presence. The frozen knight gripped the hilt of the blade tightly and as if moving on instinct, Jack tried to reach out toward the blade, his stub outstretched as if desperately trying to reach it. A crack could be heard as the knight's right gauntlet released the blade before it reached out toward Jack. As a blinding blue light erupted in the realm, Jack felt a freezing sensation where his right arm used to be.

*   *   *

Jack found himself awakened from the strange daze he had fallen into and to his surprise, his descent had halted. When he looked up, he found the right gauntlet of the frozen knight extending from his stub. The talons of the gauntlet crackled with presence which allowed them to sink into the stone effortlessly. It was on the back of his now armored arm, however, where Jack found his attention drawn for it bore an all too familiar brand that Jack had thought was lost to him.

"Arondight," Jack whispered as a cold mist escaped his lips.

"Sometimes fear is more effective than a thousand lectures," Meifeng said from atop of the mountain. "Come, our session is far from over," Meifeng said as she walked away. Jack's talons dug deeper into the stone before he catapulted himself up to the top of the mountain. When Jack landed and met Meifeng's eyes, they both knew that Jack would never doubt her again. "Take your stance."

"Yes, Master," Jack said as he raised his gauntlet in front of him.

* * *

Elysium

"So why? Why did you three choose to make the Midas Family the royal line?" Diamond questioned Juventas as she stood on the Goddess' hand. Juventas released a long breath as she thought about the question.

"When the founders were cursed, they were afflicted with a crippling madness as well as power. Our enemies sought to have the founders destroy themselves and each other with the power forced upon them. Midas, that devilish rogue, asked me to take the madness from his allies and seal it within him. His idea was that by doing this, his companions would be able to harness their cursed power and use it to bring down our enemies," Juventas explained as she looked at a stunned Diamond sadly. "He was willing to sacrifice himself for the future of the Guild. His selflessness moved my divine heart and I honored his final request to continue his bloodline just before his very soul was torn asunder. The madness ran deep, its darkness binding with his very blood and being passed down from himself to his heirs. Yet, unlike their father, because of my blood, their bodies hardened and were strong enough to contain the madness and hone it along with his cursed touch. It is because of this fortitude that your family continues to lead the Guild Diamond, and why I'll never leave your family," Juventas told Diamond pointedly. "Unlike other thieves, you are born with your treasure, you have years ahead of others to get used to it which is why your family always makes such capable thieves. In the end, however, that madness is still there. Your body keeps it contained which is why your blood must never spill," Juventas warned and Diamond grimaced. "The females of your family, in particular, have to be monitored with extreme care for obvious reasons."

"Like my schedule for drinking nectar?"

"Exactly, and why you must come to me when you are ready to produce an heir," Juventas informed her. "Not to ask for permission, but rather give me time to prepare my realm for you. Giving birth amongst the mortals will not end well. This is why it took almost two centuries for your mother to work up the courage to even think about a family. If it wasn't for my nectar, your family would have died out long ago," Juventas revealed and she smirked at the memory. "In hindsight, we owe your father a great deal. I was convinced the line would end with her."

"I…was born here?"

"And delivered by myself, as was your mother, her father, and so on and so forth," Juventas said as she raised an eyebrow. "But please, tell me once more how I abandoned you. My sisters and I are guides, we want you all to thrive but we cannot interfere too much or else we risk hindering your ability to grow and improve. That's why when things like this war with the Mages happens, we have to be creative, a trick we actually learned from you all. Many think that speed is the greatest strength of a thief, but it is your imagination. How you decide to overcome each and every obstacle is your true power."

"I'm sorry."

"You better be," Juventas said though her smile never wavered. "Each generation I am reborn, taking a form that would best relate to the next heir. I guide them but I never truly interfere with how they rule. I was there for tyrants like your grandfather and I was there for saviors like your mother, and now I am here for you as I will be for your child."

"No point, I am not having children nor am I heir to the throne."

"No children? And here I thought you were quite fond of the Frost boy," Juventas said. "I can't speak for my sisters, though Discordia is most likely too distracted by her toys to care. Laverna would most likely object, but even so, I am in your corner."

"He's gone, you know that my band fell against August."

"Funny, I don't remember letting either of them through the gates of Elysium," Juventas mused which made Diamond's heart skip a beat. "No, in fact, I actually believe they are alive now, waiting for their boss to return."

"But...I...I saw..." Diamond trailed off while Juventas chuckled as she raised her free hand.

"You saw what? The Frost boy die? Give him more credit," Juventas said as an image appeared in the sky that showed Jack sparring with Meifeng only to be defeated. However, after each defeat, he climbed to his feet quickly and began to fight back. "Or perhaps you meant Katarina?" Juventas asked and Diamond's heart clench as a second image of a broken Kat appeared. Kat's body rested in a grassy field as a massive shadow appeared over her. "She's far craftier than you give her credit for. She ripped her own Apple of Discord from her chest to protect it from August's onslaught," Juventas said as Diamond fell to her knees. "And I know you do not believe your civilian friend is dead," Juventas said as a final image appeared that showed Alice, Roy, and Eric working to rebuild Wonderland. Juventas smiled as she looked at Alice's tattoo. "Good taste, I always did favor the Cerberus. Of all the creations from the gods of old, it represents the band system the best does it not?"

"But I couldn't feel them," Diamond said unable to believe her eyes.

"Your own pain distracted you from theirs. It is simply too powerful. Let me tell you something I told your mother. Stop bottling up your emotions and just let the healing waters flow, girl," Juventas said warmly as Diamond's eyes shone with unshed tears. "Come to terms with what plagues you and become the person you know you can be."

"But my curse-"

"-Doesn't affect a Goddess like me, just let it out, you're safe here with me," Juventas said reassuringly as Diamond looked down at her gloved hand. She hesitated for a moment before she began to pull it off. Once she pulled it off, it felt as though a dam had broken as her heart no longer felt suppressed. Her nearly emotionless expression shattered as she broke down into tears while she stared at her right hand which released a bright golden light. Juventas just watched silently as Diamond cried uncontrollably while years of suppressed pain were released. Images flashed through Diamond's mind, memories both good and bad. She saw the times she celebrated a successful job with her band and she saw when she failed them when she thought each died in front of her. She saw her mother smile down at her and she saw her mother fall, her heart stopped by a wicked mage that wore Romero's face. Diamond even saw when she, just twelve years of age, celebrated her birthday with her father. She saw how she reached to grab a necklace he bought for her from a saleswoman. She saw how her hand touched the stranger's and how the woman suddenly turned into a golden dust as Diamond's curse activated. Diamond wept as she relived how her hand's light brought destruction upon anything and everything within the crowded store. The destruction only stopped when she covered her hand with her body and waited for her father to bring her a glove. So many memories passed through Diamond's mind, so much pain, and finally, she had a release. The sight moved Juventas so much that a single golden tear slid from her eye while the light continued to grow and engulf everything in sight.

*　　*　　*

Garden of Discord

Kat's eyes snapped open as she shot up to a sitting position while fear filled her entire body.

"Everything hurts," Kat muttered before she noticed that she was in what appeared to be a large orchard. There were apple trees as far as the eye could see and Kat couldn't help but be stunned when she noticed that all of the apples were gold in color. Scattered throughout the realm were nude individuals, Dolls if Kat had to guess. They all happily tended to the orchard and the few that noticed her simply waved with bright smiles before they continued with their tasks. Kat looked down and was startled to find her arms, legs, and chest covered by a black flesh-like material. Upon closer inspection, she could see what looked like her skin slowly reappear over the material. Kat ran her fingers through her hair and paused when she noticed that it now hung past her shoulders. "How long have I been out? Where am I?"

"Home," a voice said with a sinister chuckle. Kat tensed and looked up to find a brunette woman on the branch of a nearby tree. Her body was covered in a loose-fitting red toga that seemed to be made out of silk. Her eyes were covered by a red blindfold yet Kat could still feel the mischievous glint that was in the woman's hidden gaze. "You took quite the beating," the woman said as she grabbed one of the apples and bit into it.

"Discordia," Kat whispered in awe before she hugged herself when a sharp pain shook her to her core. "So, it's true, I'm a Doll," Kat murmured quietly as she realized August was right. "Did I really destroy a nursery? Did I really smile at the deaths I caused?" Kat asked desperately. For a moment, Discordia said nothing as she continued to eat the apple.

"The last war was...a dark time in the Guild's history. The alliance had to do whatever it could to protect humanity from a very powerful enemy," Discordia said after a moment. "Umbra was tasked with infiltrating a group known as the Legion of the Black Moon. They had been long-term enemies of the alliance and were the ones who started the war. Umbra was to act as a traitor and fight against us while giving us much-needed information. One task the Black Moon gave her was to destroy a supply base of the Mage's Circle," Discordia explained. "However, the man who now calls himself August made a last-minute decision and swapped the locations of the supply base and their nursery. Umbra set off a bomb on the outside and..."

"...the children died," Kat finished.

"That event broke Umbra, so much that the systems in charge of her emotions were scrambled. Her face smiled, but her heart shattered. This is why you, even now, tend to smile in dire situations," Discordia explained to a stunned Kat who even at that moment had to stop a smile. "The nursery was an unfortunate loss but it earned you their trust and thanks to you and the information you got us, the war ended in our favor. You ran into August who was understandably angry and he did damage to your apple. The damage was severe and you would never be able to be as powerful as you used to be...until now," Discordia said as she gestured toward a tree behind Kat. "After this last little adventure of yours, I planted the seeds from your apple. This tree grew from them in mere weeks and is currently producing some of the ripest fruit I have seen in a long time. Through your sacrifice, we will be able to create some of the best Dolls and bands the Guild has ever seen. I've taken the liberty of giving its first fruit to you to celebrate your new body. Unlike other Dolls, you had a badge that could be used to temporarily store your mind. You're lucky, losing your Apple of Discord would normally mean death," it was then that Discordia frowned. "That said, though your fruit can be replaced, your body cannot. Laverna made it clear that she would not participate in the creation of another Black Doll. The complete production process proved to be a bit too unsavory for her tastes," Discordia said with a scoff. "This will be your last life. A regular Doll cannot participate in the band system, and we both know you'd rather die than be transferred into a body that couldn't aid your band."

"What happened to Jack? Diamond?" Kat asked urgently as she thought about her band. "What happened to-" Kat cut herself off as she remembered who she spoke to. Discordia, however, just chuckled and gave her a knowing look.

"Your lover?" Discordia questioned as Kat averted her eyes. "You can fool those mortals, but I will always know what my toys are doing. Personally, I approve, the chaos resulting in keeping a civilian bound to you...I wonder how this will end?" Discordia said with a sinister laugh that made Kat shudder. "Doesn't matter, Laverna is who you should fear but she is not here so for now your secret will remain just that. They are all safe, your boss...well, I'm told she is strong so she will survive. You saved them."

"I did?" Kat asked with a frown. "But the last thing I remember was my treasure failing."

"Your treasure doesn't fail," Discordia said with a sneer, as if insulted by the thought. "You just didn't get the effect you wished for. As a reward for your efforts in the war, the Bandit Queen, Isabelle, gave you the chance at living a new life, a chance to live as a civilian before being honorably decommissioned. You chose a new life, wanting to forget the horrors you saw, but you refused to leave the Guild," Discordia said with a smirk. "Each Doll is born from a single memory of a thief, as a soul is nothing but an aggregate of memories. When you're forged, a memory is bound to your apple. That memory will become the basis of your personality. Your very appearance comes from the donor who gave you this gift of life. Isabelle chose to transfer the memory she had of giving birth to Diamond into Umbra's apple. A few years passed as I raised you, making sure that your damaged body was working properly before I sent you off to live with the woman you call Vivi. Still, I am not Juventas. I am not as hopelessly optimistic as she is, I knew a day would come when we would need your old self back which is why I made sure Umbra stayed with you. Your treasure is a fail-safe," Discordia informed Kat. "Good luck makes you take over and bad luck awakens Umbra. Neither you nor she remembers your time as the other, but you feel what the other felt. You probably felt like you woke up from a terrible nightmare while the inverse is true for Umbra."

"So, when I blacked out..."

"Umbra took over and did her best to keep you all alive," Discordia said and waved a hand at Kat's new body. "At any cost."

"I see, wait, what about the Doll in Prosperity Industries? Did anyone go back for her?"

"On the contrary, she came for you," Discordia said with a grin. "The Frost child incapacitated August long enough for her to sneak in and retrieve your body. In fact, she's now a part of you," Discordia said and Kat looked down at herself in horror. "Calm down, she's fine

263

but let's say she...no longer wanted to be part of your model-type. She was repurposed, her apple was removed from the black frame and placed in one more suited for servicing the Guild in more passive ways. You are now effectively the last of your model. Parts from your fallen sisters and brothers were used to repair you and upgrade you into a ninth generation Doll, the latest incarnation," Discordia said with a laugh, clearly proud of her work. "And the last for you. I can repair you, but you cannot withstand massive damage like that again my little agent of chaos."

"Heh," Kat laughed and Discordia raised an eyebrow. "Sorry, it's just, I've been called that before. So, when will I be done here? I want to see the others as soon as possible."

"Not so fast," Discordia said firmly. "You have been blessed with a new body, a superior one. You must discover your new limits and undergo many tests to make sure the transfer worked. You will be here for a little while."

"Wait, what!?"

"Yes, but do not worry. Your band is using this time to get stronger," Discordia informed Kat. "You should do the same so you don't fall behind. We must test for bugs and work out any possible flaws in your new body. You should be in optimal condition in a few more months."

"Months!?" Kat repeated with a horrified look on her face. A stern look from Discordia, however, just silenced her before her shoulders slumped. "Fine, all I gotta do is pass these tests, right? Let's see what I can do, then."

"Yes, but before we can begin preparations to help you spread havoc, I do believe you are forgetting something," Discordia said and Kat was confused by Discordia's growing irritation. Kat suddenly gasped before she kneeled and bowed her head. In her confusion, she had forgotten that she was before her Goddess. "Well, I suppose the lack of respect means you were successful at becoming like the mortals. Now, let's begin."

* * *

Elysium

"Are you alright now?" Juventas asked as Diamond wiped her eyes.

"Yes, I needed that. I feel lighter than I have in a long time, like a burden has been lifted," Diamond said kindly with a bright smile that Juventas matched only to gasp as she looked at the desolate wasteland that surrounded them. No trace of Elysium's former beauty to be found. "What have I done?" Diamond whispered in horror only for Juventas to wave off her concerns.

"The gate to Elysium still stands and that's all that matters. Everything else? It can be rebuilt, made even better now. That's the fun part," Juventas said with a smile. "Just like you, you've broken down and now you can rebuild. Become a better you. Your curse will continue to destroy but that is a small price to pay for your peace of mind."

"I almost don't want to put this back on, to turn back into that cold person…but it's for the best I suppose," Diamond said sadly. "Plus, this light is hurting my eyes," Diamond said with a giggle.

"Well, that depends, you could stay here if you want to," Juventas clearly amused by this more open Diamond.

"No, I can't," Diamond denied. "My band needs me, my father needs me, but most importantly the Guild needs me, even if I threw away my right to the throne."

"Diamond, the throne is part of you, it cannot be easily cast away," Juventas said before she tapped Diamond on her head. The Princess frowned for a bit before she felt a tingling sensation course over her body. Diamond's eyes widened when she found her hands and arms covered in strange black markings that vaguely resembled those on the Knight Order's grimoire. It was then that something seemed to click into place for Diamond.

"The Thief grimoire…is me?"

"Your body already protects your blood and the Guild. We decided to have it protect our secrets as well, tying them to the royal bloodline," Juventas explained. "As you see you have many responsibilities, your status as heir to the throne cannot be lost easily even by your own hand. Now, you wish to earn your right to go back to your band? A life is easily given up, but not easily taken back," Juventas told Diamond as her gaze hardened ever so slightly. "Can you prove to me that you're worth a second attempt at life?"

"How can I prove to you that I am?"

"Hm, let's see. I mentioned that imagination is a thief's greatest power," Juventas mused. "Nothing solidifies that more than the illusion, Dominion. Cast that, and I will let you live."

"That's impossible, that takes years to learn and decades to master! It can't even be transferred...I don't even know how to begin figuring it out!" Diamond said in shock. Unable to believe that Juventas wanted her, a first year, to do something her mother, the Queen, struggled to do. "I can't even use shadow synch properly. When my band needed me most, I froze up. So, distracted by my own weakness, I forgot to use their strength to cover it," Diamond said as she shook her head. "Dominion is impossible for someone like me."

"Shame and here I thought you cared for your band," Juventas said with a small frown.

"I do!"

"Then prove it. Did you forget your role? You are the grimoire, you literally have all the information you need to begin learning how to cast that illusion right under your nose. Without it, you'll never be able to end this war with the mages or be worthy of the throne," Juventas said and for a moment Diamond said nothing before she nodded. As Diamond put on her glove, Juventas watched as Diamond's expression hardened as the light died down. When Diamond's gaze met hers, Juventas could see a fire burning within Diamond's gaze.

"Fine then, you're on. Just watch, I'll figure this out and then, I will take back everything," Diamond said firmly. "But not before I steal everything from August."

"Now you're sounding like a true Bandit Queen," Juventas mused. "Alright, impress me. Earn your right to live."

* * *

Santa Monica, Midas Tower

"Finally, it's all set up," Alice said as she placed a pair of contact lenses in her eyes before she turned to face Roy and Eric. "Look, the world is slowly goin' crazy. Every time you turn around someone else has died, or some business made profits through the blood of someone else. Right now, it's only the three of us, but as we work together, do what we can to make a difference and build up our strength, we can make Wonderland even better than it used to be. I hope you guys are willing to work with me."

"Of course!" Eric said with a grin.

"Glad to hear it, then let's get started. Let me show you somethin'," Alice said before she typed something into a tablet and watched as a large hologram of the planet appeared in the center of the room. "See the blue?" Alice asked as she gestured toward the image, and the men noted that a good portion of North America along with a few parts of Europe was blue. "That's how far Wonderland spread the first go around. The purple is us now."

"Uh I don't see any purple," Eric said with a frown and they watched as the image shifted and zoomed in on North America, or more accurately California. The image zoomed in until they could see the block surrounding Midas tower and sure enough, it was purple. "Oh."

"Yeah, as you can see, we need some work," Alice said dryly. "Fortunately, the news of our return should help us progress faster than if we were to organize an entirely new group. Power and influence, that's what we need."

"How much are you aiming for?"

"Watch this," Alice said before she waved at the monitor which dismissed the image as she made her way toward the window. Alice held her hand out toward the city, it was night time so lights filled every building their eyes could see. When Alice closed her hand into a fist, the lenses in her eyes lit up and shifted a bit as every light on the block suddenly shut down. Even Midas Tower darkened as the block looked like it got hit with a power surge. "One...two..." Alice was barely able to finish the last number before the lights turned back on. "We need enough to make that last longer than two seconds and for it to affect a lot more than one block."

"Holy shit," Eric said incredulously as Roy let out an appreciative whistle. "Unfortunately, when P.I. rolls out their next-generation operating system with Athena up and runnin', we will not be able to do even that much and we'll be crushed quickly," Alice informed them. "The good news is that I built it so I can tear it down. I made it when I was younger and dumber. I'm still young…"

"But a little less dumb," Roy said with a laugh.

"Exactly. I can make somethin' better, safer, that can take that thing down before it can go online," Alice informed them "I'm gonna have to get my hands a little dirty if I want to do it though."

"You mean we, right?" Eric said skeptically. "No offense, you're tall but kind of scrawny."

"Hey, I picked up a few exercises. Just give me a few months," Alice said before she smirked. "But yes, I mean we, Eric."

"Well, I'm too old for all of that." Roy informed them. "I'll be here for advice, and maybe supervise here or there to help you rebuild but that's it."

"You've already done more for me than my entire family. So, thank you, we can take it from here," Alice said before she gave the older man a hug.

"Now, don't get all emotional on me," Roy said with a laugh. "If you ever need a place to hide out, you know where to find me. Just don't be strangers."

"Wouldn't dream of it, old man," Eric said with a grin.

"I'll be taking my leave now, you got my number," Roy said before he took off his straw fedora and placed it on Eric's head. "Look after her for me, lil' brother', someone has to stop her from going insane."

"Of course."

"Tell the Mrs. we said hi," Alice said which made him nod before he departed, optimistic about this new Wonderland's future. "Now come on, Eric, let's get to work."

CHAPTER 18

· · · · · · ●●● ● ●●●● · · · · ·

SPRING OF REBIRTH

Los Angeles, Warehouse

"I'm in, get the car ready."

"Gotcha," Eric said as Alice stealthily made her way deeper into the building. When Alice spotted an armed guard, she pulled up a black cloth she had tied around her neck that covered the lower half of her face. Silently, Alice made her way to the guard as the image of what appeared to be the lower half of a skull appeared on the mask in a white light. Once she was behind the guard, Alice grabbed him in a choke-hold and held him tightly until he lost consciousness. Alice made sure to hide his body and relieved the guard's weapon of its ammunition before she advanced further through the building.

"Where is it?" Alice muttered and the mouth of the skull moved with each word as if it had spoken. Alice's contact lenses shifted as she scanned the boxes and crates, unable to find her target. Before she could continue her search any longer, the sound of gunfire startled her and forced her to take cover. "What?" Alice wondered in confusion as she peeked over a crate. To her disbelief, she watched as a brunette woman ran into the scene with a compact bow held tightly in her hand. The newcomers face was covered by a mask that Alice knew all too well.

269

"God damn it, Hood, you had one job!" another voice laced thick with a Russian accent shouted. When Alice turned to it, she found a man with a black and purple mask that held a rifle in his hand. He had brown eyes and black hair with a gray streak in it. The masked man aimed at one of the guards and quickly shot him down.

"Grimm, what the hell!?" the woman called Hood shouted in alarm.

"Relax, he had a vest. Besides, aren't you the assassin? Act like it."

"You think it's that simple?" Hood questioned angrily before she loaded an arrow into her bow and shot it at a light. Alice watched as the arrow tore through the cord that kept the light suspended before it crashed down upon an unsuspecting guard.

"Can you two, please act professionally for once?" a quiet voice asked tiredly. When they turned, they found a brunette man wearing a black and gold mask, locked in hand-to-hand combat with two guards. Alice thought the man would be outmatched but to her surprise, despite his small stature, he quickly and efficiently took down his opponents. Alice frowned as she saw the man, sure that she had seen him before. That said, she knew as long as they had those masks, she would never be able to discern their identities.

"Sorry, boss!" Hood said apologetically as Grimm rested his rifle on his shoulder.

"Sorry," Grimm said before he whistled in appreciation. "You've gotten stronger."

"I have to, with Frost gone someone has to pick up the slack," the boss said quietly and Alice saw his band tense at his mention of Jack. Alice felt her heart clench at the reminder of what she lost. However, before the band could respond, more security officers quickly rushed into the room.

"God damn it, of course I run into thieves today of all days," Alice complained as she ran a hand through her hair. Alice reached into a satchel she carried on her back and pulled out a strange device along with her phone. Alice pressed a button on the device which caused it to unfold into a drone. Alice took cover behind a crate and used her phone to pilot the drone above the chaos so that she could look for her objective.

"Alice!? What the hell is happening in there!? Did you say something about thieves?" Eric questioned through her earpiece.

"Huh, oh yeah, looks like other people are stealin' somethin' from here too," Alice explained quickly. Alice winced when she saw a body land in front of her. One look at the downed guard told Alice that he would not wake up anytime soon.

"Same thing we are? Do we already have a rival group? Not surprised, we have been killing it these last few months."

"Don't know, but what I do know is that if they are goin' after what we are, we need to get it first," Alice said as her drone found her target. "I'll be out in ten," Alice said before a countdown appeared on her phone. Alice hid in the shadows as she stealthily made her way to her objective while the thieves continued to fight. Once she made it to her target, Alice broke her way into a crate and found smaller boxes all filled with the next generation of smartphones created by P.I. Alice snagged one of the phones and she placed it in her satchel before she ran toward an exit that her drone hovered over. Before Alice could escape her drone crashed down before her, pierced by an arrow. "Damn it," Alice muttered before she turned to find the band of thieves behind her. "You know that was expensive, right?"

"I'm sorry," Hood said even though her tone clearly conveyed that she was anything but. "Nice mask," Hood complimented even as she aimed an arrow at Alice.

"Back at you," Alice said as their boss gave her a calculating look.

"Who are you? You look...familiar," the boss muttered before he shook his head. "I can't get a read on her," the boss said and Alice had no idea what that meant but it seemed to put his band on edge. "More importantly, though, why are you here? You clearly don't work here."

"No, but she beat us to the prize," Grimm said as he gestured to the open crate.

"The phones," the boss whispered. "What do you want with the phones?"

"Uh, hello? Have you seen the lines for them? Figured I'd get the drop on them this generation. Plenty of them left, take them,"

Alice said as she nodded toward the crate. "Then we can go our separate ways."

"I'm afraid it's not that simple."

"And I was afraid you'd say that," Alice said before she quickly placed a pair of earbuds in her ears as the timer on her phone reached zero. At that moment, every phone that the thieves and the downed guards had on their possessions release a high-pitched noise that sent the thieves down to their knees. This made Hood release an arrow that Alice barely managed to duck under. "Hey! It wasn't personal!" Alice shouted before she left the warehouse and pulled her mask down. Once outside, she briskly walked down the side-walk and blended in with the pedestrians as she pulled the pair of mechanical earbuds from her ears. "Jack was right, these do block out everything," Alice mused. As she walked, Alice rolled her eyes when she saw a group of women fawning over an expensive looking car.

"Move, hussies," Alice said as she moved through the group and climbed into the passenger's seat.

"Sorry, ladies, gotta bounce," Eric said with a charming smile which earned dissatisfied comments from them as he pulled off. "What?" Eric asked defensively when Alice just stared at him with a raised eyebrow.

"Really?"

"Hey, they came on to me!" Eric defended. "If anything, you saved me. You know I'm a faithful person. I'd never creep on my girl."

"I didn't even know you were seeing anyone."

"Yup, ever since the nightclub gig all those months ago," Eric said as Alice vaguely recalled the text that she had gotten from him the day after that party. "I'd introduce you but she's been abroad on business."

"Long distance? Didn't know you had it in you, she must be special," Alice said with a small smile, happy for her friend.

"You have no idea, I'll show you a picture later."

"My baby's growin' up," Alice said as she pretended to wipe a tear from her eye.

"Yeah, yeah, so how did it go?"

"Successful as always," Alice said as she pulled out the phone.

"Aw, you only got one?"

"First off, Hattori Tech is better any day," Alice said bluntly. "Secondly, you want one? You go and get shot at."

"Nah, I'm comfortable being your hype man. Won't catch my ass doing half the crazy shit you do."

"What happened to being by my side?"

"That was when you were scrawny, could probably kick my ass now," Eric said with a laugh. Over the last few months, he and Alice had worked nonstop to spread Wonderland's influence. They had undertaken missions that were taxing both mentally and physically. The missions in addition to Alice's workout regimen had given his friend a very well-toned body. Between her new physique, tattoo, and hairstyle-which was shorter and sported blue highlights-his once scrawny friend had become a very intimidating looking woman. "So, you said this thing had the last piece you needed?"

"Yup, I can extract some of Athena's code from this. Once we get back to my place, I can finally finish making our trump card," Alice said with a grin.

"This calls for a celebration."

"Pizza?"

"Pizza," Eric agreed as they found themselves leaving the city, more optimistic than ever about their budding group.

*   *   *

Hollywood, Midas Manor

"You needed to see me?" Vivi asked as she walked into Roderick's study. She frowned when she saw a dark expression on his face as he slid an open letter across the top of his desk toward her.

"An informant of mine sent me some unnerving information. They've found out who August is working with," Roderick said as Vivi read the contents of the letter.

"June? Figures, he was nowhere near smart enough to rebuild the Knights' Order on his own. Between her, August, and Regina she did have the brains. She's their head healer, though, right? What interest would she have in the Knights' Order?"

"Seems like she has a dark past."

"Hold on, this says that June and her siblings…they're descendants of Morgana!?" Vivi said as a furious expression crossed her face. "I thought Merlin himself banished that entire bloodline. How did they sneak their way back into their inner circle?"

"Morgana was a cruel mage, who rivaled Merlin himself, not to mention the inner circle is just as divided as the council. There are way too many openings for her to use to slip them back in," Roderick explained. "What's worse is that I hear she's been seen with remnants of the Legion."

"The Black Moon? Damn it all, I hate to admit it but I had hoped Diamond was wrong."

"Morgana managed to get in contact with her son Mordred one last time to continue their bloodline. I'll leave it to your imagination to guess how," Roderick said as Vivi gained a disgusted look. "June, August, and Regina all have this blood. Though twisted, evil, and corrupted with incest it may be, the blood still contains that of Arthur Pendragon."

"August is still a mage," Vivi reminded Roderick. "The rules are clear. He has the blood, but only a civilian can wield Arthur's sword."

"You're right, but you forget that the Spring Equinox is soon approaching. At any time during that day, a mage has the option to give up their magic or regain it if they've given it up in the past," Roderick said as Vivi cursed when she figured out what that meant. "Spring is their season of rebirth that allows their oldest members to give up their power and live out the rest of their days humbly."

"If he gives up his magic…"

"…He can wield that sword," Roderick said with a grim expression. "Not that it matters, this whole thing with August is just smoke and mirrors, she is plotting something bigger. August is just a distraction, Morgana would never devote so much time and energy to him. No, we need to find June. My contact says she's preparing for some sort of ritual on the Equinox," Roderick explained as he rose from behind his desk. "We have two options, we can either try to find August before the Equinox or we can go to the location where my contact found June."

"When is the Equinox?"

"Tomorrow."

"Damn it," Vivi cursed as she clenched her fists. "As much as I want revenge, June's the bigger threat. Hell, if she really was in charge, then our kids' blood is on her hands as well. We'll take that bitch down."

"Exactly my thoughts," Roderick said as he stepped from behind his desk and grabbed his cane. "Let's go meet my contact, I have the Guild working overtime to find August. I even asked the Tribe for help. They don't care about our war, but if the Black Moon is involved they'll listen."

"And their Chief just…believed you?" Vivi asked skeptically.

"She and I have a …understanding," Roderick said after a moment as Vivi pursed her lips. "I wouldn't lie to her about the Black Moon and she knows that," Roderick said firmly. "Now let's get ready for a witch hunt."

*   *   *

Santa Monica, Midas Tower

"This is it," Alice said as the hologram of the planet appeared in the center of the room. This time, however, all of California was purple along with a few other spots sprinkled throughout the country. Eric watched apprehensively as Alice bit her lower lip when she pressed the enter button on her keyboard. At that moment, the image simply vanished. For a moment, they felt their hearts drop before the word Wonderland appeared.

"Did it…?" Eric trailed off quietly before the word was replaced by a large platinum M.

"Hello! I am Minerva! Are you my creator?"

"Yes, yes, I am," Alice said with a grin, feeling pride in her work.

"Wonderful!"

"That's crazy!"

"Crazy? No, I am Minerva!"

"Okay…" Eric began cautiously now a bit unnerved. "This won't end up like those classic movies right, right? A.I. going rampant and taking over the world?"

"Not with the fail-safes and reward systems I put in place," Alice reassured Eric. "That said, Athena? That has a huge possibility of makin' your sci-fi nightmares a reality. Especially with the increase in cybernetic implants among the population. "Which is why in two days, during the Equinox when they plan to launch it, I need to break into the P.I. server room and take it down with Minerva."

"Hold up, I hope you're not planning on going alone," Eric said with a frown. "You can't go into that place by yourself! Didn't you say they were the ones responsible for Kat's death? I don't care how much you want revenge, there's a limit."

"I know, relax, I have a plan and you're comin' with me," Alice reassured her friend who looked at her suspiciously.

"Damn right I am."

"Good, we'll meet up in two days, alright?"

"Alright," Eric said after a moment. "I'll head home and rest, it's been a long day."

"Sounds like a plan, thanks for the help today," Alice said as she led him out of the door. Once she closed the door, she released a long sigh.

"Creator, the Equinox is tomorrow not in two days."

"I know," Alice said with a forced smile as she turned to face the hologram. "Sometimes, Minerva, when you care about someone you need to withhold information that would get them hurt."

"I see! New knowledge, exciting!"

"Yes, it is. I'm turnin' you off for now. We need some rest."

"Why Creator? I do not require rest."

"I know, but it makes me feel better," Alice said with a small laugh.

"I see, interesting. Then would now be the appropriate time to say goodnight?"

"It would," Alice said with a smile. "Goodnight, Minerva."

"Here," Discordia said as she tossed a black cloth into Kat's face.

"Hey!" Kat complained before she grabbed it. She released a startled gasp, however, when she realized what it was. Discordia had not only found but repaired her beloved hoodie. Kat's expression softened at the sight and when she looked up, Discordia was nowhere to be found. "Thank you. For everything."

* * *

Hollywood, Midas Manor

Diamond groaned tiredly as she opened her eyes. Her entire body felt weak as she tried to collect her bearings. The first thing she noticed was that she was in her room while a heart-monitor beeped nearby. The next thing she noted was the amused form of Crystal that sat on the side of her bed.

"Juventas…"

"Ah-ah, it's Crystal when I'm in this form," Crystal said teasingly as she helped Diamond sit up. "When I'm with you like this, I am not your Goddess. I am your best friend, Crystal."

"Don't tell Dominique that," Diamond said, her voice hoarse as Crystal just chuckled.

"She'll just have to deal with it. Come on," Crystal said as she raised a flask to Diamond's lips. "Drink and regain your strength, your muscles have atrophied a lot. You passed my test but now I have a little favor to ask of you."

"What?" Diamond asked only for Crystal to shake her head.

"I'll get to that later. First, we seriously need to do something about your hair, girlfriend," Crystal said as she poked at the fluffy disheveled mess that had become Diamond's hair. "You seriously need some work done," Crystal said sadly. Diamond groaned when she realized that Crystal was right. Externally she was a complete mess. Internally, however, she had never felt stronger. She felt reborn.

* * *

San Diego, Magnus Manor

"Finally, done," Xavier said proudly as he held Eve's core and showed it to Lilia, the gold that had surrounded the crimson orb now a magnificent platinum. "With this, we can finally fight back," Xavier said before he glanced down at the core. "Incredible, now I see I had only barely scratched the surface of Eve's power."

"So, this is your Mastercraft? I hope it's enough," Lilia said as she looked at the orb. "I can feel the power coming from it from over here. A wonderful feat, as expected of you."

"Thank you," Xavier said sincerely, still not quite used to Lilia's kinder attitude toward him. "Lilia, if you don't mind me asking, what is your Mastercraft?"

"I don't have one," Lilia answered as she averted her eyes.

"What!? But you're a brilliant healer, wait, that means you're not officially part of the Circle," Xavier said as Lilia closed her eyes as if pained by a memory that had resurfaced.

"My Mastercraft wasn't a feat like yours, but rather a theory. It was the application of infusing light from the sun and moon into our spells," Lilia revealed. "Though we could never harness light like the Knights' Order, surely we could do something with it, I thought."

"What? Lilia...that was revolutionary..."

"I know, I was so proud of it that I showed August, thinking that for once I could get my actual father to be proud of me, a foolish girl I was," Lilia said with a bitter laugh. "He took my idea, presented it as his own and earned all of the praise. Because of this, it was made to seem as if I tried to pass his work off as my own. I don't know why he did it. Whether it was for the glory, to be cruel, or simply as an excuse to stay in this house as non-Circle mages can't be left unsupervised. Whatever the reason, he destroyed my future."

"Why didn't you tell someone!?"

"Who could I have told?" Lilia asked quietly. "You were but a child, Xavier, and by the time you gained power our relationship was not good enough for you to take my word over our dear uncle's. Though I treated you with disdain to protect you, I will admit to feeling genuine jealousy at times," Lilia said as she placed a hand on her brother's shoulder. "Xavier, you must save House Magnus. In Romero's absence, an evil has infiltrated it that must be cleansed. You have all the tools you need now and I know you have Romero's might. Avenge our brother, don't let August win tomorrow."

"I won't, *mia sorella,* I promise you that."

"Good," Lilia said with a smile. "Now, he's moved Faith to Prosperity Industries. He believes that if thieves attack, we'll fight them off to keep Faith safe."

"Coward."

"Indeed," Lilia said with a scoff. "I will be trying to finish replacing his magic with mine so I can keep her alive. He's giving up his magic tomorrow so that he can wield Excalibur, once he does that, his enchantments on me will disappear. You have to take him down when he completes the ritual."

"Should be easy without his magic."

"Don't think that. His magic shield made him invincible and being an Arch-Mage allowed him to perform miracles without incantations," Lilia began as she looked at him firmly. "Do you know how much power he must be getting in return to give that up? Don't underestimate Excalibur or the strength it bestows upon its wielder."

"You're right, sorry, I just want this over with," Xavier said quietly which made her chuckle before she kissed him on his cheek.

"Me too, brother, me too," Lilia agreed. "For better or worse, our family drama ends tomorrow."

*   *   *

Silicon Valley, Prosperity Industries

The next evening, Alice stood across the street from the Prosperity Industries building, the building that took away everything she loved. The sight of it alone caused a storm of emotions to whirl within her, but she managed to keep her composure albeit barely.

"I don't see any pedestrians or workers, even the air-traffic is clear…yeah this isn't ominous at all," Alice said sarcastically. No matter what scenario she ran in her head, she could guess that tonight would only end badly for her. That said, she couldn't walk away, if her death was what was needed to stop the weapon that she created then so be it. "Minerva."

"Yes, Creator?" Minerva said through the phone.

"If something bad happens to me…tell Eric I'm sorry, alright?"

"As you wish."

"Good," Alice said before she pulled up her mask. The skull pattern glowed brightly in the shadow of Prosperity Industries. "Well then, let's get started.'

*   *   *

Spain, Valencia

"This it?" Vivi asked as they stepped through the gates of what appeared to be an old cemetery.

"According to my source," Roderick answered. "What the hell is she doing?" Roderick wondered as they walked.

"This could be a trap, who is this source of yours anyway? It's not like you to be this secretive with me about anything."

"Someone we can trust, believe me," Roderick answered vaguely. "She will meet us here soon."

"She?" Vivi repeated and her eyes narrowed when Roderick suddenly held up a hand to silence her.

"Wait, you see that?" Roderick asked quietly as they hid behind two dead trees. Before them, a group of twelve individuals garbed in black cloaks knelt in a circle. In the middle of the circle they could see the twelve-pointed star of the Mages' Circle. However, while the usual star was a vibrant blue, this was a sinister looking green. Behind them, they could see June garbed in one of the cloaks. "June."

"And that is definitely the Black Moon," Vivi muttered. "But what are they doing?"

"No idea, but whatever it is it clearly must be stopped," Roderick said as he began to pull his cane apart which revealed a hidden blade.

Purple presence sparked from his ring and danced across the blade's edge before his body shot forward like a bolt of lightning. In an instant he was behind the unsuspecting June and rammed his blade through her back with the intent to pierce her heart. For a brief moment June stood and looked down at the blade that pierced her chest in wonder before her body exploded into a flock of ravens. "Damn."

"Ah, thieves, I was wondering when you would make your move," June's voice echoed throughout the cemetery as the ravens circled the area. "To be greeted by the Bandit King himself, I'm honored. That said, clearly you are not the assassin of your band, she got far closer," June's voice continued before a flash of green light temporarily blinded the thieves. When their visions cleared, they looked up in alarm to find Julia trapped in the air, unconscious in a bright green sphere. June laughed when she saw the thieves freeze at the sight. "Seems I was right to keep her alive, helps ensure her back up behaves," June mused. The cultists continued their chanting as the ravens merged together on the branch of a nearby by tree and reformed June's body.

"Julia!" Vivi shouted as a myriad of emotions crossed over her face before they settled on anger. When Vivi turned to Roderick, her eyes were a bright orange. "She was your informant!?"

"Later!" Roderick snapped which made Vivi grit her teeth before they both turned to an amused June. "What are you after June?"

"Rebirth," June said serenely as she stood up on the branch. A black staff then appeared in her hand, its end bore a skull that had a green gem clenched in its teeth. June spread her arms and she looked up at the moon with a large smile as she bathed in its light. "The resurrection of the Black Moon is this planet's best chance at survival you see. I realized this over the years as I walked the path of a healer."

"Survival!?" Vivi asked incredulously. "The Black Moon has done nothing but brought death since it was created!"

"Exactly," June said as she looked down at Vivi as if she were a child. "Rebirth, resurrection, revival…do you know what these all have in common? By definition they are impossible without death. Death, you see, is the greatest healer of all. The ultimate end to suffering and the chance to fix what is broken," June explained reverently. "Everything must end at some point, so why not use this inevitability to aid my mother one last time? She alone has the power to resurrect humanity as something greater but to do so she must bring an end to it in its current form."

"And what of August? What role does your brother and his plans to bring back the Knights' Order play into this?" Roderick questioned.

"A grandiose distraction, nothing more," June said dismissively. "Something to keep you and the Circle busy while I searched for the Circle's anchor that helps keep my mother's servant sealed away," June explained. "Misdirection, a common tactic of yours I heard. If he actually succeeds, well good for him, but that is just a bonus," June said as the chanting stopped. "He bought me enough time to get here, and using your little assassin bought me the last few moments I needed to finish the ritual."

At that moment, twelve black spikes erupted from the ground and pierced each cultist through their chests. Soon the spikes retracted and viciously ripped out their souls and dragged them into the ground. The ground trembled and cracked as a massive green ethereal chain burst out from the earth and flew up endlessly into the night sky. June cackled at the sight before the chain exploded into countless particles of green light that rained down harmlessly over the city.

"It worked, twelve sacrifices each born in a different month. To have them sacrificed on this night of all nights where the magic is strongest, nothing else would be powerful enough to shatter such a powerful seal," June said before she gazed down at the thieves as Julia floated in between them. "Now I will bless you each, one by one with the gift of death starting with my sister's murderer," June said as Roderick bowed his head slightly at the sight. "Any last words to your precious assassin oh great Bandit King?"

"Yes…Julia, now!" Roderick ordered as he snapped his head back up. Gone was the hazel in his eyes and in its place was an electric purple. Black pooled in the whites of his eyes as he activated shadow synch. June's eyes widened in alarm when Julia's image vanished from inside the sphere only for the assassin to appear next to June. Julia glared at June with bright purple eyes, an ornate dagger clenched tightly in her hand that was covered in Roderick's presence. In an instant, the dagger was buried up to the hilt inside June, pierced between her ribs. June lurched forward as blood spilled from her lips while her shield shattered like glass. "It doesn't take much to shatter a mage's shield, does it? If the weak spot is hit with sufficient force, the entire thing goes down rather easily."

"You let me release the anchor…why?" June questioned as a look of morbid fascination covered her face.

"Information," Roderick answered easily. "No matter how strong Morgana's servant was, she still lost in the end due to information. Information is the greatest weapon in any war, and it's why you're dying now. Julia has been tailing you for a lot longer than you knew, waiting until she could identify your shield's weak point. Then when the time was right, she allowed herself to be 'caught'. The loss of the Circle's anchor is indeed a tragedy, but we have three more and it was worth it in the grand scheme of things. Now that we know who is once more our enemy and what assets need the most protecting," Roderick said with a smirk as Julia twisted the dagger. "So, let me be the first to thank you for your aid."

"The trap I laid for you ended up being a trap for me…your reputation does not do you enough justice, Your Majesty," June said weakly as she glared at him. "Let me bless you with some more information before I go, since you find it so precious. My death? Is only the beginning to your suffering," June said darkly as she raised her staff at Vivi. "Obsessio!" June shouted with her last breath. A purple bolt of magic immediately blasted from the staff, right at the enforcer. Before the blast could connect, the gem on Vivi's buckle glimmered and a ring of orange presence erupted from around Vivi's body and intercepted the spell. The resulting explosion made Vivi cough as June fell lifelessly from the tree. A tense silence followed June's failed attack on Vivi as the thieves' shadow synch ended. Eventually Julia simply sat on the branch and swung her legs as she smiled down at them.

"I almost forgot how much fun working with you was, Roderick," Julia mused before she gazed down at Vivi. "If it isn't my old flame, did you miss me, love?" Julia asked playfully and if looks could kill, Vivi's glare would have reduced Julia to ashes.

"You…"

"…will both settle this later," Roderick ordered as he stepped in between them. "Right now, we have one more of those siblings to kill before the night is over. Stay focused so we can avenge our children," Roderick said as he began to walk away. "I'll request some Dolls to clean this mess up," the two women glanced at each other briefly one last time before they followed their boss. Roderick was right, their children came first.

CHAPTER 19

••••••••●••••••••

THE PROSPERITY
INDUSTRIES JOB

Silicon Valley, Prosperity Industries

"Minerva, help me out," Alice said quietly when she spotted a guard that blocked the entrance of the server room. "Get me his info."

"Right away!" Minerva said before Alice's contact lenses began to shift while various data was displayed in her field of vision. Alice watched in satisfaction as she saw the guard's name and personal information. Alice quickly called a number she saw below his name and the guard was startled when his phone began to ring. The moment he pulled his phone out, Alice chose that moment to attack. Alice moved quickly and slammed a stun-gun into the side of his neck that took him down instantly. Alice looted his keycard and used it to enter the server room.

"Finally, we made it in," Alice said as she dragged his body into the room.

"Query, why did we have to come to the server directly?"

"Because although you're superior to Athena, it has had more time to evolve than you have. Athena can fend off any attack I can think of except for a direct one on her servers, an attack from the inside. Athena can make endless changes to its software but it is still limited by its hardware," Alice said as she pulled off her cross and plugged it into the server. "Nothin' is invincible, if you can't attack it from the outside then attack it from the inside," Alice said as she glanced around the room, and noted the gold "A" emblem on the monitors. "Athena's not online, you're going to destroy it and take its place. Transfer any information you find about P.I. and all of its business partners to the Wonderland servers."

"Creator, when the upload begins, I will be unavailable and you will be compromised. Query, what is your plan of escape?"

"You let me worry about that, darlin. When I leave, seal this door and begin the upload," Alice ordered as she made her way to the door. Nearly as soon as she stepped out of the room, alarms began to ring loudly throughout the building as the door behind her slammed shut. This was all the warning Alice needed before she made her escape.

∗   ∗   ∗

"Alarms?" Lilia wondered as she aimed her staff at a sleeping Faith. A stream of healing energy released from the staff and covered the younger woman with a golden glow.

"Must be thieves. After what happened to their Princess, they will kill you both if they make it here," Xavier muttered. "Damn I can't afford to be wasting my magic on them, how much more time do you need?"

"At least an hour." Lilia said with a grimace. "She was worse than I thought."

"Shit," Xavier said before he shook his head. "Doesn't matter, right now you and Faith's safety is what matters most."

"Or perhaps, just Faith's," Lilia said quietly. "I have a spell that can transfer my life force to her. I can save her right now. My hands aren't clean when it comes to this, I helped August-"

"Anything wrong you've done was to protect your family," Xavier interrupted. "You don't get to die for trying to do the right thing. Just wait here, believe in me," Xavier pleaded which made Lilia frown as she seemed to search his eyes for something. For a moment, she no longer saw her younger brother but rather their father. Her heart clenched painfully as she forced herself to nod.

"Just be safe," Lilia said as she hugged him tightly.

*   *   *

Visibly exhausted, Alice made her way down the numerous flights of stairs in an attempt to make it back to the ground level. When Alice spotted security on the stairs, she pulled a collapsible baton from her satchel and hit one of the guards over his head with it. Alice quickly snatched his handgun from its holster and took aim at the second guard. Before he could react, Alice shot him in his vest which knocked him off balance and made him crash down the steps. Tiredly Alice made her way down the stairs as the guard struggled to reach his weapon. Just as he grabbed his side-arm, Alice kicked it out of his hand and knocked him out with a well-placed kick to the head.

"Holy shit," Alice gasped out as she weakly opened the door to the main lobby. Nearly as soon as she stepped through the door a large man quickly grabbed her. He lifted her up with ease as he ran toward a pillar. Alice panicked and tried to hit him with her stun gun only to find him unaffected by it. Pain exploded in Alice's head when he slammed her back against a pillar with enough force to crack the marble. Alice groaned when he released her and slid down to the ground as he stood above her. Alice cursed when she saw a faint glow in his eyes and noted his almost lifeless demeanor. It was clear that this guard was not human. Just as he prepared to bring an end to her, his head suddenly exploded much to Alice's surprise. She watched incredulously as she saw a small crystal in the remnants of his head before it shattered, reducing the man to rubble.

"What the hell are you doing here, Stone?" Diamond asked softly as she stepped from the shadows and made her way to the injured hacker. Though her mod-suit covered most of her body, and she now sported a silky bob cut, Alice recognized that golden gaze instantly.

"Oh, you know me, always searching for a new hobby," Alice joked despite her pain.

"Here, drink," Diamond ordered as she handed Alice her flask. Alice pulled down her mask to take a sip of the nectar and shuddered when she felt her wounds stitch themselves back together. "I'll admit it, part of me never expected you to actually use that mask."

"Hey, it serves its purpose," Alice said as Diamond helped her to her feet. "Damn it," Alice muttered as dozens of guards entered the scene.

"Get down," Diamond ordered as she stepped in front of Alice while both of her handguns formed in her palms. Diamond began to shoot down her opposition with deadly precision. Whether they were human or golem, Diamond showed them no mercy. Even shots Alice could swear Diamond missed exploded from the shadows and took down the security guards from impossible angles. Suddenly a few guards aimed at Alice and Diamond immediately jumped in front of her and shielded Alice with her body. "Are you okay?" Diamond asked when the gunfire died down. The sound of bullets hitting the floor echoed throughout the silent lobby as flattened bullets fell harmlessly off of Diamond's body.

"Yeah."

"Good. I'm going to go…"

"…yeah go do you." Alice said as she scurried off to take cover while Diamond went on the offensive. Within moments, Diamond eliminated the rest of the security in the lobby. Alice was relieved but she couldn't help but feel as if it were too easy. That feeling was soon proven correct when a massive fissure formed in the floor which Alice would have fallen into if she hadn't jumped to the side at the last moment. The sound of a galloping horse was all the warning Alice had before the familiar form of the Dullahan sprung out from the fissure. Its horse landed on the ground with enough force to be felt by all those in the lobby. It raised its golden head at Diamond, its golden visor releasing an all too familiar light. "Watch out!" Alice shouted as the massive servant released a crimson beam of pure magic at Diamond who hadn't turned around. Instead, she simply threw her guns to the side, as a black blur intercepted the Dullahan's attack.

"This thing again?" Jack asked as presence crackled along the length of his gauntlet as Arondight absorbed all of the energy. When the attack ended Jack formed a frozen spear of ice in his left hand and raised it high. Jack threw it across the lobby and watched in satisfaction as it pierced the golden servant through its chest with ease. The ice spread rapidly and effectively turned the servant into a frozen statue. Diamond glanced back at the statue approvingly as its frozen helmet fell from its grasp and bounced toward Alice.

"You're late."

"Fashionably late," Jack corrected. Diamond rolled her eyes while the severed head of the servant began to glow red, prepared to explode with the small amount of power it had left. "You know me, I have to make an entrance, unlike a certain girl we both know who's always late to the party."

"Uh...guys..." Alice trailed off as she tried to get away from the head. However, before it could explode, Kat rushed into the scene from behind Alice and kicked the head toward the frozen statue. Upon impact, both exploded and sent small crystals of ice flying harmlessly throughout the lobby. This was the sight that Xavier teleported into as the thieves bickered amongst themselves.

"First off, how can I be late to the party when it doesn't even start until I show up?" Kat asked as she placed a hand on her hip. "Secondly, that is how you make an entrance, Jack."

"Whatever," Jack said as Kat turned to face Alice. It was only then when their eyes met that time seemed to come to a standstill. To say there was a lot Alice wanted to say would have been an understatement. The fact that Kat, and even Jack, were alive and there before her was almost too much for the hacker to handle. She wanted to say something, but when she started to do so, Xavier spoke first.

"Jack!? You're alive!" Xavier exclaimed, unable to believe his eyes. The sound of Xavier's voice seemed to flip a switch within Kat as she suddenly placed a finger over Alice's lips.

"Hold that thought," Kat said quietly before she quite literally vanished before Alice's eyes. It was an eerie feeling for Alice because she knew Kat hadn't moved, she could still feel her finger on her lips which meant that her lover had become invisible. When she felt Kat move, Alice had no idea what to expect from her. That said, when Kat suddenly reappeared in front of Xavier and kicked him into a wall, Alice realized that she probably should have expected something like that. "You son of a bitch!" Kat snapped as her whip formed more than eager to interrupt the would-be family reunion as she prepared to fight the surprised Xavier. When Kat swung her whip back, green presence coursed along its length while its serrated blades cut through the floor.

"Wait! We don't have to fight! We want the same thing!" Xavier said urgently. "You want to bring down, August, right? I want the same thing!"

"Explain," Diamond said coldly.

"Excuse me!?" Kat asked incredulously, surprised Diamond would even speak to the mage. In response, Diamond held up her hand to silence her as she clearly wanted to hear what Xavier had to say.

"He's gone too far. I know the truth, everything he's done. He's the reason you lost your mother. He's why Jack and I lost our parents, and now he's endangering our sisters!" Xavier explained, his anger evident. "He started this war!"

"I know."

"Then you see that we have a common goal. We can work together and stop him!"

"No," Diamond said bluntly. "I'm afraid you can't be trusted."

"I understand your hesitancy, but you can't defeat him alone," Xavier tried to persuade her. "Do you even have a plan?"

"I do."

"You do?" Jack and Kat asked their boss simultaneously.

"But surely this plan of yours can work better if I were to join you."

"It would," Diamond admitted. "But the risk is too great. You didn't know it was us, you came down here to fight thieves. You're protecting August's ritual which means you are still under his control."

"I came here to fight thieves, not to protect his ritual but to protect my sisters who August has trapped here," Xavier explained. "If it were anyone else, they would not show them mercy. Not after everything that has happened in this war. However, you all I can talk to. We can work together. We can save them and stop August," Xavier said as he turned to face Jack. "Your mother's poison has spread and Lilia is doing her best to keep it at bay. When Lilia finishes Faith's treatment we can face down August without any reservations."

"Faith?" Jack said, momentarily lost in thought. "Bloody hell it's been over ten years, she's still kicking?"

"How long will this treatment take, Magnus?" Diamond asked after she felt Jack's relief.

"Roughly an hour."

"That's far too long, August will be done and gone by then," Diamond said as Xavier shook his head.

"We have no choice, we cannot risk their safety!"

"Look at the big picture, Magnus. You're close to your sisters, I get it, you care about family. A lot more families are going to be destroyed if August gets control over a new Knights' Order," Diamond said firmly. "Your sisters mean the world to you, but my entire Guild is at risk. Their lives aren't worth it. We may never get a chance like this again," Diamond said before she turned to Jack. "Please, talk some sense into your brother," Diamond said only to pause when she noticed Jack disappeared. "Frost?" Diamond asked again as she looked around for her missing bandmate. Diamond grimaced when she turned to Kat only to see that both she and Alice were just as confused about Jack's sudden disappearance. "Juventas, help me," Diamond muttered, clearly annoyed as she rubbed the bridge of her nose.

*   *   *

"Sorry, Xavier, but he needs to be stopped. We can't waste any more time on this," Lilia said quietly, a grim resolve on her face as she aimed her staff at Faith. "Hopefully, I can be a better person in the next life."

"Why wait that long?" a voice asked and Lilia looked up to find Jack at the entrance of the room. Lilia frowned as she aimed her staff at him, prepared to defend her sister from the intruder. Jack chuckled and let his mask dissolve so that he could put Lilia at ease.

"Jack..." Lilia said breathlessly. "I thought you were dead! How did you get here!?"

"As if August could take me down," Jack said cheekily as he gave her a wink. "As for how I got here, all I had to do was feel around a bit for your magic. It's gotten powerful, but it still has the same warm feeling it did when we were children. I must say though, that serious expression, I would have never pictured you wearing that," Jack said as he made his way to her and wiped her tears away.

"Look who's talking, since when do you smile?" Lilia asked before she frowned and grasped his gauntlet gently. "And what the hell happened to your arm?"

"It was the price I had to pay to be here," Jack said dismissively. "A small price compared to whatever the hell you were just about to do," Jack said quietly as he looked down at the slumbering Faith and brushed some of her hair away from her face. "What are you doing, Lily? Didn't you once tell me that us bastards have to stick together?"

"Jack...I..." Lilia started before stopping. "I have no choice, there aren't any more options. The poison has spread too far."

"You're wrong, but I can't fault you, the most obvious options tend to be the most overlooked," Jack said as he pulled out his flask. Lilia said nothing as he leaned over the table and nudged Faith awake.

"J...Jackie?" Faith asked quietly, her eyes opening tiredly as he smiled down upon her. "You've gotten...bigger..."

"How have you been, little bird? I need you to do me a favor and take your medicine for me. It'll be hard, but I need you to drink all of it, we need to flush all of this mess out of you," Jack said as he lifted her up gently and pressed the flask to her lips. This was the sight Xavier and the rest of Band 13 walked in on. "Sorry, you two would have been there forever. Decided to nip this in the bud."

"That's right, you all have the elixir of life! Of course, thieves have the antidote to their poison," Xavier muttered. "I...why didn't I consider you earlier?"

"Too busy throwing fireballs at me, thinking that I was the spawn of Satan," Jack answered dryly. "Not like I would have helped anyway, would have thought it was a trap. I mean I can barely believe she's still kicking now."

"Elixir of life?" Alice repeated. "As in the key to immortality?" Alice questioned skeptically. Of course, she had begun to have her suspicions but to hear the truth said so bluntly was unexpected.

"Told you, you wouldn't believe me," Kat said as Alice shook her head. They could all see Faith's body heal before their very eyes and for the first time in years, Faith looked healthy.

"That's my girl," Jack said with a smile. "So, where's August?"

"The roof," Lilia answered. "I'd teleport you to him myself but he erected wards to prevent teleportation. You'd have to destroy either him or the building to get rid of them. Insurance against the Arch-Mages who are probably trying to figure out why he missed tonight's meeting."

"So, what? We take the stairs?" Kat asked curiously only for Lilia to jerk a thumb backward toward an elevator.

"No, we take the elevator."

"Hold on, we? No, you need to take Faith and Abbie out of here, we'll deal with August," Jack said only for Lilia to shake her head.

"What did you just say about sticking together? You're going to need a healer. If you think August will let you drink from your flasks you're mistaken. I'll fly them to safety, but we finish this together," Lilia said as she glanced at Alice, or more specifically, at her tattoo. "And something tells me it's best if your civilian friend stays nearby. Call it a hunch," Lilia said before she made her way to the elevator. "Let's go."

*   *   *

"Should have taken the stairs," Kat muttered as they were all crammed into the impossibly slow elevator. "This is so awkward," Kat said before she found herself pressed against Alice. "Though I can't complain too much. Really love what you did with the hair."

"Back at you," Alice said as she ran her fingers through Kat's longer hair. "So…you're…a Doll?"

"Apparently…" Kat muttered, looking obviously uncomfortable about that topic. "Hope that doesn't…freak you out."

"Freak me out? This might be the coolest thing ever. This is like, every sci-fi nerd's dream," Alice said before she gave the surprised Kat a wink. It was then, however, Alice frowned. "But…did you lose an inch?" Alice questioned noting that Kat seemed a bit smaller.

"Don't remind me," Kat muttered. "Apparently the idea that upgrading tech makes it smaller, applies to Dolls too."

"Also, it is you, right? Like you and not some backup or copy?"

"Fortunately, Dolls don't work like that. I'm Kat, the one and only."

"But how…" Alice was cut off when Kat placed a finger to her lips to silence her.

"Shut up and trust me," Kat said before she kissed Alice. Alice smiled a bit at the all too familiar taste of apples as she pulled away.

"I missed you."

"Can you two please save your reunion for when we're able to get more than a few inches away from you?" Diamond asked, though with her mask removed they could see her place a smile on her black painted lips in order to show them that she really didn't mean it.

"Speak for yourself, please, continue," Jack said as he wiggled his eyebrows suggestively. Lilia laughed at his antics while Kat and Alice proceeded to do just that.

"Please, don't," Xavier groaned as he tried to keep a curious Faith faced toward him and not the two women that were busy re-familiarizing themselves with each other. "I thought you thieves were more professional."

"It's been months since we've seen each other, let the lovers have a moment, we might all die anyway," Jack said with an eye-roll. "Goddesses know, I'm going to make up for lost time myself if we survive this."

"Is that right?" Diamond asked only to get a wink from Jack. Xavier just shook his head before he turned to Diamond.

"What is this plan you have?"

"I plan on using Dominion," Diamond answered and both her band and the mages looked at her in alarm.

"You've mastered Dominion!?" Xavier asked incredulously, a silent awe on his face.

"I can use it," Diamond corrected him before she held up her right arm. The mod-suit dissolved enough for them to see strange black markings on the skin of her arm. "I'm a long way from mastering it which is why we need to fight him for as long as possible so that I can prepare it."

"Dominion?" Faith asked curiously.

"The thieves' strongest illusion. It's the only thing Arch-Mages like August fear," Lilia answered. "It takes decades to master, but even using it at her age is unheard of no matter how much of a prodigy she may be."

"I'm no prodigy," Diamond began firmly as the elevator came to a stop before the doors opened, Band 13's masks all reformed as they stepped out. "That's Katarina. I'm the heir to the throne, the future Bandit Queen," Diamond continued "This much is to be expected. Frost, Umbra, it's time we end this."

"I take it back," Lilia said to Xavier after a moment, an amused expression her face. "If it's them then it's no wonder you got beaten so badly by rookies," Lilia teased. Xavier rolled his eyes at her while Faith looked at her siblings in confusion.

"Are all of you going to hurt uncle August?" Faith asked cautiously.

"You bet," Kat said darkly as she slammed a fist into her palm. "I'm swinging on sight, just like how we did things back in Chicago, right Jack?"

"Just leave some for me this time," Jack said before he glanced down at Faith. "He's hurt a lot of people, he's a bad man Faith. Bad things happen to bad people."

"I see, well if all three of you say so then I'll trust you," Faith said as she looked at her older siblings. "It's not often you three can agree on anything," Faith explained and the three in question glanced at each other before they averted their eyes. Their poor sister didn't even know the beginning of how bad their relationship was.

*　　*　　*

"Finally, everything has come to fruition," August said as he stood in front of the Lady and Haylen who floated in the air in front of him with their arms bound by chains. His staff was covered in a sickening green magic. "With the blood of the Lady," August began before he stabbed the Lady in her abdomen with a curved dagger. "Tonight, on the night where magic shines brightest, I can break the seal that traps your true power," August said before he stabbed the blade through the emblem on Haylen's abdomen. Haylen screamed in agony as the emblem began to release a golden light.

"You will be stopped!" the Lady shouted angrily. As the lady thrashed against her chains, blue sigils began to appear on them, making her scream as they shocked her and sapped away her power. August just laughed at the sight.

"And here I thought Gods couldn't bleed or feel pain," August said before he turned back to Haylen who continued to scream in agony. However, just as he did so he felt a blow to his shield. With a frown, August turned to find Kat who pulled her fist back. "You!?"

"Me," Kat said before she kicked him and flipped away. He glared darkly at his nemesis as she landed in a crouched position. Kat's image flickered for a moment before she cloaked herself and disappeared from sight. Beneath August a card was stabbed into the ground which immediately exploded in a bright flash of light that blinded him and left him open for a powerful blow from Jack. Jack's talons scratched against the surface of August's shield and siphoned off some of its magic.

"Damn you!" August growled out as he rubbed his eyes. August grimaced as he felt Diamond's bullets slam into his shield. "You children just don't learn, do you!?" August snapped as his body exploded with a blue light. The force of his magic shattered the ground beneath him as he floated up into the air. He shot a fireball at Diamond only for her to barely dodge the spell. "It's already too late!" August roared as Haylen screamed louder while a golden flame engulfed her very being.

"Haylen!?" Alice shouted in confusion. Alice had no idea what just happened to her sister. Haylen looked down at Alice weakly and a tear slid down her cheek when she saw her.

"Run," was all Haylen managed to say before her body simply exploded into a golden fireball. Gone was Haylen, and in her place an ornate sword that was engulfed in a golden flame.

"Protection!" Lilia shouted as she quickly slammed her staff down and created a wall of magic that protected everyone but August from the explosion. When the explosion ended, the thieves immediately resumed their attack on August who had landed back on the roof unscathed. No matter what they did, their attacks had no effect on him. Even when Jack and Kat both attacked him at once, his magic simply pulsed and knocked them back as he made his way toward the sword. Golden runes glowed on top of its beautifully crafted blade which bore a crimson jewel at its center.

"Finally!" August said as he stood in front of the sword, his own body completely engulfed in a blue light as his magic began to leave his very being. "Excalibur," August said as he gripped the sword's golden handle. As August pulled the blade free, he laughed as he felt its power fill his very being. Lilia wasted no time and grabbed Faith and Alice before she flew them away to place them on another building out of harm's way.

"Lilia!?" Faith asked in confusion as Lilia gave her a weak smile.

"I'll be back," Lilia said before she turned back toward her uncle's location, or more accurately, toward the Lady.

"Now, who shall I destroy first?" August asked darkly as he raised the flaming blade toward Band 13, golden flames poured from his eyes as Excalibur's golden light filled the entire area.

"No one, because the only one who falls today is you!" Xavier declared as he got August's attention.

"Oh really? I have to say, boy, after all of this time you have yet to give me a reason to be impressed. Exactly who do you think you are to stand before me, the Champion of Light?" August asked as Xavier walked toward him while his magic flowed from his body in waves. The Mages' Circle's star shone beneath his feet as he summoned Eve who appeared behind him with a cold expression on her face.

"I am Xavier Romero Magnus, Head of House Magnus, Son of Arch-Mage Romero," Xavier began as the straps on Eve's straitjacket broke and freed her arms. Eve's power skyrocketed as she landed next to him while her chains shattered into countless particles of light. "His light flows through me," Xavier said as he and Eve released a silver light from their bodies.

"Silver magic? So you really do possess his magic," August muttered as Xavier and Eve's eyes both turned silver. At that moment, Eve's core flew from her chest while a platinum ring formed around it. The Core then connected to a platinum rod that appeared in Xavier's hand in a flash of light. "Don't tell me, this whole time, your servant was your staff!?"

"Like my father, and his before him, I am the heir of Merlin!" Xavier boomed as his magic clashed against Excalibur's power as he slammed his staff into the ground.

"Holy shit! Has he always had this much power!?" Kat asked incredulously as Band 13 braced themselves after they felt the power that poured from Xavier. Jack narrowed his eyes at the sight. "He would have killed us if he took us seriously!"

"So, he did inherit Romero's power," Jack murmured before he glanced at Diamond. "How much longer?"

"A bit, come on, let's show them our power," Diamond said before she activated shadow synch. Both August and Xavier looked at the thieves in alarm when they felt the golden storm of presence erupt. The nature of Diamond's presence felt like a massive weight on their bodies as they resisted the urge to submit. "Don't be so surprised, August, you're in the presence of royalty."

"For your sins against my family, your life is forfeit! *Bolide!*" Xavier boomed before he aimed his staff at August which created a massive fireball that fired from its end. August glared at the attack before he swung Excalibur at it which created a golden arc of light that cleaved the spell in half. The light continued on to Xavier but he didn't so much as move as Jack suddenly appeared before him and absorbed it. At that moment Jack activated his third circle causing the stolen energy to now fill his very being. Jack formed a frozen spear in his hand and threw it at August who cleaved through it, only to be frozen solid when it exploded into a storm of ice. The ice soon blew off of his body when Excalibur's power surged through him. August switched his attention to Jack only to shout in pain when Kat whipped him across his back. The whip ripped August's back open and made him stumble back.

"Seems he's not used to pain," Diamond said before she dashed toward Kat and slid into her shadow. Diamond reappeared on top of a nearby building and she tossed her guns to the side. The weapons dissolved into ash along with the right sleeve of her mod suit. The back of her mod-suit and a part above her chest vanished as well as the ash formed together to create a high-impact sniper rifle that was identical to the one used by Jezebel. On the side of the new weapon, was the name "Jezebel" etched into its side in a pale gold. "Learn from your enemies," Diamond muttered to herself as she aimed down the scope of her rifle and pulled the trigger. A powerful shot tore from her weapon and into August's shoulder with enough force to nearly rip it apart. Diamond quickly fired two more shots, one hit him in his chest and the other in the side of his head. His body was torn apart by her attacks but to her disappointment, Excalibur's light healed the damage nearly as soon as he received it. Still, it was obvious that August could no longer think straight as he swung his blade around him randomly in a desperate attempt to fend off his attackers. When he finally managed to spot Diamond, August swung the blade in her direction and released an arc of light that destroyed her vantage point. Fortunately, Diamond managed to escape and reappeared from Jack's shadow. Diamond jumped back and turned her attention to Xavier. "We need to separate him from that blade, he won't die unless we do! Rip his damn arm off if you have to!" Diamond called out. Xavier nodded and began to whisper an incantation as he felt his magic build inside of him.

"Like I'd let you," August growled out as he charged forward to attack Xavier only for Kat's whip to wrap around his arm and pull it back. A bright light shone from her chest as she drew on the power of her Apple of Discord. Enraged, August swung at her which made Kat duck beneath the arc of light. Kat dove forward to avoid his follow-up attack and pulled out her treasure before she threw it high into the air. Much to Diamond's relief, Kat's treasure released a golden light. Kat's body gained a golden glow as her apple began to pump out even more presence through her body. August moved to cleave her in half, but tripped over an upturned piece of concrete that made his attack miss. Jack chose that moment to attack and slammed his left fist into August's face. The power Jack had stockpiled was released at once as a storm of ice and presence ripped from his fist. Jack felt a satisfying crunch beneath his fist before August was blown away from Kat. August's body bounced on the ground but he managed to catch himself before he fell off of the roof.

"You damn bastard!" August growled out while Kat began to throw a barrage of cards at him. Each exploded like bombs when they hit him but he managed to stab Excalibur into the roof to brace himself enough to prevent being knocked off of the building. When she saw this, Kat threw a card that said "Steal" but unfortunately for her, the blade reacted negatively to her attempt to steal it and released a pulse of light large enough to knock her back as her card was incinerated. Quickly, Kat recovered before she ran toward August alongside Jack. August released another arc of light at them but before it reached her, Kat ducked and slid under it as Jack caught it with his gauntlet which immediately absorbed the power. Kat slipped into her shadow which slid toward August quickly. Once the shadow was close enough, she emerged from it and kicked his legs which knocked him off balance. However, before he could hit the ground Jack appeared with Arondight shining brightly as he formed a frozen short sword and pierced August through his chest with it. Nearly immediately, the short sword exploded and encased August in ice as Xavier aimed his staff at his uncle.

"*Esplosione*," Xavier chanted before a massive explosion erupted from beneath his uncle's icy prison and sent him up into the air. August's skin was charred from the damage it took even as Excalibur tried to heal his wounds. Eve flew up above August before she stopped and descended upon him as she slammed her foot into his chest. August felt his ribs crack before he slammed into the roof. Lilia, who had managed to safely extract the Lady reappeared and slammed her staff into the ground and covered the thieves, herself, and Xavier with her magic. "Now!" Xavier shouted as Eve aimed both of her hands at the building, or more specifically at August. Her body exploded with magic as a massive concussive force suddenly slammed into the roof. The impact hit August full force as the first five floors of the towering building were simply crushed and blown away. Xavier glared at August who still desperately clung to Excalibur. *"Stella Cadente!"* Xavier shouted as he slammed his staff down into the ground. Eve's body was completely engulfed in the silver magic as she flew higher into the air. The moon shone brightly behind her as the rubble from P.I. began to form around her and encased her in a sphere of debris. The sphere soon engulfed itself in a silver flame before it simply fell toward the building like a meteor. Its descent was silent but its impact was not. The force of its impact shattered every window of every building surrounding Prosperity Industries which found itself completely destroyed as Eve tore through every floor and essentially reduced the tower to dust.

"Get down!"Alice said as she quickly held Faith to protect her from the debris. When she realized she didn't feel any pain, Alice looked up to find the that the Lady had shielded them with her body.

"Hey, you okay!?" Alice asked as she caught the Lady. Alice grimaced when she saw the shards of glass and stone that stuck out from the Goddess' back.

"Do not worry about me. I am a Goddess, a patron of humanity," the Lady said weakly. "If I couldn't do this much, I would be undeserving of my rank."

"Just what the hell am I lookin' at?" Alice asked, her hands trembled a bit after she saw one of the tallest buildings in the country wiped from existence before her very eyes. When Alice looked down she was relieved to see that Band 13 and the mages had climbed to their feet. They all looked ready to keel over, but at least they were alive. "Why is my sister a fuckin' sword!?"

"So you're her sister," the Lady mused. "You know she never lost faith that you would come for her."

"Well it was an accident."

"Or was it?"the Lady asked omniously. "Fate works in mysterious ways, the bond between siblings is more sacred than you know."

"She's right, I mean my brothers are at war and Xavier and Lilia never got along yet here all three of them are, together," Faith added. Alice frowned but she decided not to think about it at the moment.

"Regardless, it's over right? That should have killed him."

"That's what I'm afraid of, as much as I detest him he does have Pendragon blood in his veins. I make all of my blades with a jewel, a focus, to allow my knights to channel light directly from the sun and moon. Like the treasures of the thieves each focus has a unique power depending on what it was forged from," the Lady explained. "Excalibur's was forged from dragon blood that only reacts when in contact with Pendragon's bloodline. Excalibur has had many wielders in the Order but no one since Arthur himself could bring out its full potential. With that blade in his hands he can survive death and keep fighting," the Lady said as a crimson energy engulfed August's corpse. A chill went down Alice's spine at the sight. "In this state, he'll become unstoppable," the Lady said as August stood up, there was no life in his eyes as the crimson light stitched his body back together. "The real fight has only just started."

"Seriously!?" Kat asked, shadow synch broken, as she watched the man stand up. She grimaced as she tried to resume the fight but found herself unable to move as her body completely overheated. "Son of a bitch!"

"I'm running low, how much longer do you need?" Xavier asked Diamond tiredly while Lilia seemed to struggle to maintain consciousness.

"Just two minutes," Diamond said as she thrust her rifle into the ground to support herself. "How is he still standing?"

"Dragon blood. Make no mistake he is far deadlier now," Lilia said as Eve dug herself out of the rubble completely exhausted, her body heavily damaged from her last attack.

"M...Master, win," Eve whispered before her body suddenly vanished, no longer able to stay in the battle as her magic returned to Xavier.

"Thank you, Eve," Xavier whispered before he glared at August.

"I will destroy all of you!" August boomed and his power nearly forced them to their knees. However, it was not just the overwhelming energy that flowed from him, but the sheer bloodlust that made them tremble. It was as if they truly stood before a dragon.

"Focus on Dominion, I'll buy you time," Jack told Diamond before he faced Lilia and held out his gauntlet. "Give me everything you have, Lilia. If it's a couple of minutes, I can hold on for at least that long," Jack said. Lilia nodded when she saw his resolve and grabbed his armored hand. Lilia shuddered when she felt Arondight steal away the rest of her magic. Jack's body trembled as the fourth circle was filled with presence. The color of Jack's presence changed from blue to violet as his eyes did the same. Jack shivered as his hair turned silver in color while his heart froze. The black ice of his gauntlet seemed to spread as his left arm, legs, and chest were covered by it. Even as the ice slowly but surely began to spread across his body, Jack was pleased to feel his power grow. Jack cracked his neck as he stood next to Xavier who was also prepared to continue the fight.

"Let's end this," Xavier said as his shield finally broke and returned the magic to his body. Xavier glared at August as he aimed his staff at him. His magic transformed the staff into an all too familiar spear of silver light that made August glower. Together the sons of Romero stood, one covered in a blinding light while the other was slowly encroached by his own darkness. For the first time, the two finally found common ground. "Now Jack," Xavier said as Jack formed a two-handed sword, as August charged them. Like his frozen armor, the ice that covered the blade was black in color and appeared to be cracked. However, within each crack, violet presence could be seen crackling within. August laughed as he saw Jack prepare to parry his strike.

"Idiot boy, this sword cuts through anything! I'll cleave you in two!" August shouted as the two blades met. However, to August's confusion, Excalibur went straight through the black blade as if it were intangible. At the last moment, Jack ducked and was barely able to avoid being beheaded by Excalibur before his blade cut through August's chest. Jack then aimed his gauntlet at August before it shot from his body. August stabbed the blade into the ground to block it, but the gauntlet simply phased through the blade and tore through August's side. "What!?"

"A little something I stumbled across in my training, I like to call it black ice," Jack said as the gauntlet reformed around his stub. Jack raised his gauntlet and a massive spike of black ice that nearly shot up from the ground ran through August's chest. August grit his teeth in frustration as he realized that even though he couldn't touch the strange new ice it could very well touch him. It was then August was forced to dodge a strike from Xavier who attempted to skewer him with his spear. August raised his blade back to attack Xavier only to leap back when black spikes of ice exploded from the ground beneath them.

"Thank you," Xavier said before two more spears of light appeared above the young mage. *"Bombardare,"* Xavier said as he snapped his fingers. The spears shot toward August and exploded upon impact which made him scream in pain before Jack slammed his left black ice-covered fist into the man's jaw. The stockpiled power once more released and knocked August back into a broken-down wall. As one, both Jack and Xavier rushed him down and stabbed him in the chest with their respective weapons.

"Yield already! You can't win against us!" Xavier said as August found himself slowly being encased in ice while the two men pushed and twisted their weapons deeper into his chest. "The sword is powerful on its own, yes, but think! All of its previous wielders were masters of their craft! They spent years mastering their skills! They earned their power, you don't honestly think you can be just as powerful as them just by picking up the blade do you!?"

"Though you were granted their power, you still have to master it," Jack said as he recalled Vivi's words.

"Silence! I will not be lectured by someone who was born into great power! You have no idea how it feels to be powerless. To be born with nothing!" August sneered. "You're just like that fool Romero, claiming he understood my pain while taking everything I ever dreamed of having!" August shouted as the red energy exploded from his body and forced both Jack and Xavier back. August ripped Xavier's staff from his torso and threw it to the side as Jack's blade simply vanished. "The fame, the power, the respect, he even took the woman I loved and you sit there, his sons who inherited everything he owned and try to lecture me!?" August said before he raised the blade. "With this sword, I am immortal! Pain only serves to make me stronger! I will use this sword to destroy everything Romero once loved. Starting with his precious children!"

"Enough, father! This is madness!" Lilia shouted as she stood in front of her brothers. "You may have always hated Romero, but he genuinely saw you as his brother, his best friend. Does that mean nothing to you!? Can you really destroy his legacy!?" Lilia questioned as August glared at her. "What about me? Yes, he took the woman you loved, but I am your daughter by blood and Romero's by name. To destroy his legacy, you must destroy me too, can you really do that? Do I truly matter that little to you!?" Lilia questioned as tears ran down her face while August schooled his expression.

"You remind me so much of her, of my Regina," August said quietly before a grim expression crossed his face. "And just like her you chose to be a whore of House Magnus," August said before he brought his blade down. A powerful wave of energy rushed at her as it prepared to blow through both her and her brothers. She watched heart-broken as the light raced toward her but before it could connect, she was suddenly pushed to the side by Jack who raised his hand to absorb the energy. He gritted his teeth as he felt his body become covered with black ice.

"Jack!" Xavier shouted as he forced himself to his feet as the ice continued to spread and cover Jack. When the light died down, August smirked as he saw Jack once more trapped inside his own ice, unable to move.

"Once more you bit off more than you could chew, attempting to absorb a power far too great for you," August declared as he made his way toward Jack. "This time your whore of a mother isn't here to save you, boy," August said as he raised his blade to behead Jack only for a bullet to slam into the side of his head. August grimaced before he glanced to the side toward Diamond as the bullet fell from his head while the wound healed.

"You say you're immortal with that sword?" Diamond asked as she raised her gloved hand and revealed an orb made of a black glass. Its shape was slightly distorted as it rested in her palm while a golden presence raged within it. The energy thrashed wildly as cracks appeared on the orb's surface. Soon the raging presence vanished and was replaced by a foggy image of a throne room as the orb continued to crack. "Then I'll take it from you."

"No...impossible! A child like you!?" August shouted, fear in his eyes as she gripped the sphere tightly, making more cracks appear on its surface. "Don't tell me, this was your plan!?" August shouted as he glanced around at his opponents who all smiled, even Lilia. "You...you were just trying to waste time!? Such treachery!"

"Like you said, I'm just like mother," Lilia said with a sneer.

"This is the end," Diamond said as she threw the sphere down and shattered it. Soon waves upon waves of a dark energy was released that obscured the visions of all that saw it. They felt a harsh tugging sensation as their bodies were sucked into what appeared to be a rift in the air that was created by the shattered orb.

"A child like her?" the Lady whispered breathlessly as her vision began to darken. The whites of her eyes turned black along with everyone else's while a golden presence coursed over their surroundings and trapped them within a dark void. Suddenly, Alice released a scream as she felt her shoulder burn.

* * *

"Welcome to my Dominion," Diamond said as they found themselves in a new realm. The very floor made up of countless gold coins, each with Diamond's face on them. The coins seemed to shine and release their own light which illuminated the realm that was filled with dozens of gray statues. Each statue depicted a different Bandit King or Queen that had their eyes and right hands forged from gold. At the opposite side of the realm were two statues that stood above the rest. One male, carved from onyx that lacked the gold present in the other statues. The other was female and seemingly carved out of ivory with the exception of her golden eyes and right hand. Both of these statues stood tall next to a massive gate that shook as something thrashed against it.

"Incredible," Xavier whispered in a silent awe along with Lilia. It was then they noticed that Jack was missing. When they looked around, they saw that Kat was as well. Even across the realm with the Lady and Faith, they found themselves unable to locate Alice. "Will it be enough?"

"Dominion is said to be the thieves' answer to both Excalibur and Merlin's magic," Lilia said quietly. "However," Lilia continued as she narrowed her eyes when she noticed the realm's appearance flicker slightly as if trying to force itself to stay focused. "This is clearly far from perfect; your guess is as good as mine."

"What are you?" August asked as he glared at Diamond.

"We've been over this, I'm the Queen," Diamond answered before she released a loud whistle and soon the massive gate burst open. August turned around at that moment and watched in a silent horror as a massive black Cerberus landed before him that sent gold coins flying everywhere.

"A Cerberus," Lilia said breathlessly as her eyes watered. "Forged from his mistakes…this…this is it," Lilia said quietly as Xavier looked on at the scene with wide eyes.

"Umbra," Diamond began as she faced the leftmost head that had bright green eyes. "Stone," Diamond continued when she faced the centermost head that gazed back at her with shining gray eyes. "Frost," Diamond said as she saw the rightmost head that had cold blue eyes. Diamond noted that the right paw looked exceptionally sinister as its blue talons crackled with presence. The three heads howled in unison as all six eyes of the beast turned golden in color. "Sic 'em," Diamond said coldly as the massive beast lunged at a terrified August. It swiped its massive right claw at the man, a wave of ice ripped up from the gold. August cleaved to the ice only to find himself kicked in the side by Diamond. Diamond pulled out her mother's knife and spun it in her hand for a moment. Diamond tossed it from hand to hand before she gripped it tightly in her right hand and charged forward. August brought his blade down upon her only for her to parry it with her blade which was charged with her presence. Despite the clear difference in both strength and size, Excalibur couldn't even scratch the smaller blade.

"How!?"

"Magic," Diamond taunted before her image faded. August realized then that she was never really before him. "My world, my rules," Diamond said as she reappeared behind him, and attempted to stab him only for him to jump away at the last moment. For a small moment, the two found themselves locked in close-quarters combat. Diamond danced around him and dodged his strikes before she sliced him across his chest whenever she got close. August cursed when the Cerberus landed behind him and created a wave of gold that knocked him back as Diamond vanished and reappeared on top of the Cerberus. Its left claw suddenly swiped at him and large black chains sprung from the ground and attempted to crush him. August cut through the chains quickly and rushed forward before he leaped into the air. Excalibur was raised high as August released a large wave of light at the beast which jumped to the side at the last moment to avoid the attack. Taking aim Diamond threw her knife which he barely managed to block with his blade. Diamond formed her sniper rifle in her hands and took aim before she shot him in the chest. The force of the bullet slammed into Excalibur's light and created an explosion that blew him onto his back. The Cerberus barked loudly before all three-heads released a loud howl that forced the bystanders to cover their ears. The sheer force of it knocked August through three statues. His body destroyed each of them until he hit the fourth one. August looked up in a daze as his ears bled while they rang. August watched as the Cerberus raced toward him, prepared to finish him off. Desperately, August dodged to the side when the central head bit down at him, attempting to end him. August managed to survive, but not without a cost as his right arm was bitten off, sword and all.

"No..." August screamed as the beast circled back and stalked toward him. "Not like this!" August shouted before his body exploded in a blue light. The realm shattered like glass as the Cerberus tried to land one last attack.

* * *

Diamond shouted as she hit the ground as Jack, Kat, and Alice all fell down before her as they once more found themselves in the ruins of the P.I. headquarters.

"You bitch!" August roared angrily, his staff held tightly in his left hand, his right arm nowhere to be found.

"What happened?" Faith asked in confusion as the Lady grimaced.

"The Equinox, he desperately wished for his magic back and the sudden surge of power was enough to shatter the already unstable illusion," the Lady answered as she watched August stand tall, his shield was back and it shone brighter than ever.

"Immortality," August said with a scoff as he glared at Excalibur which found itself stabbed into the ground. "Worthless excuse for a blade. I was better off as I was. After all, why be immortal when you can be invincible?" August taunted while a blue light covered his stub. Alice groaned weakly as her head pounded. Alice wiped the corner of her mouth in a daze and removed blood she wasn't sure was hers.

"Damn it, we were so close!" Lilia forced out as she and Xavier tried to regain their bearings.

"How does he have his shield back already?" an exhausted Kat wondered as Jack grimaced while rising to his feet.

"It was never destroyed so the casting penalty never applied, he simply took it off when he got rid of his magic," Jack explained. His appearance had now returned to normal and his right arm had vanished as he was unable to conjure up the presence needed to keep it in tact. "A desperate move from a desperate man."

"Silence boy, my patience has finally reached its limit with you," August said as his power continued to rise. "I'll just wait until after I've crushed you to reclaim that blade."

"Thirty minutes," Xavier said suddenly as he got their attention after he checked his watch. "That's when the Equinox ends. If he beats us before then, he wins."

"Fool, I win either way. Even if you can somehow last, I'll just wait until next year. Look at you all, you can barely stand while I have more than enough power to spare," August said with a dark grin. "Still before you all die, take satisfaction that you fell before me, August Gladius the Invincible! The Champion of Light!"

"Invincible? Query, why does he keep saying that?" Minerva asked as Alice tried her best to sit up. Quickly, Alice reached into her pocket and pulled out her phone. Alice was relieved to see that

despite the destruction the upload had completed. *"You said nothing was invincible. If an external attack doesn't work why not try attacking internally?"*

"Not sure that…applies…here…" Alice trailed off slowly. Alice's eyes widened in disbelief as she looked up at the gloating August in disbelief. "Oh my God," Alice whispered incredulously as she pocketed her phone. The lights in her contacts shifted and flickered as she spotted an electronic signal from the pocket of August's pants. Pants which he wore beneath his apparently unbreakable shield. She felt her jaw go slack as she identified that the signal came from his phone. It was then she did something that caught everyone off guard.

She laughed.

She laughed loudly.

"Are you serious!? It can't be that simple!" Alice said as she laughed despite the seriousness of the situation. Alice couldn't help it even as August turned to face the civilian as if she had lost her mind. "Fuck it, this is gonna be a hell of a gamble," Alice said tiredly after she calmed down and forced herself to her feet. That rebellious fire she came to love, coursed through her veins as the skull on her mask seemed to grin at the Arch-Mage. "I'll take you on, darlin'," Alice said as she pointed at him, and made an "L" with her thumb and pointer finger. Alice then aimed at him as if she had a gun.

"Stone?" Diamond asked with a confused frown as Jack shut his eyes tightly.

"Bloody hell, she's done it, she's finally lost her damn mind," Jack said as even Kat looked at Alice as if a screw had come loose.

"Babe, what are you doing?" Kat asked nervously as Alice just grinned at the Arch-Mage who didn't look the slightest bit amused by the civilian.

"If you're that eager to die," August began before he turned his staff into a spear of light. "Then so be it!" August said as he raised his spear but before he could throw it, Alice just winked at him.

"Boom," Alice said before his hip suddenly exploded. August screamed in agony as the spear he threw missed her head by mere inches. His indestructible shield shattered like glass as he simply collapsed much to everyone's surprise. Alice blew the tip of her finger as if it were a pistol as the now charred remnants of his phone fell from the gaping hole in his waist.

"Holy shit, what the fuck!?" Kat asked incredulously as Band 13 looked at their hacker in shock. Hell, even the mages looked at her as if she had two heads as Alice just smirked at the downed Arch-Mage.

"His shield was unbreakable," Alice began tiredly while a small smirk graced her lips. "But only from the outside. His shield did have a weak spot, he just moved it out of your reach. In the end, his greatest strength wasn't nothin' but an illusion. Not that his weak spot is even a factor here. A bomb in anyone's pants will take them down."

"Not like this…not at the hands of a civilian!" August raged as he tried to summon his staff back to his hand only to scream in pain when he felt his palm sliced. August felt the blood drain from his face when instead of his staff he saw a single electrum coated card that had the word "Steal" on it. He glared up at Kat who now held his staff. Kat tossed it to Jack who froze it in his grip before snapping it over his knee. Now more desperate than ever, August tried to crawl his way toward Excalibur. August smiled more and more the closer he got, his magic left him as he sacrificed it once more. Not once did August wonder why they let him get so close to the powerful blade. He soon found his answer, however, when he looked up. His smile dropped when he saw that Lilia stood on the opposite side of the blade. August trembled when he saw her magic leave her body, given up to the Equinox as she tightened her grip on the blade's hilt.

"Do it," the Lady said tiredly as she watched Lilia grip the blade tightly as her broken father tried desperately to grab on to it. August's hands bled as he gripped Excalibur's burning edge. "Take away from him, everything."

"No! Don't you dare!" August snarled as Lilia, with a visible show of effort, pulled the blade from the ground and out of her father's grasp before she held it high into the air. Light engulfed her as a wave of gold flaming energy fired from the blade and shot up into the night sky. "No!" August roared as Lilia felt her body become engulfed with power. "What do you think you are doing!?"

"Getting even," Lilia said quietly, a slight edge to her voice as he froze with fear, "You took away my dreams so I'll take yours," Lilia said as she gazed down at her father sadly before she turned away. "Curse my bleeding heart. I can't bring myself to kill you. Despite everything you've done to me, to my family, even at your worst you are still my father."

"But you aren't mine," Diamond said darkly as she kicked him over. "Tell me again how you're unaffected by my skill set," Diamond said as he looked at the barrel of her gun fearfully.

"Wait!"

"Did you wait when you murdered my mother?" Diamond questioned before she pulled the trigger. Diamond's aim was true and August's terrified expression was frozen on his face even as the life left his eyes. Diamond closed her eyes and raised her head up toward the night sky as she dropped her gun. "Finally, it's over," Diamond said quietly as the group of misfits simply stood together in a comforting silence. The war, their bad relationships, everything that divided them simply forgotten for a moment as their common source of suffering had finally been removed. At that moment, she could imagine her mother smiling down upon her and allowed a single tear to slide down her cheek. "Your honor has been restored. Now, you may rest in peace."

EPILOGUE

••••••••●•••••••••

PRESENCE

Thieves' Guild, Dorado, Council Chambers

"And that's everything that happened," Diamond said as she stood before the council with her band and Alice. The council members either looked at her incredulously or appeared pensive about the information she had just given them. "After that, my father's band found us as the Arch-Mage Enero appeared," Diamond said as she gestured across the room where her father and his band sat on their thrones that overlooked the proceedings.

*   *   *

Silicon Valley, Prosperity Industries, Three Hours Earlier

The clouds darkened and lighting flashed violently before a bolt slammed into the ground a few feet away from them. When the dust settled, the gathered individuals looked on with wide eyes as all three members of Roderick's band stepped out from the smoke.

"What the hell happened here!?" Vivi asked before she paused when she saw Band 13. Roderick appeared just as perplexed as she was while Julia simply whistled in appreciation.

"Not bad, I give the carnage a seven out of ten," Julia said as she looked at the destruction. Julia then turned to face Band 13 and winked at Jack. "I'm proud."

"Julia!?" Jack asked incredulously while Xavier instinctively grabbed his staff. A storm of conflicting emotions raged inside the young man. Before Xavier could do anything, he was blinded by a blue flash of light. When the light faded a tall man with tanned skin, black hair, and hazel eyes stood in front of him.

"What happened to my building!?" Enero questioned as Xavier, Faith, and Lilia looked at the Arch-Mage in surprise before they realized that with the building gone, August's wards had vanished as well. At that moment, Arch-Mage Enero and Roderick's band spotted each other. Stars filled Enero's now black eyes as the force of his magic exploded from his body and forced everyone but Roderick's band down to their knees. Unlike when they faced August, Band 13 felt genuine fear as a black staff appeared in Enero's hand. The end of the staff was sculpted into what appeared to be a black goat that held a blue gem in its mouth. Enero cursed something in Italian before he made his way to Roderick's band. "This was bound to happen eventually."

"Agreed," Roderick said as purple bolts of lightning continuously struck the soon to be battlefield. "We'll make it quick."

"Oh, it will be quick my old friend, of that I have no doubt," Enero sneered. However, before the two sides could potentially lay waste to each other, Diamond and Xavier forced themselves up and got between Roderick and Enero respectively.

"Uncle, stop!"

"Father, calm down!" Diamond said as she and Xavier stood back to back. They hoped beyond hope that the situation didn't escalate any further. "They're not our enemies...well...not anymore," Diamond corrected as she presumed Xavier said something similar to his uncle in Italian. For a moment, no one said a thing as they watched the encounter with baited breaths. Roderick's frown deepened when he looked up from his daughter and made eye contact with Enero. When Roderick returned

his attention to his daughter, Diamond realized that it wasn't her father that now stood before her but rather her King.

"Explain."

*   *   *

Thieves Guild, Dorado, Council Chambers

"As I told you after my first encounter with August, everything, from my mother's death to every single life lost in this war was not the fault of the Mages' Circle. It was the fault of one twisted man jealous of power he was too lazy to earn for himself. The Circle is now also aware of this. There is no reason to continue this farce," Diamond said firmly as she addressed the council. "He turned ally against ally, destroying the alliance and endangering the lives of every civilian on this planet. That man is now gone, I've made sure that he can never return. I've done my job not only as an assassin of this Guild but as the rightful heir to the throne," Diamond declared. "Now it's time for you to do yours. Right now, the Mage's Circle is discussing the possibility of a cease-fire. It's a long way from the alliance we once had, war is not easily forgotten, but it is a step in the right direction. A chance to end this bloodshed and focus on protecting the civilians. Make the right decision."

"And you honestly think the Circle will uphold that ceasefire, girl?" Heathcliff asked skeptically.

"It's not easy having the cause for this war come from your own faction. Especially when you preached about being in the right for as long as the Circle has," Diamond explained. "Their members will notice August's disappearance, this simply can't be covered up. They'll need to save face to maintain order within their faction. Their inner circle will probably change the tale a bit to save face, but that doesn't matter. What matters is that this fighting stops," Diamond said as she gazed at the council. "So yes, I believe they will uphold it. They have no choice with the loss of not only August but June as well," Diamond said making the council whisper amongst themselves.

"And what of the sword?" an older heavy-set man asked quietly, his eyes cold as he sat garbed in a black pin-stripe suit. This man was Antonio Insegnare, Head of the Insegnare Familia.

$*$ $*$ $*$

Silicon Valley, Prosperity Industries, Three Hours Earlier

"There," Lilia said after she used Excalibur to cut the chains that sealed the Lady's power. Now free, the Goddess' body began to glow blue as she felt her power return to her. "How do you feel?"

"Exhausted, but better," the Lady answered tiredly. "It will take a bit of time for me to regain my strength."

"I am so sorry," Enero said as he bowed before her. "For you to have been harmed by the Circle, and inside my own property, causes me no small amount of shame. If you need anything, I will get it for you if it's within my power."

"Anything?" the Lady questioned as she looked at the remorseful form of Enero. "Two things. One, twenty percent of the Circle's current wealth, give it to me so that I may restart rebuilding my Order."

"Consider it done. When we bring an end to this war, we should have more than enough to spare. Though we would do it anyway to see our closest ally return to its former glory," Enero said passionately. "What else?"

"The second thing is, I need you to turn a blind eye," the Lady said which confused all that heard her.

"A blind eye?"

"One of your members has impressed me with their strength, I would like to take them for myself to rebuild my Order with them heading the next generation of knights," the Lady said and it was this request that seemed to give Enero pause.

"My Lady, with all due respect, Xavier is important to not just myself but the Circle as well. He's the heir of Merlin and head of House Magnus. We simply can't afford to lose him, August, and June all at once," Enero explained, his eyes pleaded for the Lady to understand.

318

"I understand that. The boy does his blood justice, but it is not him I was referring to," the Lady reassured Enero. "It's her," the Lady said as she gestured toward Lilia who looked at her in surprise. "She has shown a level of compassion I have thought impossible from blood as twisted as hers. That said, in that twisted blood she has the blood of a dragon and a virtuous heart to match. I cannot allow my biases of the past to negatively impact the future of my Order," the Lady said pointedly. Enero averted his eyes as he thought about the situation between the Circle and the Thieves' Guild. "She is a light in the darkness that I wish to cultivate," the Lady said before she turned to Lilia along with Enero and the others. "Every action she makes is with another's well-being in mind. Such compassion is most humbling to me," the Lady explained and she smirked a bit when she saw Enero look at her a bit skeptically. "Girl, no, Lilia…you can have one thing as a reward for the kindness you have shown me. Whatever it is, when I regain my power I will give it to you. What do you desire?" the Lady questioned as Lilia frowned in thought. After a moment, Lilia approached her with the burning blade in her hand and handed it to the Lady.

"Fix her, she had a life before my father destroyed it," this request made the Lady beam proudly at Lilia as even her own siblings and Enero looked at her in surprise.

"Are you sure?"

"Yes," Lilia said without hesitation.

"Very well," the Lady said as she raised a hand over the blade. A bright blue liquid formed around it before it shot toward the blade and doused its flames. They watched, stunned, as the blade transformed back into an exhausted Haylen who barely looked conscious.

"You!" Alice said angrily as she made her way toward Haylen only to get held back by both Jack and Kat.

"Relax! She's barely holding on as it is!" Kat said urgently. Alice struggled against them as they did their best to stop her before she committed fratricide.

"Listen to Kat, love, for once she's right," Jack said before he glanced at Xavier. "And I thought we were bad," Jack said as Xavier just shook his head in wonder at the civilian's blatant hostility. Then again, after he got to know Haylen as he had he couldn't really blame the younger Stone sibling.

"I want Lilia as the next leader for my Order and I will train this one," the Lady trailed off as she gestured toward Haylen. "To control her power. I do believe the two of them can do great things together if led in the right direction."

"If…if that's what she wants," Enero said eventually as he turned to Lilia. "With your magic gone, you have a year to wait. You can use that time to see if this is a good fit for you."

"I think I will," Lilia said after a moment which made the Lady smile.

"Good, now you two will be gone for a while and we will be leaving here soon so that I may rest and recuperate in my Lake. Say your goodbyes."

"Wait, what!? Do you really have to go now?" Faith asked Lilia, sad that her sister would leave so soon. "I've just gotten better, there are so many things I wanted to do with you and our brothers!"

"It won't be forever," Lilia said with a small smile. "We'll see each other again, and when we do, I will have some exciting stories to tell you. Stories, that will make Xavier's look like nothing," Lilia said as Xavier rolled his eyes. "Look after her."

"I will," Xavier said before he hugged her tightly. "You just look after yourself. You were a terrible mage, let's pray you're a better knight."

"Ass," Lilia said with a laugh as she separated herself from him and turned to face Jack. "Keep beating him up for me."

"Will do," Jack said before he winked at her. "Be safe, we bastards have to stick together," Jack said. Lilia smiled at him brightly before she turned to make her way toward the Lady who manipulated the strange blue liquid once more and transformed it into a portal.

"You have anything to say?" the Lady asked Alice while Haylen passed out in her arms. Alice gritted her teeth as she looked over at Haylen.

"When she wakes up tell her…" Alice trailed off before her expression hardened. "…to stay the hell away from me," Alice said coldly. The Lady just sighed sadly in response.

"If that is what you wish," the Lady said before she picked up Haylen and stepped through the portal with Lilia right behind her.

* * *

Thieves' Guild, Dorado, Council Chambers

"The sword is with its rightful owner. The Lady of the Lake will rebuild the Knights' Order when she recovers her strength and they will be a neutral party when it comes to matters between the Guild and Circle much like the Tribe is currently," Diamond explained and Antonio appeared satisfied with that decision.

"Hmph, well better than the Circle having control over it I suppose. Even if we don't," Heathcliff admitted. His eyes then narrowed as he gazed down upon Band 13, or more specifically Alice. "Now let's talk about the number of rules you've broken which include the number of unregulated jobs you've taken as first years that have surrounded this whole mess and the exposure of the Guild to a civilian, who may I remind everyone is still not unmarked?" Heathcliff said while the council talked amongst themselves. "You claim to be heir to the throne, a position you've given up willingly. That said, let's pretend that you didn't do that. Would we really want a Queen, or even a thief, this reckless? Is this the leadership we want for our children? The leadership that nearly got her own band killed?"

"That's enough, Ardent!" Vivi boomed, flames exploded from around her throne that burned brightly. Band 13 tensed at the sight and Alice couldn't help but look up at her fearfully. Kat's fear of Vivi was now much more understandable for the hacker. Heathcliff smiled smugly at her even as a few other councilors looked a bit uneasy.

"I'm just speaking facts, lass. The Victoire girl clearly doesn't want the position and Midas is not fit for it. We've all agreed it's time for a change, I say we put an Ardent on the throne, hell we already have one close enough as it is," Heathcliff said as he gestured toward Vivi.

"They're in the same band so that would be pointless. Also, Rose doesn't want it either and don't you dare use me to further your goals!" Vivi snarled. "You disowned me, you can't claim me as a part of your family only when it's convenient!"

"She's right. Besides, the jobs Diamond took were because I asked her as her father and King. She simply did her job," Roderick spoke up, his voice firm. "Don't use my mistakes as an attempt to illegitimatize her position."

"But he has a point," a younger man with pale skin and brown hair said as he and his band sat across from Roderick's band. He was an ambitious man named Ronaldo Avarice, elected representative for the Outsiders in the Guild. "Like father, like daughter. Though I disagree with the notion that an Ardent should lay claim to the throne, I say it needs to be abolished altogether."

"Not this again," Antonio muttered from his seat. This served to make Ronaldo angry as he glared at the man.

"Us outsiders make up sixty percent of the Guild! Why should you all have so much power?"

"Of that sixty percent, how many of you are actually in our top bands?" the head of the Hattori family asked. Alice looked at the man who was one of her biggest idols in silent awe. Hattori Hanzo was an elderly looking man but even despite his age Alice could see the resemblance between him and Akira. "The greatest one that ever walked among you is the one you're trying to dethrone this very moment. Logic like that is why you all do not have a bigger say. We bring in the most capital, the most power. We were born and bred for this while you all were picked off of the street, deemed worthy by us more times than not. You exist to pad our numbers. You wouldn't even be here if it wasn't for us, so how about you sit down and know your place? You claim the outsiders don't have a voice, you're wrong, it's just your voice in particular that we ignore."

"Wow," Kat said as her band looked at Akira's father in surprise. They hadn't expected him to come to their defense.

"That said," the Hattori patriarch continued as he faced Band 13. "You saw a problem that was being ignored and acted accordingly. Without you, a dangerous man would have a dangerous weapon with him this very moment. And that's not even mentioning the fact you helped reveal that the Black Moon is not as gone as we thought," the man continued as a few of the councilors flinched at his words. "However, we cannot ignore the fact that you willingly compromised the Guild. You kept a civilian marked and unsupervised for months. This is an action you must be reprimanded for. Normally you'd be expelled, and in my family, you'd lose a finger. That said, that would be too much for the very thieves that saved us and defeated an Arch-Mage."

"So, what do you propose we do?" Heathcliff asked sarcastically. The response, however, came from an unexpected source.

"With all due respect councilors, fuck you," Diamond said after a moment. Stunned, everyone, even her own band, looked at her in shock.

"What did you say to me girl!?" Heathcliff boomed, gray smoke pouring from his mouth as he glared down at her.

"I apologize for being unclear," Diamond said apologetically before she cleared her throat. "I said, fuck you, councilor Ardent. You don't get to sit up there and judge my leadership when none of you have done a single job in at least a decade. You come from a time where civilian technology was primitive and you could learn what you needed to as you went along. The world no longer operates that way. Jobs are becoming more and more impossible to undertake and you are all unwilling to adapt to the world that is changing around us so that we can rectify it. Too content to rely solely on the Hattori family and their connections! Ask any thief that is still active when the last time they accomplished a job without contracting a civilian in some fashion. Odds are each thief you ask will be unable to answer that such a job occurred in the last year. That is unless they come from the Hattori family who actually knows how all this new technology works," Diamond said as she narrowed her eyes. "You say I exposed us to a civilian? I ask you, where is this civilian? Because all I see next to me is my band."

"Heresy! Are you honestly claiming that civilian to be your bandmate!?" Heathcliff shouted, the temperature around him rising while his eyes turned a bright orange. "If it wasn't for the mark, she wouldn't even know what a band is!" Heathcliff said as the councilors spoke up in agreement. "A four-person band simply does not exist."

"There's a first time for everything," Diamond said firmly.

"Yes, but not that," Antonio said with a sigh as Julia perked up.

"How about a test?" Julia spoke up as she got their attention. Vivi glared at the woman but said nothing, a silent request from

Roderick who wanted to see where Julia was headed. "Remove her mark yourself Heathcliff, if she still recognizes what's going on, Diamond is right. If she forgets, you're right. We can solve this now."

"The traitor has a point," Heathcliff said as Julia just smirked at him while a dark expression crossed his face. "Don't get too comfortable, Frost, we still must deal with you. Come here, lass, I'll remove that mark and we can see if your so-called boss is right," Heathcliff said as Alice suddenly found herself put on the spot. A shiver ran down her spine as she realized that there was no way out of this. Not when she was in a room filled with the most powerful thieves the Guild had to offer. Shakily she stepped away from Band 13 and nodded her head. Alice took a deep breath before she hardened her expression. After everything she had been through with Band 13, she refused to show her fear.

"Fine," Alice said as Heathcliff stepped away from his seat. Alice went to meet him halfway, but found her wrist grabbed tightly by Kat. She closed her eyes when she found herself kissed by the thief while Kat's hand slid up the back of her shirt.

"Sometime today, please," Heathcliff called out impatiently clearly disgusted as Kat broke the kiss before she raised her middle finger at him. Alice calmed herself down as she made her way toward him. Alice turned around when she stopped in front of him and raised the back of her shit. Heathcliff's eyes narrowed when he saw the mark that rested in the middle of her back between her shoulder blades. Heathcliff smirked as an orange presence coursed over his hand. Heathcliff moved to burn the mark off once and for all only to find himself paralyzed. Startled, he looked up at Band 13 and shuddered slightly when he saw a seething Diamond. Diamond's glare froze him in place as her anger overtook her. It was only after Kat whispered something in her ear that he found himself free of her suffocating presence. Heathcliff shrugged off the dark feeling he felt from Diamond and slammed his hand into Alice's back. Alice screamed in pain as she felt her skin burn as he violently ripped the mark off. When he ripped his hand free, Alice collapsed to her knees both dazed and hurt. Band 13 immediately rushed toward her, and Kat quickly pulled out her flask.

"Here drink this," Kat said quietly as she put the flask to Alice's lips. "This might sound weird but do you remember me?"

"Y…Yes," Alice said with a weak smile which Kat returned.

"And what am I?"

"My kitten," Alice began which made Kat smile brightly at her. "And a thief," Alice added as Heathcliff looked down at them incredulously. The council whispered amongst themselves.

"Where are you?"

"The Guild, right? The council chambers?" Alice answered with a frown and Kat smiled brightly as she pulled Alice in for a hug.

"Well, that's that," Julia said with a shrug while she ignored how the council erupted in pandemonium. "Let them go home and rest, yeah? They should enjoy their time off until their second year begins."

"Not just yet," a new voice said as the door to the chambers opened up. Everyone in the room froze when they saw a human-sized Juventas enter the chamber. The Goddess made strong confident strides toward them as her divine presence made them instinctively bow. "You'd let these heroes go unrewarded for their troubles?"

"L-Lady Juventas!?" Heathcliff stuttered out surprised to see her after her long absence. Quickly, those assembled bowed before the Goddess. "Rewards?"

"Arise," Juventas commanded as the thieves scrambled to their feet. "Yes, Band 13 has completed a job that was given to them by my sisters and me. We gave them a contract, calling for the assassination of the Arch-Mage, August," Juventas said with a warm smile as she turned to face the stunned members of Band 13. "We have decided that you all shall each receive ten thousand Honor along with a boon of four thousand gold coins for your band," Juventas said and Alice was glad that she could stand on her own now because she was positive that she would have been dropped.

"Holy shit, we can almost skip two years with that!" Kat exclaimed.

"In addition," Juventas continued as her smile seemed to grow. "Young Frost, your strength has impressed my wayward sister. Laverna wishes for you to tell whoever trained you that they are to be considered a Master, effective immediately. Laverna expects great things from this school of…Hēishǒu, was it?"

"Yes, my Lady," Jack said as he bowed respectfully. Julia and Vivi both looked at him proudly before they glanced at each other. Julia's smile faltered slightly as Vivi outright glared at her.

"Katarina and…" Juventas trailed off as she stared at the civilian with a small frown.

"C-Call me, Alice," Alice said after she got over the shock of being addressed by an actual Goddess. "It's a long story," Alice said when she noticed the confused expression on her friends' faces.

"Katarina and Alice, Discordia wants it to be made clear that as long as Katarina considers you a member of the band, you shall be treated as such," Juventas revealed. It was then that a tense silence seemed to come over the council which in turn made Juventas frown as she swept her gaze over the council. "I do not particularly enjoy being one left out of the loop. Would someone care to explain what it is that I am missing?" Juventas asked as Heathcliff felt his heart plummet when more than few glanced his way before they looked away. Even those who were on his side avoided eye contact with the man. "Ardent, is there something I should inform Discordia of?"

"I…I…" Heathcliff stuttered out as even Band 13 felt bad for the man.

"Usual council inefficiency, nothing more," Diamond finally answered her Goddess as Heathcliff looked at her in surprise. "Nothing I can't handle when I ascend," Diamond said pointedly as she made it clear that she would hear no more of Heathcliff's claims against her position, less he wished to face the wrath of Juventas.

"I see, speaking of which, would you like to?" Juventas asked almost as an afterthought as if it didn't matter. Diamond blinked owlishly as Juventas' words registered in her head.

"Excuse me?"

"Your ascension, would you like to become the Bandit Queen now?" Juventas asked as she gestured toward Roderick and his band. "Your mother was your age when she first claimed the throne, would you like to give it a try?"

"Lady Juventas…nothing would bring me more joy," Diamond said after a moment before she clenched her fist. "But I must refuse," Diamond said and Juventas didn't seem surprised in the slightest. "My mother was forced to take the throne early when she was not prepared in a time of desperation. It caused her no small amount of stress and personally, I believe it ended up inhibiting her full potential. Everything worked out in the end but she made plenty of mistakes on that seat because she wasn't ready. Please allow me to finish my training so that I can ascend when I am truly ready and with a council that will stand by me."

"I see," Juventas said while her eyes shone with pride as she stared at Diamond. "You've grown wise my child."

"Only because of your light."

"Still, I do not wish to leave you without my own gift, having the member from my sect being the only one without something special will portray me in a bad light," Juventas mused. "Name one thing and it will be yours as long as it is in my power to give it to you."

"Anything?"

"Anything."

"Then please allow me to reverse one of my mother's mistakes," Diamond pleaded before she gestured toward the council. "This… This is a mess, my Goddess, one that stemmed from my mother believing she was doing the right thing but I see it as her gravest error. Please restore power to the throne, make it a seat that matters once more."

"What!?" Ronaldo shouted before Juventas leveled him with a piercing stare.

"Do not yell in my presence child," Juventas warned only once which made Ronaldo nod nervously. Juventas' eyes never left him as she continued speaking to Diamond. "Why would you wish to overturn one of your mother's biggest actions as Queen?"

"She took away its power to make sure another tyrant like my grandfather didn't sit on the throne. That said, even if he was a tyrant, a mad king…the Guild was still standing when she overthrew him. He did his job, Diamond said firmly. "She had a council that

327

loved her and as a result, was given a false impression that she made the right choice because she could get things done. But look at the council now? Plotting, scheming, and stopping my father at every turn to the point he had to put me at risk just to get something done! I don't want to be put in that position, I don't want to have to risk my own heir one day because the council doesn't agree with me," Diamond said passionately as Jack looked at her in surprise. There was so much raw emotion in her voice that he had to check whether or not her glove was still on. "You, Discordia, and Laverna created this Guild, its very structure both physically and politically. My mother had no right to change something you set in place. In a way that one act was far madder than anything her father had done."

"Isabelle was young, you are right," Juventas said after a moment. "However, with youth comes a level of naiveté that can be both good and bad," Juventas said as she rested a hand on Diamond's shoulder and smiled down at her. "So be it, as of this moment the council will work as it did before Isabelle's reign. Perhaps now your father can get things done," Juventas said as both Heathcliff and Ronaldo looked ready to faint. "I expect great things from you, Roderick and eventually you as well Diamond," Juventas said before she prepared to leave only to stop suddenly. "Also, before I forget," Juventas said as she turned to face Julia this time. "In light of recent revelations, consider your sins forgiven. The Frost family's honor is restored but also, as an apology, everything you lost shall be returned with interest. Laverna just has one last mission for you," Juventas said before gesturing toward Jack. "Guide your child."

"Understood," Julia said quietly as she gazed down at Jack from her throne while Juventas disappeared.

"Well, then shall we bring this meeting to a close?" Roderick asked before a grinning Vivi nudged him.

"What are you doing? You don't need their permission anymore!" Vivi said as his eyes suddenly shone with mischief. The members on the council who had continuously opposed him now looked at him with apprehension.

"You're right," Roderick said as he stood up. "We're done here," he said before he and his band convened with Band 13 and led them out of the chambers. Roderick didn't care if the councilors went home or not. "It's great to be King," Roderick said as he wrapped an arm around Diamond's shoulder. "But it's even greater to be able to call myself your father. Isabelle would be proud, I know I am."

"So how did you two pull that off?" Vivi couldn't help but ask Kat who just smirked in response.

* * *

Council Chambers, Minutes earlier

As Kat kissed Alice, she slid her hand up the back of her shirt. In between Alice's shoulder blades, Kat quickly placed a second mark on her. It was at that moment, Alice caught on to her plan when she felt the familiar sensation of the mark being etched into her body. Once they were forced to end their moment, Alice approached Heathcliff bravely. As Alice pulled up her shirt, she showed the man the false mark and hoped beyond hope that the ruse would work. If it wasn't for the searing pain from his hand, she was sure she would have let out a sigh of relief when she felt him rip away the false mark.

* * *

"I'm just that good."

"Now you sound like the lad," Vivi said as Kat laughed before she glanced at Julia who tried to reconnect with Jack. It was ironic, really, Kat only just met the woman but could tell she was like an older more experienced Jack. Confident if not a bit cocky and could charm whomever they wanted. To see them act so awkward around each other almost made her laugh.

"Hey, are you gonna be okay with this?" Kat asked Vivi with a frown.

"I hate her with every fiber of my being, lass," Vivi said though her heart wasn't in it. If anything, she just sounded tired and for once, Kat felt that the woman actually looked her age when she saw the exhaustion on Vivi's face. "That said, he's a grown man like you're a grown woman. Who you two let into your lives is up to you, I raised you two good enough to trust your own judgment," Vivi said as she glanced at Alice who smiled shyly. "Doesn't mean I won't still give you the third degree later, lass," Vivi told Alice which immediately wiped the growing smile from her face. Amused by Alice's blatant fear, Vivi looked back at Kat. "She's a shitty person, but I'll be damned if she wasn't a good mother while she was there. It's hard to pinpoint what a Frost is truly like, everything you know about them ends up being a façade. However, one thing I do know is that she loves him. That bond is something you can't fake," Vivi said quietly before she shook her head. "So, what do you all have planned for the summer?" Vivi asked which made Kat and Alice pause before they grinned at each other.

*　　*　　*

Mages' Circle, Inner Circle

"To think we were led astray and lost not just one but two members of our inner circle. June's replacement has been chosen, but what about August? That position has always been a symbol of hope for the Circle, but after this…" a man garbed in a white cloak trailed off uneasily.

"It can still be such a symbol, Rhagfyr. What our people need now is a new champion, a reminder of the light that can come from the darkness," Enero said before he turned to Xavier as the other nine Arch-Mages looked down upon him. "That is if you're up for such a task?"

"I am."

"Then come, take your position amongst us," Enero said with a smile. "You are young but your power is great and there is much we can teach you," Enero said as a silver light shone beneath Xavier's feet. "Welcome to the inner circle, Xavier…or should I say, August?"

"Personally, I prefer *Agosto,*" the new Arch-Mage said using his native tongue as Enero smiled in response.

*   *   *

Moscow, Drakenova Corp.

"It seems that August failed his mission, defeated by the same ones that killed your father, Alexie," an older well-dressed man said as he stood in front of a desk, his crimson eyes piercing the darkness of the office. On his neck was a crimson heart shaped tattoo with the letter "K" inside of it.

"That weakling was no father of mine. He simply donated his venom, nothing more and nothing less," a woman responded as the chair that was facing the window turned to face him. In the chair sat a blonde woman wearing a pair of round framed sunglasses. The crimson lenses seemed to shine in the darkness. On her neck was a red heart shaped tattoo that had the letter "Q" inside of it. The woman smiled at her companion, her white fangs seemed to glimmer in the moonlight as she swirled a wine glass filled with a dark red liquid in her hand. "August's failure was to also be expected, but to think some first-year thieves had a part in it. Perhaps the Guild truly has gotten less pathetic since I left?" the woman mused. "Has Morgana been informed of her son's failure?"

"Yes, but she doesn't care. She's more interested in your project."

"And for a good reason. For too long the Black Moon has depended on ancient weapons and myths," the woman said with a scoff. "So, distracted by them, they ignored the perfectly capable tools that the civilians leave hanging around. Speaking of which, were you able to salvage the program?"

"I was," The man said as he placed a phone on the desk. Soon the screen turned on as a golden "A" appeared.

"Perfect, Morgana will be most pleased. This year will prove to be very interesting, won't it?" the woman asked as she pocketed the phone.

"It will indeed, Elizabeth."

* * *

"Road trip!" Kat said with a cheer as they climbed into the car. "I can't believe you kept this baby in such good condition!" Kat said as she laid across the dashboard and rubbed her hand against it affectionately. "There, there, mama missed you. I'm never leaving you again," Kat whispered and Alice could swear she saw a tear or two.

"Honestly," Diamond said with a shake of her head as Jack climbed into the back with her. "So, you wanted to be in charge of this since we're on a break, where are we headed?"

"Where aren't we is a better question," Kat said with a grin. "We're thieves, we're supposed to be traveling yet we got stuck in Cali for how long? I'm stir crazy, Diamond!"

"Just remember, you promised to show me as many lights as possible," Alice said and Kat grinned in response before she moved closer to Alice.

"And I plan to," Kat said before she claimed Alice's lips for her own while Jack groaned good-naturedly.

"As much as one can enjoy this sight, please don't tell me this is going to be the whole trip," Jack complained.

"Hey, bite me, I'm making up for lost time," Kat said as she flipped him off before she started the car. "You should do the same, I mean it's just your band here, no point in trying to be professional on break. Indulge yourself a little, we're off the clock!" Kat pointed out and before Jack could say anything, a hand grabbed him by his collar. Jack's eyes widened as he found himself being pulled down and kissed by Diamond. The moment their lips met, his mind seemed to explode with a pleasure that seemed to last an eternity. That said, it was gone all too soon. When they broke apart, Jack looked at Diamond incredulously.

"What? What happened to-" Jack was cut off when she placed a finger on his lips.

"Jack, just shut up and let me have this," Diamond said as Kat and Alice smirked as they drove.

"Jack?" Jack said, not used to being call by his first name by Diamond. He looked at her with an amused smile as she rolled her golden eyes.

"We're on break, right?" Diamond asked rhetorically. "There's no need for professionalism amongst friends if there is no job to be completed."

"I can work with that," Jack said before he kissed Diamond once more. As they left the city, Alice received a text from Eric.

Eric: Hey out of town visiting my girl.

Eric: We'll have to communicate overseas to coordinate our next moves.

Eric: Also, before I forget, my girl says hi.

"No way," Alice said breathlessly as she saw a picture attached to the last message. When they stopped at a red light, she showed her bandmates her phone. Kat and Jack laughed loudly as Diamond's eyes widened. The picture showed a happy Eric with his arm around a smirking blonde woman who was all too familiar. Diamond just shook her head as she realized that perhaps she and Dominique had a lot more to catch up on than she realized.

"Looks like we're heading to France at some point," Kat said and they all agreed. It was then Kat frowned when she saw a few air-shuttles flying overhead. "Fuck it," Kat said suddenly. The tone in her voice filled her friends with dread as they saw a grin on her face. Alice felt the blood drain from her face when she saw Kat's hand reach for a button it had no business going near.

"Kitten, don't-" Alice was cut off when Kat pressed the button. Kat's grin widened as the car suddenly began to hover off of the streets, its wheels folding within the body of the vehicle. Diamond grimaced while Jack and Alice shouted in fear when the vehicle suddenly took off and raced high into the skies. Kat laughed as she shouted that they'd reach their next destination in no time. It was then that despite Kat's words, and current feelings of terror, Alice realized she didn't care that much about the destination. Because as long as she was with them, she felt complete. She had friends, a family, and love thanks to them. She had become a far stronger person than she thought she was capable of and lived a life that was far beyond her wildest imagination. No, she realized, where they ended up didn't matter because the only thing that she needed was their presence.

End.